9/19

LP
PER
ZM

✓ **W9-BRJ-365**

#3 House of Secrets

DISCARDED

HOW SECRETS DIE

Center Point
Large Print

Also by Marta Perry and available from
Center Point Large Print:

Search in the Dark
Abandon the Dark
The Rescued
The Rebel
Where Secrets Sleep
When Secrets Strike

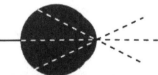

**This Large Print Book carries the
Seal of Approval of N.A.V.H.**

HOW SECRETS DIE

—*House of Secrets*—

Marta Perry

CENTER POINT LARGE PRINT
THORNDIKE, MAINE

This Center Point Large Print edition
is published in the year 2019 by arrangement with
Harlequin Books S.A.

The text of this Large Print edition is unabridged.
In other aspects, this book may vary
from the original edition.
Printed in the United States of America
on permanent paper.
Set in 16-point Times New Roman type.

ISBN: 978-1-64358-330-3

The Library of Congress has cataloged this record
under Library of Congress Control Number: 2019943641

Dear Reader,

I'm so glad you decided to read the final book in my Blackburn House series. I've especially enjoyed writing this series because I've been able to pick up pieces from real Pennsylvania small towns to incorporate in the stories, which makes the setting very real to me.

In *How Secrets Die*, police chief Mac Whiting finally meets his match in a woman who is just as stubbornly determined to do the right thing as he is. After getting to know Mac in the two earlier books, I hope you enjoy watching as he and Kate battle each other as well as the forces of wrong to find their own happily-ever-after.

Please let me know how you feel about my story. I'd be happy to send you a signed bookmark and my brochure of Pennsylvania Dutch recipes. You can email me at marta@martaperry.com, visit me at www.Facebook.com/martaperrybooks or at www.martaperry.com, or write to me at HQN Books, 195 Broadway, 24th FL, New York, NY 10007.

Blessings,

Marta Perry

This story is dedicated to my husband,
who always believes in me, with much love.

HOW
SECRETS
DIE

Death isn't the greatest loss in life.
The greatest loss is
what dies inside of us while we live.
—Amish proverb

CHAPTER ONE

A cemetery should be a place where people were buried—not where they died. Kate Beaumont, confronted so unexpectedly with the place Jason had chosen to end his life, stopped the car in mid-traffic, earning an irritated honk from the driver behind her as he was forced to come to a halt, as well.

The driver circled her, looking annoyed but refraining from the rude gesture she anticipated. Apparently drivers were a bit more polite in a small town like Laurel Ridge, Pennsylvania, than they were in the city. Her hands were shaking, and not from the sudden stop. She pulled off the road near the stone wall that encircled the graveyard.

Ridiculous, to let just the sight of the place send her into a tailspin. She was tougher than that, wasn't she? But while she could face down a recalcitrant politician or an irate citizen in search of a story, she couldn't maintain that level of detachment where her younger brother's death was concerned.

Kate took a long breath, fighting to still the tremors that shook her. She focused on the scene facing her, thinking of how she'd describe it for a newspaper article.

Laurel Ridge's cemetery covered the top of a rounded hill at the eastern end of town. Spreading maples, their leaves already turning color, shielded gray tombstones. Some of the stones were worn and tilted, their lettering eroded, while others were new enough to make it obvious the cemetery was still in use. The whole place had a well-tended air, the grass mown, with beds of gold-and-burgundy chrysanthemums blossoming here and there.

Which was the stone Jason had leaned against when he'd taken that fatal dose of pain meds and swallowed that final mouthful of whiskey? She could find it, she supposed, since the name had shown clearly in the newspaper photo she'd scanned online. But looking at the spot wouldn't lead her to any answers.

Movement reflected in the rearview mirror startled her, and her stomach tightened as she realized a police car had pulled up behind her. Great. All she needed was to draw official attention to herself before she'd even begun the task that brought her here.

An officer slid from the vehicle and started toward her. Taking a firm grip on her nerves, Kate planted a smile on her face and hit the button to roll down her window.

She was about to speak when a closer look at the man's uniform gave her another shock. The lettering on his pocket read M. Whiting.

McKinley Whiting, then. Chief of Police in this backwater town, and the man who'd dismissed her little brother's death as just another druggie overdosing himself.

Kate gritted her teeth, fighting to keep her feelings from showing as she looked up at the man. Tall and lean, he had dark hair in a military-style cut and a jaw that conveyed determination. He didn't affect the dark sunglasses so many cops did, and his brown eyes studied her, missing nothing, she felt sure.

"Are you having car trouble, ma'am?" His voice was a bass rumble.

"No, not at all. Is there a problem?"

"You can't park here." He nodded to the no-parking sign directly in front of her fender. "If you're interested in the cemetery, you can turn in at the gate just ahead. You'll find a gravel pull-off where you can park, if you want."

"I don't." Kate's tone was sharper than she intended, but she couldn't seem to control the spurt of temper. "Can't a visitor to your town stop to get her bearings without being harassed?"

Reading the surprise in his face, she clamped her lips shut before she could make matters worse. She'd overdone it—lost her cool and let her feelings show. The last thing she wanted was to rouse the suspicions of the local cop before she'd been in town for five minutes.

15

"Sorry," she muttered before he could speak. "I didn't mean . . ."

"No problem." He said the words easily, but his brown eyes were watchful. "I wasn't trying to harass you. If you're lost, I'll be glad to help you find your way, Ms. . . ."

He left it hanging there, obviously intent on learning her name. For the first time she was glad her name wouldn't connect her with Jason Reilley.

"Kate Beaumont."

"Nice to meet you, Ms. Beaumont. I'm Mac Whiting." She could see him stowing her name away in the filing cabinet of his mind. "Coming to visit someone here in Laurel Ridge?"

"No." Guilt and grief were a powerful combination. She should have. If she'd come to visit Jason the summer he'd spent here, maybe he'd still be alive.

That was the danger of loving someone. It hurt too much when you let them down.

Whiting's eyes were probing again. If she'd worn a sign, it probably wouldn't have been more obvious that she was hiding something.

Kate swallowed hard and tried for a normal tone. "I've been driving for several hours. I just thought I'd find a place for lunch."

He nodded, again with that watchful look. Protective, that was what it was. As if his town might need protecting against her. Well, maybe it did.

16

"Turn left just ahead, and you'll be on Main Street. There's a café a few blocks down on your left, across from the bed-and-breakfast." He pointed, leaning against the car as he did so, and she had a sudden sensation of masculine power in his nearness. "The Buttercup. I can vouch for the food, and the prices are reasonable."

She hadn't expected that casual reference to the bed-and-breakfast, and it shook her. Would it be the same one where Jason had stayed when he came to Laurel Ridge? If so, it was going to be one of her first stops.

"Okay, thanks." She managed a cool, dismissive smile. "I appreciate the recommendation." She turned the ignition key, her fingers brushing the silver dragon charm Jason had given her, and put her finger on the window button.

Whiting looked at her for a moment longer, and then slowly stepped back so she could close the window. She put the car in gear, glanced behind her and pulled out. It was simple enough to watch Whiting in her rearview mirror. He'd drawn out a notebook and was jotting down her license number.

She doused a flicker of anger. A search of her license wouldn't tell him anything except her address in Baltimore. She'd never been arrested, so a query to the police there wouldn't help him, even if he went that far.

But this encounter had clearly shown her that

she'd have to do better. True, she hadn't expected the first person she'd meet in Laurel Ridge to be the policeman who'd been quoted in that article about Jason's death. She might be excused for losing her grip just a bit, but it was unfortunate. She'd made herself an object of his interest before she'd had a chance to do a single thing.

But what difference did it make in the long run? Sooner or later she'd have to divulge the relationship between her and Jason. If she didn't, she'd have no reason for asking questions about him.

She'd toyed with the thought of trying to conceal her identity. She could have claimed to be writing a newspaper story about Jason's death, but that didn't sound credible even to herself, not after over a year had passed.

Kate made the turn onto Main Street and drove down it at a sedate speed, reading signs as she went. There, ahead of her on the left, was the café Whiting had mentioned, and on her right the bed-and-breakfast. She slowed, peering toward the rear of the white clapboard building, and caught a glimpse of a small building nearly hidden by the trees. That had to be it—the cottage where Jason had lived during his three months in Laurel Ridge.

And next to the bed-and-breakfast rose the imposing Italianate building that was Blackburn

House, where Jason had worked. The place where he'd lived, the place where he'd worked. That was where she had to begin.

She hadn't been here when Jason had needed her, but she was now. She'd find the answer to the question that haunted her, because if she didn't, she'd never be satisfied. What had happened in this seemingly quiet, peaceful town that had led to her brother's death?

Mac drove down Main Street, keeping an eye on the compact car ahead of him. He wasn't following the woman exactly, but she had stirred his curiosity. Something had been just a little off-kilter about their conversation, and her defensiveness had startled as well as intrigued him.

He frowned, trying to put his finger on the exact source of his unease. Kate Beaumont had seemed vaguely familiar to him, but he couldn't quite place her. Thick, honey-blond hair was pulled casually back on the nape of her neck, allowing wavy tendrils to escape and curl around her ears. Her lightly tanned skin seemed touched by the gold in her hair, and even her eyes were a golden brown. Surely, if he'd ever known her, he'd remember. A man didn't run into that many brown-eyed blondes—and especially not one carrying a chip the size of a mountain on her shoulder.

19

The familiarity remained stubbornly elusive, so he put the resemblance on a back burner to percolate. It would come through, sooner or later. Meantime, it looked as if his mystery woman was going to take his advice. She'd pulled into a parking space across from the café.

A moment later he realized he'd jumped to conclusions. Ms. Beaumont wasn't headed toward the café. Instead, she was walking up the sidewalk of Blackburn House. Now what, exactly, was she up to? Unless she had a sudden yen to buy quilt fabric or a book, there wasn't much in Blackburn House to attract a casual visitor.

Curiosity had him turning in at the driveway that ran along the side of the building. At the rear of Blackburn House stood the old carriage house, converted into the workshop of Whiting and Whiting Cabinetry. Not that he was the Whiting or the son involved in the business. Dad might have had hopes in that direction at one time, but when Mac had come back from a stint in the military, he'd known the carpentry trade wasn't for him. Still, Dad seemed content with one son in partnership, and the business suited Mac's brother, Nick, perfectly.

Parking, Mac eyed the back door into Blackburn House. That might be a bit too blatant, running into the woman so quickly. She really would have cause to cry harassment if he did that, wouldn't she?

Instead, he headed into the cabinetry shop, prepared for the usual din of saws and hammers. But all was fairly quiet at the moment. One of the Amish carpenters who worked in the shop sat on a bench in the rear, his lunch bucket beside him. He raised a thermos in Mac's direction, and Mac grinned and nodded.

He'd forgotten it was lunchtime. No doubt Nick was lunching with his fiancée, Allison, assuming she'd been able to get away from the quilt shop.

His father, instead of eating the lunch Mom had packed for him, was bending over a rocking chair, carefully hand-sanding a spindle. The normal work of the shop—custom-designed kitchen cabinets—sat all around him, but he was focused on the rocker instead.

"Hey, Dad. Is that for Mom?"

His father looked up at his approach, pushing his glasses into place. Folks said Nick looked more like their father, but all three of them had the same lean, straight-featured faces. Dad's eyes crinkled at the sight of him.

"Your mom says she has enough furniture, thank you very much." He grinned. "This is a gift for Allison. The way those women are fussing over this wedding shower, you'd think no one had ever gotten married before."

"Better not let Mom or Allison hear you complaining." Mac leaned against a handy workbench. Since he was safely removed now from the farmhouse that his brother, Nick, and Nick's young son shared with Mom and Dad, he could take a more detached view of Nick and Allison's wedding preparations.

His father raised an eyebrow. "Bet you haven't even thought of setting up the bachelor party yet. That is a best man duty, you know."

"I know, I know. But Nick doesn't like any of my ideas. Especially not taking off to Vegas for a weekend."

Dad swatted at him as if he were a pesky fly. "Be nice to your brother. He's taken long enough to decide to risk marriage again. And as for you . . ."

"Don't start," Mac said quickly. "I hear enough of it from Mom. She's taken to reminding me that I'm not getting any younger, as if I were teetering on the doorstep of the nursing home."

"She wants more grandkids." Dad eyed him severely. "You're supposed to do your part."

Mac shrugged. "I've got a whole town to look after already. That's enough for me at the moment."

"Here." Dad tossed him the fine sandpaper he'd been using. "Do a little work for a change while I pour out my coffee."

Mac bent obediently over the chair, hands caressing the smooth curves of the fine maple. He might not want carpentry for his life's work, but he still enjoyed the calming nature of the skill. Seeing the grain gleam in response to his movements was satisfying.

"What brings you in here at this hour?" His father took over his spot, leaning against the workbench. "Not enough to keep you busy at the office?"

Mac shook his head, not looking up. "Just a funny thing that happened. I had to speak to a woman parked in the no-parking area up by the cemetery. She seemed . . . I don't know . . . upset, maybe. Annoyed at me for speaking, that's for sure."

"And?" Dad seemed to be waiting for more. He had to know that that was the sort of thing that happened too often to cause comment.

"It was just odd, that's all. She's a stranger, but she seemed kind of familiar to me."

He could feel his father's gaze on him. "A looker, was she?"

Mac grinned. "You could say that. A striking brown-eyed blonde, if you want to know."

"That's the answer, then." Dad sounded amused. "She probably had a starring role in one of your dreams."

He chuckled, as he was meant to, but then he shook his head, running the sandpaper smoothly along the grain of the wood. "Sounds like it, but that wasn't it. I've got a good memory for faces, and I'm sure I've seen her before."

"If she was visiting someone in town, you

might have noticed her. In fact, it sounds as if you could hardly miss her."

"She said she wasn't visiting anybody. Asked directions to a place where she could get lunch, as if she was just passing through."

"You told her the café, I suppose." Dad spoke with the experience of one who knew there were few other places in Laurel Ridge where you'd be likely to get a good lunch.

"I did," he said slowly. "But I saw her going into Blackburn House instead."

"So maybe she wanted to look around the shops."

Mac didn't respond. Slowly, very slowly, a memory was stirring in the back of his mind. An image. A rainy day, the kind of steady downpour that managed to trickle down your neck no matter how protected you were. Soggy grass underfoot, and drooping, saturated flowers, the ribbons around them stained with water. A cemetery, but not the one at the top of the hill.

"That's it." He straightened, one hand on the back of the chair, gripping it tightly as the impact of the memory hit. "I saw her a little over a year ago at a cemetery in Philadelphia. At the funeral of that young guy who worked in the financial management office. The one we found dead of an overdose right up there on the hill where she'd stopped."

Dad met his eyes, startled and sympathetic. "That poor kid? Is she some relation?"

He nodded, the memory clarifying now. "I didn't speak to her, but someone pointed her out to me. His sister—no, his half sister. The names are different, but I'm sure of it."

The picture was stamped so firmly on Mac's mind that he wondered why he hadn't realized it the minute he'd seen Kate Beaumont. Maybe he would have, if she'd been named Reilley, like the half brother.

Funny how much you could tell about a situation just from body language. The half sister and the father had stood several feet apart, obviously not touching, not even looking at one another, each one isolated in his or her own grief.

Tom Reilley, presumably Kate Beaumont's stepfather, had been a retired cop. That had been one reason why Mac had driven to Philadelphia for the funeral. Professional courtesy, if you will. The man's son had died on his turf.

Mac realized his own father was studying him, an expression of concern on his face. He'd known—he always seemed to know—how hard Mac had taken the death. This was his town. He was responsible for it. That meant never letting a situation get out of control, because if it did, then as a peacekeeper, you'd failed.

Jason Reilley, lying dead against a gravestone in the oldest section of the cemetery, a fatal combination of alcohol and pills in his system, had been out of his control.

Another memory flickered, just for an instant. Another town, a world away—flattened homes, the smell of burning in the air, a small, huddled body . . .

His father stirred. "Well, no reason for the woman not to come here, I suppose. Maybe she felt as if she wanted to see for herself where he died. Sort of a pilgrimage."

It struck him then. Kate Beaumont hadn't looked to him like a woman on a pilgrimage. She'd looked like a woman on a crusade.

His uneasiness was full-blown now. His sudden movement set the chair rocking as he headed for the door.

"Where are you going?" Dad put out a hand to still the rocking.

"To have a talk with Ms. Beaumont." Mac's course of action solidified. "Maybe you're right. But I want to know why, when she saw who I was, Kate Beaumont was so careful not to mention her relationship with Jason Reilley."

Kate hadn't gone more than a few steps inside Blackburn House before she realized that checking out the business that had hired Jason as an intern wouldn't be unobtrusive. The building was smaller than she'd expected, though impressive with its marble entrance hall and

26

Victorian woodwork. To her right was a quilt shop, and through the window she could see several women in Amish dress browsing along rows of fabric.

The business on her left checked her for a moment. Whiting and Whiting Cabinetry. Related to Chief of Police Mac Whiting? Probably. It wasn't that common a name, and Laurel Ridge was a small town.

She walked toward the back, past a graceful staircase that clearly led to offices on the second floor. That must be where the financial consultants had their offices. The rear of this level housed what appeared to be a storage room and a bookstore.

Kate paused, looking at the display of bestsellers in the window. It was unusual to find an independent bookseller thriving in a small town, but this one appeared to be doing fine. Several customers wandered through the aisles, a toddler stacked blocks in a corner with children's books, and an elderly man seemed to be having an animated conversation with the woman behind the counter.

Upstairs, then, for a look at the offices of Laurel Ridge Financial Group. No one else was on the stairs, and Kate felt conspicuous as she hurried her steps.

The second floor was quiet. Two offices on the right, two on the left and what seemed to be a private area separating them. Rejecting the attorney's office and the door marked with only the name Standish, she turned left and found a real-estate company and then the offices she'd been looking for.

Kate stationed herself in front of the posters of available properties displayed in the plateglass window of the real-estate office, trying to appear absorbed in the description of what was called a desirable four-bedroom residence and the photo of a decrepit-looking farmhouse, optimistically labeled a fixer-upper. From there, she could glance into the windows of the office next door.

The first thing she noticed was that something was missing. Jason had mentioned, when he'd first accepted the internship one of his professors had helped arrange, the names of the two partners who comprised the professional staff: Russell Sheldon and Bartley Gordon. Now there was only one name listed on the door—Gordon. Below it, in suitably smaller letters, she read, Lina Oberlin, Assistant and Office Manager. What had happened to the other partner?

The room beyond the window told her nothing. A reception desk, where a twentysomething with improbably red hair sat filing her nails, another desk behind hers, which might once have been Jason's, and three uncommunicative doors.

Kate sensed movement in back of her, and before she could turn, she saw a face reflected in the glass. Mac Whiting stood behind her, his jaw especially uncompromising.

She swung around. "Are you following me, Chief Whiting?"

"Looking to ask you a question." He seemed to make an effort not to sound as intimidating as he appeared. "When we met earlier, why didn't you mention that you were Jason Reilley's sister?"

"Half sister," she pointed out, her mind scurrying busily. How had he identified her with Jason so quickly? She'd never even been to Laurel Ridge before. She had gone straight to Philadelphia when she'd heard the news of Jason's death. "That's why our names are different."

He inclined his head at that obvious statement, but his eyes never left hers. "I'm sorry for your loss."

The phrase sounded a little stilted, but Kate thought she detected real regret in his voice, and she warmed toward him before she reminded herself who he was.

"Thank you." She hesitated, but curiosity was stronger than her desire to keep the man at arm's length. "How did you know who I am? Or is it your practice to run a background check on everyone who comes to Laurel Ridge?"

Surprisingly, he didn't seem to take offense at that, although his face didn't relax. "I didn't have to. I recognized you from—" he hesitated, his straight brows drawing down "—from the funeral."

She was probably gaping at him. Kate gave herself a mental shake. "You were at my brother's funeral? Why?"

"He died in my town." The words were clipped. "Call it a courtesy."

"You didn't speak to me."

"Under the circumstances, I thought it was better not to. I figured you and your father didn't need the reminder of what happened."

"Stepfather," she corrected automatically. "You mean your assumption that Jason was just another druggie who'd overdosed in your town."

He stiffened. "It wasn't a question of assuming anything. The postmortem confirmed the cause of his death."

She wanted to protest that Jason had been clean for nearly three years before he died, but told herself bitterly that it was hardly likely a cop would be convinced by her opinion. Not when Jason's own father hadn't been.

Kate rubbed her arms, chilled by the vivid reminder. Jason had looked so young by the time she'd been able to see his body at the viewing. With every care and stress wiped from his face, he might have been a sleeping child again.

When she didn't speak, Whiting frowned at her with a look of frustration. "Weren't you satisfied with the coroner's findings? Is that it?"

"No." She could hear the reluctance in her voice. She'd like to argue, but she couldn't. Jason had died of a combination of powerful prescription painkillers and alcohol. It was only too likely. But it didn't answer the important question. It didn't tell her why.

"Ms. Beaumont?" Whiting's voice had gentled, and he reached toward her tentatively. "I'm sorry. I wish it had been different."

He sounded convincing, but she wasn't going to take anything at face value here.

"Yes." Different. If she'd come before, if she'd known or even guessed . . . But there was no point in going down that road again.

"When I spoke to you earlier, at the cemetery—" he paused "—did you want to see the place? Is that why you're here in Laurel Ridge?"

Whiting was bound to ask that question, of course. And she'd have to answer him, but she wasn't about to trust him with the real reason she was here. He would, inevitably, be on the side of his town, his people.

"I'm taking some time off before I start looking for a new job." That, at least, was more or less true. The Baltimore paper that had employed her suffered, as most print papers did, from dwindling circulation. They'd resorted to what they euphemistically called retrenchment. "My stepfather passed away recently, so I don't have

31

any other family left. I wanted to spend a little time in the last place my brother lived."

That might sound morbid, but it was the best she could do in terms of an explanation.

"I see." Whiting was studying her face, as if measuring exactly how much he believed her. "I'm sorry about your stepfather."

She nodded, accepting the sympathy wordlessly. He would, she supposed, expect her to regret Tom Reilley's death, and she didn't have anything to say that was likely to make sense to a man like Whiting. Another cop, another man with hard edges and no tolerance for someone who didn't live by his rules.

He took a step back, and Kate felt as if she could breathe again.

"I hope you find whatever it is you're looking for here."

Her gaze flew to his face, but he apparently didn't mean anything specific by the words. He was just attempting to console. He couldn't possibly have any idea what she was really looking for in Laurel Ridge.

I want to know why. I want to know what happened to my little brother in your town that led to him taking his own life.

CHAPTER TWO

Since her identity was already known to Chief Whiting, Kate didn't see much point in being less than open with the owner of the bed-and-breakfast. She paused on the sidewalk, taking in the white-frame building, its welcoming porch lined with pots of yellow-and-burgundy chrysanthemums. Jason had mentioned Mrs. Anderson in one of his infrequent phone calls last summer, and Kate had formed the impression from his words of a bustling busybody, intent on knowing all about her guests and everyone else in town.

Well, the woman wouldn't have to pry if Kate was up-front with her—relatively speaking, at least. And if Mrs. Anderson spread the word about Kate's presence, it might pave the way to conversations with people who had known him. Of course, Mac Whiting might already be talking about her. She grimaced, not sure she wanted to know what he thought.

The front door stood hospitably open. Kate rang the bell once and stepped inside, onto a braided rug bright against wide, gleaming oak floorboards. An archway on one side of the hall led into a sunny living room—or maybe *parlor* was a better word, given the Victorian settees,

33

marble-topped tables and grandfather clock. To her left, a drop-leaf table apparently did duty as a reception desk, and a heavily carved staircase wound upward behind it.

No doubt alerted by the bell, a woman emerged from a swinging door that must lead to the back of the ground floor—probably the kitchen and private area. Plump and graying, the woman had a beaming smile for her visitor.

"I hope I didn't keep you waiting. I'm Grace Anderson. Passing through, are you? Were you looking for a room for the night?" She hurried to flip open an old-fashioned register on the table, sounding hopeful.

"Actually, I'd like to stay for a bit longer than that." She paused, oddly reluctant to take the plunge now that she was here. "I'm Kate Beaumont. Jason Reilley was my brother."

"Oh, my dear." The smiling expression crumpled, and Mrs. Anderson's eyes filled with tears. She came around the table, holding both hands out to Kate. "I'm so very sorry for your loss."

The woman's obvious distress pierced Kate's armor, and she fought back her own tears. "Thank you." Her voice was husky, and she cleared her throat. "Jason spoke of your kindness."

Actually, Jason had seemed annoyed by her fussing over him, but coming from a young man finally out on his own, that was only natural.

He wouldn't have been eager to trade what he considered an overprotective big sister for a mothering landlady.

"He was a dear boy." Mrs. Anderson wiped away tears with the back of her hand. She hesitated, studying Kate's face and then glancing away. "Did you come . . ." She let the question fade away, obviously curious but hampered by good manners from probing a sensitive subject.

Kate had a wry inward smile for that convention. It was one of the first things to go for a reporter. Well, the story she'd told Whiting had better stay consistent.

"I'm taking a little time off before looking for a new job, which will mean relocating. I thought I'd like to spend some time in Laurel Ridge. This place seemed to mean a lot to Jason." She paused, but she may as well go after what she really wanted. "I hoped your cottage might be available to rent for a few weeks, maybe a month."

The woman's expression grew wary. "Are you sure that's wise? Maybe it's not . . . not healthy."

Was she afraid Kate would kill herself with drugs and alcohol, the way Jason did? The thought stung, and Kate had to force a smile.

"The cottage sounded so charming from the way my brother described it. And I'll be writing several freelance articles while I'm here, so I'd appreciate having the extra space to work."

That seemed to mollify the woman, but there

was still a trace of doubt in her eyes. "Yes, well, why don't we take a look at the cottage first? Maybe it won't be what you want at all, and I have several lovely rooms in the house."

"Thanks. I'd like to see the cottage." She waited, the smile pinned to her face, letting the silence grow between them. She'd guess Mrs. Anderson wasn't very good with silences.

"Yes. Fine." The woman gestured toward the door she'd come in. "We'll go out the back."

A dining room lay behind the parlor, complete with built-in cabinets containing an elaborate china service. An oval cherry table was large enough to seat a dozen, making her wonder how many guests were in residence. The place seemed very quiet.

The kitchen beyond was obviously Mrs. Anderson's own domain, with a corner devoted to a computer and filing cabinet and another turned into a cozy nook with a television and a recliner. On the opposite side a glassed-in sunroom looked out on flower beds.

Mrs. Anderson gestured toward the long table that occupied the sunroom. "I serve breakfast there from seven to nine on weekdays and eight to ten on Saturday and Sunday. Or if I have a party that wants to meet together, I can set up in the dining room." What sounded like a routine announcement was interrupted by a sudden smile. "Well, really, you can let me know

36

what time you want breakfast, as long as I'm not too busy."

Encouraged by the thaw, Kate ventured a question. "Did Jason usually have breakfast here, or did he fix his own in the cottage?"

Mrs. Anderson shrugged, sailing on out the back door and dangling a set of keys. "Sometimes one, sometimes the other. On workdays, he'd often just have cereal in the cottage, even though I told him he ought to have a good hot breakfast."

The words conjured up an image of Jason, hair rumpled, eyes sleepy, crouched over a bowl of his favorite cereal. There were days when he'd eat nothing else for breakfast, lunch and supper unless she intervened.

It was a matter of twenty feet or so to the cottage, but the small building was almost screened from view by an overgrown hedge of lilac bushes that surrounded it, to say nothing of the ivy that climbed up the walls and over the door.

Mrs. Anderson pushed back a lilac branch as she fumbled with a key.

"Sometimes I think I ought to have the dratted things cut to the ground, but they smell so lovely in the spring that I haven't the heart." She darted a look at Kate. "Your brother said it was like the hedge around Sleeping Beauty's castle. He liked it."

"I'm sure he did." From childhood, Jason had

37

escaped life through myth and fantasy, and she wasn't surprised he'd thought of it in that way. "No thorns, thank goodness," she added.

The door swung open, and Mrs. Anderson vanished inside. "Just let me get some lights on, so you can see the place properly, although there is light from the windows, of course."

Kate hesitated on the doorstep, one hand on the frame. A tendril of ivy entangled her fingers as if to restrain her. *This is it,* a voice seemed to be saying in the back of her mind. *Once you're committed, there's no going back.*

I don't want to go back, she insisted. *I'm already in this to the end.*

The only possible thing worse than knowing the truth of why Jason died would be never knowing at all.

Mac was still thinking about that odd encounter with Kate Beaumont when he headed into the café for coffee. He should be concentrating on the recent explosion of illegal prescription meds surfacing in town. Trouble was, he had a suspicion Kate Beaumont might be likely to set off a few explosions of her own.

"Uncle Mac!" The high, young voice of his nephew cut through the chatter of the lunchtime crowd. "Look what I have!"

Grinning, Mac wended his way through tables to where his mother sat with his brother's boy,

Jamie. Jamie was holding a sticky bun in an equally sticky hand.

"Do you want some, Uncle Mac? I'll share."

Mac stepped back out of range of Jamie's waving hand. "No, thanks. If I eat that in my uniform, I'll have the bees following me around town."

Jamie, at eight easily impressed, found that hilarious. While he was doubled up with giggles, Mac raised an eyebrow at his mother. "No school today?"

Ellen Whiting, slim and attractive, shook her head. "Dentist appointment. I'll drop him at school after lunch."

"I didn't have cavities," Jamie announced proudly around a sticky mouthful.

"So you're making up for that by eating lots of sugar, right, buddy?" Mac ruffled Jamie's fair, silky hair.

"*Ach*, such a sweet boy can use some sugar." Anna Schmidt, the Amish owner of the Buttercup Café, set a mug of coffee in front of Mac and gestured him into a chair. "I'll put your coffee refill in a to-go cup, but for now sit down and visit like a normal person."

"*Denke*, Anna." He slid easily into the Pennsylvania Dutch expression he'd heard all his life. "You scold me as much as my mother does."

"I don't scold," Mom said. "I just suggest."

"Over and over," he teased. He glanced toward

39

the door at the sound of the bell and stiffened. Kate Beaumont had just come in.

She spotted him and stopped midstride, making him think that she was fighting the inclination to turn around and walk back out again.

His lips twitched. She probably didn't know how obvious she was. Perversely, he rose, nodding to her and forcing her to recognize him. "Ms. Beaumont, it's nice to see you again. Come and meet my mother."

If anyone had a talent for making people thaw, it was Ellen Whiting. He'd be fascinated to see how long Kate held out against her.

Kate approached somewhat unwillingly, he thought.

"Kate Beaumont, Ellen Whiting."

His mother held out her hand. "So nice to meet you, Kate. Won't you join us?"

Before Kate had a chance to respond, Jamie burst into the conversation. "Hi, I'm Jamie Whiting. Not James, 'cause that's my grandpa's name. Sometimes Grammy calls him Jimmy to tease him, but she always calls me Jamie. Does anybody call you Katie?"

Kate looked a bit stunned at Jamie's conversational style, but she managed to make a recovery. "Hi, Jamie. No, nobody calls me Katie. Just Kate, okay?"

"Okay. Grammy says you should always call people what they want to be called, because nicknames can hurt people's feelings. Aren't you going to sit down?"

Under the pressure of that wide, innocent blue gaze, Kate sat in a chair, but she perched on the edge of it, as if ready to make a quick retreat.

Mac reached across to hand Jamie another napkin. "Maybe if you'd slow down a bit, somebody else could talk."

Jamie just grinned at him, but he subsided.

"Mom, Kate's brother was Jason Reilley. You remember—the young man who passed away last year." He glanced at Jamie, but his nephew was deeply engaged in eating the last crumb of his treat.

His mother's eyes filled with quick sympathy. "Oh, my dear, I'm so sorry. That was just tragic. You must miss him terribly."

As usual, his mother had moved straight to the heart, and he saw Kate's lips tremble for an instant. "Yes," she murmured. "I do miss him."

"Losing someone is never easy, but I always think it's especially hard when it's a young person." His mother clasped Kate's hand. "Naturally you must have wanted to see where he lived."

Funny. He'd assumed she'd wanted to see where her brother had died, but Mom jumped to the opposite conclusion. And she must be right, judging by the way Kate was looking at her—with a kind of startled surprise at meeting understanding from a stranger.

His mother never stayed a stranger with anyone for long. In a few minutes she'd elicited the fact that Kate had lost her job with a Baltimore newspaper in a series of cutbacks.

"I'm not the only one." She shrugged off an expression of sympathy. "People seem to rely on the internet for their news these days, not the daily paper."

"Laurel Ridge must be the exception, then." He decided it was time he got back into the conversation. "We still have to have our daily dose of the *Laurel Ridge Standard*, don't we?"

Mom chuckled. "How else would we know what was going on in town? The grapevine is good, but we have to see some things in print to believe them."

"Myself, I'd say gossip is more interesting." Anna appeared, setting a mug of coffee in front of Kate without being asked. "But there's nothing like the newspaper for seeing who's got what for sale. My boy Luke just got a perfectly good harrow from someone who was going to pay to have it hauled away as junk."

Kate looked startled at the server's entering the discussion, as well she might. He suspected Laurel Ridge had a few surprises in store for her.

"Anna, this is Kate Beaumont. She's visiting Laurel Ridge for a bit."

"*Ach, gut.*" Anna's round face beamed. "*Wilkom.* I'll be seeing you in the Buttercup, then, ain't so?"

"I guess so. I'm staying right across the street."

"Mrs. Anderson's." She nodded. "I guessed as much. Will you be having some lunch? The chicken pot pie, maybe?"

"Just a salad, please. To take out."

"I'm sure you're busy getting settled in," Mom said, wiping Jamie's hands and face despite his protests. "We've delayed you long enough, and I must get this boy back to school."

"Do I have to . . ." Jamie began, but he subsided at a look from his grandmother. Sliding from his chair, he gave Mac a throttling hug and turned to Kate. "See you again soon, okay?"

Kate smiled, her expression softening. "It was nice to meet you, Jamie."

"I hope we'll have a chance to get better acquainted while you're here," Mom said, touching Kate's shoulder lightly. "I know Grace Anderson will make you comfortable. Her rooms are lovely."

"I'm sure they are. I'm actually renting the cottage, and it's . . . charming."

Did he really hear an infinitesimal pause before the final word? It seemed to him it was far from charming for her to be living in the very rooms where her brother had spent his last days.

He waved to Jamie, who'd paused at the door

43

for a last look, and then turned back to Kate.

"Your little boy is a sweetheart," she said quickly, maybe to forestall any criticism from him.

"My little nephew," he corrected. "Jamie is my brother Nick's boy. I'm not married."

"I see." She seemed to be readjusting her thoughts.

It wouldn't be any of his business where she stayed, if it weren't for his instinct that she was hiding something. He couldn't shake his conviction that a big-city reporter wouldn't be spending time in Laurel Ridge without an agenda. Bluntness was probably the only way he'd get an answer.

"Why are you living in the cottage? What are you after in Laurel Ridge?"

Kate flared up at that, as he'd expected. "I'm not after anything. Besides, wouldn't you do the same, if it was your brother?"

What exactly was the passion that flamed in her eyes and made her skin flush? Not grief, he thought. Or at least, not only grief. Something more.

He took a moment, and then tried to respond honestly. "If I lost Nick all of a sudden, I don't know what I'd do. It would be like losing part of myself."

Their eyes met. Held. She looked stunned, vulnerable, and that very vulnerability had the power to draw him in. To make him want to touch her, comfort her.

But he couldn't. Not when he didn't know what she was going to bring to his town.

Deliberately he went on. "But I'm pretty sure I wouldn't try to retrace his final steps. Not unless I was looking for something. What are you looking for, Kate?"

Watching her face then was like watching ice form on the river. She stared at him as if he'd just crawled out from under a rock. Not bothering to deny it, she rose, slung her bag strap over her shoulder and headed for the counter, probably to wait for her order.

He gazed at her for a long moment. No good trying to get anything more from her now. The rigid line of her back told him that much.

Maybe it was just as well that he'd said something to infuriate her again, because when she'd looked at him with vulnerability in those golden-brown eyes, he'd have had a tough time holding on to his own good judgment.

By the time Kate entered Blackburn House that afternoon, she'd tried a dozen times to dismiss Mac Whiting from her thoughts. Unfortunately, he wouldn't stay gone. She had no doubt he'd be an obstacle in her path if she let him.

She wouldn't. She'd already dealt with one hard-headed cop in her life, and she could deal with Whiting. Anybody who'd been raised by a difficult man like Tom Reilley had developed a tough shell. Except Jason, of course. Maybe if he had, his life wouldn't have ended the way it had.

The important thing was to get on with her plans, and that meant starting at the place where Jason had worked. He'd spent every day there, and judging by what she'd been able to decipher of his video diary, he'd had a lot of opinions about the place.

Preoccupied, she headed for the stairs, passing an Amish woman standing in the doorway of the quilt shop. The woman smiled and nodded as if Kate were known to her. The power of the grapevine in a small town? Maybe so. At least she seemed friendly.

Movement behind the glass door to Whiting and Whiting Cabinetry made her nerves jump irrationally, and she turned her face away as she hurried past, gaining the stairs without incident.

Whatever activity there was in Blackburn House seemed concentrated on the ground floor. Once again there was no one on the steps, and the upper hallway was deserted. A murmur of conversation came from the real-estate office, but Laurel Ridge Financial Group was empty, save for the same young receptionist behind the front desk, her head bent over a printer that was spewing out papers.

She looked up at the sound of the door

opening, seeming to brighten at the prospect of an interruption. "Welcome to Laurel Ridge Financial." Abandoning the printer, she flipped open a pad on the desk. "Do you have an appointment?"

"No, I'm afraid not." Kate glanced at the nameplate on the desk. "I just dropped in. I hope I'm not interrupting you. Are you Nikki?"

"That's me." Nikki jerked an impatient nod toward the printer. "Just boring routine, even if the office manager does think the printer will jam when somebody's not watching it every minute. You're new around here, right?"

Kate couldn't help smiling. "How does everyone I meet know I'm a stranger?"

Nikki rolled her eyes. "Easy to see you don't know what it's like in a burg the size of Laurel Ridge. Everybody knows everybody. Boring." She managed to insert a wealth of meaning into the word, which seemed to be one of her favorites.

This kid couldn't be much more than seven or eight years younger than her, but Kate felt aeons older. With that improbably red hair and the matching scarlet nails, Nikki looked like a fifteen-year-old trying for a fake ID. She had a small, sharp-featured face and an obvious disdain for the job she held.

Had she thought Jason boring, too? Or had he been interesting, an urban stranger, someone she hadn't known all her life? Kate didn't think Jason had mentioned Nikki, but he may have. He often didn't bother with names when he talked about people.

Only one way to find out. "I wonder if you remember my brother. He worked here for the summer last year."

"Jason?" Nikki's pointed features seemed to tighten. "Jason was your brother?"

"That's right. I'm Kate. Kate Beaumont. I suppose you got to know him, with you two being the only young people working here. Did he mention me?"

"He said he had a sister who was a reporter someplace." Nikki pushed a curl out of her face with a scarlet fingertip. "That's you, huh?"

Kate nodded, debating with herself about how much she wanted to say to the receptionist. Maybe it was better not to let Nikki think she wanted anything in particular, at least until Kate knew how close she'd been to Jason. "He seemed to enjoy his job."

Nikki shrugged. "It's an okay place to work, if you don't mind routine. And I took him around a little bit. You know, showed him what passes for nightlife in a place like this."

"He told me you'd been friendly." He hadn't, but let that pass in the interest of establishing a rapport with Nikki. "He appreciated it, especially since he didn't know anyone here."

"Maybe. But he sure didn't like partying all that much." Nikki didn't seem to realize that a big sister might consider that a good thing. "That's why it was so strange when he—well, you know." She lowered her voice, as if speaking of death required softer tones.

"You didn't have any idea he'd been into drugs?" In Kate's experience, someone like Nikki was more likely to recognize the signs than one of the bosses would have been.

"I didn't think—"

One of the doors behind Nikki opened, and her voice cut off immediately.

"Nikki, why didn't you tell me there was a client waiting?" The man who surged forward, hand extended, had the kind of professional smile usually worn by anyone who had something to sell—his slightly puffy cheeks creasing, eyes crinkling in welcome as if she were a long-lost relative. "I'm Bart Gordon." He clasped her hand warmly. "And you are?"

"Kate Beaumont." How long would it take for the jovial welcome to wear off once he knew she wasn't a client? Not long, she suspected, but maybe she was being too cynical.

"She's Jason Reilley's sister," Nikki said before Kate could.

Gordon stiffened, his hand releasing hers. "I see." The smile became noticeably artificial. "What brings you to see us, Ms. Beaumont?"

49

"I happened to be in Laurel Ridge and thought I'd like to introduce myself to my brother's friends and colleagues here. And to thank you for the beautiful flower arrangement you sent for the services."

The man's tension seemed to ease. "The least we could do. Such a sad loss," he murmured.

"I see that Mr. Sheldon is no longer active in the firm. I did want to express my thanks to him, as well." *And ask him about my brother.*

"Russell Sheldon retired last year. Poor fellow—the work was getting beyond him. I'll be sure to give him your message when I see him. Thanks for stopping by." Gordon's fingers brushed her elbow, as if he'd usher her out.

Not yet. She ignored the hint. "Jason's death was a terrible shock, of course. Especially since he'd been so enthusiastic about his internship. Was there some issue at work that might have disturbed or upset him?"

Gordon's already flushed face reddened alarmingly. "Are you trying to blame us for what your brother did? If you think you can hold the firm responsible, you've got another—"

The door to the other office opened behind him, a woman emerging. Kate's wayward imagination presented her with an image of a Bavarian clock, with figures appearing and disappearing through their little doors.

"Bart, I'm sure you're misunderstanding the

situation." She smiled at Kate, extending her hand. "I'm Lina Oberlin, Mr. Gordon's assistant. Did I hear him say that you're poor Jason's sister?"

In other words, she'd been listening behind the door. Maybe, as Nikki had said, things were so boring that any interruption was welcome.

The female assistant was fair, blonde and fortyish, with hair drawn back from a pale, nearly colorless face. Lina Oberlin had small, even features and a trim figure that could have been appealing in anything other than the plain gray pantsuit she wore. It was as if she'd deliberately set out to fade into the woodwork.

"That's right . . ." she began, but Bart Gordon's voice ran over hers like a steamroller.

"The idea of it. We're the ones with a complaint. Here I was, giving the kid a second chance, and he goes and brings the worst kind of publicity down on the firm."

Her brother was dead, and he was worried about publicity. Kate's fingers tightened into fists. Before she could cut loose, she happened to catch a glimpse of the receptionist's face. Avid, blatant curiosity—an eagerness, even, to see a drama unfolding in front of her.

And more, perhaps? If Nikki was glad to see the apparently forgotten situation raked up, that might mean she knew something.

"You don't mean that." Lina Oberlin's voice

seemed to hold a warning for her volatile boss. "I'm so sorry." She touched Kate's arm lightly. "We were all stunned by what happened to your brother. Jason was such a nice boy. I'm sure he was happy here. Perhaps you and I could have a quiet talk later?" She glanced at Gordon, as if to ensure that he wouldn't burst out again.

"I'd appreciate that." Kate let herself be led to the door. She couldn't accomplish anything more here now, but she wasn't dissatisfied with this first encounter. Outright anger was more revealing than bland sympathy.

Her presence angered Gordon. Why? And why did Lina Oberlin feel the need to intercede? Mere politeness, or something more?

And what about the receptionist? She'd have to make a point of talking to Nikki away from the office, little though she wanted to satisfy the girl's keen curiosity. She didn't doubt that if there was something to tell, Nikki would seize the chance to be involved.

CHAPTER THREE

The few belongings Kate had brought with her were quickly unpacked and stowed away in the cottage. She slid a suitcase into the back of the bedroom closet to get it out of the way. The rest of her things had gone into storage in Baltimore.

She hadn't taken anything from Tom Reilley's house except for Jason's things. The rest had gone to a sale. The fewer reminders of life there, the better, as far as she was concerned.

Jason had probably felt the same way when he'd left his father's house for the last time. It couldn't have held too many happy memories for him. Although she hoped he might have cherished, as she did, the after-school hours they'd spent at home together.

Kate walked back into the living room. The cottage was small and compact. The living room had just enough space for a television, sofa and chairs in one end and a bookcase and desk at the other, where she'd immediately set up her computer. Jason would no doubt have set up in the same place. He couldn't bear to be off-line, and he wanted a laptop for gaming.

If a person liked cottage style, the place was perfectly decorated, with cheerful chintz fabric on the furniture, white end tables and Cape Cod curtains on the windows. There was a small kitchen with a nook for a table and chairs, and a bedroom and bath. The shrubbery and vines she'd noted on the outside increased a sense of isolation, especially where they brushed against the windows.

It was quiet—too quiet for her tastes. She was used to the constant noise and movement of the city. This much solitude would take some getting used to.

Jason wouldn't have minded it, she knew. As introverted as he'd been, he'd have welcomed it. Close contact with other people stressed him almost beyond bearing. College dorm life must have been a nightmare for him. It had taken time and maturity for her to understand that, but Tom never had. He'd always insisted Jason could be like other kids if he just tried harder.

Small wonder Jason had taken refuge in his fantasy world. There, he could be in control. He could shut out the outside world and focus on the voices in his imagination. If she'd understood that earlier, if his father had grasped it at all . . .

She pushed the thought away. She couldn't go back. All she could do for Jason now was find out why he'd died, and the key to that had to be in his video diary.

Reluctantly, Kate turned her laptop on. The video diary had been Jason's closely guarded secret. She'd known it existed, but she'd never had so much as a glimpse of it until two weeks ago, when she'd started clearing Tom's house for the sale. It still felt as if she were violating Jason's privacy by watching it.

She clicked the diary file, and Jason's face appeared on her screen, looking as he'd so often looked in reality—soft brown hair standing on end as if he'd been running his fingers through it, hazel eyes magnified by his dark-rimmed glasses, his sensitive mouth unsmiling.

The first time she'd watched it she hadn't been able to get all the way through even one entry— she'd been crying too hard. It wasn't that much easier now, but at least she was able to control the tears. Now a session of trying to understand just left her wrung out and exhausted, her throat tight, her eyes burning.

Even if it hadn't been for the grief, under-standing would have been difficult, due to Jason's refusal to be ordinary in referring to people. He almost never used names, instead dubbing the people he met with the identities of the mythic characters from his favorite books and games. Some Kate could understand a little, like the characters from fairy tales or Tolkien's books, while others left her banging her head against the wall.

Now that she'd met the cast of characters at Laurel Ridge Financial, she might have a chance of identifying the people he referred to. Maybe even begin to understand what was happening in his life that disturbed him so toward the end of that summer that he would have turned to pills to dull the pain. Or to end it permanently.

She'd like to believe the overdose had been accidental. Unfortunately, she couldn't convince herself of that. Jason had been clean for so long. He knew, if anyone did, the results of combining alcohol with those strong prescription meds.

Telling her stepfather her feelings would just have made the whole situation worse. Better to keep her opinion to herself until—unless—she knew for sure.

She clicked the video to start it, and Jason's soft, diffident voice sounded, wrenching her heart.

"The King was upset today, and I'm not sure why." Jason's eyes were serious, concerned. This had been about midway through his internship. She paused the tape and pulled out a notebook to jot down her impressions.

The King. Well, that would probably be Bart Gordon, wouldn't it? He seemed to be running things now.

But what had been his position relative to Russell Sheldon? She didn't know, and such a simple thing could mean a world of difference in interpretation. She noted a query—find out who was in charge when Sheldon was still with the firm. Probably anyone would know. Like

Mac Whiting, for instance, but she dismissed the thought. He was the last person she'd go to for help.

A firm knock on the door interrupted her line of thought. Mrs. Anderson again? She'd already been here twice, once with a freshly laundered blanket and again with a loaf of pumpkin bread. It was easy to see why she'd gotten on Jason's nerves.

Kate got up, then turned back and closed the file she'd been watching. No one need know about the diary, not now, maybe not ever.

She opened the door, prepared to be polite to her landlady, and found the woman from the financial group, Lina Oberlin, waiting.

"Ms. Oberlin." She was frankly surprised. She'd hoped the woman meant her comment about getting together, but she certainly hadn't expected a visit so soon. "Please, come in. How did you know where to find me?" She hadn't said a word about where she was staying while she'd been in the office, had she?

"It's all over Blackburn House already, I'm afraid." With a restrained smile, the woman stepped inside. "Please, call me Lina."

"Lina," she repeated. "How would anyone at Blackburn House know?" If she sounded a little suspicious, it was nothing to how she felt. Were people watching her?

"Obviously you're not used to the way news

spreads in a place like Laurel Ridge. After all, we're right next door. I'm sure someone saw you moving in." Lina shrugged. "People in a small town are interested in their neighbors."

"Obviously so." Kate gestured to the sofa. "Please, sit down."

Lina had apparently come straight from work, since she still wore the tailored suit she'd had on earlier. She sat down, looking around the room with frank curiosity. "This is really quite nice, isn't it?" Her gaze seemed to linger on the desk, and Kate was relieved that she had closed the file. "I haven't seen the inside before, but it's roomier than I'd have expected."

"You were never inside when Jason lived here?" Kate sat down opposite the woman.

Lina's lips twitched in what might have been a smile. "I can just imagine the talk that would have spread if I'd come to visit a young male colleague. I'm afraid financial consultants are expected to be models of rectitude in a place like Laurel Ridge."

"Yes. I'd say Mr. Gordon made it clear that adverse publicity was frowned on." She couldn't seem to keep the resentment from her tone. Gordon's facile sympathy had disappeared very quickly at any faint suggestion of fault on the part of the firm.

"That's really why I've come so quickly." Lina leaned forward, her pale face intent. "I'm afraid

Bart reacted badly, and I wanted to explain. It's not entirely his fault, you know. Our clients didn't like seeing the newspaper stories about one of our staff in such a situation." She shook her head, rueful. "Sorry. I don't want to hurt you, but that's the truth."

Kate suppressed her irritation as best she could. "I understand being concerned for the reputation of the firm." But Bart Gordon had overreacted, it seemed to her, and she really wanted to know why.

"But you think he was over-the-top." Lina seemed to know what she was thinking. "I'm afraid he was so annoyed because he was the one who suggested taking Jason on as an intern. He talked Mr. Sheldon into it. Apparently Jason's adviser was an old fraternity brother of Bart's, and Bart agreed as a favor to him. Then, when things went badly . . ."

She let that trail off, and Kate managed not to point out that things had gone far more badly for Jason than for the firm. She hoped to get information from the woman, not antagonize her.

"Aside from the way it ended, how was Jason doing as an intern? I'm sure you have an opinion, working so closely with him."

"Well, not really all that closely, I'm afraid. It was actually Russell Sheldon who seemed to take the most interest in Jason. He took the time to work with the young man, and according to him, Jason did very well. He always seemed very conscientious to me—almost too preoccupied with his work at times, I'd say."

That sounded like Jason. He'd focus on a task to the exclusion of everything else.

"I'm glad Jason found a mentor here. I really should thank Mr. Sheldon personally, then. Is he still living in town?" It would be as good an excuse as any to probe into what the man remembered of Jason's time here.

Lina looked doubtful. "Yes, Russell Sheldon is quite a fixture in town. Everyone knows him. But I don't know that it's a good idea for you to visit him."

She paused, then seemed to realize she'd have to explain further if she expected Kate to drop the idea.

"The trouble is that Russell has been failing mentally for the past few years. He probably should have retired earlier than he did, to be honest, but he had such a good rapport with our older clients that we hated to see him go. They'd trusted him for years, and it wasn't easy to convince them that they'd be quite safe in Bart's hands."

"Surely a short visit with him wouldn't hurt . . ." Kate began, but Lina was already shaking her head.

"I understand the poor man is becoming increasingly erratic. Apparently the least disruption of his usual routine causes him to react very emotionally. In fact, his son has been trying to get him into an assisted living facility. I'm sure you wouldn't want to cause Mr. Sheldon any distress, and I don't imagine he even remembers Jason at this point."

"I see." Somehow she didn't think she wanted to take Lina's word for it, as helpful as she seemed. "I've hoped people who knew my brother during those last weeks might have noticed some indication of trouble. Anything that seemed out of his normal routine, any change in his attitude . . ."

There had to be something—something that had pushed Jason into his final act.

"I wish I could be of more help." Lina spread her hands in a gesture of helplessness. "In retrospect I do think Jason seemed a bit more preoccupied than usual toward the end of the summer, but then he'd been sending out résumés and looking for a position, so that's only natural."

Kate nodded. In one of his phone calls, they'd talked about the possibility of Jason getting a job near her. He wouldn't have wanted to move in with her again, but she'd wanted to be close enough to provide some support, at least.

She tried another tack. "I suppose you don't know any of the friends he made here?"

"I'm afraid not. Jason didn't seem like the social type. He was more serious than a lot of young men his age." Lina's smile seemed to freeze. "I'd be wary of anything Nikki has to say about your brother, by the way. From what I saw, he was usually trying to evade her attentions."

"Thanks. I'll bear that in mind."

"Well, you don't need my advice. I'm sure a woman of your experience could see at once just how much you can rely on Nikki for the truth." A smile warmed her rather restrained manner. "What was she doing when you came in? Filing her nails?"

Kate had to laugh. "Actually, I did spot her doing that earlier."

"We'd get someone better, but there isn't really all that much choice. The bright kids take off for college after graduation. At least Nikki knows how to operate the office equipment, and she's better on the computer than Bart is." Lina smiled. "Although that's not saying much."

"I sometimes think a five-year-old could teach me something new, despite my job." In the interests of possibly getting more from the woman later, she should respond to any friendship cues.

Lina reached for her bag. "I won't hold you up any longer, but if there's anything I can do, please, let me know. Jason's death must have been a terrible shock as well as a devastating loss."

The woman's sympathetic tone got to her, and

for a moment Kate considered taking Lina into her confidence. But only for a moment. Her native caution reasserted itself. She didn't intend to give too much away to anyone in this town, not until she had a better idea of where she stood.

Mac pulled into his parking space in front of the police station the next day, fuming. The meeting he'd had with the district attorney had been an exercise in frustration. They both knew of the increasing presence of drugs in their community, and of illegal prescription meds in particular. But the problem wasn't solved by talking about it—or at least, not by talking with a DA who was up for reelection this fall and wanted to be able to show voters he'd been actively involved in fighting drugs. All the DA wanted to do was give lip service to the problem.

Mac spared a passing thought to appreciate the crisp, clear weather that was so typical of fall in Pennsylvania. He didn't have time to enjoy it today, unfortunately. He headed for the door of the solid redbrick building that had housed the station for the past century. The cement block addition along one side might not have the beauty of the original structure, but it gave much-needed space for police cars as well as the paramedics.

A glance at the clock on the bell tower of Town Hall informed him that the morning was nearly gone, eaten up by talk that led nowhere. Marge

Bailey, their dispatcher/receptionist, gave him a sympathetic look as he came in out of the bright fall sunshine. Marge was fond of telling people how she used to babysit for Mac and his brother, and her motherliness with him was balanced by the crisp, no-nonsense way she dealt with police matters.

"No fun?"

He grimaced. "Maybe it'll satisfy him for the moment, so I can get some work done. Did the state police crime stats come in yet?"

"On your computer." She glanced toward his office door. "But first, you have a visitor." Marge rolled her eyes. "Bart Gordon. All het up about something. I told him you were tied up in a meeting, and that if he had something to report, another officer could speak with him, but he insisted on waiting for you."

"Right." Bart was one of those people who always had a list of complaints, most of them not police business at all. Looked as if the last shreds of his morning were being swept away. Well, his job was to protect and serve the community, even when they wasted his time.

Mac strode into the office, tossing his cap onto the desk. " 'Morning, Bart."

Bart Gordon shot out of the visitor's chair that took up too much space in Mac's tiny office, already crowded with desk, chair and files, made to seem even smaller by the framed photos of various town dignitaries and events that covered most of one wall.

"It's about time you're getting back. I've been waiting." Bart looked prosperous, self-satisfied and florid, as usual. He was enough older than Mac that their lives hadn't really touched at any point.

"Didn't Marge tell you I was at a meeting with the DA?" he asked blandly. "I'll have to speak to her about it."

Taken aback, Bart sat down again. "She mentioned it," he said reluctantly.

"Well, what can I do for you?" Mac edged around his desk and sat in the creaky swivel chair he'd inherited from his predecessor.

Bart seemed to get up a head of steam again. "Are you aware that Jason Reilley's sister is in town?" He made it sound like an accusation.

Now, what was there in Kate Beaumont's presence to make Bart so hot under the collar?

"Yes, I've met her." He kept his voice carefully neutral. "Is there a problem?"

"A problem? When a perfect stranger walks into my office and starts prying into my business?" Bart seemed to take a breath, maybe deciding that wasn't the way he wanted to present himself. After a moment he leaned forward, an earnest expression on his ruddy face. "Now, Mac, you know I always have the best interest of Laurel Ridge at heart. Adverse publicity about a

65

prominent business like ours can't do anyone any good. I'm just trying to protect the reputation of our town."

More intrigued by Bart's attitude than anything else, Mac raised an eyebrow. "Is Ms. Beaumont threatening you with bad publicity? How?"

"Not exactly." Bart hesitated as if balancing the wisdom of confiding in the police against his obvious irritation with the Beaumont woman. "But she's stirring up talk about her unfortunate brother's death. You know how uncomfortable that was. I think it best that it be forgotten, not dragged into the public eye again."

In other words, Bart Gordon had the wind up because of Kate Beaumont's interest in her brother's death. But why? There'd never been any suggestion of involvement on the part of the company.

"I can't run the woman out of town because she makes you uncomfortable," he pointed out.

"I know. But it's just so inconsiderate. We've already dealt with all that unpleasantness, and it certainly wasn't our fault. If I'd known the boy was likely to go back to drugs, I'd never have agreed to give him a chance." He was beginning to sound petulant, and Mac's supply of courtesy was running dangerously low.

He rose, hoping to indicate that the interview was over. "I'll have a talk with her."

"Yes, well, I suppose that will have to do." Bart

made it as far as the door before his grievance burst out again. "What does she want here, anyway? And why did it take her over a year to decide she had to come?"

Muttering a soothing word or two, Mac eased him out the door and closed it firmly.

But the question lingered in his mind. Little though he wanted to admit it, Bart Gordon did have a point. Why had Kate Beaumont waited over a year to come to the place where her brother died?

Kate walked the flagstone path to the cottage, disappointed but not deterred by the failure of her effort to speak to Russell Sheldon. Apparently it was true that the retiree was in poor health, since a caregiver had opened the door at his house and politely but firmly declined Kate's request to speak to him.

Very firmly—almost as if she'd been warned that Kate might come calling. Someone from the financial office had probably tipped off the woman, and it would be interesting to know who it had been.

She passed into the shade cast by the tall hedge along the side of the bed-and-breakfast, chilled when she stepped out of the bright autumn sunshine. She glanced up. The clear, crisp day seemed to accentuate the bright colors that appeared here and there on the ridge that isolated the town. She wasn't sure she'd enjoy living in a place where the hills crowded so close.

One refusal didn't spell the end. The caregiver had to leave sometime. She'd just have to catch Sheldon at a time when he was alone. No good reporter would ever give up after the first rebuff.

The walkway led to the stoop at the front door, where she exchanged the shadow of the hedge for those of the shrubs that overhung the cottage. Had Jason ever felt claustrophobic, living in such an enclosed space?

Kate drew out her keys, her fingers caressing the silver dragon on the key ring before they selected the door key. But when she touched the door, the key wasn't necessary. The door was unlocked, and it swung soundlessly open a few inches.

She stepped back, her heart pounding. She hadn't left the cottage unlocked. Double-checking the locks was second nature for someone who'd spent her life in an urban area, and Tom had drilled safety and self-defense into both of them.

No sound came from the cottage, but that didn't mean it was safe to go in. She threaded her fingers through her keys, almost hearing her stepfather's voice instructing her, and grasped her cell phone with the other hand. She pushed the door wide with her foot and peered inside, senses alert.

Nothing. At this point, Tom's instructions

would have stressed moving away and calling the police, but she had no desire for another encounter with Mac Whiting.

Kate took a cautious step inside, then another, and listened, holding her breath. After a moment or two, tense muscles began to relax. Whoever had been here must be gone.

Even as she thought it she sensed movement behind her. She whirled, striking out with the hand holding the keys—*get out, scream, run—*

Iron fingers grabbed her wrist before the blow could land. She froze, face-to-face with Mac, staring breathless into his narrowed eyes. For a long moment they stood very close, and the air seemed to quiver between them.

Then he stepped back, releasing her, his eyebrows lifting slightly. "You always greet visitors that way?"

"Visitors generally knock." Kate grabbed for the shaken fragments of her composure.

"The door was open." Whiting took hold of her wrist again, turning it to examine the points of the keys extending through her fingers. "Very effective weapon."

The touch of his hand made her too aware of the fierce physical presence behind his lazy smile and small-town manner. She drew away, and he didn't attempt to stop her.

"My stepfather was a cop. He taught us both self-defense."

"You must have been his star pupil." He studied her face for a moment. "You want to tell me what this is all about? I was just coming to talk to you. You came into the cottage as if you were expecting an attack."

Kate turned away, rubbing her fingers against the silver dragon. "I locked the door when I left earlier," she said shortly. "When I came back just now, it was unlocked."

"You're sure?" He shot the question at her.

"Of course I'm sure," she snapped. "I didn't grow up in Hicksville. I learned to lock doors as soon as I was tall enough to reach the knob."

Before she'd finished, he was giving her a firm push toward the door. "Go outside while I check the house." Without looking to see that she obeyed, he moved toward the bedroom, staying to the side as he opened the door.

Nothing happened. He disappeared into the room. Kate followed to find him surveying the clothes she'd tossed on the bed. Mac gave her a sharp look. "I thought I told you to go outside."

"I don't follow orders well." She glanced around and shrugged. "Doesn't look as if anything's disturbed in here."

He'd moved to the dresser, and she spoke again, impatient.

"I didn't bring the crown jewels with me this trip. The only thing of value here is my computer." The computer. She spun and fled back to the other room. The computer still sat on the small side table she'd appropriated to use as a desk.

"It's still here." Mac spoke behind her. "So apparently you haven't been burgled."

"It's here." Quickly she checked her files. Jason's diary was there, all right.

"Everything okay?" Mac had moved close enough that she felt his breath on her neck when he spoke. Close enough, most likely, to read the titles of the files. She shut the laptop.

"Okay. Except that I left it turned off, and now it's on."

But he was already moving to the kitchen, most of it visible from where they stood. "Easy to make a mistake about a thing like that, isn't it?" he said. "And I think I've solved the mystery." He held something up. "Your burglar left you a present. Smells like nut bread."

"Mrs. Anderson." Kate's jaw was tight, and she struggled to relax it. "She means to be kind, but . . ."

"But you'd rather she didn't," he finished for her. His face took on the amused look that annoyed her so. "I've never heard of locking doors to keep out kindness."

Kate took a deep breath, trying to think of a response that didn't sound petty. She couldn't. "Was there some reason you came over, Chief Whiting?"

His smile suggested he knew what she was thinking. "Mac, please. It seems you've ruffled the feathers of one of our prominent residents."

She looked at him blankly for a moment. "Who?" She couldn't imagine Russell Sheldon's caregiver going to the police about her visit.

"Bart Gordon seems to think you're planning to stir up bad publicity for his company." He raised an eyebrow. "And he's not yet aware that you're a reporter."

That comment seemed to come from left field. "My profession has nothing to do with it. My reasons for being here are purely personal."

"And they are?"

Her fingers clenched, nails biting into her palms. "I've already told you. I want to see the place where my brother spent the last months of his life."

"Yes, you told me. But I don't think you mentioned why you waited a year to come."

If she threw the computer at him, he'd probably arrest her for assault. She glared at him instead. "Not that it's any of your business, but this is the first opportunity I've had to get away from work for any length of time."

Mac seemed to be weighing her words, his eyes noncommittal.

Nettled, she couldn't keep from responding to what she suspected was disbelief. "I think that's all I have to say on the subject. So unless you intend to arrest me for making the good residents of Laurel Ridge think about something they'd rather forget, I'd appreciate it if you'd leave."

His smile flickered. "I'll buy that, for the moment. But if you ever decide to confide in me . . ."

"I won't." Her tone was tart.

"In the meantime, take my advice and steer clear of Bart Gordon. We wouldn't want him charging you with harassment, would we?" He gave her another extended look, then turned and walked out.

Kate let out a long breath. She hadn't seen the last of him—there was no doubt of that in her mind.

In the meantime, she had a more immediate problem. Obviously the landlady had come in, bearing food. But would she have started the computer? Somehow Kate didn't think so.

At least whoever had done so hadn't been able to get past the password, as far as she could see. But who? And why?

CHAPTER FOUR

Kate stood frowning at the computer for another moment. Then, realizing she was standing right in front of the window, she looked out, half expecting to see Mac Whiting staring in at her.

No one was there. She moved away from the window, and then went back and pulled the curtains closed. It made the small room dark, but it eliminated the sense that someone was watching her.

Rubbing her arms, she stalked into the kitchen. Mac had been right, of course. He seemed to make a habit of that. The neatly wrapped loaf on the counter bore a label. Nut bread, it proclaimed, in Mrs. Anderson's already familiar writing.

Drat the man. She'd already been shaken at finding the cottage door unlocked, and the immediate confrontation with him had really knocked her off her balance. That was probably why she'd had that intense awareness of him as a man. That, and the brief glimpse he'd given her of an intense protectiveness lurking under his professionalism.

He'd rocked her, and she didn't want that. Didn't have time for it, and really didn't welcome it. There was no space in her thoughts right now for anything but her mission.

Why, Jason? Why? She had nothing but the last journal entry to go on. If only he'd been clearer, just that one time.

He'd been upset, that much was evident. He'd talked about something wrong, something that had rocked him to his very soul.

Something so serious that he had taken his own life. She'd come reluctantly to that conclusion over a number of sleepless nights. It would be so much easier if she could believe he'd died of an accidental overdose. But she couldn't.

Someone had hurt Jason beyond bearing. She had to know who. Why.

Shaking her head, she forced herself to concentrate on more immediate problems. Like who had been in the cottage while she was out.

Kate rested her hand on the smooth, rounded surface of the loaf. Granted that Mrs. Anderson had been in the cottage, she still came back to the conviction that the woman would not have turned on Kate's computer. Naturally Mac would assume she'd been mistaken about turning it off, but she distinctly remembered doing so.

There was no point in going over and over the same ground. Kate grabbed her bag and went quickly toward the door. She'd thank Mrs. Anderson for the nut bread and add, very politely, that she'd rather the woman didn't come in when she wasn't there. Even a temporary tenant had a reasonable expectation of privacy, didn't she?

Crossing the yard, Kate tapped on the back door. Mrs. Anderson, busy with something at the stove, turned and waved her in.

The door was unlocked, and the first thing Kate noticed in the back hallway was a wooden rack attached to the wall, containing a row of keys, all neatly labeled. She hadn't noticed it when they'd come out this door the first time, probably because she was too intent on persuading Mrs. Anderson to let her have the cottage.

Obviously she didn't have to look far for a means by which someone could get into the cottage. That person had only to wait until Mrs. Anderson was in the front of the building, open the back door, reach in and lift the key from its hook. Apparently people here didn't have much concern for security.

Mrs. Anderson, wiping her hands on a towel, hurried to meet her. "Sorry. I thought I'd get a few coffee cakes baked to put in the freezer. Weekends get busy during the fall foliage season, you know."

"I didn't realize," Kate said. And she had no idea what Mrs. Anderson considered busy. "I just wanted to thank you for the nut bread you left for me today. That was so thoughtful." *And I wish you hadn't.* "The thing is . . ."

She ran out of words. Maybe Mac had been right about this. How could a person lock the door against kindness?

"It's nothing at all." The woman waved her to a seat in the breakfast area. "Goodness, I'm baking all the time, it seems. And I worry about you, alone back there, just like Jason was. Now, you'll stay and have a cup of coffee or tea, won't you? Or iced tea or cider?"

Kate started to shake her head but changed her mind. In the interest of keeping good relations with Mrs. Anderson, she should accept. If they started chatting casually, she might find a way of suggesting that the cottage key be kept in a more secure location.

"Iced tea, thanks." She settled into a chair and looked out on a flower bed filled with a colorful array of mums and asters.

Mrs. Anderson hurried to the refrigerator, returning to the table in moments with a tray holding a pitcher of tea, ice-filled glasses and fresh sprigs of mint. The woman must have been born to be a hostess.

"It's nice of you to stop and visit." Mrs. Anderson poured tea into the glasses. "How are you getting on, dear? It's not upsetting you too much, living where Jason did?" Her round face crinkled with what seemed genuine concern.

"Not at all." To Kate's surprise, she realized that was true. She didn't have a sense of Jason in the cottage, not the way she'd had when she'd cleared the house where they'd grown up. That place had been filled with memories, too many of them unhappy ones.

"That's good." The woman's worried look didn't vanish completely, but she seemed satisfied at the moment. "I noticed that Lina Oberlin stopped by to see you." There was a bit of curiosity in the words.

"She knew I wanted to hear about how Jason got on there." Kate paused. Apparently Mrs. Anderson kept tabs on who went to the cottage. Annoying, but it meant she might be able to provide information Kate needed. "I had hoped Ms. Oberlin might know about any friends Jason made at Blackburn House, but she didn't seem to."

"At Blackburn House? Well, let me think. He must have met Nick Whiting and his father, who run the cabinetry business, and Sarah at the quilt shop, but I don't think any of them ever got close. And of course the bookshop owner was much older." She seemed to brighten a little. "There's Nikki, the receptionist. She'd have been more his age, and I think she stopped by a few times. And Rich Willis, the young attorney whose office is upstairs. He might have known Jason."

"I hadn't thought of him. I might stop by and introduce myself." She couldn't remember that Jason had ever mentioned the man, but it was a possibility. And she'd have to cultivate Nikki's acquaintance.

Mac's warning about staying away from Bart Gordon slithered into her mind. Too bad she'd managed to make an enemy of Gordon at their first meeting. But that hadn't entirely been her fault. Gordon had overreacted to her presence, badly overreacted. That had to mean something.

While Kate had been busy with her speculations, Mrs. Anderson had been burbling on, seemingly an inexhaustible source of local information. ". . . previous bookshop owner was killed, right there in Blackburn House." She leaned forward, emphasizing her words with a tap on the table. "Right next door, can you imagine it? Such a scandal, it caused."

Wheels turned. "Was that when Jason was here?"

"Oh, no, dear. That happened just this past spring. It turned out he'd been blackmailing someone."

Impressive, but it didn't seem to have any possible relationship to her brother. "Who runs the bookshop now?"

"That would be Emily Waterston. She'd clerked there for years, and he left everything to her. Poor Emily." She shook her head. "I'm afraid it's all been overwhelming for her. And now the high school girl who helped her part-time has gone off to college, leaving her in the lurch. Well, I mean, of course the young woman had to go on

79

to college, but Emily hasn't been able to find anyone reliable to fill in."

A bell rang in Kate's mind. A part-time job at the bookshop—what could be better? It wouldn't tie her down, and it would give her a legitimate reason for being in Blackburn House whenever she wanted.

"If she hasn't filled the position, do you think she might be interested in taking me on, just for the month? I . . . I could stand to have a little extra money coming in until I start a new job." Actually she was fine financially since Tom had so unexpectedly left everything to her.

But as a reason, it seemed to satisfy Mrs. Anderson. "Why, I'm sure she would. That would give her time to look for someone more permanent. She'd be so relieved." The woman rose as she spoke and headed for the telephone. "I'll call her right now and tell her."

"You don't need . . ." she began, but Mrs. Anderson was already punching in the number.

Kate made an effort not to listen to Mrs. Anderson's side of the phone call, but it was hard not to hear. She got the impression the unknown Emily was jumping at the chance of immediate help.

In a few minutes Mrs. Anderson hung up, turning to Kate with the satisfied smile of one who has done a good deed. "She's so pleased.

You can go over and talk with her right away and set something up."

"That's great." Really great, that it had fallen into her lap so easily. Too easily? She had an almost superstitious mistrust of anything easy. Still, she couldn't ignore the opportunity. Draining the rest of her iced tea, Kate stood. "Thanks so much."

Mrs. Anderson flapped away her thanks. "No trouble at all."

Kate couldn't stop the triumphant smile that curved her lips as she headed out the door. So much for Mac Whiting's warning. Not even he could turn a job at the bookshop into a matter of harassment. She'd like to see his face when he heard.

Not that she cared, of course.

Mac told himself he'd done everything he could about Kate Beaumont's troubling presence in his town. Unfortunately, his efforts hadn't amounted to much. As for Kate herself, she made him think of nothing so much as a barricaded fortification—impenetrable walls bristling with weapons, ready to fire at the slightest provocation, or even at nothing at all.

Kate had every right to be here in Laurel Ridge. He just wished he could get rid of the feeling that she was nothing short of a roadside bomb, ready to explode at the slightest vibration.

Kate lingered at the back of his mind throughout the routine on his plate for the afternoon. Plans for the usual fall safety talk at the elementary school reminded him of Kate, saying that her stepfather had drilled self-defense into her. A meeting with the downtown merchants' association over a rash of shoplifting made him think of her insistence that someone had tampered with her computer.

By the time he went back to his office, Mac had made up his mind. He had to find out more about Kate Beaumont, even if it meant letting her know he'd been inquiring about her. His lips twisted wryly. The words "police harassment" would undoubtedly be heard.

Marge lifted her eyebrows at him as he walked in. "Something funny?"

"Not really. Be sure all the usual stuff is collected for the elementary school safety talk, will you? We're supposed to do it Friday afternoon."

Marge nodded. "Will do. Johnny is down at the bank. A fender bender in the parking lot."

Johnny was young John Foster, a raw patrolman who showed little signs of ripening. He sighed. "Maybe I'd better get down there."

"You told me to remind you that he has to learn to do a few things on his own, remember?"

Marge was right. She usually was.

"Okay. I guess he can't mess up a minor

accident report too badly." Doubt assailed him even as he said the words, but the kid had to do something to earn his salary.

Besides, Mac had something else to do. "Tell him to check in with me when he's finished." He headed into his own office. "I need to make a couple of calls."

Actually there was one call on his mind. Phil Durban had served with him briefly in Afghanistan before returning to the Philadelphia PD, and he'd been Mac's contact point over the whole disturbing business of Jason Reilley's death. Phil knew the family, and if there were any rumors floating around about Kate Beaumont, he'd be aware of them.

Luckily Phil was in the station. Mac leaned back in his chair, which creaked in protest, propped his feet on the pulled-out bottom drawer and prepared to exchange the usual backchat with an old comrade.

The genial exchange of friendly insults over with, Mac got down to business. "Listen, Phil, I need some information."

"Don't tell me one of our local boys has ventured as far as the middle of nowhere to cause you trouble." There was the ordinary gibe in the words, but he could sense Phil's attention sharpen.

"Nothing like that, but someone has shown up here unexpectedly. Kate Beaumont." He waited for a reaction. Phil might look as bright as a trout, but he had a brain that never forgot a thing.

"Tom Reilley's kid." Phil's voice had slowed. "I wondered."

"Wondered what?" Mac prompted. "Don't be too forthcoming now, old buddy."

"It's not like I really know a lot, but I did stop by and see Tom once in a while. Poor guy." Mac could almost see him shaking his head. "He took the boy's death hard, and then when the cancer showed up, it was like he didn't have the will to fight it."

"Rough." There wasn't really anything else to say.

"Yeah. Not easy to be a cop's kid, I guess. My wife not only carries the load, she knocks sense into me when I start bringing job issues home. Tom wasn't so lucky."

He'd had a vague notion Kate's mother was out of the picture, but nothing more. "What happened to Tom's wife?"

"Alcohol. She tried to drive on the expressway in the wrong direction. Left Tom to raise the kids the best he could." Phil made a complicated sound in his throat that might have expressed either sympathy or regret. "Suppose he made some mistakes. Who wouldn't?"

"Right." He let the word hang for a moment, and when Phil didn't speak, he prompted him.

"What do you know about why Kate decided to come to Laurel Ridge?"

Another silence. When Phil finally spoke, he sounded reluctant. "Understand, I'm only saying this because you're the one who's asking."

"Got it." A man owed things to the people he'd served with— trust, for one.

"I stopped by to see if I could help when Kate was clearing the house. She'd found a lot of her brother's stuff, including his computer, that Tom had put away. She didn't confide in me. Well, she wouldn't. But I got the idea she'd found something in her brother's things that raised questions about the boy's death."

There was a sour taste in the back of Mac's mouth. "Found what?" He ground out the words.

"Don't know. She didn't say. Maybe I'm wrong about the whole thing."

"No. I don't think you're wrong."

Phil had good instincts when it came to people. So did Mac. And he'd thought from the first moment he'd set eyes on Kate Beaumont that she was hiding something.

"Listen, about Kate . . ." Phil hesitated. "Whatever she's up to, she's a cop's kid."

"Yeah, I get it." Professional courtesy again, he supposed. Kate, like it or not—and he suspected she didn't—was part of the fraternity. *Protect and serve.* He owed that to every person in his community, yes. But he also owed it, and more, to someone like Kate.

So whatever it was she thought she'd found out about her brother's death, he had to take it seriously. To help, if he could. And to do that, he had to convince her to open up to him.

"Thanks, Phil. I'll do what I can."

By evening, Kate was feeling less than satisfied with her progress. She'd been hired by Emily Waterston with no problem, but the woman hadn't been as forthcoming as Kate had hoped.

Emily, as she'd insisted Kate call her, looked like the stereotypical chatty elderly lady, with her halo of curly white hair and bright, inquisitive eyes. However, when Kate brought up the subject of her brother, Emily had shied away like a skittish cat that didn't trust a stranger's hand.

Kate would have to take time to earn the woman's trust. Patience. Unfortunately, patience wasn't her strong suit.

Tomorrow, she decided, she'd find a way to make contact with Nikki, the receptionist. Nikki might not be entirely reliable, but she'd clearly been ready to gossip. In the meantime—

Kate rubbed the back of her neck, where tension seemed to be setting up permanent residence. The only useful course at the moment was to go back to the video diary once more. Painful as it was to watch Jason alive again, she might begin to understand some of his esoteric references now that she'd met a few of the people he'd known.

Pushing past her reluctance, she settled in front of the computer, a notepad ready at hand. A few clicks brought up Jason's image. She'd start with the one posted on his arrival in Laurel Ridge and work through them.

Jason's hope and enthusiasm for his new start came through so clearly in the first entry that it brought hot tears to her eyes. This was how he'd looked when he'd discovered a new fantasy game or a wonderful author. He'd seen a new world opening up in front of him. What had gone wrong?

Listening intently, she began jotting down every reference to the people he'd met in Laurel Ridge. She'd get them down, then try to figure out what they meant.

When a sound impinged on her concentration, Kate glanced up, startled to see that darkness crowded against the window. She'd been so intent she hadn't noticed the passing of light. The noise had come from outside, she thought, and her heart thudded uncomfortably.

A second later someone knocked at the door. Cautious, she advanced to within a couple of feet of it. "Who's there?"

"Mac Whiting. I'd like to speak to you."

I don't want to speak to you. But she opened the door.

"Sorry to bother you so late." He was coming in even as he spoke. His movement was casual, but beyond that Kate had the sense that he held himself under tight control.

Whatever this was, she didn't want to deal with it now. "I don't want to sound unwelcoming, but it's late." She managed a smile. "And I have it on good authority that the neighbors will talk."

Mac's face tightened, all planes and angles. "They'd talk more if I asked you to come to the station to meet with me."

"You can't be serious." She was instantly poised to fight. "You can't have any possible reason—"

She stopped, realizing he wasn't paying attention to her words. He was focused on something beyond her. Kate spun to see Jason's face looking out at them from the computer screen.

She sped toward the computer, but even as she reached for it, Mac caught her hand.

Her breath caught. "Let go of me. That's private."

"Not just yet. What is it?"

"Nothing. Just a video clip of my brother." She tried to twist away, to no avail.

"Something you found among your brother's belongings when you cleared the house?"

Her gaze met his, her temper flaring. "How do you know about that? Who told you?"

His eyes shifted. She felt his reluctance and knew the answer.

"Don't bother." Bitterness laced her words. "I should be able to guess. Phil Durban, I suppose. You cops stick together, don't you?"

"We have to." Answering anger flashed in his face, and she saw him fight to control it. She suspected he didn't often let impulse get the better of him. Unlike Tom, who would have exploded by this point in the conversation. He'd had a short fuse, and it wasn't until she'd grown and gone that she'd appreciated the stress that went into his temper.

"Whatever your buddy guessed, he doesn't know anything. I wasn't foolish enough to confide in him." She threw the words at him, clinging to the enmity between them.

But Mac didn't flare back. Instead he studied her face, and his expression softened. "Phil's a good guy. If you needed help, he'd have been the first to offer it."

That sudden gentleness got under her guard. She turned away, and this time he didn't try to stop her. "I don't need help. Not from him. Not from you."

"Well, now, that's too bad." The country-boy casualness was back in his voice again. "Because Phil thinks you found out something that made

89

you suspicious about how your brother died, and I can't leave it alone. If I made a mistake, I have to fix it."

Kate hadn't expected that, and the admission jolted her. "You mean that?"

He lifted an eyebrow. "Do you have any reason to think I don't?"

"No, I suppose not," she admitted. Even Tom, as much as they'd fought, had always meant exactly what he'd said.

"Okay." He made it sound as if they'd taken a giant step forward. "Let's start over. What makes you think there's something I didn't find out about how Jason died?"

She tried to arrange her thoughts. Her instinct was to tell him nothing, but that had become impossible. But she didn't have to say she suspected suicide. "It's not a question of how he died. But *why* he died."

Mac seemed to process the difference instantly. "An overdose . . ." he began, his voice gentle.

"An overdose, yes." Her throat tightened. "I don't imagine any coroner could miss that. But why? He'd been clean for nearly three years. He'd graduated with honors. He had a bright future. Why would he throw all that away?"

"Addiction is a day-by-day battle." Mac rubbed the back of his neck, and frustration threaded his words. "Twenty years ago the worst thing Laurel Ridge cops had to deal with was a Saturday night

90

drunk. Now we fight drugs like every other place in the country."

"Do you think I don't know that? I helped him through a couple of relapses. But he was doing so well. Something happened to him while he was here in Laurel Ridge that summer. Something that ended with him lying dead in that cemetery." What? A breakup? A fresh battle with his father? Trouble at his job? There had to be something. Each time he'd relapsed, something had triggered it.

And if she never found that trigger? Either way, the responsibility came back to her. Her throat closed entirely, and she fought to hold back tears, shaking her head as she turned away from him.

He touched her arm in mute sympathy and guided her to the sofa. He drew the armchair closer and sat like a man prepared to wait as long as it took.

Kate sucked in a breath and swallowed hard. "All right," she muttered.

"The coroner did confirm that there hadn't been drugs in his system for some time before the overdose." Mac's tone was carefully neutral, as if he understood she needed that to hang on to her precarious control. "But what makes you think it was something that happened here that pushed him into it? Did he say anything to you about dealing?"

His attention seemed to sharpen on the question.

Naturally that would be his first thought—that someone was bringing drugs into his town.

"If you're thinking it was Jason, you're wrong," she said flatly. "He wouldn't. And he hadn't left here all summer, anyway."

That had been part of Jason's determination to make it on his own this time, without leaning on his big sister. He'd stay here for the duration of his internship. Phone calls only—no visits. And Jason never had expressed himself well on the phone. She needed to see his face to know what was happening with him.

"I know that. Obviously we looked into it—the drugs had to come from somewhere. Since he didn't go anywhere to get them, someone brought them in. We never found out who."

That had frustrated him. She could see it in his suddenly taut face.

"You don't know who. But you must have some idea." She leaned toward him, suddenly urgent. "There can't be that many potential dealers in a place like this."

"You'd be surprised." His lips twisted wryly. "I had some ideas, yeah, but they all came up empty." He jerked a nod toward the computer. "That file—what does that have to do with it?"

Kate rubbed her forehead as if she could scour away some of the confusion. "Jason kept a sort of video diary. Not every day, but most of the summer."

"You didn't find it until your stepfather died."

She nodded. He was putting the pieces together. "Tom had kept everything that was returned to him, but I doubt he ever looked at it. When I started watching the diary . . ." She paused, not wanting to say more than she had to. Still, the time for that might have already passed. "I could see how excited and enthusiastic he was at the beginning of the summer. But something changed. He was worried, maybe even scared, about some situation. I think at his work, but I can't be sure."

"What precisely did he say? You must know that much." Mac glanced at the computer again, probably longing to wrest the truth from it.

"It's not as easy as that. Jason wasn't exactly direct. He had a way of talking about places and people in a kind of code. I doubt you'd understand any of it." Just in case he was thinking he'd walk away with her file.

Mac stood, as if he couldn't pretend to relax for another moment. "Let me see it."

"No." She rose as well, facing him. "It's personal, and you have no right . . ."

"It could be evidence in a drug case." He left implied the threat that he could get a subpoena if she didn't cooperate. "Whatever this code is, it can be broken."

She'd laugh if this were anything but deadly serious. "It's not that kind of code." It was no good—she'd have to tell him more, or she'd never get rid of him. "Jason always loved fantasy—books, games, movies, whatever. I tried to keep up, just so I could share something with him. He'd refer to people and situations with references from fantasy that even I didn't always understand." She nodded toward the image of his face, frozen on the screen. "That's what he did in the diary. He would have known what he meant, but the chances that anyone else could figure it out are slim to none."

"But that's what you're trying to do. That's why you came here. To see the layout for yourself, to meet the people, to figure out what or who led your brother to his death."

There was no point in denying it. "It's my own business," she repeated stubbornly. "If I find anything that looks like a police matter, you'll be the first to know."

"Not good enough." Mac could apparently be equally stubborn. "You're not going to be conducting any sort of crusade in my town. Not unless I'm involved every step of the way."

"You can't force me . . ."

He raised an eyebrow. "Force? Who said anything about force? But either you let me in on it, or I'll make it impossible for you to find out anything about anyone here. It wouldn't even be hard. A few words to a few people, and you won't find a soul in Laurel Ridge willing to talk to you."

She didn't doubt he could do it. "That's blackmail."

"That's me, doing my job, whether you want me to or not." His lips quirked, but his eyes were intent. "Take it or leave it."

Kate wanted to kick him out. To say she'd manage this herself. Trouble was, he held all the cards.

"All right," she said finally. "You win. I'll take it."

CHAPTER FIVE

Mac walked slowly out to the street, his mind and emotions churning. He'd gotten a lot more than he'd expected from his confrontation with Kate, and he wasn't sure what to do with it.

His immediate instinct was to deny—deny her opinions, deny the possibility that he had missed something, deny the possibility that Kate was right and something in Laurel Ridge had led to her brother's death.

That would be the comfortable thing to do, but he couldn't. He'd insisted that he'd work with Kate Beaumont to uncover the truth, wherever that might lead. Sounded good, but at the moment, he didn't even know where to start.

A light glowed through the trees lining the drive that led alongside Blackburn House. Someone was in the cabinetry shop. On impulse, he veered in that direction. He needed a sounding board right at the moment, and nobody was more trustworthy than family.

Blackburn House was dark and still except for the usual hall lights left on for safety's sake. There were a few more on than there used to be, ever since the bookstore owner had met an untimely end, dying on the marble floor of the hallway.

Maybe he was growing superstitious after everything that had happened in that building. Now Jason Reilley—did his death have anything to do with the office where he'd interned? Far more likely, surely, that it was his extracurricular activities that contributed to what happened to him.

Giving a quick tap on the shop door, he swung it open. Nick, his brother, glanced up from the cabinet he was attaching doors to.

"Working late?" Nick asked.

"That's my line." Mac crossed to where his brother was occupied, tossing his uniform cap onto the nearest workbench. "Don't you get enough hours in during the day? What's your fiancée think of you working overtime instead of spending time with her?"

Nick grinned and gestured to the cabinet. "Make yourself useful and hold this door in place. Allison and Mom requested the pleasure of my absence. They're baking cookies for the school bake sale."

"Hmm, I might have to stop in and taste-test those." He held the door steady as Nick screwed the hinge into place. He could feel his brother's gaze on his face and knew his casual air hadn't deceived Nick.

"You want to tell me what's up?" Nick's question confirmed his thought.

Nick would have heard all about Kate after

Mom and Jamie had met, so there was no point in being restrained. "Turns out I was right about Kate Beaumont. She does have an agenda for being here. She thinks something happened in Laurel Ridge that led to her brother's death."

Nick didn't need to ask why that troubled Mac. "What makes her think so? Does she have any proof or just suspicions?"

"Apparently she discovered a video diary young Jason kept during his internship. She claims he was worried about something that was happening here, and she's determined to find out what."

Nick didn't speak for a moment. "Have you seen this video?"

"Not yet. I just came from talking to her." He shook his head, Kate's defiant face forming in his mind. "I did push her into letting me in on what she's doing, and I'll have a look at it tomorrow. See if I can make any sense of it."

Nick straightened. "You didn't insist on taking the file with you or viewing it immediately?"

"I felt like I'd already pushed as much as I was justified in doing." He frowned, thinking of the vulnerability Kate had shown him in those moments. She was probably already hating the fact that she'd revealed so much. That tough facade must be very important to her.

"You getting soft, by any chance?" Nick asked. "What if she destroys it?"

Soft? Again he flashed back to a hot, dry afternoon in Afghanistan and the rubble of what had once been a welcoming home. It wasn't soft to feel that need to protect the needy. And while Kate wouldn't admit to any such thing, she needed help.

"She won't destroy it." He was confident of that. "It's all she has left of her brother."

"Guess I'll have to take your word for that." Nick glanced at his watch and began putting tools away. "But I don't see what you're going to uncover after over a year. You followed up every lead at the time."

There might have been a slight question in Nick's voice.

"It seemed fairly clear-cut." Mac frowned, running his fingers along the smooth curved edge of a cabinet. "The main thing we focused on was where the drugs came from. I had my suspicions, but that's a long way from having proof."

"No reason to doubt that the kid died of an accidental overdose, was there?" Nick leaned against the workbench, arms folded over his chest in a movement that reminded Mac of his father.

Mac shrugged, meeting his brother's eyes. "There was no note, but to tell you the truth, I wondered if it might have been a deliberate act. Choosing the cemetery as a place to get high just seemed unlikely. People don't normally pick a public place for that. Still, with no proof either way, it seemed kinder to the family to declare it accidental."

"Let me get this straight. The Beaumont woman isn't suggesting someone deliberately gave him an overdose, is she?"

"No, that would be crazy, and Kate is perfectly sane and logical. She seems to think that something happened here that pushed the kid into turning to drugs. She wants to know what." He spread his hands, palms up. "Wouldn't you?"

"I guess. But I don't see what you're going to do about it." Nick frowned, and it was like looking into a mirror.

"I wish I knew. I just want to keep Kate from hunting down potential drug suppliers and putting herself in danger. And maybe prevent her from alienating half the town with her accusations."

"Yeah, I already had an earful from Bart Gordon." Nick grinned. "The man seems to think I have some control over you, either as your big brother or as the mayor, I'm not sure which."

"The answer is neither," Mac retorted. It figured that Gordon wouldn't be content with complaining to him.

Nick hesitated. "Do you actually have some idea who might have brought the drugs into town?"

"There are a couple of possibilities." Much as he trusted his brother, he wasn't about to name names. "I don't know how she'd get on to them, but I wouldn't put anything past her."

Nick raised an eyebrow. "It sounds like you're going to have your hands full with Ms. Beaumont."

"You've got that right." He picked up his cap and followed Nick to the door, stepping out into the cool air and waiting while Nick locked up.

He stood for a moment, glancing over his town, dozing in the autumn evening. The moon was approaching full, and it glinted from the top of the clock tower on Town Hall, giving it a ghostly gleam.

His hands were going to be full for sure. Keep Kate out of danger, don't let her stir up a hornet's nest with her questions and above all, find out the truth, if that was even possible.

And then what? It seemed to him that no matter what the answer to the riddle of Jason's death was, Kate was going to be hurt.

Kate felt a bit conspicuous, lingering in the front window of the bookshop watching the stairs that came down from the offices above. But catching Nikki when she left the financial office for lunch seemed the best and most casual way of approaching the woman.

She straightened the display of current books in the window, hoping Emily wasn't watching her. The two hours Kate had worked this morning had gone well, with Emily warming up and becoming chattier, and she didn't want to rouse any suspicions now.

Five after twelve—surely Nikki would take her lunch break soon. She might, of course, have brought lunch with her, but Nikki hadn't seemed so eager to get on with her work that she'd want to eat at her desk.

"You don't need to tidy the window."

The voice behind her startled Kate. She hadn't heard Emily's approach. The thick-soled, sensible shoes she wore allowed her to move like a cat.

"I was looking at this." Kate picked up the latest volume by a popular fantasy author, her fingers tracing the embossed lines of the green dragon on its cover. "My brother loved this series."

Emily's crinkled face softened, her china-blue eyes filling with easy tears. "He did, didn't he? He always browsed through the fantasy section, and what he didn't know about the books and authors wasn't worth knowing. I told him he'd missed his calling, going into finance the way he did."

The tears may have been facile, but there was no doubting that Emily had been touched by Jason's death. Strange, wasn't it? She'd come here intent on her own private grief, only to find that his passing had affected people she hadn't even known. Mrs. Anderson and Emily had both shed tears for him.

As for Mac—unless he was putting up an awfully good front, he had been wounded himself, either by the fact of someone dying on his watch or by his inability to trace the drugs that had killed Jason. Her nerves clenched. She'd struck a bargain with Mac that she had yet to fulfill, and she was already regretting it. And yet what choice had she had?

"Jason did enjoy fantasy. I always thought he'd end up designing fantasy games or maybe writing graphic novels. But his father always pushed him toward doing something practical."

In that, as in so many things, Tom had shown his lack of understanding of his son. Jason had never been, maybe couldn't be, practical. But he'd wanted, just once, to please his father.

"I suppose finance is practical, all right." Emily looked a little doubtful. "It's all I can do to make sure my income balances at the end of the day. Russell—Russell Sheldon, that is, from the financial services company—used to say that we should hire a teenager to look after the computer records for us. He claimed they were the only ones who really understood computers."

"Jason mentioned Mr. Sheldon. He was one of the partners when Jason worked there."

"Not just one of the partners," Emily corrected. "Why, Russell founded that firm. Always very successful, it was, and he was the soul of integrity. Everyone was sorry to see him retire so abruptly. I'm sure Bart and Lina do fine work, but it's not the same. Russell was a real *gentleman*." In Emily's phrasing the word seemed to convey an image of an era in which gentlemen adhered to a code that others might not.

Kate was about to follow up with a question when a flicker of movement caught the corner of her eye. Nikki was coming down the stairs.

"I liked being here this morning," she said quickly. "Thanks again for the opportunity. I'll see you tomorrow." With a quick smile, she hurried out. Now that the ice was broken, she could lead Emily on to talk about the business again. Right now, she'd better try to manage a casual encounter with Nikki.

Kate reached the staircase just as Nikki arrived at the bottom. Nikki smiled, then gave a quick, apprehensive glance up in the direction of her office. Kate had no difficulty in translating it— she didn't want to be seen by her boss talking to the enemy.

"Hi, Nikki. I'm glad I ran into you." Not wanting to be suspected of lurking, she quickly added, "I'm working part-time at the bookshop now."

"I know." Nikki grinned. "You should hear my boss—he about had a fit over the idea."

"I guessed he wouldn't like it, but I don't know

what he's worried about. It's not as if I accused him of anything." Kate gave her own glance upstairs, but no one was visible. "Listen, you're one of the few people I know in this town. Want to have lunch? On me," she added.

Nikki hesitated for a moment, then grinned. "Sure. Only someplace where Bart won't see us. You know the Lamplight Tavern, out on the edge of town? Just go on down Main Street, and you'll see it on the right."

"I'll find it." She felt ridiculously triumphant that she'd pulled it off. "I'll meet you there in a few minutes."

Kate hurried to the front door, forcing herself not to look toward the Whiting Cabinetry showroom just in case Mac should be in there. It took only moments to get to the spot alongside the bed-and-breakfast where she'd left her car, and not much more than that until she was pulling into the gravel parking lot at the Lamplight Tavern.

It looked like, and probably was, a neighborhood bar. Cement block, it squatted at the very end of a row of houses, and beyond it, Main Street turned into a country road. The neon sign that proclaimed it the Lamplight Tavern seemed a contradiction in terms. Neon, not lamplight, was the order of the day.

Nikki pulled in and parked as Kate walked toward the door, so she stopped and waited for her. "Not the best food in town," Nikki said, approaching. "But I guarantee Bart and Lina wouldn't dream of being caught dead here."

"I bet." She could well imagine that the fastidious Lina didn't frequent neighborhood bars.

Nikki, on the other hand, seemed to be well acquainted with the place. She waved to the bartender as they passed, exchanged joking comments with a couple of guys holding up the bar and led the way to a booth against the back wall.

Kate didn't miss the fact that she'd chosen a spot well away from anyone who might overhear. She trusted that meant Nikki intended to be open with her.

Nikki slid into place and plucked two plastic-covered menus from behind the napkin holder. "The burgers are safe. I wouldn't order anything fancy."

Fancy wasn't the word for the menu. She decided to follow Nikki's advice.

The bartender apparently doubled as server. Once they'd ordered, Kate focused on the girl's pert face. Her sharp features weren't enhanced by the overdone makeup, but her grin made her look both impish and younger than she probably wanted to.

"Okay, it's safe to talk. I guessed you had more questions about Jason." Nikki sobered. "He was a good guy."

"Yes." Kate sucked in a breath. "I was hoping you might have some ideas about what happened to him."

Nikki looked blank. Obviously that was too general a comment.

"For instance, the days before he died. I assume he was coming to work as usual."

"Oh, sure." Nikki brightened. "He never missed a day. Always early, too. I told him he made me look bad."

"Did you notice any change in his mood around that time? Was anything different that last day?" It was hard to keep her voice level—to talk about this as if Jason had been a stranger.

There was a long pause—long enough to be noticeable. Finally Nikki shrugged. "Guess I don't owe the old firm all that much loyalty. Yeah, something was going on that day, but I don't know what. There was a lot of hush-hush talk behind closed doors. Lina went around looking like she'd been sucking on a sour lemon. Bart blew up at everybody—'course, that's not unusual. You saw that. And Mr. Russell . . . well, I thought we were going to have to call an ambulance for him. He was so pale he looked gray."

"What about Jason?" She held her breath, not sure she wanted to hear it. "Did this involve him?"

Nikki's gaze met hers and slid away. "Yeah, I

guess. They called him in. I couldn't hear what went on." She grimaced. "I tried, but no dice. When Jase came out he was white as a sheet, and his eyes looked all funny—like he wanted to cry, you know?"

Kate nodded. She knew that expression. It had meant Jason had been hurt beyond bearing. And she hadn't been here to soothe away the pain, the way she'd done when he was small.

"Did Jason leave the office then?"

"Right away. Packed up his stuff and left." Nikki examined a chip in her scarlet nail polish, as if to distract herself. "I wanted to talk to him, you know, but everything was in an uproar, and I figured it was safer to keep my head down." She darted a look at Kate.

"I understand." She forced the words out. Would some expression of kindness at that moment have helped Jason? Maybe, maybe not. They'd never know.

"The next thing I heard was the next day when . . . you know. It was awful. Everybody was really shaken up."

Here was the chance she'd been looking for. "What about the other people in the office?"

"Oh, yeah, them, too. Lina was nervy all day and looked like she'd been crying, and she never shows any emotion."

That had been her impression of the woman, as well. Despite the sympathy she'd expressed when she'd talked of Jason, Lina had impressed her as the type of businesswoman who considered emotion would put her at a disadvantage.

"What about Bart Gordon?"

Nikki shrugged. "Well, he was shook up, for sure. 'Course, he kept saying that it wasn't his fault. He's always trying to find somebody else to blame."

Their burgers arrived then, creating a diversion. Kate waited until the server had left and Nikki had started eating before venturing another question.

"I understand that Mr. Sheldon retired shortly after Jason's death. Was that unexpected?"

Nikki took a moment, considering. "Sort of. I mean, he'd talked sometimes about retiring, but usually in kind of a joking way, saying he was getting too old to deal with the difficult clients and that kind of thing. But I never thought he really would. That place was his baby, you know?"

That was the impression Emily had given her, too. "Do you think what happened to Jason had anything to do with it?"

"Maybe so." She darted a quick, suspicious look at Kate. "Hey, you're not thinking about suing the firm, are you? I don't want to get involved in any trouble."

She shook her head, smiling. Had Gordon been worrying about that possibility? "Believe me, that's the last thing on my mind. I'd just like to understand what happened that pushed Jason into what he did."

"Well, it was funny, Mr. Sheldon leaving just then. I wasn't actually there. After the news broke about Jason, the office closed for the day, and then Lina called and told me not to bother coming in the rest of the week. When I got back on Monday, Mr. Sheldon's office was empty. At first I thought he was just taking some time off, but then I heard he wasn't coming back." She shrugged. "Like I said, it was funny, but it wasn't my business."

Kate's mind was spinning busily. Here was something that had to be explained. Surely people had talked about the fact that the man had retired so abruptly after Jason's death.

"Your lunch is getting cold," Nikki pointed out between French fries.

Reminded, she bit into the burger, finding it surprisingly good. "Nice," she said. "You were right about what to order."

Nikki glanced at her watch. "I'll have to leave before long. Lina gives me that fish-eye look of hers if I take an extra minute."

"Right. I don't want to hold you up. But I wondered if you might know of anyone else who was friendly with Jason while he was here." He might have talked more to another guy than he would to Nikki, especially if he'd found a kindred spirit.

But Nikki was flicking through her phone and seemed to have lost interest in the conversation.

"Nikki? Anyone else Jason knew?" The server was approaching, and she wanted another lead, no matter how tentative.

"Huh? Oh, yeah. Jason was sort of . . . like a loner, you know?"

Given much more of Nikki's conversation, and Kate would start inserting "you know" into her every sentence.

"You said that you'd shown him around a few times. Maybe you brought him here. Introduced him to some of your friends?"

"We did do that." Nikki glanced around. "This place is pretty dead during the day, but it livens up after about nine or ten. I don't think he . . . Well, yeah, I did see him talking to a couple of guys who are into those computer games. And Larry Foust." Diverted, she rolled her eyes. "What a slacker he is. Always talks big about how he's going to get out of Laurel Ridge as soon as he gets some money, and he still lives with his mother. Probably gets an allowance from her, because he sure doesn't work." Her voice was filled with disdain.

"So, where might I find them?" Kate mentally filed the name.

Nikki shrugged. "Not sure I remember who any of the gamers were. I'll give it some thought. Maybe it will come to me but, you know, they weren't exactly my type. As for Larry . . . he used to come in here most nights, but I haven't been seeing much of him." Before Kate could stop her, Nikki hailed the bartender. "Hey, Pete, you seen Larry Foust around lately?"

Pete revolved a stained cloth slowly around a glass, his gaze moving from Nikki's face to Kate's. "Who wants to know?"

"I'm asking, okay? I just haven't seen him around much."

Pete shrugged ham-like shoulders. "Not my job to keep track of him. If he finds someplace else to drink, it's okay by me. He did come in last night, round about midnight."

"Well, if you see him, tell him I was asking about him." Nikki turned to Kate. "That'll bring him out of the woodwork. He's always hitting on me, like I'd have time for a loser."

Kate nodded. "I'd appreciate a chance to talk to him, even for a few minutes."

Nikki glanced at her watch and gave a little shriek. "I gotta run. Thanks for the lunch, Kate. I'll see you around." She grinned. "Just not where my bosses will notice."

"Right, thanks, Nikki."

She watched as Nikki scurried to the door, realizing that the men at the bar were doing the same. Was there anything else she might usefully have asked? Surely there had been other people present on those nights when Nikki had taken

Jason out, but apparently she wasn't eager to give up those names. Still—

"You're looking for Larry Foust, then?" Pete made it a question, his heavy frame leaning toward her.

"I'd like to talk to him."

A frown settled on Pete's pudgy face. "Somebody like you doesn't want to hang around with the likes of Foust."

She zeroed in on him, surprised. Was that well-meant or a veiled threat? She didn't read any antagonism in his manner. "I want to ask him a couple of questions, that's all."

"Last night he had a couple of guys with him I didn't like the look of. I told him. Don't bring people like that into my bar. I got a respectable place here."

"I'm sure you do." Kate's pulse quickened, and she chose her words carefully. "You wouldn't want anybody undesirable in here. But what was wrong with them?"

But Pete seemed to have dried up as a source of information. His face went blank. "Didn't like the look of 'em. That's all. You ready for the bill?"

She'd push, but that might lose her the opportunity to get more from him another time. "Just about. You make a good burger."

He didn't respond to the compliment, instead pulling a pad from his apron pocket and slapping the bill down in front of her. "Pay at the bar."

All right, then. She wasn't going to get anything else from him now, but her brain teemed with possibilities. She needed to connect with this Foust character and find out about his friendship with Jason. And maybe he could lead her to those gamers Nikki mentioned.

And then there was the truth about what had happened that day at the office. Something had happened, and whatever it was, it sounded as if Mac Whiting hadn't known about it. If Jason had been fired, why keep it a secret?

She didn't cherish any hopes that Bart would open up about it, or even Lina. Somehow, she had to get to Russell Sheldon. And as much as she hated to admit it, Mac Whiting might be her best hope.

CHAPTER SIX

It was nearly four that afternoon when Mac stalked back the walk toward the cottage. He paused to inhale a breath, reminding himself that he couldn't take the lousy day out on Kate. Still, he couldn't stop seeing the terrified faces of the parents whose teenage son had collapsed in the high school hallway, hit by a seizure after taking who knew what. A few pills had been found in his jeans pocket, nicely packaged in cellophane.

The state police crime lab had those now, so sooner or later he'd get their report, but the ER doctors suspected a cocktail of prescription pain meds mixed in alcohol. Mac's fists clenched at the sheer stupidity of it. The kid was an honor student—what on earth would make him take such a risk? And God only knew what the final outcome would be. Possible brain damage, one of the EMTs had told him privately.

Would that have been the result with Kate's brother, had they gotten to him sooner? As chance would have it, Jason had taken his deadly dose where he wouldn't be found very quickly.

He blew out a long breath, consciously trying to clear his mind. Going through that video diary might be his best chance of finding the conduit of drugs into his town. That was worth just about any concession he had to make, even to taking Kate Beaumont's mission seriously.

Kate came to the door almost before he had a chance to rap on it. Clearly she'd been waiting for him.

"I expected you an hour ago." She stepped back to allow him entrance.

"I got held up," he said shortly. "Ready to let me see the video?" He removed his cap and tossed it onto the sofa, glancing around the small living room. The computer sat open on the table by the window.

He could sense her reluctance in the way she hesitated, fingers brushing back through that honey-blond hair. "I warn you—you're not going to understand a lot of what Jason says."

Mac forced a smile. "So we'll work on it together. You know how your brother thought, and I know the people in this town. We ought to be able to figure it out."

But a few minutes into the first entry, he had to admit, to himself at least, that Kate had a point. He glanced at her. They sat side by side on kitchen chairs pulled up to the computer, and her hand brushed his as she paused the video.

"What?" she said, reacting to his stare.

"I thought I had a pretty good handle on fantasy—Tolkien, and all that. Obviously I was wrong."

A smile tugged at her lips, and he had to gaze away from the appeal.

"Tolkien was his favorite when he was younger. I didn't consider it suitable bedtime reading then, but he was so determined, I figured it was safer to read it with him. But he's up on all the modern authors, too. Emily was just saying that today."

"Yes, I heard you're working in Blackburn House now." He tried to keep his tone neutral and probably failed.

Kate lifted her eyebrows. "Do you have an objection?"

"Several, but let's stay focused on the task. What do you think of these references to the old king?"

Maybe she didn't like his refusal to argue about her new job, because the look she flashed him was challenging. But when he didn't respond, she turned back to the screen, frowning a little.

"At first I thought it referred to Bart Gordon. I suppose he's the boss now. But from what Emily said, the firm was really Russell Sheldon's."

"Right. If he's talking about the business, he has to mean Sheldon."

"It had to be. The firm was the only thing he was involved with that early in his stay here," Kate pointed out.

"I suppose." Impatience rode him. "I assume you've been through the whole thing. Is there any reference to someone who might have provided him with drugs?"

Her fingers clenched on the edge of the table. "That's all you're interested in, isn't it? Any talk about helping me find out why was just a smoke screen. You just care about making an arrest."

He swung round to face her. If he tightened his jaw any more, it would probably break. "That's right. I care. I'm a cop, and somebody, probably several somebodies, are wrecking lives with their dirty trade."

"My brother was a victim, not a dealer!" Anger flared dangerously in her eyes.

"He wasn't the only victim. Try riding along to the ER with a kid found seizing on the floor of the high school. Try talking to his parents, the way I did today. You—" He stopped, knowing he'd gone too far.

For a moment she just stared at him, her face filling with pain. Then she reached out to cover his hand with hers, gripping it hard. "Oh, Lord." She breathed it like a prayer. "I'm so sorry. Those poor people. Is he . . . Will he be all right?"

"Too soon to tell." He exhaled some of the tension away. "He's alive, anyway. But if I can't find out who is peddling prescription painkillers to kids, he won't be the last." Sheer frustration had him pounding one fist on the table. "Why? Why would a bright kid do something like that? That's what I don't get."

Her fingers tightened on his, and something strong and elemental seemed to flow between them, shaking him. "I know." Her breath caught. "That's what I keep asking. Why?"

Their gazes met, clung. He leaned toward her, driven by something he couldn't name. Close—so close he could feel her breath on his skin.

He pulled back, fighting the heat that rushed through him. "Sorry," he muttered, not sure what he regretted most. *Get a grip,* he told himself. "I know. At least, I *should* know."

Kate rubbed her forehead. "All right. You want to find the person who is distributing drugs. I want to find out why Jason died. That's clear, isn't it?"

"The two things aren't mutually exclusive. We work together on this, and we have a better chance of finding out anything there is to learn. Right?" He tried to sound casual, tried to ignore the feelings that sizzled along his skin.

"Right." She took a deep breath. "It sounds like you've had a miserable day. If you want to put this off . . ."

"Let's push on a bit more. Maybe I can trade one guilt for another."

Shaking her head, she reached toward the computer. "You can't take responsibility for everything that happens. If there was one thing I learned during Jason's hard times, it was that you can't prevent people from making bad decisions. No matter how much you care."

"Yeah." He tried to close the door on the memories that haunted him, but it refused to stay closed. Each time he felt that he let someone down, it was a reflection of that terrible failure.

Kate clearly felt she had let her brother down, whether she admitted it or not. How did that stack up against a whole village razed to the ground, with old people and children slaughtered?

Not that they were in a contest for who carried the most guilt. One life lost needlessly was too many.

He studied Kate's averted face, in profile as she looked at the computer screen. He'd told her something he'd had no intention of spilling, but in an odd way, it had brought them closer. He wanted to trust her, even though his logical mind was telling him not to take the risk. Still, if he didn't trust, how could they possibly work together?

"That's enough," Kate said, reaching across Mac to close down the file. They'd been at it for an hour, watching each segment and trying to figure out what had been in Jason's mind.

Mac glanced at his watch. "I can give it another half hour."

"I can't," she said shortly. As always when she'd been watching Jason on-screen, the reminder that this was all she had left of him ate at her, frazzling her nerves and tightening her chest until she felt she couldn't take a deep breath.

"Sorry." Mac's voice went deep on the word, and his eyes seemed to darken. "I wasn't thinking. This has to be hard on you."

Grief caught at her throat, and she nodded.

"I could take a copy of the file . . ." he began.

"No." She nearly barked the word and was instantly sorry. There was no reason to expose more of her emotions to Mac, with his steady cop's gaze. "I'd rather not," she said, managing a softer tone.

"It wouldn't do much good anyway, I guess." Mac leaned back, still studying her face. "Without your help trying to figure it out, I wouldn't get anywhere." He grinned, his expression softening. "I wonder how Nikki would like it if she knew he saw her as a chameleon who changed her persona by the moment."

"She's young enough to be still figuring out who she wants to be." Kate didn't remember being that way, but it didn't surprise her.

"You, on the other hand, always knew who you were," he said.

Kate didn't bother denying it. Given her early life, she hadn't had a choice.

Mac stood, stretching, his lean body looming over her until she stood as well, taking a step back.

121

It was on the tip of her tongue to tell Mac about her lunch with Nikki and what the Lamplight's bartender had said about Larry Foust and his buddies, but she hesitated. If she did that, it might get back to Foust and destroy any chance she had of finding out what he knew.

"I'll touch base with you tomorrow. Will you be working?"

"Just in the morning."

He nodded, opening the door. "Okay, thanks. I'll see you . . ."

If he finished that sentence, Kate didn't hear it. She was staring at the stone slab that served as a step outside the cottage.

"Kate?" He caught her arm. "What's wrong?"

"Nothing." It couldn't be anything. An optical illusion, created by the fact that she'd been so focused on Jason for the past hour. She drew her arm free. "I'll expect to hear from you tomorrow, then." Putting a note of finality in her voice, she moved back into the cottage and closed the door.

But once Mac had disappeared around the bed-and-breakfast, she opened it again, went out and knelt by the stoop. The stone—slate, probably—was scratched and scarred from years of use. But there on the doorstep was the scratched image of a dragon, like the dragon on her key chain. Like the dragon her brother had always carried with him—the one that disappeared when he died. She ran her hand across the marks, but she couldn't tell how recent they were. Had Jason done it? Or someone else?

Kate frowned. Jason might have scratched the dragon image there. He often doodled that shape. But if he had, why hadn't she noticed it earlier?

And if it was more recent than that, then who? And why? She didn't have answers, only questions.

Thinking about Jason and the silver dragon made her restless. To say nothing of those moments when she'd felt that current of desire flowing between her and Mac. Impossible, she reminded herself. She had no energy to spare for anything but the task at hand. And if she were in the mood for romance, it certainly wouldn't be with someone like Mac Whiting—a cop down to his bones.

To her, *cop* meant Tom Reilley, with his rigid insistence that everything had to be done his way. He'd been like that even before her mother died, and he had only become worse. He'd done his duty by her, she supposed. Like Mac, he'd always do his duty. But it had been a cheerless thing with him, with no wiggle room for anyone who approached life differently.

Like Jason. Poor Jason had spent his brief life torn between his own instincts and his father's expectations. Her jaw tightened so much that her teeth clenched.

As an adult, she'd been able to understand, at least a little, how difficult it must have been for him to deal with an angry adolescent girl. But his mistakes with Jason—those she couldn't forgive.

Eventually she found herself clicking through late shows, unable to keep her interest focused on them long enough to follow a single monologue or interview through to its conclusion. She switched off and tossed the remote aside.

Maybe, if that had been a dragon's shape scratched into the doorstep, Jason had done it. She couldn't think of any reason why, but still . . .

Or someone else had put it there. Perhaps someone who conceived it as a warning.

Far-fetched, her logical mind insisted loudly. *You're getting as fanciful as Jason was.* Chances were it was an accidental resemblance, only there because she imagined it, the way people saw a face in the moon.

The phone rang, startling her, and she glanced at the clock. Nearly midnight. Who on earth would call her at this hour?

Most likely a wrong number, given how few people knew she was living here. Her friends would call or text on her cell. She picked up the landline phone.

"Is that Ms. Beaumont?" The voice was male and muffled by what sounded like country music and laughter in the background.

"Yes. Who is this, please?" she asked crisply.

"You wanted to know when Larry Foust came in to the Lamplight. He's here now." The caller hung up.

Kate stared at the phone for a moment. The bartender, she supposed. He and Nikki were the only ones who'd have reason to call—not that she'd expected it after what he'd said about Larry.

A few minutes later she stepped out into the chilly darkness, pulling the door closed behind her and checking the lock automatically. If this was someone's idea of a joke, she was going to be seriously annoyed.

And speaking of annoyed, she hadn't mentioned Larry Foust to Mac. If he heard of this private expedition, he wouldn't be happy. Still, she'd never agreed to tell him everything. And she didn't doubt that there were things he'd kept from her.

The streets were deserted when she drove toward the bar, and the ridges loomed darkly over the town. Only the clock tower on what she supposed was the town hall was brightly illuminated, its face declaring the hour.

The silence and solitude didn't extend to the Lamplight, however. Apparently the night was young there, since there were still plenty of cars in the dimly lit parking area, and the orange-and-green neon signs glowed.

She pulled in, finding a space at the far end of the second row of vehicles. Pickups outnumbered cars by a wide margin, and when someone opened the door, country music spilled out into the night.

Kate glanced back at the sleeping town, quiet under the crescent moon. Every place had to have its equivalent of the Lamplight, most likely.

Near the door, she slowed her steps. She hadn't really planned how she would approach Larry, and maybe she should have. If he knew she was Jason's sister—well, she'd begun to think everyone in town knew it by now. She'd have to play it by ear, she supposed, but she never liked going into an interview unprepared.

The Lamplight lived up to Nikki's implication that it was where the action was at night. Crowded and smoky, with a roar of talk, it stunned the senses for an instant after the dark stillness outside. The crowd seemed to be a mix of twentysomethings flirting with each other, a few older, lone drinkers and a couple of convivial clusters of men who looked as if this were a second home.

Kate worked her way through the crowd toward the bar. No sense in looking for Larry, since she didn't know him by sight. She'd have to depend on Pete to point him out.

But when she reached the bar, Pete wasn't there. A younger man sauntered over, wiping the

126

bar as he came. "What'll it be, honey? Beer?" He gave her a long, assessing look. "Or you one of the white wine crowd?"

"Neither. I'm looking for Pete. Is he in tonight?"

The bartender shook his head, turning away, obviously not interested in someone who didn't plan to spend money. "Off." He headed toward the end of the bar to someone who was beckoning.

"Pete works nights on the weekend," a voice volunteered. She glanced to her right, and the speaker grinned. "Have a drink with me and my buddy instead, why don't you?"

Late thirties, she'd guess, with a dark stubble he probably thought was sexy and the faded jeans and flannel shirt that seemed the wardrobe here. He leaned closer. "Pete's an old married man, anyway. We're more fun. I'm Mike, and this is Stan."

Stan was a carbon copy of his friend, but he looked uncomfortable, as if picking up girls in bars were new to him.

On the slight possibility they might know the man she was looking for, she tried an encouraging smile. "Actually, I thought Pete might have some information for me."

Odd, no matter how she considered it. If Pete hadn't called her, who had? She felt sure the call had come from here—the background noise fit.

The man drew back slightly. "What kind of information?"

"I'm been trying to catch up with a friend of my brother's. His name is Larry Foust. Do you know him, by any chance?"

Mike whatever-his-name-was shrugged. "Know who he is, yeah. Dropout, lives with his mama. Your brother doesn't have much taste in friends."

"Has he been in here tonight, do you know?"

He exchanged glances with his friend, who shook his head. "I don't . . ." he began, and then seemed struck with a thought. "Come to think of it, I might have seen him going out a minute ago. He could still be in the parking lot. Let's go have a look."

She doubted his sincerity, but with her self-defense training, she was confident she could rebuff anything he might try. Plus, it was better than wandering around a noisy crowd looking for someone she couldn't identify, although she suspected Mike was more interested in pursuing a hookup than being helpful.

"Okay, thanks."

Elbowing their way back through the crowd, she and Mike reached the door and stepped outside. Kate sucked in a breath of cool, clean air. Her clothes probably already smelled of cigarette smoke.

"I don't see anyone. If he did come out, he must have gone."

"Maybe not." Mike snaked a hand around her waist. "Let's walk down to the end of the lot. Make sure he's not in one of these cars."

She sighed, detaching his arm. "Nice try. No, thanks."

He shrugged, apparently not offended. "Hey, can't blame me for trying. I was just telling Stan he should pick up a conversation with a woman. Poor guy just got the boot after seven years with the same woman. Then you walked up next to me. Thought I'd show him how it was done."

"Nice of you."

He didn't seem to notice the sarcasm in her tone. "Well, hey, no hard feelings?"

She couldn't help smiling. "No hard feelings. Do you even know Larry Foust?"

"Oh, hey, yeah, I wasn't lying about that. But I didn't see him tonight. Sorry."

"Okay. Thanks." She nodded to the door. "Maybe you'd better get back to Stan before he loses his nerve entirely."

Grinning, he went back inside.

Well, at least she hadn't had to use her self-defense skills on him, but this looked to be a futile trip. If Pete hadn't called her, who had? The more she thought about it, the odder it seemed.

Frowning, she started along the gravel lot toward her car. It was even darker at this end farthest from the pole light, and she fumbled in her bag for her key ring, intending to hit the unlock button so the lights would flash. The ring had slipped from its usual position in the upper pocket, and she fished in the bottom of the bag, exasperated.

Headlamps flared suddenly—but not hers. A dark vehicle swung out of a shadowy space at the end of the lot, its high beams striking her in the face. She put up her hand to shield her eyes, muttering imprecations against drivers who used their high beams to blind unwary pedestrians.

And suddenly it accelerated, the engine roaring, heading straight toward her. For a stunned second she didn't move, unable to believe what was happening. Then she lunged to the side, feet scrambling for purchase on the loose gravel, heart thudding against her chest. She wasn't going to make it—it would hit her—

She landed hard—hands and knees scraping gravel, but clear of the vehicle. Swinging around, she tried to focus on the car. If she could get a look at the license plate, she'd—

It was backing, accelerating again, swerving toward her. She was helpless, sprawled on the ground—

Her fingers closed on the smooth silver of the dragon charm. She clasped it, fumbled for the panic button on the key and pressed it.

Her horn began to blare, lights flashing. The vehicle stopped with a scream of brakes, a crashing of gears, and then it went spinning out of the lot, sending up a spray of gravel just as the bar door opened and several people looked out, probably wondering if their cars had been hit.

Kate slumped back on her elbow, wincing at the pain in her hands and knees, struggling to accept the truth. Someone had tried to run her down. Deliberately. But who? And why?

CHAPTER SEVEN

Mac took advantage of the empty streets to reach the Lamplight in record time, not that he expected to find anything too alarming. It wasn't unusual to get a late-night call from the Lamplight, but that was generally on a Saturday night, not a weeknight. The caller hadn't been making much sense. Still, he was there now.

He pulled into the parking lot, illuminating the scene with his high beams, flashers on. The lights showed him a cluster of figures grouped around something on the ground. Adrenaline pumped as he strode toward them.

"What's going on?" he demanded.

The crowd parted, revealing the figure in the center. With what felt like a kick in the chest, he realized it was Kate. She was sitting on the ground, a woman bending over her. The shock of wild bleached hair was enough for him to know her—Sheila Hileman, openhearted, generous, uneducated but shrewd as they came.

"How is she, Sheila?"

"She'll do, Mac." Sheila looked up from whatever she was doing to Kate's hands. "Painful scrapes, but no bones broken."

He squatted beside Kate, taking her hand and

turning it palm up to shine his flashlight on it. Raw abrasions showed red in the light. "Maybe a doctor better have a look at this."

Kate snatched her hand away. "I don't need a doctor."

The anger in her tone reassured him. "A doctor might think otherwise."

She drew herself up with as much dignity as was possible for someone sitting on the ground. "Ms. Hileman took care of it. I just want to go home and wash up."

"That's right," Sheila said encouragingly. "Get all this nasty gravel out of it. The owner ought to repave the whole lot, but catch him spending any money he doesn't have to."

"I'll take you home in a minute," he told Kate. "First, I want to know what happened."

A babble of voices answered him.

He raised a hand and silence fell. "Sheila, what do you know about it?"

She stood, wiping her hands on tight jeans. "I saw her—Ms. Beaumont—come in a while ago. Looked like she was asking the bartender something. Then Mike here started talking to her, and they went out together. He came back after a couple of minutes, and then somebody near the door heard all the fuss out here—the car alarm, wheels spinning and all. We went out and . . ." She shrugged. "That's all."

He zeroed in on Mike Corliss. "Well, Mike?"

Mike's ruddy face grew redder. "I was just . . . I just . . ."

"He was trying to pick me up," Kate said. She made a move as if to stand. Mac grasped her arms and lifted her to her feet.

"You want me to think you came to the Lamplight to pick up men?" He lifted an eyebrow, and she glared at him.

"She wanted to find Larry Foust," Mike volunteered. "So I . . . I said I thought . . ." He trailed off and stared at his feet.

"There's no point in asking them anything else," Kate said. "No one was out here when it happened. A car nearly ran me down." She clamped her lips shut so decisively that he knew there was more to it.

"I caught a glimpse of the taillights, turning away from town," Sheila said.

"Anyone see anything more of it? Or notice who came outside during that time?"

Silence and shaking heads. Naturally, no one had seen. That was always the way. Either people saw more than was there or they saw nothing.

"Anyone think of anything, call the station," he ordered. He turned to Kate. "I'll take you home."

"I can drive myself." She closed her palms and winced. "I'll be fine."

"No," he said shortly.

"I'll bring her car along," Sheila volunteered. "Me and Alice are leaving now, anyway." She grinned. "Don't worry. We only had a beer each."

He picked up the key ring, lying on the ground where Kate had been, and handed it to Sheila. "The cottage behind the B and B."

She nodded, and he took a firm grasp on Kate's arm. "Come on. I want a few words with you."

"Can't it wait?" But she went along with him to the squad car.

"No." He helped her in and shut the door firmly. She was lucky he didn't lock her in the backseat. After agreeing she'd tell him what she was doing, she'd gone off on her own. And what did Larry Foust have to do with anything?

Mac slid into the driver's seat, turned and pulled out of the lot, with Sheila following in Kate's car and her friend trailing along behind.

"Well?" she demanded.

"When we get to the cottage. I don't want to be interrupted."

She glared at him and then sat mute, her hands lying palm up in her lap.

Mac spent the few minutes' drive trying to get a grip on himself. He was furious with Kate for putting herself at risk, and he was quite sure she hadn't told him the whole story yet. But at the same time he knew that his anger had its roots in fear for her. The situation was spiraling out of his control, and that triggered all his alarms.

Reaching the cottage, they paused long enough to get the keys from Sheila. Standing in the spill of light from the car's interior dome, he could plainly see Kate rubbing her fingers over and over the silver ornament on her key chain. Something important to her, clearly, and he wondered why.

Mac followed her inside, closed the door and swung to face her. "Why Larry Foust? And what else have you been keeping from me?"

Kate rubbed her forehead with the back of her hand. "Can't this wait until tomorrow?"

He hardened his resolve against the pity that came close to swamping him. "No. But it can wait until you clean those scrapes completely. I have a first-aid kit in the cruiser. I'll get it."

When he returned with the kit, she was emerging from the bedroom, patting her hands with a small towel. She'd swapped her jeans for a pair of soft knit pants, which probably meant her knees were beat up, too.

"Sit down over here in the light." He opened the kit. Somewhat to his surprise, she obeyed without argument.

He took her hand in his, checking to see that there were no tiny bits of gravel left to fester. "Larry Foust?" he said, squeezing some first-aid cream over the scrapes.

Kate hesitated, probably wondering how little she could get away with telling him. "According to Nikki, he was a friend of my brother's. Or at least, someone she'd seen him talking to. Do you know anything about him?"

"He's familiar enough," he admitted, smoothing the cream over her palm with the lightest possible touch. Even so, she took a quick, indrawn breath when he went over the worst of the scrapes. "A local kid. Father deceased, totally spoiled by his mother, who thinks he can do no wrong. He dropped out of college after one semester and has been hanging around town ever since."

"Have you suspected him of drug use?" She started to pull her hand away, but he held it firmly.

"You'd better have a sterile pad over that bad spot, at least for the night. Hold still."

She conceded, and he opened the packet and held the sterile pad in place, securing it with tape. Only then did he return to her question. "Not hard drugs, no. But I wouldn't be at all surprised to find out he uses pot when he can get it."

"I wondered, after Nikki mentioned seeing him with Jason, whether he might have something to do with the drugs. Jason had to get them from someone in town."

He began working on her other hand. "If he's a dealer, he must be the least successful one in the history of the world. He's always hard up for money, always cadging drinks from people. I heard recently that his mother threatened to cut off his allowance if he didn't get a job, but I doubt that she'd follow through."

Kate watched the movement of his fingers, frowning slightly. Was she as aware of the sensations when they touched as he was? If so, she seemed determined to show no signs of it. But when he'd finished, she looked relieved, as well as pale and tired.

He reminded himself that he was going to get straight answers from her. "So you went to the Lamplight tonight looking for Larry Foust. What made you think he'd be there?"

"Nikki said it was a popular hangout." She paused.

"Don't bother stopping there. I'm not leaving until I hear the whole story."

"All right," she snapped, but it was an echo of her usual force. "I had lunch there today with Nikki. I wanted to talk to her about what she remembered about Jason's . . . about the last few days he was at the office. And we went to the Lamplight because she didn't want to be seen by her bosses."

"Go on." He thought she was telling the truth, but not necessarily all of it.

"Well, we talked. And I asked her about any other friends Jason made or people he knew." An expression of exasperation crossed her face. "That girl has the concentration of a butterfly. But she did come up with Foust's name. And the bartender heard us talking. He said Larry Foust had come in late the previous night with a couple

138

of guys he didn't want in the place. He wouldn't say why."

"That was Pete, I suppose. He manages the Lamplight for the owner. If he didn't want people in there, it was because they were troublemakers of some variety. But that still docsn't explain why you went there tonight."

"I had a call saying Larry Foust was there." She frowned. "I thought it was Pete, but it turned out he wasn't even working tonight. And Foust wasn't there. I'd almost think it was a practical joke, except who else could have known I wanted to talk to Larry? And . . ." She stopped abruptly.

"And somebody almost ran you down," he finished for her.

His anger rose again—anger that she'd broken her word to him, anger that she could have been badly hurt.

Kate nodded, not meeting his gaze.

He resisted the urge to grab her and force her to look at him. "What happened to letting me in on what you were doing?"

"I never agreed to tell you every little thing I do," she said, flaring. "Anyway, if you'd been with me, it would have been hopeless trying to get anything from Foust."

"You didn't get anything, anyway. Except a bad scare and a painful set of scrapes," he pointed out. "Do you want me to have to follow you around town?"

She glared at him. "I could charge you with harassment."

"You could. And I could tell everyone in town what you're doing." He let her mull that over for a moment and then leaned closer. "Listen to me. I'm still willing to cooperate with you, but no more Lone Ranger stuff. Now, tell me what happened with the car."

After a long look, Kate nodded. "You've heard how we went outside. Mike claimed he'd seen Larry leaving, but it was just an excuse." She shrugged. "He took it pretty well when I sent him back to his buddy. And he seemed sure Foust hadn't been in at all, so I decided not to waste any more time on a wild-goose chase. I was going to my car when a vehicle came roaring around from the end of the lot, headed straight for me. I had to dive out of the way. That's how I got this." She gestured, palms up.

He was frowning, trying to picture it. "Could have been somebody who'd had one too many and didn't notice you, then ran when they realized what they'd done."

"Could have been," she said. "Except that while I was on the ground, the car reversed and came at me again."

Everything in him stilled, trying to make sense of it. Things like this didn't happen in his town. Except that Kate's pallor was very convincing.

"If he was trying to hit you, why didn't he?

If you were on the ground, you were a sitting duck."

"I had my keys out. I hit the panic button, and my car alarm went off. And I think I yelled. He must have thought he'd be caught. He roared off just when somebody looked out."

Mac didn't want to believe it, but somehow he did. "Did you get a glimpse of the vehicle at all?"

"I was too busy trying not to get hit. I think it was either a pickup or an SUV—the lights seemed higher than a car, anyway."

"That narrows it down to about three-quarters of the population," he muttered. "If it was Foust . . ." He shook his head. "It doesn't make sense."

"It doesn't make sense no matter who it was. But somebody apparently doesn't like my being here."

He studied her face, not sure how much of this he was buying, and yet swayed by the fact that she obviously believed it. "There has to be some other explanation. Maybe the driver was backing up out of panic, thinking he'd hit someone. Maybe he was too drunk to know what he was doing."

Kate didn't respond, and she clearly didn't believe it.

"Look, on the outside chance that you're right, the best thing you can do is get out of Laurel Ridge. Go home, and leave this business to me."

She was already shaking her head. "I'm not going anywhere."

He wasn't really surprised. He leaned toward her, grasping her wrists with both hands, careful not to touch her palms. He could feel her pulse pounding against his hands.

He forced himself to ignore the sensation. *Concentrate on the job at hand.*

"Then you're going to tell me everything you're up to, everything you suspect," he said firmly. "And you're not doing any more investigating on your own, or so help me, I'll lock you up. That's a promise."

Kate reconsidered that confrontation with Mac the next morning as she walked into Blackburn House. It hadn't been as bad as she'd expected. She grudgingly admitted Mac had every reason to be angry with her, but he'd been almost mild.

He'd probably felt sorry for her at the moment. That didn't mean further questioning wasn't coming. Still, she could do some pushing of her own. She wanted a talk with Russ Sheldon, and she meant to have it, no matter what she had to do.

The sunlight streamed through the windows on the door, laying patterns on the marble hall floor. Kate hadn't gotten more than a few steps inside the building before a woman in Amish garb emerged from the quilt shop, headed right for her.

"You'll be Kate Beaumont, ain't so?" The woman's smile brought beauty to a face that at first Kate had considered plain. "I'm Sarah Bitler. I have the quilt shop." She gestured toward the store window, filled with a colorful display of fabrics and one orange cat which stared at Kate unblinkingly.

Apparently most of the town knew who she was by now. "It's nice to meet you, Ms. Bitler. Your shop looks very intriguing."

"Sarah, please. You're working in the bookshop, so we're almost neighbors." Her blue eyes darkened in concern. "But we've heard about your accident. Should you be working today? Allison or I could help Emily if needed."

"We'd be glad to." Another woman had come out of the store while they'd been talking. She was the opposite of Sarah in appearance, with dark red hair stylishly cut and a silky teal top worn over expensive-looking slacks. "I'm Allison Standish, Sarah's partner. I'm sure Emily doesn't expect you in today."

Kate gave her a blank look. "But she told me to work this morning."

"She'll have changed her mind after she heard." Allison smiled. "Obviously you're not used to the small-town grapevine. Neither was I, when I first came to Laurel Ridge. Word spreads as if by

143

magic, especially about something as dramatic as a newcomer being knocked down by a car."

"I wasn't really knocked down," she began, and then wondered why she was explaining to these strangers. "Thanks for your concern, but I'm fine."

"You'll let us know if you need a break, now." Sarah's worry seemed genuine. "We never mind looking after each other's businesses here in Blackburn House."

"Thank you." She beat a hasty retreat toward the bookshop, wondering how far the story of last night's adventure had spread. It had never occurred to her that anyone would think it worth repeating. Would it make her task more difficult? Nikki might well be regretting her cooperation if gossip linked them together.

The sympathy she'd received from two complete strangers prepared Kate somewhat for Emily's fluttering over her. First, she insisted Kate go home and rest, and when Kate declined, Emily insisted she'd put off the errands she'd planned to run this morning until another day.

Kate finally persuaded her to go ahead with her plans, and with her departure, the bookshop settled down to a somnolent late morning. Blackburn House in general seemed deserted, making her wonder how people stayed in business with so little foot traffic.

She was dusting shelves when she heard the

door and turned to welcome a customer at last. But it was Mac Whiting, and she doubted that he'd come to buy a book.

"I thought you'd be at the cottage resting this morning," he said, frowning as he approached her. "Surely Emily can get along without you for a few hours."

All this concern was starting to grate. Did they think she was as feeble as all that? "I'm perfectly all right. A few scrapes won't keep me from doing my job."

"Let's have a look." Before she could stop him, Mac had her hand. "Seems all right. But you've probably got a few bruises elsewhere from hitting the gravel."

She snatched her hand away. "My bruises aren't any of your business."

Mac rested an elbow against the nearest shelf, his face relaxing in a smile. "Your injuries might be important if we catch up with the driver. Maybe I ought to have a few photos."

"Dream on," she scoffed, not appreciating the effect his smile had on her. "If you don't have anything more important to say, I'd like to get on with my work while Emily is out."

"The dusting can wait." He glanced around. "This seems as private as anyplace. So let's get a few things straight about Larry Foust. Does your brother mention him in the video diary?"

"I'm not sure." She straightened a row of

paperbacks. "You saw what it was like. There are a few mentions of someone who might be him, but nothing that indicated he was a source of drugs, if that's what you're after."

"His name didn't come up at all in the initial investigation. Odd, if they were friends. Still, a talk with Larry is needed."

"Not by you," she said immediately.

Mac resumed his impassive cop's expression. "This is police business."

She resisted the temptation to point out that he wouldn't even know about Foust if not for her. "If you talk to him, he'll be on his guard, right?"

He shrugged. "Past experience tells me he'll give me a few smart-ass answers. But if I lean on him . . ."

"Then he'll never say a word about Jason. Look, doesn't it make more sense for me to approach him? I can just say that I wanted to meet him because he was a friend of my brother's. Chances are he'll talk to me."

"Aren't you forgetting your experience last night?" Mac raised an eyebrow. "I thought you were convinced it was an attempt to scare you away because you were looking for Larry."

Mac was annoying with that way he had of using her own words against her. "I don't know that's what was behind it, at all. Maybe it really was an accident, like Jason's death. Look, if Larry was Jason's friend, he may have some insight into what made him turn back to drugs. And if he supplied them, then I want him to pay."

"That phone call doesn't make much sense unless you assume the incident wasn't an accident." He was frowning as he pieced it together.

"Or maybe someone else has reason to want me to leave." She studied his face to see how he'd react to that. "Seems to me you're a member of that party, right?"

She'd succeeded in nettling him. She could tell by the look he gave her.

"I think you should leave because, on the very slim chance you're right about last night, you could be in danger. If you start poking around Larry Foust, you'd make things worse."

"That's my responsibility, isn't it? Anyway, you have to admit that he's more likely to talk to me than to you, at least where Jason is concerned, which is all *I'm* concerned with."

Mac obviously didn't want to admit any such thing, but finally he gave a reluctant nod. "Only if I have your word you'll let me know when and where you're meeting him. That way I'll know where to pick up the pieces."

She smiled with relief at her success. "You're forgetting my self-defense skills."

"They didn't help you much with that car last night," he snapped.

"Wrong." She couldn't help a little smugness in

her reply. "Dive and roll. My stepfather had us practicing that in the backyard until it was second nature." She grimaced, glancing at her hands. "The grass was considerably softer than gravel, though."

"You're determined to have the last word, aren't you?"

She didn't bother answering what was obviously a rhetorical question. And just as obviously, Mac wasn't done yet.

"What else did you get from Nikki? Anything useful?"

She'd equivocate, but he looked ready to stand there propping up the bookshelf all day if necessary.

"Nikki said everything at the office seemed to be going fine until that last day. Did you know they'd fired Jason?"

He nodded. "Bart finally came out with that when I pressed him. He kept insisting everything was fine. Didn't want to be blamed, I'm sure."

"You didn't tell me you spoke to Bart." A thought occurred to her. Had her stepfather known about Jason being fired? Could Tom's reaction have pushed Jason back into drug use? No one in Laurel Ridge would have the answer to that.

And, she and Tom hadn't had much of anything to say to each other by then. Jason had been their only meeting point, and when he was gone, neither of them had tried.

Mac looked uncomfortable. "I'm sorry. I suppose, at the time, Bart thought it best. He was never very clear about why they'd let him go. He just kept insisting that Jason's work wasn't acceptable."

"Then why did they keep him so long?" She shook her head. "It doesn't add up. From what Nikki said, there was a big blowup that last day. She said Russell Sheldon looked devastated. And that he never came back to the office after Jason's death. That has to mean something."

"Not necessarily. Russ is a tenderhearted guy. It may have been the incident that pushed him over the top toward retiring." But Mac didn't sound as confident as he might have, and she was quick to push the advantage.

"Nikki thought it was strange. And as far as I could tell, so did Emily. She said Sheldon sometimes talked about retiring, but never seriously. She implied that the business was his life."

"I suppose it was." Mac frowned, and she could see that her words had made an impression. "Still, the truth is that he's been going downhill ever since he retired, and probably before that. You can't tell what a person like Russ Sheldon might do if he felt his mental powers failing him."

"Did you talk to him at the time of Jason's death?"

His frown deepened, his firm lips pressing together. "No."

"Didn't you think it might be important to speak to him?" If that sounded critical, it was meant that way.

"He was extremely upset about your brother's death. Bart said it would be dangerous to question him." He glared at her. "And, no, I didn't take his word for it. I spoke to Russ Sheldon's doctor, and he was clearly worried about the man. In his opinion, it could be harmful. Frankly, there didn't seem to be anything he could tell me that I hadn't already heard from Bart and Lina."

"Like Jason being fired? I'd very much like to talk to Russell Sheldon."

He studied her face, seeming to consider her determination. Finally he lifted an eyebrow questioningly. "I already gave in about Foust. You think you could let me have this one?"

Something that had been stretched to intensity in her began to relax. He wasn't going to prevent her.

"I promise to be tactful. I'd just like to hear for myself what he has to say about Jason. Surely after all this time, it wouldn't upset him to talk about it."

"I'm not so sure that your idea of tactful is the same as mine, but I'll set it up." He seemed to regret having conceded that. "But remember, if I think he's getting too upset, I'll call a halt and you don't argue."

"If I went by myself . . ."

"No." The firmness of the word said Mac wasn't to be moved. "We do this together or not at all."

Once again, he'd left her without a choice. Still, she was getting what she wanted, wasn't she?

"Fine. We'll do it together."

Mac should have looked relieved at her capitulation. Instead, he just looked stressed.

CHAPTER EIGHT

Kate pulled a box of records off the top shelf in the back room of the bookshop, stirring up a cloud of dust. She sneezed, nearly losing her perch on the rickety step stool. Emily said it had been a long time since this area had been cleaned, and she'd been right.

Despite the dust, it was somehow relaxing to work in silence, even at something as mundane as dusting. Emily must be with a customer—Kate could hear the birdlike chirping of her voice. Odd, how quickly she and Emily had settled into a routine. There was nothing challenging about the work, but it allowed her imagination time to play with the article she was writing for an online magazine.

If Mac came through with his promise to set up a meeting with Russell Sheldon, she could be on her way to finding some answers. Come to think of it, she didn't doubt that Mac would do as he said. He wasn't a person to promise what he couldn't deliver.

The door closed sharply behind her. Kate swung around, losing her balance entirely this time, and hopped from the stool just as it toppled.

"Hey, sorry." The intruder seemed abashed at the havoc he'd wrought with his entrance. He rushed to set the step stool upright, giving Kate a chance to have a look at him.

Early twenties, probably, with a round, youthful face that didn't seem to match the black pants, T-shirt and jacket he wore. His straw-colored hair was longish in the back, curling despite his likely efforts to subdue it.

"Were you looking for something?" she asked. *Or someone?*

"You, if you're Kate Beaumont." He tried to assume a menacing look that didn't work well with his blue eyes and the dimple in his cheek. "You've been asking around about me. Lay off."

"Larry Foust, I suppose. I've been asking because I want to talk to you about my brother."

"Yeah, well, I don't want to talk, so quit poking around asking questions, or . . ."

"Or what?" She took a step closer, resisting the impulse to grab him by the shirt and shake the attitude out of him. "If you want me to leave you alone, just answer my questions."

"I don't know anything." The words turned into a whine. He moved a step back, as if they were involved in an odd dance.

"You knew Jason. Pretty well, I understand. How can you say you don't know anything when you don't know what I want to ask?"

He shot a look toward the door, probably regretting the bravado that had prompted him to close it. "Look, I'm sorry about your brother.

153

He seemed like a good guy. But you'll get me in trouble if you go linking us together."

Kate was on that in an instant. "Why would you be in trouble? Unless you encouraged him to get back on drugs. Or maybe you know something about where he got the drugs he took."

"I don't, honest, I don't. But nobody wants to be mixed up in trouble, maybe have the cops coming to the door asking questions. You can't say I had anything to do with Jason dying. Honest." He tried for a boyish look that probably worked well on older women.

But she had no desire to mother him. She tried an appeal of her own. "You knew Jason. You're about the same age. I thought if anyone knew why he did what he did, it might be you. Won't you help me?"

"I don't know. Honest, I don't." For an instant she seemed to see the confused kid behind the facade. "It seemed like Jase had everything going for him. Good job, enough money to get by on, a place of his own. I don't get it."

"Do you think he took an overdose deliberately?" It was a struggle to say the words.

Larry shrugged helplessly. "I don't know. I mean, I know he wasn't using before that. I tried to give him a joint or two, and he wouldn't touch them. No harm in that," he muttered. "Everybody does it."

That was one of the things she'd learned in

helping Jason through his crisis. People who used had to believe that it was normal, that everyone did it, so that meant it wasn't so bad.

"Did you see him that last day?"

He shook his head violently. "Not me. Last I saw of him was the night before. He just had a beer at the Lamplight and went home early. He seemed fine. Honest. It was strange that . . ."

"That what?"

Larry shrugged. "Well, that he had a beer, even. He didn't drink anything alcoholic. Said he couldn't, so I figured he had a problem. But something pushed him over the line."

So if Larry was to be believed, and that was a big if, something happened that last day that had pushed Jason into an overdose, deliberate or accidental. What could it be other than his firing? Unless, of course, his father had found out. She could imagine the brand of sympathy Tom would offer.

Why hadn't he called her? She backed away from the answer to that question and turned on Larry instead.

"If he'd wanted something stronger than the marijuana you offered, where would he get it in Laurel Ridge?" She snapped the question at him.

"I don't know." Panic flared in his face. "Honest, I don't."

Her stepfather used to say that people used the

word *honest* when they really meant the opposite. Of course, Tom had been a cynic about humanity.

"Listen, I have to go." Larry scrabbled at the door, missing the knob in his haste. "I can't tell you anything else. Just leave me alone."

"One more thing." She planted her hand on the door. He probably could have yanked it open against her, but he didn't try. "Were you at the Lamplight last night?"

"No, no, I swear I wasn't." His expression told her he'd heard what happened to her, and beads of perspiration appeared along his hairline. "Whoever did that, it wasn't me. I didn't have a thing to do with it."

Kate wasn't sure she entirely believed him, but she doubted she'd get anything else from him. She stepped back from the door.

This time his hand landed on the knob. He yanked the door open and catapulted through it. A moment later she heard the outside door open and close.

Kate stood where she was for a moment. She didn't think she'd gotten the entire story from Larry, but it was clear there was someone or something he feared more than he did anything she could do. She'd give a lot to know who or what that was. Her thoughts ricocheted to the incident Mac had told her about with the high school kid. She'd been so focused on Jason that she hadn't even considered the bigger picture.

156

· · ·

Supper at his parents' place tended to be a noisy affair, Mac knew, and tonight it was louder than ever. But it was a break from the thrown-together suppers he usually ate in his quiet second-floor apartment in town. He'd wanted his privacy when he got back from the military, and his job had made a good reason to move into town. No one would hear him there when the nightmares got bad.

Nick and Allison had taken Jamie for a hike through the woods after school to collect autumn leaves, and he bubbled over with enthusiasm, as always.

"Grammy's going to show me how to make place mats with the leaves, Uncle Mac. I bet you don't know how to do that."

Mac grinned, ruffling his nephew's silky hair. "You'd lose, then. Grammy did that with me when I was a little boy. And your daddy, too."

Jamie ducked away from his hand and smoothed his hair back into place. "What happened to yours?"

Mac exchanged glances with his mother, who smiled and shrugged.

"They don't last forever," she explained. "But we'll enjoy them this fall, won't we?"

Jamie nodded, apparently satisfied, and spooned the last bite of his apple dumpling between his lips. "Can I be excused?" he muttered, mouth still full.

"May I," Nick corrected. "Okay. But don't run."

The addition was too late, since Jamie took off as if jet-propelled in his eagerness to get back outside before dark. The door slammed, punctuating his flight.

His mother shook her head indulgently and turned back to her conversation with Allison about wedding plans.

Mac lifted his eyebrows at his brother. "Do those two ever talk about anything else?"

"Not that I've noticed," Nick admitted.

"Weddings take a lot of planning," his mother informed him. "Not that you'd know anything about that."

Mac rolled his eyes at the inevitable jab at his unmarried state. "Seems like the Amish do it a lot simpler. I don't hear Aaron and Sarah talking about flower girls and bouquets."

"If you think it's simpler to provide a wedding supper for upwards of two hundred family and friends in the Bitlers' farmhouse, you'd best think again," she said.

"That reminds me, I promised Sarah's father I'd put together a few extra trestle tables for the wedding," his father said. "I said you boys would help."

Mac nodded. "Just let me know when. It'll be nice to see those two happy after all they've been through." Sarah and Aaron had had a difficult time of it this summer, but at last they were free to look forward to a life together.

Nick nudged him. "All these weddings giving you any ideas, little brother?"

"Not yet, thanks," he said firmly. "I don't plan . . ."

He lost the rest of that thought when his cell phone vibrated. Pushing back his chair, he answered as he moved away from the table. At least he'd gotten through the meal before being interrupted.

"Whiting," he said briskly. "What's up?"

"Nothing important."

At the sound of Kate's voice, he could almost sense her in the room with him. Keeping his back to the table, he moved into the living room. "You haven't been dodging any more speeding vehicles?"

"No." She hesitated, making him think she was considering how to put whatever it was she'd called to say. "I wasn't going to bother calling you about this, but I don't care to listen to any more lectures about keeping secrets."

"Glad to hear it." He moved to the window and glanced out at the rolling fields, golden now in the last of the afternoon's sun. "What's happening, then?"

"I had a visitor at the bookshop today. Larry Foust came to see me."

"That's a surprise. I thought he was avoiding you."

159

"He said he'd heard I'd been asking around about him. He wanted me to knock it off."

She said it lightly, but still his hand tightened on the phone.

"You mean he threatened you? Right out in public?"

"It wasn't exactly in public. I was working in the back room when he suddenly showed up. As for threatening . . ." A thread of amusement ran through her voice. "With that baby face of his, he can't really manage to look menacing."

"That doesn't mean he's harmless, especially if he's the one who supplied your brother with drugs." His jaw hardened. He'd known Kate's presence would stir things up. Still, if she hadn't found her brother's journal, the case would still be at an unsatisfying end. "Are you at home? I'm coming over."

"That's not necessary. I just wanted to tell you, so you couldn't complain."

"I'll be there in fifteen minutes." He ended the call before she could answer and stalked back into the dining room, to find every member of his family looking at him with interest.

He tried to ignore them. "Thanks for supper, Mom. It was great. I'm afraid I have to leave now."

"Was that Kate Beaumont on the phone?" his mother asked. "If you're seeing her, tell her I'd like for her to come to dinner this weekend."

160

"Mom." It was the harassed tone that made him feel like a teenager, trying to keep his parents from embarrassing him. "I don't think that's a good idea." He didn't want a possibly dangerous situation touching his family.

She tilted her head slightly as she studied his face, reminding him of Jamie. "Maybe you're right. It should come from me. I'll call her."

"That isn't what I meant." He shook his head, giving it up as a lost cause. No one ever stopped his mother from exercising her gift for hospitality. "I have to go."

It took less than fifteen minutes to reach the bed-and-breakfast, park and start back the walk toward the cottage, but in that time the sun had slid behind the ridge, and the shadows were thick under the trees and around the buildings. He strode to the stoop, noticed something white fluttering against the door and tugged it free as he knocked.

Kate yanked the door open immediately, looking ready for battle, her hair pulled ruthlessly back from her face to a knot at her nape. "I told you . . ." she began, but he walked past her.

"If you had an encounter with Larry Foust, I want to talk to you face-to-face." He thrust the paper at her. "This was stuck in your door."

She took it, still frowning at him. "Larry didn't scare me."

"No, he wouldn't." Unwilling, he felt a smile tug at his lips. "I'd guess it was the other way around."

Taken by surprise, she blinked, and her face relaxed. "You mean I scared him. I meant to, I suppose. But really, isn't it stretching things to picture him as some kind of drug kingpin? I wouldn't think he'd have either the brains or the nerve."

"Probably not, but that doesn't mean he's guiltless. If he introduced your brother to the person who provided the drugs he took, he's still morally responsible. And legally, as well." He moved a little farther into the room, glancing at the computer screen. He wouldn't have been surprised to see Jason's face, but it was a page of text.

She caught the direction of his glance. "I was working on a magazine article. Anyway, there's no reason for you to get hot under the collar because I talked to Larry. I was fine."

"You were alone with him." His exasperation grew. Didn't the woman have any sense? "After what happened to you last night, you shouldn't have put yourself in another risky position."

"I didn't." Kate sounded as exasperated as he felt. "I was in the storeroom of the bookshop in the middle of the day. And Emily was right in the next room. Why would I think that dangerous?"

Mac knew perfectly well why he was so

irritated. It was because she was right. And because she should have been safe in his town.

"You wouldn't," he admitted. "But when you saw Larry, why didn't you walk right out into the shop?"

Kate just stared at him for a moment, and then a smile teased her lips. "And ask him about supplying my brother with drugs in Emily's presence?"

He threw up his hand in a gesture of surrender. "All right, you win. So, did you learn anything from all of that?"

"Not much. Except that—well, I did get the sense that he wasn't telling me everything. He did say, or imply anyway, that he'd offered Jason pot, and Jason refused."

Mac nodded. "I'm not surprised. There's too much of it around to suit me. As soon as we stop one channel, another one pops up." He zeroed in on her face, trying to penetrate the barrier she put up whenever the conversation turned to her brother. "You said you thought Larry was hiding something. Any idea what?"

"I can't be sure," she said slowly, as if she thought back over the conversation, trying to tease out any further meaning. "When I pushed him about where Jason might have gotten the drugs, it seemed to me that he panicked."

He considered. "If that's so, it sounds as if he knew."

"And didn't want to say. Or was afraid to say." She finished the thought for him, and her gaze met his. "So Larry knows where Jason got the drugs that killed him." Her voice shook just a little. "We have to make him tell us."

"Not we," he corrected quickly. "This is a job for the police. I'll lean on Larry." After he'd gone back and questioned people at the bar more closely, he'd been convinced that Larry hadn't been around at all that night. Obviously he shouldn't have accepted that. Maybe he'd become too confident that he knew his town and its people.

Mac expected an argument and was surprised when he didn't get one. Instead, Kate gave a rueful smile.

"Much as I hate to admit it, I don't think I'll get anything more from him. I'm sure you'll be a lot more impressive."

He masked his surprise with a smile. "It's the uniform that does it."

"And the man who wears it," Kate added.

Coming from anyone else that would have been a compliment. Kate made it sound more like an insult. Obviously her relationship with her stepfather hadn't been a good one. Maybe she was transferring those feelings to anyone else in uniform.

Well, there wasn't much he could do about it. His job was clear. If any doubt existed about Jason Reilley's death, he had to clear it up. And if he had any chance of finding the person who'd supplied the drugs, he'd never let go.

He studied Kate's averted face for a moment and decided it was time to change the subject if he could. "I've arranged for us to meet with Russ Sheldon tomorrow at eleven. I hope that works for you."

That news kindled enthusiasm that made her golden-brown eyes sparkle. "Great. That'll be fine. I'm not working until the afternoon tomorrow, anyway. I'll meet you there."

"I'll pick you up," he said firmly. "I'll be here about ten to eleven."

As anticipated, that raised an instant objection. "I know where he lives. I can walk."

He let his lips quirk just a little. "You walk beautifully, but I'm still picking you up."

His compliment hung in the balance for a moment, but then she smiled. "Okay, have it your way. I'll see you then."

The words were a prelude to dismissal, and he didn't want to go, at least not yet. He nodded toward the scrap of paper he'd carried in with him. It lay on the corner of the desk where she'd tossed it.

"Was that trash, or has someone been leaving you love notes?"

"Hardly that, I think," she said, unfolding it.

She glanced at it, then stared, the warm color draining from her face.

"Kate?" He'd reached her in an instant, putting his arm around her waist. She looked pale enough to pass out. "What's wrong?"

In answer, she shoved the paper into his hand. He frowned, staring at it. A dragon, crudely drawn in pencil, the lines a bit smudged from lying on the step. No words. It seemed meaningless, but obviously it wasn't.

"Come on, Kate. Snap out of it." His grasp tightened. He was suddenly, inappropriately, aware of the slim body brushing his. "What does it mean?"

She took a deep breath, then another, seeming to force her emotion back under control. But it was a precarious control—he could sense that in the tremors that passed through her.

"This is something connected with your brother." Obviously. Jason was the only one who could make her expose her feelings. "Why? What is there about a dragon that upsets you?"

Kate put up a hand to rub the crease between her brows. "Sorry. It just . . . it shook me. I'm all right." But she didn't move out of the circle of his arm.

He waited. She'd tell him now. She couldn't help it.

Another quick glance at the paper, and then she met his gaze. "Jason had a silver dragon charm.

166

It was like a mascot. It always hung on his key ring. But it apparently wasn't with his keys when they were returned to his father." She stopped, and a thought seemed to strike her. "Unless Tom got rid of it. I suppose he might . . ."

He shook his head, even while wondering why she'd think her stepfather would do that. "No. I've been through all the reports I wrote at the time, trying to refresh my memory." Not that it needed much refreshing. "There wasn't anything like that on Jason's key ring or on his person. Or in his belongings, for that matter."

She drew away from him, and he suppressed the urge to pull her back. Reaching into her bag that lay open on the desk, Kate pulled out her own keys. She fingered them, singling out a silver object, and handed it to him.

"It was exactly like this. He . . . Jason bought matching ones with his first paycheck. One for himself and one for me."

He turned it over in his hand, noting the weight of it and the sterling mark on the underside. Not cheap, was his first thought. "It wasn't here, so it wasn't returned to your . . . to his father."

Kate stared at him blankly for a moment. "But it's impossible. I know he had it on his key ring. It was his lucky charm. If he'd lost it, he would have told me."

She might be overestimating the object's importance to her brother—a young man, busy

167

with life and on his own for the first time, could easily have shed some of the things that tied him to his younger self.

"You don't think it was important to him." Kate seemed to read his thoughts without difficulty. "You're wrong. He often mentioned it. On the rare occasion that he sent something to me in writing, he signed it with a drawing a lot like this one." She gestured to the note. "Someone who knew how important it was left that for me."

"Kate, you can't know that . . ."

"Don't you believe me? You can even see his key ring with the charm in some of the diary entries. He'd have mentioned it if he'd lost it." Her voice was ragged, and she threw the words at him like a challenge.

"Okay, I believe you. But I'm still sure that it wasn't here to be collected with his effects."

"It was on his key ring," she repeated stubbornly.

He shook his head, taking a step to erase the space between them. Clasping her hand, he put the dragon charm into it. "I'm sorry, Kate. When we found him, his key ring was lying on the grass about a foot from the . . . from his hand. There was nothing on it but his car keys and a couple of door keys." It showed up plainly enough in the photographs of the body, but he didn't want to show her those.

"Then someone took it." She said the words defiantly.

Mac had no desire to reply in kind. This was hurting her too much. "That would mean someone had taken it before I reached the scene. If so, I'd think they'd have cleaned out his wallet, too, and it appeared to be untouched."

Kate's hand lay passive in his, and then her fingers tightened around his. "Don't you see? That means someone was there when he died. Someone who knew the dragon had sentimental value to him. And to me. What if that person set up the whole thing? Gave him the drugs and left him to die."

"Kate." He held her hand between both of his, trying not to let pity show in his tone. She was jumping to conclusions, wasn't she? Reading something into the absence of the dragon from Jason's keys.

Still, here was the drawing, right in front of him. His skeptical cop's mind toyed with the thought that she'd put it there herself for him to find. But what could she hope to gain from it? He tabled the thought for future consideration.

"I'm sorry. Tell me why it was so important to you." And still is, he added silently.

She took a shaky breath, the muscles in her neck working. "Jason . . . Jason was different. From the time he was small, he wasn't like other kids." Her lips twisted wryly. "He certainly wasn't the outgoing, athletic son his father expected. Tom never understood Jason."

"Your mother . . ." he ventured, and she shook her head sharply.

"My mother was an alcoholic, not that I knew the word when I was small. After my father left, she couldn't handle being alone. The drinking got worse. When she met Tom, she saw in him all the strength she needed. But she couldn't handle the hours when he was gone, imagining all sorts of things happening to him. She killed herself driving under the influence when Jason was only five. Killed herself, like Jason did." She winced. "Jason was devastated, and Tom didn't help."

He could hear the anger at her stepfather in her voice, and he knew this wasn't the time to suggest that the man might not have known how, struggling with his own grief as he must have been.

"How old were you?" he asked.

"Eleven. Jason . . . Jason turned to me. We felt as if all we had was each other."

Mac tried to imagine himself in that situation and failed. His folks had always been such a solid, loving influence in his life. He and Nick were close, but not the way Kate had been with her brother. She'd been more of a mother to him.

He moved his fingers over the backs of her hands, soothing and comforting. "Why the dragon? What did it mean?"

Kate actually smiled, tilting her head to meet his gaze. "Silly, I guess. But I used to read to Jason. He was what the teachers called a reluctant reader, right up until the time I read him a fantasy book. He was fascinated. He begged for those stories every night, and then he started reading them on his own."

"So you tried to keep up with his interests." It wasn't hard to guess that his devoted sister would do anything to stay close to Jason.

She chuckled. "I can't say I enjoyed all of them, but I tried to steer him to the better books— C. S. Lewis, J. R. R. Tolkien, Lloyd Alexander. Eventually he drifted into playing fantasy games and that sort of thing. Well, you must know that from the little bits of the diary you've seen."

"Definitely." It would have been helpful if Jason had left a little of the fantasy behind when recording his diary, but he couldn't have everything. "You said he bought the matching dragons with his first paycheck."

"Yes." Her fingers, still enclosed in his, moved over the charm. "There had been a silver dragon on the cover of one of those early books. Every time I touch it, it reminds me of Jason." Her voice broke on the name. "I should have been here for him. He was desperate enough to take his own life, and I wasn't here."

That jolted him. He'd tried to be careful not

to hint at suicide, and apparently she'd been thinking it all along.

"You believe it was deliberate," he said softly.

"I don't want to, but I can't believe . . ."

"I'm sorry." The words were inadequate, especially when the tears she'd been holding back spilled over.

Kate made an inarticulate sound, her hands trembling in his. His heart twisted in sympathy, and he drew her into his arms, unsure whether she'd welcome it or not. But she didn't pull away.

Mac murmured whatever soothing words came to his mind. Probably the words didn't matter at all. Right now, Kate's proud self-sufficiency had broken down, and she just needed another human being to hold her.

Not necessarily him, he told himself. And the stirring of his own senses he felt with Kate in his arms was completely selfish.

She leaned into him, clutching him as if he were the only stable thing in a suddenly rocky world. He stroked her hair, curling against his fingers, and then the long curve of her back, wishing he could do more and knowing the only thing he could possibly do for her was find out the truth of Jason's death—always assuming there was anything left to learn.

After a long moment she drew away, averting her face. Embarrassed, he supposed, both that she'd let her control slip and that she'd turned to him. He wanted to tell her he understood. He knew what it was like to feel you'd failed someone. His own guilt stabbed at his heart.

He almost spoke. But then her head lifted, and she managed a slight smile.

"Sorry," she said. "I didn't mean to fall apart on you."

"Anytime." He tried to keep it light.

She shook her head. "It won't happen again. Let's just get on with what has to be done." Kate glanced toward the door, and it was a clear invitation for him to leave. "I'll see you tomorrow, then."

Mac couldn't blame her for wanting to be alone with her grief. After all, he was the same way, wasn't he?

He had the door open and was halfway out when he knew he couldn't leave it at that. He turned, saw the pain in her eyes and leaned forward to kiss her lightly.

Her lips were cool. Unresponsive. And maybe he just imagined that they warmed and softened for an instant before he drew away.

"Lock this door," he said shortly. "And put the dead bolt on." After waiting only to hear the locks click into place, he strode to his car.

CHAPTER NINE

Kate walked past the window, allowing herself a casual glance out. She was ready early, and she suspected Mac would be right on time. He wasn't the sort to take any commitment lightly, even a trivial one.

Thinking of him brought his face to mind—his eyes dark and intent in that instant before he'd kissed her last night. Her lips warmed at the memory, and Kate shook her head. Where had that come from? She hadn't been sending out any signals she'd been unaware of, had she?

She'd deny that the physical attraction was there if she thought she could get away with it. But a person ought to be honest with herself, if not with anyone else. She just hadn't realized it had been reciprocated.

Still, how could she? Mac had a shield every bit as impervious as hers was, except that he hid it behind a smiling, easy manner.

Movement outside caught her eye. There he was. She snatched up her bag and opened the door before he could reach it, stepping outside to meet him. It might be just as well, under the circumstances, to avoid being alone with him whenever possible.

"A woman who's ready on time," he said, giving her that casual smile of his.

She wasn't deceived. His eyes were watchful, always watchful, behind it.

"You're not a male chauvinist, are you?" She matched her steps to his as they went out toward the street.

"God forbid," he said with an expression of mock horror. "My mother would never put up with that. I vividly remember being sent to my room without dessert for referring to a classmate as 'only a girl' when I was about eight. That cured me."

"Good. I like a woman who teaches her sons not to discriminate." They'd reached the street.

"Walk or ride?" Mac lifted an eyebrow with the question. "It's only a few blocks."

"Walk, by all means. I haven't had enough exercise since I've been here."

Mac nodded, and they headed up Main Street in the direction she'd come when she arrived in town, toward where the clock tower rose like a sentinel over the trees that bordered Main Street.

Mac caught the direction of her gaze. "Admiring our town hall tower?" He grinned. "It's a fine example of a community overreaching itself."

"How so?" She raised her eyebrows.

"Our town fathers thought we'd be named the county seat, so they built to match their dreams. Unfortunately, it didn't work out that way."

"It's impressive, even so." During the short time she'd been in town she'd noticed how often people glanced up at the clock, as if it was bound to be more accurate than their watches. "How old is it?"

"Built in 1842." He broke off to exchange greetings with a pair of elderly women exiting the bank. "Local stone, same as the church on the corner," he finished as they resumed walking.

Kate realized that the women had turned to watch them. "We seem to be attracting attention."

"Keeping an eye on us, are they?" Amusement threaded his voice. "The female half of the population is always trying to marry me off. We could hold hands." He gave her a challenging glance. "That would really give them something to talk about."

"No, thank you," she responded, ignoring the way her palm tingled at the suggestion. "According to Lina Oberlin, people will have started talking the first time you came to the cottage."

He stiffened. "When did you get a chance to exchange that sort of advice with Lina?"

"Relax, it was nothing that should concern the police," she said, answering the tone rather than the words. "She stopped by to apologize for her partner's attitude. We talked about Jason a little."

"Did she have any insights?" His voice gentled as it always did when he spoke to her about her brother. That alone could undermine her defenses if she weren't careful.

Kate shook her head. "Nothing that helped any. She said that bit about people noticing when I asked if she'd ever visited him. She implied that financial consultants had to be like Caesar's wife—above reproach."

Mac nodded, his lips quirking in amusement. "It's hard to believe anyone's imagination could conceive of a romance between a kid like Jason and a woman Lina's age."

"She's just middle-aged, not dead," she retorted. "Still, I can't think of anything less likely. Older women usually wanted to mother him, if anything."

They were approaching a hardware store, where a number of men lounged outside in the sunshine, many of them obviously Amish from their clothing and beards. Kate made an effort not to stare.

Mac clearly didn't find it unusual. He exchanged passing greetings with everyone, including a few laughing words she didn't understand, accompanied by a glance or two at her.

Once they were safely out of earshot, she turned on him. "That sounded like German. And it looked as if you were talking about me."

"Pennsylvania Dutch," he said. "It's the Low German language the Amish brought with them to this country. Joseph asked me if I had a new girl."

"What did you say to him?"

He grinned. "I said, well . . . the equivalent of 'Don't count your chickens before they're hatched.' "

"You should have just told him no." She tried for a firm tone despite the little curl of pleasure inside her at his implication.

"Then they'd assume we were together on police business," he responded. "Seems to me it's better to keep a low profile on that."

"Yes, of course," she muttered. It wasn't personal, in other words.

He glanced at her. "About last night," he began.

She was ready to turn off any conversation about that kiss with a laugh. The words she'd prepared were on her lips.

". . . I meant to ask if you'd deciphered anything else in your brother's diary," he continued.

She'd been so prepared for mention of the kiss that it took a moment to adjust. "There was something, but I have no idea what it means. In one of the last sessions, Jason makes a reference to someone called something like Baldicer. I have no idea what it means, but whoever it was, his attitude toward that person was . . . well, uneasy is the best way to describe it."

"Man or woman?" Mac automatically snapped into cop mode.

She shook her head. "It wasn't clear. I couldn't even tell if he was referring to someone at work or elsewhere. It would have been clear to him, of course, but not to me."

Mac considered. "No idea to where that character appears or what it represents?"

She shook her head. "It's not in any of the classic fantasy we read. I'm sure of that. Could be from one of the online games he played, I suppose."

"You didn't join him in those?" His lips quirked.

"I figured a thirty-year-old woman could never keep up." She smiled. "I probably would have embarrassed him."

"So, what we need is a young person who is as into that world as Jason was. To serve as an interpreter."

"You want me to let someone else look at Jason's private journal?" Despite herself, her voice rose a little, drawing a glance from a man watering a pot of mums outside the pharmacy.

"Well, think about it," Mac said. "The best way into that world is through someone who knows it. And isn't it easier if it's a stranger? It wouldn't mean anything to him or her, and you'd never have to see them again."

She could see the sense in what he said, but she still didn't like it. "I . . . I don't know. I'll think about it."

Mac nodded as if satisfied with that answer. "I'll do some quiet looking around for someone who fits the job in the meantime."

They turned off Main Street, immediately in a residential area of Victorian houses, neatly kept behind their hedges or fences. Chrysanthemums and marigolds bloomed along porches, and trees flaunted gold-and-red banners.

Russell Sheldon's house was a half block down, she knew from her previous visit. "Are you going to let me ask whatever questions I want?" she said abruptly.

"Within reason." Mac's tone was wary.

"What does that mean?" She was ready to do battle. This visit would be worse than useless if she couldn't be free to follow whatever turned up.

Mac stopped, turning to face her as if to give added emphasis to his words. "Look, I've already told you about Russ's condition. If he starts getting agitated or upset, we call a halt. No arguments. Agreed?"

"It's only when people are upset that the truth comes out," she countered.

He seemed to consider for a moment. Then he gave a short nod. "I'll give you some leeway. But I can't risk getting us both charged with harassment, either. Agreed?"

"I suppose I don't have a choice, do I?" She resented his efforts to control her, but the sneaky thought intruded that there was something admirable about his protectiveness for his town and the people in it.

They headed up the walk and the few steps to the porch. The yard was well cared for, presumably by someone hired to deal with it.

"Just one other thing." Mac paused again. "Let's start out with something innocuous. I'm afraid if you say something about Jason right away, we'll risk upsetting him so quickly we won't get anything out of him."

Kate studied his expression and found nothing more than genuine concern. And he was probably right—easing into the conversation she wanted to have might be the way.

"Okay, as long as you don't try to take over."

His lips quirked. "I'll try."

The caregiver must have been watching for them, because she opened the door the instant Mac knocked. Kate blinked.

"You're—"

"Sheila." The woman beamed. "Sure thing. Glad to see you up and around after your accident."

It was the woman who'd come to the rescue the night she'd nearly been run over at the Lamplight. Sheila's obviously bleached hair frizzed in a halo about a round face that beamed with friendliness.

"So, are you all better now?" She waved them inside as she spoke.

"Fine, thanks. Just a bruise or two to show for it. I wanted to thank you for your help . . ."

The woman waved her to silence. "Forget it. No trouble at all. Gave us all a little excitement that night."

"I could do without that kind of excitement," she said ruefully.

"Well, if Mac here had caught the guy, it would have been even more exciting." She elbowed Mac. "You're falling down on the job."

"It's all your fault, Sheila. If you'd managed to get a description of the vehicle, it'd be a different story."

He sounded as if the joking exchange was second nature to him, but Kate could sense the frustration beneath his words. He did feel as if he'd failed.

"Next time, I'll arrange to have my accidents where there are more reliable witnesses," she said, and then feared Sheila would think she meant her. "Sheila was the only one who kept her head, and she was busy with me."

Sheila shrugged. "Most of the boys had had a few by that time of the evening, and nobody could say that parking lot is well lit." She grinned. " 'Course there's those who like it that way."

"You can never please everyone," Mac said with a return of his official manner. "So how is Russ doing today?"

"Pretty fair. He's pleased to have company. The thing is, there's no telling what'll set him off. Gets upset and starts to cry sometimes, and all I can do is hug him and tell him everything is okay." Sheila shook her head. "Sad to see a smart gentleman turn out like that, but we'll all come to it sooner or later, if we live long enough."

There didn't seem to be any appropriate answer to that comment, so Kate just nodded.

"I told him you were Jason's sister. He seemed to understand, but . . ." She let that trail off with a shrug. "Come on in the living room." Sheila ushered them into a room to the left of the center hall with its typical Victorian hat stand and mirror.

"Mr. Sheldon, here's Mac Whiting, come to bring you a visitor." She raised her voice, but there didn't seem to be a need. The face that turned toward them was alert and intelligent.

Russell Sheldon rose immediately at the sight of Kate, and the dog that had been dozing at the side of his armchair rose, as well.

"How pleasant to have visitors . . ." he began, but the dog, apparently recognizing Mac, rushed toward him with the obvious intent of jumping up.

"There's a good dog, Ruffy." Mac caught the paws that would otherwise have landed on his chest. "No, I don't want a kiss, and Kate doesn't want one, either."

The dog, with every appearance of under-standing, padded over to Kate and nuzzled her hand. She patted him.

"What a nice-looking dog." She tried to find something else that would appeal to a dog lover. "What breed is he?"

Mac chuckled. "That's a good question."

Mr. Sheldon gave him a reproving look. "Golden retriever on his mother's side. Alas, the father remains unknown, but I have my suspicions." He held out his hand to Kate. "It's nice of you to come to visit me, my dear."

Mac, reminded of his duty, cleared his throat. "Russ, this is Kate Beaumont. She's new in town. Kate, Russell Sheldon."

Kate found her hand shaken firmly while she was assessed by still bright blue eyes. Despite the alertness, something in the man's appearance said he wasn't well. Maybe it was the parchment-like color of his skin or the slight quaver in his voice.

"Please, sit down and visit." He gestured to two armchairs at angles to his. "Sheila . . ." he began.

"Tea will be ready in a minute." Sheila hustled toward the back of the house. "Just have to bring the water back to the boil."

"I hope you don't mind tea," Sheldon said, sitting down. "I've never been able to like coffee, no matter how I try. The doctor seems to think it would be good for me, but I can't stand the taste."

"Tea is fine, thank you." She glanced at Mac, and he gave a slight nod.

"Kate is working for Emily at the bookshop in Blackburn House."

Kate smiled, trying to still her jittery nerves. "It's a fascinating place."

"It is that." Sheldon turned to her attentively. "Emily has a nice little shop. Of course, that space was once occupied by the back parlor."

"So the place was originally a private home, was it?"

"Oh, yes. The grandest place in town." He chuckled. "At least, that was the original Blackburn's intent. It was a showpiece, with that marble center hall and all those large rooms. Josiah Blackburn was one of the original timber barons. He made a fortune out of harvesting timber from the ridges."

Kate couldn't help a glance out the nearest window to the wooded ridge that overlooked the town.

He seemed to interpret her look.

"Second growth, all of it. The only stand of virgin timber left in the area is in the state park. So the era of the timber barons passed, and eventually his heirs sold the house to the Standish family. They converted it to its present form. Did a good job with it, too. Many's the time I walked up that staircase to my office and thanked Heaven they had sense enough not to pull it apart. Allison Standish is the current owner."

So Allison was more than just a partner in the quilt shop. "You worked in the building for a long time, then?" She made it a question.

"More years than I care to count," he said.

Kate nodded. "You're retired now, are you?"

"Yes." He looked down, plucking at the arm of the chair. "Yes, I am." Sheldon fell silent, his gaze directed inward.

Kate glanced at Mac, not sure how to proceed in the face of his abstraction.

"Ruffy has trouble adjusting to retirement," Mac prompted. "Sometimes he slips out and goes trotting down to Blackburn House just as if it's a workday."

Ruffy, hearing him name, came and pushed his head against Mac's hand. Mac patted him absently, his gaze focused on Sheldon's face.

"Yes, yes. Ruffy didn't want to quit." He'd lost some of the focus in his eyes.

"Maybe you didn't want to retire, either," Kate suggested.

"No. I mean . . ." He seemed to lose the thread and then grasped at it again. "Things changed. They said . . . we agreed it was time." His voice faded on the last few words.

"What changed?" She rapped the question and then bit her lip. Easy, she reminded herself.

186

Sheldon's gaze wavered, as if he looked for an answer in the air. "Everything," he muttered.

With a clatter of dishes, Sheila emerged from the rear premises carrying a tray. She assessed her patient before setting the tray on the coffee table.

"Now, you're not getting too tired from talking, are you? Let me pour your tea. That'll make you feel better." She fussed around, handing out cups, passing sugar, pressing a piece of coffee cake on each of them. She was giving him time to recover, Kate realized. Sheila had good instincts—caretaker instincts, obviously.

Kate sipped at the aromatic brew and tried to contain herself. With both Sheila and Mac giving her warning looks, she couldn't do anything else, but she had to ask Sheldon about Jason.

"Your brother was part of the firm initially, wasn't he?" Mac asked when he'd apparently decided that they'd avoided the topic long enough.

Russell Sheldon smiled, nodding, his face regaining some of its animation. "That's right. George. But George never was one to stay in one place for long. He got restless. He went out to California and started a business out there. He was always after me to join him, but I never could see relocating."

"So you carried on with the business here,"

Kate prompted. She wasn't interested in roving Brother George.

"I couldn't manage on my own as the business grew, so I brought in the younger folks to help. Naturally, they have their own ideas." He paused, wiping a hand across his face as if to wipe away cobwebs.

Mac shuffled his feet, and with a flare of panic she thought he was going to suggest they'd been here long enough. But it seemed he was just preparing another question. "What about Jason Reilley? Did he have his own ideas, too?"

"Jason?" His voice was suddenly old. "Why are you asking about Jason?"

"Kate is Jason's sister, remember?" Sheila prompted. "She just wants to talk about him."

"You remember him, don't you? Tell me about him." Kate leaned toward him, trying to hold his wavering gaze.

"Jason was a good boy. He wasn't . . . He didn't . . ." He fell silent.

"What do you mean? What didn't he do?" Need pounded at her. He knew something. She was sure of it.

Sheldon shook his head, and it trembled as if he couldn't control it. Tears welled in his eyes, and his lips trembled. "He didn't. It wasn't fair." The words seemed to be wrenched out of him, and his tears spilled over.

188

Kate was shaken by pity for the elderly man and loathing for herself.

Mac stood. "I think it's time we were going." His tone left no room for argument.

Tears gripped her throat, too. She stood and then knelt next to Sheldon's chair, her hands covering his. "Please, Mr. Sheldon. I have to know about Jason."

For an instant his hand gripped hers. He shook his head frantically. "No. I can't. Poor Jason. He didn't do it. He didn't, he didn't." His voice rose with each repetition.

Sheila hurried to him, wrapping her arms around him. "It's all right. Don't be upset. Sheila's here to take care of you."

Kate's arm was seized in a grasp of iron. Mac pulled her to her feet. "That's enough. We're going." He propelled her to the door, not pausing until they'd reached the outside.

Then he let go of her arm as if she carried the plague. "You don't care who you hurt, do you? I told you he was fragile."

His contempt stung her, but she couldn't let that matter. "He knows something—couldn't you see that? They're hiding the truth about Jason."

He didn't respond, and she wanted to shake him.

"You're the one who doesn't care who you hurt as long as it's not someone in your precious town." She threw the words at him. "If you were any kind of a cop, you'd be the one looking for the truth."

She spun and walked away.

Mac's anger with Kate hadn't abated by afternoon, but it had been tempered by the niggling fear that there was some truth in her accusation. Had he been too ready to conclude the investigation into Jason's death? He had a feeling that question wasn't going to go away easily—not until he honestly felt he'd done everything possible.

But as for Kate's conviction that Russ Sheldon knew anything . . . well, she was reading into his ramblings what she wanted to hear. What did she expect him to do—bring a senile old man in for interrogation?

He clicked out of the file he'd been working on and shoved his chair away from his desk with unnecessary violence. There was one thing he could follow up on. He'd have done it by now if Kate hadn't distracted him with her fairy tales.

Kate distracted him on too many counts, and that was the truth. Time to ignore that and get some work done.

He tracked down his patrolman, Johnny Foster, in the cluttered back room that was dedicated to all the files that pre-dated digital copying. He was supposed to be sorting a stack of unfiled reports, but he actually seemed to be using the wastebasket for a basketball hoop.

Foster halted in the middle of a free throw and attempted to look busy. "Something I can do, Chief?" His tone was hopeful.

"I doubt it, but you're better than nothing. Come on. We're going to go lean on somebody."

Foster brightened at once, all his ideas of police work having come from intense watching of television series. He rose to his gangling six feet, hand going to the firearm at his side.

"I'm ready, Chief." He fingered the weapon.

Mac couldn't help wishing that the Commonwealth of Pennsylvania hadn't seen fit to grant Johnny the authority to carry a loaded gun. Maybe he ought to ration the kid's ammo.

"No weapons are going to be needed, Foster," he said firmly. "I'm doing the questioning. Your job is to keep your mouth shut and look menacing. Think you can handle that?"

"Sure thing, Chief." He rounded the desk, managing to trip over his erstwhile basketball hoop. "Look menacing. Scare the perp into talking, right?"

Mac suppressed a sigh. "Something like that. Is Larry Foust still working on rebuilding that old T-Bird of his?" Foster's only value, as far as Mac had been able to determine, was that he usually knew what was going on with the kids his age.

"Sure is." He shook his head as he followed

191

Mac toward the door. "He'll never do it, though. He hasn't got the touch."

He wasn't concerned with Larry's abilities as a mechanic, but at least it gave him an idea where to find him at this time of day. Of course, he might equally well be lounging on the sofa in his mother's house, watching television, in which case this interview would have to be postponed until later. No one with any sense wanted to accuse Ethel Foust's little lamb with wrongdoing in her presence.

It was a few minutes' drive in the patrol car to the Foust place, with Johnny lamenting most of the distance that he so seldom had the chance to turn the siren on. When they reached the block, Mac directed him down the alley in the back. That way they could reach the garage without drawing undue attention.

The two-car garage held the conservative sedan belonging to Larry's mother and the candy-apple-red T-Bird that was the love of Larry's heart. Too bad the engine needed a rebuild that was beyond Larry's capabilities. Or maybe not. He didn't want to envision the patrol car with Johnny at the wheel in pursuit of Larry in the T-Bird.

Larry was bent over the motor, aiming a light at its innards. He didn't move at the sounds of footsteps. "I'm busy, Ma."

"It's not your mother. It's the police." Mac had the satisfaction of seeing a flicker of fear in Larry's face as he jerked upright, narrowly missing cracking his head.

For an instant Larry seemed torn as to what attitude to present to the police. Then he settled on the good citizen.

"Chief Whiting. What can I do for you?" He rubbed his palms on a pair of greasy coveralls.

Mac had considered his approach, too. "You can tell me where Jason Reilley got the prescription meds that took his life."

Fear and anger chased each other across Larry's face. "Kate Beaumont sent you here, didn't she? She's got it in for me. I knew she'd cause trouble."

Mac took in the way Jason's hands knotted into fists, and his own anger edged up a notch. Maybe Kate had been wrong about how harmless Larry was. He moved toward him, taking satisfaction from looming over the kid.

"You're causing trouble for yourself. Where did Jason get the drugs?" He let the question fall like a hammer.

"Not from me. Honest." He backed up until he bumped into the wall and sent a longing look beyond the two cops to the door. "I'm not into that stuff. Jason must have bought it himself. He probably had contacts back in the city. Not me."

"So you don't know anything about anybody doing drugs in Laurel Ridge. What about the odor of marijuana that clings to those overalls you're wearing?"

Larry turned a sickly shade of green and looked from one to the other of the police who'd closed in on him.

"Somebody else," he stammered. "Not me."

"If we searched the garage and the house, we wouldn't find anything? Like maybe some joints, or some prescription meds from your mother's medicine cabinet?"

"You . . . you can't do that without a warrant." Larry's bluster was wearing thin.

"I can get a warrant. And I can leave Foster here to keep an eye on you while I do it. Or maybe it's a setup for cooking meth we'll find."

"I'm not dumb enough to try that, honest, I'm not. Anyway, Ax says—" He stopped, and it couldn't be more obvious that he'd said more than he'd meant if he'd clapped both hands over his mouth.

"Ax? Who's Ax?" The name, if that's what it was, raised a question in his mind. Had he heard it before?

"Ax Bolt." Johnny broke the prohibition on speaking. "He's been hanging around town off and on. Lowlife. Fake prison tattoos up to his eyebrows."

Mac suppressed the urge to ask him how he knew they were fake. Television, most likely.

"What about it, Larry?" He leaned in, knowing

194

what he smelled was fear. Larry hadn't been seriously afraid until that name surfaced. "Is this Ax Bolt dealing?"

"I don't know anything about him. You can't— you can't let him think I said anything. You don't know him. You can't . . ."

Panic overtook Larry, and he squirmed past the two of them, running from the garage.

Johnny started after him, but Mac grabbed his arm.

"I can catch him, Chief. He'll get away."

"He's running into the house," Mac pointed out. "We don't have anything on him, and if you want to go in there without a solid case and tell Ethel Foust her darling boy is in trouble, you're just asking for trouble."

"He might know where to find this creep." Johnny's face, almost as ingenuous as Larry's, clearly showed his disappointment.

"If he does, he's too scared to tell us." Mac headed for the patrol car. "From the sounds of it, Bolt will have gotten into somebody's records somewhere. Let's go find out. And in the meantime, you can tell me everything you know about him."

Mac slid into the car, energized. At last, something concrete to work on. And his satisfaction didn't have anything at all to do with wanting to prove to Kate that he was doing something.

CHAPTER TEN

It only took moments to tidy the small cottage kitchen after Kate had had breakfast the next morning. She was supposed to work for a couple of hours this morning, which would give her plenty of time afterward to pursue the most pressing of her preoccupations—investigating the financial group.

The only question was, how? A couple of possibilities had come to mind. Talk to Nikki again, prepared with questions this time. And get in touch with Morris Vail, the financial reporter at her last job. Morris had information about investment markets at his fingertips, and if he didn't know anything about Laurel Ridge Financial specifically, he'd know where to find it.

The other possibility was to approach Lina Oberlin. She, at least, seemed kindly disposed toward Kate. Maybe she'd open up about what happened that last day.

The only other hope was that Mac had had a successful encounter with Larry Foust. And if he had, would he be inclined to share with her, given the heated words they'd exchanged yesterday?

Thinking about that quarrel roused mixed feelings in Kate. She was sorry if she'd caused

Russell Sheldon pain. But surely just the fact that he'd become so upset meant that he knew something—if not about why Jason had taken his life, then about what had happened at the office that last day.

She'd called Sheila this morning to check on Mr. Sheldon's condition. Sheila had been cautious at first, but when she realized Kate wasn't trying to pump her, she loosened up.

Apparently he'd recovered fairly quickly, but Sheila said he'd been a little withdrawn the rest of the day. She seemed to think something was troubling him, and Kate would give a lot to know just what that something was.

Mac's anger had probably been justifiable in his own eyes. He was trying to protect people he cared about.

If he did refuse to cooperate with her—well, it just showed that she'd been right all along.

Leaving the cottage, she locked it carefully, double-checking to be sure. She crossed the grass, heading to the shortcut between the two properties that Mrs. Anderson had pointed out the previous day. A grassy path led through a gap in the hedge and came out onto the driveway at the side of the building.

Lina first. Then after she finished up at the bookshop, she might try to call Morris. If there was anything to be found about the financial group, he'd find it.

She stepped into the narrow pathway between the hedges. Before she'd gone more than a few feet, a shadow filled the patch of sunlight at the other end. Bart Gordon was coming toward her, and something in his purposeful stride told her this wasn't an accidental meeting.

Her jaw set, and she went forward to meet him. If Gordon thought he could intimidate her, he was dead wrong.

Gordon stopped a couple of feet from her, his bulldog face set in a way that probably frightened his subordinates. Certainly he was the sort to bulldoze his way through life, running over anyone he considered beneath him.

Kate waited, eyebrows slightly raised, knowing that silence could sometimes be the more effective of weapons.

Sure enough, her failure to speak first seemed to throw him off stride for a moment, but he made a quick recovery. "You harassed a sick old man. People can't get away with things like that in Laurel Ridge."

No point in pretending to misunderstand him. "If you mean I talked with Mr. Sheldon about my brother, I did it in the company of the police chief and Sheldon's caregiver. I don't think that constitutes harassment."

"We'll see what a lawyer thinks about that," Gordon snapped, face reddening as he glared at her. "I've already advised Sheldon's son to file a complaint against you. We've had about enough of this witch hunt of yours."

She raised an eyebrow, a look calculated to annoy. "Who is 'we'?"

That didn't sidetrack him. "Laurel Ridge Financial Group, to say nothing of Russell Sheldon's many friends. He's done a lot for this town, and he deserves better than to be bothered and upset by you over something he knows nothing about."

She pounced on that. "Nothing about what? According to you, my brother's job had nothing to do with his death. But you fired him that day. How do you know it had nothing to do with what happened to him?"

"It wasn't our responsibility if he was so unstable he turned to drugs because he failed at his job."

That had the bite of truth in it, but it wasn't the whole story. "What did Jason do wrong? Why did you fire him?"

"I don't owe you any explanations. His work wasn't satisfactory. That's all." He clamped his mouth shut.

"What about Mr. Sheldon telling me Jason wasn't to blame? Wasn't to blame for what?" It was her turn to glare. "What was it? What did you accuse Jason of?"

If it was possible for the man to get any redder, he did. He took a step toward Kate, and she was suddenly aware of how isolated they were. The street wasn't more than thirty yards away, but they might as well have been in one of Baltimore's dark alleys for how alone she felt.

"There was nothing. Your brother was a druggie who found life too much for him and tried to escape. You shouldn't have pushed him into coming here to begin with. You should have known he was too weak to stand on his own."

Here was a counterattack with a vengeance, hitting too close to home, but she wasn't about to let him see he'd scored. "Jason wasn't weak. Something forced him into what happened. If it was you . . ."

"This a private quarrel, or can anyone join in?"

The quiet, casual voice from behind her was a marked contrast to their heated tones. Mac seemed to have a genius for turning up at moments like this.

Gordon got in first. "You allowed this woman to harass Russell Sheldon. What were you thinking? Russell's a respected citizen of this town."

"I don't think Russ came to any harm." The distaste in Mac's voice came through to Kate. He hated having to defend her, especially on this subject. "Ms. Beaumont has some questions about her brother's death. She deserves a few straight answers."

"She's had all the answers she's going to get from me." Gordon transferred his anger to Mac.

"If you know what's good for you, you'll make sure she leaves town and doesn't come back." He turned and barreled away, apparently considering he'd had the last word.

Kate took a cautious look at Mac's face, wondering if it was safe to speak. She didn't think so.

He grabbed her arm. "Come on." He headed back toward the cottage, tugging her along.

"Where are we going? I have to go to work," she protested.

"I told Emily you'd be a little late today. We have to talk." He propelled her toward the cottage.

"Not there." She didn't think she'd risk another private chat in the tiny cottage when emotions were at such a pitch.

She could tell by his expression that he knew why not. His jaw tightened even more, and he tugged her over to the police car. Opening the front door on the passenger side, he gestured for her to get in.

Kate slid inside. "Am I under arrest?"

"If you were, you'd be in the backseat," he snapped and shut the door.

By the time Mac had rounded the car and gotten behind the wheel, he seemed to have his feelings under control. He started the vehicle, drove out to the street, and glided into a parking space in front of Blackburn House.

"There. We can be seen by anyone passing by, and I won't be tempted to make love to you in full view of half a dozen residents. Satisfied?"

She rejected several comments and finally just nodded. Mac might not want to agree with Bart Gordon, but he also didn't want to defend her. She suspected she was about to hear about that little fact.

Mac discovered he was angry with Kate, Bart Gordon and himself in about equal measure. He didn't like being off balance, and it struck him that since Kate's arrival in Laurel Ridge, he seemed to be in one of those amusement park rides that turned you upside down and spun you around until you didn't know which way was up.

"So you don't mind being alone with Bart in a secluded spot, is that it?" It wasn't how he'd intended to phrase the question, and it annoyed him doubly to find he'd made it sound personal.

"It wasn't exactly my idea." Kate responded mildly enough. "I was just taking the shortcut to Blackburn House when he waylaid me."

Mac shot a quick look at her face. "You mean deliberately?"

She shrugged. "I don't know what the odds are of him being there at the same time I was, but I'd suspect astronomical."

He had to agree. "What did he want?"

"About what you'd expect." Kate grimaced.

"He'd apparently heard all about our visit to Mr. Sheldon yesterday. I take it that wasn't from you?"

"No. I didn't go around broadcasting that fact." He shrugged restlessly. "But word gets around. Did Gordon say anything useful or just shout at you?"

"Mostly the latter. But I did get a reaction from him when I tried to find out why Jason was fired."

Mac turned in his seat to face her more fully. "When Bart admitted to me that he'd had to let Jason go, he said it was because his work hadn't been satisfactory." He felt his jaw harden. "If there was more to it, I need to find out what."

"Finally something we agree on," Kate said.

He forced a smile despite the tangle of worry in his mind. "Here's something else we'd better agree on. You don't seek out any more encounters with either of the partners until I've had a chance to get to the bottom of this."

"I didn't seek out this encounter," Kate protested.

"I believe you." But that didn't help the concern he had for her. "See that you don't go wandering along any lonely roads or poking in dark corners, though."

Her lips tilted slightly, and her wary mask disappeared. "And here I thought small towns were law-abiding places."

"Don't kid yourself," he retorted. "We have the same problems big cities do these days, and only me to deal with it in Laurel Ridge."

She looked surprised. "But you have a staff."

"A staff." He had a pitying look for her lack of understanding for small-town finances. "One patrolman and three part-timers who mainly direct traffic."

"If there's a drug problem . . ."

"That's not enough to deal with it," he finished for her. "You're so right. There's a state police task force, but they can't be everywhere. And in the meantime, lives are being ruined."

"I'm sorry." She reached out a tentative hand toward him and then drew it back, making him too aware of how close they were in the confines of the front seat. Maybe this hadn't been such a good idea, after all. Even the curious gazes of passersby didn't seem to deter him. "It's hard to feel so helpless."

Mac studied her face, seeing a depth of feeling in her eyes, and he knew they understood each other. He propped his elbow on the console, his arm brushing hers.

"On that front, at least, I might have made some progress." He put some energy into his tone. "I had a little semi-official chat with Larry Foust."

Kate's head came up. "What did you find out? Did you get him to talk?"

He had a wry smile for that. "He babbled, but not about anything very useful." He hesitated, not sure how wise it was to tell her more. But she'd been open with him, as far as he could tell.

Kate seemed to put her own interpretation on his hesitation. "Still angry with me about yesterday?"

"Cops can't afford anger. It clouds the judgment." He took a breath and made his decision. "Larry let a name drop . . . one we could find in police files. Apparently this guy has been on the fringes of the drug scene for a while now. A couple of departments in this part of the state have been keeping an eye on him."

"He's been here in Laurel Ridge?"

Mac frowned. "Not permanently, but showing up every so often over the last couple of years, from what we've found out. Needless to say, we're looking for him."

In her eagerness, Kate leaned toward him. "Are you going to tell me his name?"

He studied her face, reading the passion in her eyes, and dismissed the stray thought that having that passion directed toward him might be overwhelming. "Only if I have your word that you won't go looking for him on your own. Tap any newspaper resources you like, but no personal encounters. Right?"

"I'm not afraid."

"You should be." His careful control slipped a

little. "This Ax Bolt is no Larry Foust. He's got a record and a reputation for violence."

"Ax?" She raised an eyebrow in doubt.

"Right." His lips twisted. "Apparently Andrew Xavier Bolton wasn't a sufficiently intimidating name for him. But don't let that mislead you. He's been convicted of breaking and entering twice and been charged with assault three times but not convicted."

"A small-time pusher . . ." she began.

Frustrated, Mac grabbed her wrist. "Maybe not so small-time. Kate, the assaults were ugly. Vicious. And the only reason he wasn't sent up was that the victims refused to testify. If I find you've gone anywhere near him, so help me, I'll lock you up."

"You wouldn't." She tried to pull her wrist free, but he didn't let go. He felt her pulse pounding against his palm.

"I'll do what's necessary to keep you safe." His voice went unexpectedly husky on the words.

Kate's eyes widened. Darkened. And her breath caught with a sound he could hear. The pulse that beat against his palm seemed to be driving his own, as well. The very air grew thick around them, and his gaze was drawn irresistibly to her parted lips.

He managed to wrench his hand away from her wrist and leaned back against the door, his breath coming too quickly.

It seemed even the precaution of parking in full view of the town wasn't enough to block out the attraction that pulsed between them. He wasn't sure what would be.

Kate glanced at her watch and then took a last look at herself in the mirror to be sure she was suitable for supper with the Whiting family. This had to be the worst possible time to be going to supper with Mac's family.

After those charged moments in the police car this morning, she'd managed to beat a hasty retreat, muttering something about the need to get to work and fleeing. Mac hadn't made any attempt to delay her.

Neither of them could possibly deny the power of the attraction that had flared between them. But they could decide not to act on it, couldn't they?

Kate grabbed her bag and headed for the car, locking the door behind her. She hadn't had any difficulty in putting emotions on hold in the past—at first because she'd been so preoccupied with taking care of Jason and more recently because grief seemed to have left her emotionally numb.

Even Casey, her closest friend in Baltimore and an inveterate matchmaker, had finally stopped trying to fix her up with someone. She'd declared that until Kate got over being so prickly and guarded and started giving out some signals that she was interested, it was hopeless.

Well, she hadn't deliberately sent out any signals to Mac, and she suspected he'd say the same. And look what had happened—they'd still been ambushed by desire.

As she followed the directions Ellen had given her out of town, Kate tried to console herself that at least Mac was in the same boat she was. He hadn't intended to feel anything, either, and might even now be getting out of the prospect of having dinner with her and his family. Apparently he didn't live at his parents' farm, and he could always plead the need to work, unlike her. And if he were there, she'd been warned now. She could certainly keep her guard up.

An hour later, Kate was finding it all much easier than she'd expected. The Whiting clan, including Nick's fiancée, Allison Standish from the quilt shop, was gathered around a long table in the sprawling farmhouse dining room, but the talk stayed general, and even though Mac was there, he was seated at a safe distance from her.

At the moment, they all seemed intent on hearing from Nick on the subject of the recent town council meeting.

"Have a little pity on Kate," Jim Whiting, seated next to her, interrupted his sons. "She doesn't have the least interest in your battles with

208

the council." Jim, a leaner, grayer version of his sons, gave Kate a smile that was uncannily like Mac's. "Do you?"

"Well, I might if I knew why Nick is involved. Are you on the council?"

Nick grinned. "Heaven help me, I'm the mayor."

"Easiest job in the world," Mac said. "All he does is sign a few proclamations once in a while and smile for the camera."

"Better than riding around all day in a police car or sitting at a desk with your feet up," Nick retorted.

"Behave yourselves, boys," Ellen said, looking as if she'd said the same words, with the same smile, a few thousand times. "Remember we have a guest." She turned the sweet smile on Kate. "I did try to teach them how to behave, though you'd never know it the way they turned out."

Mac threw his arm around her in a hug. "Don't let her fool you. She secretly thinks her kids are the smartest, best-looking—" He stopped, dodging the napkin his brother threw at him.

Even as she smiled at their teasing, Kate's heart ached, just a little. How differently might Jason's life have turned out if he'd enjoyed this kind of family life? Jim and Ellen obviously adored their kids, and the feeling was just as obviously returned. Did Nick and Mac know how lucky they were to have a family like this behind them?

It struck her that it explained a lot about Mac. He had that secure, settled outlook on life, that solid acceptance of his responsibilities, because he had this family life behind him.

"Being mayor of Laurel Ridge isn't a full-time job," Ellen assured her, as if she might have taken Mac's words seriously.

"I only ran because no one else would, except for a couple of the local cranks," Nick put in. "The most difficult part of my job is to try to get the council to ignore personalities and cooperate on things important to the town."

"See, I said you wouldn't be interested," Jim interjected, his eyes smiling.

She shook her head. "Oh, I get it, all right. One of my first reporting jobs, while I was still in college, was to cover local school board meetings. I learned, to my cost, that if you didn't know who was second cousins with whom, and whose wife had just left him, and who wanted taxes lowered no matter what, that you'd never make sense of anything they did."

"Nailed it," Mac said, and the other adults laughed.

Jamie looked up from his cherry pie and vanilla ice cream. "What's a school board? Is it like a paddle?"

That raised another laugh, and Allison gave Jamie a quick hug. "It's just a bunch of boring grown-ups, sweetheart. Finish up your pie, and then you can show Kate the baby goat."

"Do you actually have a baby goat?" Kate asked him.

Jamie nodded, mouth full of pie. He swallowed quickly so he could speak. "Grandpa says baby goats are supposed to come in the spring. So we call him Tardy."

"I'd love to see Tardy." She managed to suppress the urge to laugh, because Jamie's little face was so serious. "Do you take care of him?"

" 'Course I do. He's mine, so I take good care of him."

The child's words seemed to say it all. You took care of what was yours. She began to see where Mac's sense of responsibility came from. It seemed to be bred in this family.

Mac pushed his empty pie plate away and stood, stretching, then came to her, grasping her hands. "Come on. We need some exercise to work off that pie."

"I'm not the one who had a second piece," she reminded him. "And I should help with the dishes first."

"No, you don't," Ellen said quickly. "It's Jim's turn to do the dishes, and Nick will help him. Go on now, before it's time for Jamie to get ready for bed."

With Mac tugging one hand and Jamie the other, Kate let herself be pulled out the back door.

She paused for a moment on the porch, taking in the scene around her. The setting sun turned the fields to gold, and the ridges were turned to flame with the light on the orange-and-yellow leaves.

Mac's gaze met hers. "My favorite time of the year," he said. "I don't think any spot on earth is more beautiful than home."

"I can see why." The farmhouse nestled into the land as if it had grown there, and the lawn stretched out to the red barn behind it. A cluster of smaller red outbuildings surrounded the barn like chicks around a mother hen.

"Come on." Jamie grabbed her hand and tugged. "Hurry up."

Mac grinned. "At his age, there's no such thing as standing still and enjoying the view. Okay, come on, buddy. I'll race you to the barn."

They set off—Jamie running full tilt while Mac jogged along effortlessly. His long legs could easily outstrip his nephew's pace, but he obviously wouldn't do that. She liked the way he moved, with such graceful control that it seemed he'd never tire. Kate followed more sedately, reaching the barn after they were already inside.

She paused, letting her eyes adjust to the dimmer light. Jamie was hanging over a pen built at the end of a couple of stalls occupied by two horses that leaned their heads over the doors to watch them curiously.

"Does your dad use the horses for farming?" she asked. How could Jim Whiting run the cabinetry business and a farm?

Mac chuckled low in his throat. "He's always threatening to do it, but, no. We don't really farm, not like our Amish neighbors do. Dad just likes to grow enough to fill the freezer and feed the family. Both Mom and Dad think it's good for kids to grow up on a farm. Teaches responsibility."

"I'd say it worked with the two of you." Her gaze entangled with his.

"This is Tardy," Jamie said. "Don't you want to pet him?"

"Sure thing." She knelt next to Jamie, who was reaching through the bars to pat the small brown goat. "Show me what to do."

"Just put your hand in like this. But be gentle," he warned.

Kate slid her hand between the bars, reflecting that being introduced to a pet goat hadn't figured in her image of what she'd be doing in Laurel Ridge. The goat sniffed at her fingers delicately, and then licked them, its tongue surprisingly rough for such a dainty creature.

"Tardy likes you." Jamie grinned. "Know what? I'll get a handful of grain, and you'll see how he'll eat it right out of your hand."

He jumped up and darted for the door. Mac looked down at her, his lips curving slightly, and then reached out, caught her by the elbows, and raised her to her feet.

"What are you doing?" She glanced at his face, seeing the warmth that filled his eyes, and her breath caught.

"Taking care of some unfinished business," he said. He leaned in, until she could feel the warmth of his skin and capture the masculine smell of him. Slowly, very slowly, his lips found hers.

For an instant the kiss was almost tentative, as if he waited for her to pull back. And then his arms came around her, pressing her against him as the kiss deepened. She couldn't pull back now if she wanted to, and she didn't want to. She grasped his shoulders, feeling the strength of him as she returned passion for passion. This was what she'd been waiting for, she knew through the dizzying emotion that took possession of her. And she hadn't even realized it until now.

Finally she freed her lips with an effort. "Jamie," she murmured. "He'll be back."

Mac loosened his grasp, drawing his head back enough to give her that teasing smile. "He has to go to bed eventually."

"What about the rest of your family?" Kate took a retreating step, trying to match the lightness in his tone. Not easy, when she was shaken down to her toes.

"They—" His cell phone went off, interrupting

him. Making a face, he pulled it from his pocket. The instant he put the phone to his ear, he became again the cop. "Whiting," he snapped. He listened, a frown carving lines between his brows. "Right. On my way."

Even before he'd clicked off, he was turning, heading for the door. "Sorry."

She followed him out, to see Nick bolting from the house, the rest of the family gathered on the porch.

"I'll pick up Reuben and meet you there," he shouted to Mac.

Mac was already headed for his vehicle. "Sorry," he said again over his shoulder. "Fire. I have to go."

She nodded, then crossed the yard back toward the porch. This was the sort of thing that her mother hadn't been able to tolerate—the constant calls, running off to face danger, leaving her behind to cope. Her mother hadn't been able to. Maybe that hadn't been Tom's fault, but it had happened. How did anyone know how they'd react until they were in that situation?

Jamie was already on the porch, hanging on his grandfather's arm, telling him something excitedly. He'd obviously forgotten about letting her feed the goat.

"You poor girl," Ellen said warmly when she reached the others. "I'm sure you're not used to the way everyone runs when the fire alarm goes."

"Is Mac a fireman as well as police chief?" It seemed unlikely, but everything at Laurel Ridge was out of her experience.

"No, although he went through the training just like Nick did, so he can lend a hand if they need it." Ellen sounded cheerful enough, but Kate didn't miss the worry in her eyes.

"Volunteer firefighters," Jim explained. "We can't afford a professional company. So when there's a fire, everyone turns out. Maybe I should—"

"No, you don't," Ellen said firmly. "You know what the doctor told you about that kind of stress. And don't bother telling me you'd just watch, because we both know you'd jump in the minute you got there."

Jim shrugged, putting an arm around his wife. "No wonder my heart skips a beat now and then, married to a woman like you." He kissed her temple. "Okay, I'll stay put. Let's go listen to the scanner to see how bad it is."

Allison gave her a sympathetic look as the others headed into the house. "Sorry. There's no way you'd know, but we had a terrible time with a firebug earlier in the summer. He was caught, but somehow we all still overreact a little when the alarm goes."

She nodded. "I can understand that. And really, it's time I was leaving, anyway."

But when she went inside to say her goodbyes,

she found she wasn't going to get away that easily. First she had to listen to the police scanner, learning that the incident was a chimney fire in a farmhouse on the far side of Laurel Ridge. No one was injured, but it sounded as if they'd be on scene for a time yet.

Kate could sense the relief in the room at the report. They must worry every time the alarm went, but this time, at least, everyone was safe.

Ellen insisted on packing up several pieces of pie for her to take home, and Kate barely escaped having an entire dinner pressed on her again. Finally, after hugs from Jamie and invitations from Ellen to come again, Kate got on her way.

The sun had long since disappeared behind the ridge, and darkness was gathering in. Kate pulled carefully out onto the country road, turning toward Laurel Ridge. The drive back to town wasn't going to be long enough, she decided, to process everything that was on her mind.

CHAPTER ELEVEN

Kate pulled into her parking space along the side of the bed-and-breakfast. As she'd expected, her thoughts were still in a state that could only be described as chaotic. She couldn't pretend that Mac's kiss hadn't been welcome. It had been a long time since she'd responded to a man that way. Maybe ever.

Always before, she'd had the sense that some little part of her held back, in control, watching what was happening but not participating. Not this time. She'd been completely involved in the moment, her emotions overwhelmed with the touch and smell and feel of him.

There was no future in a relationship with Mac. She knew that. So did he. Eventually she'd have her answers, and then she'd move on. Mac would stay here, in the place where he belonged.

Where did she belong? The thought came out of nowhere, and she didn't have an answer.

The back porch light Mrs. Anderson usually left on was turned off, so that the lawn between the main house and the cottage lay in darkness. Kate stifled a faint reluctance to move. Pulling out her key ring, she turned on the tiny penlight attached to it and stepped into the dark.

It was quiet—almost too quiet. She'd already

noticed that Laurel Ridge seemed to close down quickly after about six o'clock. Lights reflected from cars moving along Main Street, but otherwise, all was dark and still.

The penlight produced a narrow tunnel of illumination along which she walked. When she reached the step she paused, fumbling for the key and then trying to keep the light focused on the lock while she opened it.

But the instant she put her key in the lock, she realized it hadn't been needed. The front door to the cottage was unlocked, swinging open a few inches at the slight touch.

Alarm flared. She stepped back, cautious as a cat, making no sound, and reached for her cell phone. But even before her questing fingers located it in her bag, she paused. Mac was at the fire scene, and he'd told her how small his force was. If she dialed 911, who would she get? One of the part-timers he'd mentioned, who had no idea who she was?

She eyed the door. Nothing moved. She couldn't hear anything, not from the cottage. But there was a sound—so faint it was on the very edge of her hearing. A rustling noise, as if something disturbed the thick bushes along the property line.

If she took the penlight off the cottage door, someone might come out. But it was surely more important to know if someone was already here with her. A quick glance at the bed-and-breakfast was enough to tell her that Mrs. Anderson wasn't home. There was no point in running to her door.

The sound came again, louder this time. She tried to tell herself it was a stray cat or a night bird, but she wasn't convinced. Her fingers closed over the phone with sudden decision. She'd call Mac directly, no matter where he was. She'd rather feel foolish for raising a false alarm than fail to call when there was danger.

But before she'd even pulled the phone free, she heard it again—unmistakable this time. Someone was there, behind her. She darted a glance back to see a dark figure emerge from the shadows. It—he—whatever—was between her and the street. That left only the cottage. Gripping the phone in one hand and her keys with the other, she bolted for the cottage door.

Footsteps came behind her, with no attempt to conceal them now. Kate dashed up the two steps to the door, plunged inside and slammed it shut just as something reached toward it. She flicked the dead bolt, then backed up a couple of steps, staring toward the door.

Not that she could see much. She'd been sure she'd left the small lamp on the end table turned on, but it wasn't on now. Fumbling with the penlight, Kate focused its beam on the door.

A cold hand seemed to grip her throat as the knob turned slowly—first one direction and then the other. She could almost feel the pressure against the door as she imagined a dark-clothed figure pushing against it.

But the lock held, and she could breathe again. Her mind started to work as the adrenaline she'd been running on tapered off. Larry Foust, maybe? If he knew she'd told Mac everything she knew about him, he'd have good reason to hold a grudge.

Brushing away futile speculation, she listened for any sound from outside. The scrape of a shoe on the step and then—nothing. If he'd gone . . . but, no, she could hear movement along the front of the cottage. Then nothing.

She stood where she was, torn. If she went to the window, she might catch a glimpse of him. But what if she pulled aside the curtain and found him looking back at her?

Idiot, she chastised herself. If she stood any chance of identifying the man, she had to try, didn't she? But first—she punched in Mac's number.

While she waited for the connection, she used the feeble beam of the penlight to work her way toward the window. With one hand on the back of the sofa, she moved silently. But the danger was outside, wasn't it? What was she afraid of in here?

And then she knew. She wasn't alone. The sound was so soft it barely registered, but when she held her breath, she could hear it . . . a faint, brushing noise.

It took all her nerve to swing the penlight toward the source of the sound. The narrow beam touched fingers, scratching at the rug. Traveled up an arm toward a head, gleaming with blood that nearly obscured the face. Nearly, but not quite.

"Kate! Where are you? Answer me!"

They must have been connected for several seconds before her mind registered Mac's voice, shouting in her ear.

She swallowed hard and kept her voice steady with an effort. "Mac. It's Larry Foust. He's lying on the floor of the cottage. Hurt. It's . . . it's bad." Her voice quivered on the last word.

"Kate, I want you out of there." Mac's voice was steady, but she could almost sense his movement. He'd be racing to his car. "Go over to Mrs. Anderson's."

"I can't." She shot a quick look at the blackness outside the windows and knew nothing was going to get her out there. "There's someone out there. He came at me."

Mac muttered a few words he'd probably just as soon no one heard. "Stay put and keep your phone with you. Is the door bolted?"

"Yes."

"Good. Don't touch anything." He must have turned away from the phone for a moment to speak to someone else. Then he was back. "We'll be there in a few minutes. Okay? I'm coming."

It's all right to be afraid. The voice of her stepfather sounded in her head. *But use the fear to be smart. Don't let it master you.*

"Okay."

Fingers scraped along the windowpane, as if seeking a way in. She sucked in a breath and shouted. "The police are on their way. Hear that? They're almost here."

She swung the penlight back to focus on the inert figure, her mind starting to work. *Don't touch anything,* Mac had said. But the blood still flowed, slowly, from the wound in the back of the boy's head. He was still alive, then. She had to do something, and she would.

When Mac pulled up in the driveway, he left the headlights on. At least it illuminated a fraction of the yard.

"Search the area," he told Foster. "Look for any signs of someone hiding in the bushes. And if you find any footprints, don't put your own feet on top of them. Just mark the location and come and tell me."

"You think the guy is still here?" Foster swung the beam of his heavy police flashlight around the yard.

"Not if he has any brains." Mac strode quickly to the door.

Kate was already opening it. "Did you call an ambulance?"

"They'll be right behind us." He took a moment to study her face. Pale but composed. Whatever had happened, she had control of herself. "You weren't hurt?"

She shook her head. "No one touched me. But Larry—" She gestured, and he strode quickly to the inert form on the floor.

Larry lay facedown, one hand reached out as if to ask for help. A blanket had been tucked around him, and a blood-saturated towel lay next to him. There was blood on Kate's hands, as well.

"I see you didn't follow my instructions not to touch anything."

"I couldn't just let him bleed." She looked down at the boy, pity filling her face. "It's nearly stopped now. I hope that's a good sign. He's just a kid." Her lips trembled, and she pressed them together.

Was she thinking of Jason? He'd been just a kid, too.

The wail of a siren was followed in short order by a couple of paramedics pulling a stretcher between them. Mike Callahan, the senior of the two, squatted next to the figure, his deft fingers checking the injury.

"You determined to produce more work for us?" His attention didn't leave his patient, but he flickered a glance from Mac to Kate.

"Not my doing," he said. "How bad is it?"

"Not my call," Mike said quickly. He looked at Kate. "You stopped the bleeding?"

"I did what I could." She looked at her hands and shivered.

"Good job. We're going to transport him pretty quickly. The head injury should be looked at by a surgeon. You coming along, Mac?"

As usual, he was hamstrung by his lack of personnel. Someone should go to the hospital on the slim chance that Larry spoke and named his attacker. But someone had to question Kate and investigate the crime scene, and that had better be him.

"I'll call Harry Young and ask him to meet you at the hospital." Harry was pushing the age limit for part-timers, and he didn't have the energy to chase down a toddler, let alone a criminal, but he was steady and responsible. "I'll have to keep Johnny Foster here to help process the scene."

Though now that he and the paramedics, to say nothing of Kate, had already traipsed through the area, the chances of finding anything were lessened.

As the stretcher was moved out through the door, Kate seemed to wilt. "I'd like to go wash up," she murmured, looking at her hands in distaste.

"Not yet." In answer to her questioning look, he went on, choosing his words carefully. "I'll need to take a swab from your hands to match against Larry's blood."

"I don't see anyone else bleeding around here." Her temper flared, and he could see she was on the edge of losing that carefully detached facade she prized.

"It's just routine. We don't want to leave any loopholes for a defense attorney to drive through. Just hang on until I get the kit from the car. Okay?"

She managed a nod.

Mac strode outside and gestured to Johnny. The people who made up the guidelines for processing a crime scene apparently hadn't heard of police departments like his.

"Anything?"

Foster shook his head. "Some scuff marks over there by that big bush."

"Lilac," he corrected automatically. "Any identifiable footprints?"

"No. And I was careful, Chief. Looked like maybe the perp scuffed it up himself."

He was more thorough than most criminals they ran across in Laurel Ridge, in that case. Foster was looking at him as if he had a question he hesitated to ask.

"What?" he snapped.

"You buy Ms. Beaumont's story?"

Mac's jaw clenched. "We investigate. We don't make judgments. But on the face of it, I doubt she'd have had time to meet Foust, get into an argument and bash his head in. We'll be looking to see if anyone saw her car arrive and can establish the time."

"You want me to start on that now, Chief?"

"No. We process the scene first. Get the camera and crime scene kit."

Mac headed back inside, trying to find the detachment he so desperately needed. Right now he had to be the police officer investigating, not the man who'd held Kate in his arms such a short time ago.

Soon after he'd swabbed her palms and put the result into an evidence bag, Mac realized that if Kate had anything to say about it, he wouldn't need to worry about keeping her at arm's length. She was looking at him as if he were a lower life-form. Obviously, she hadn't bought his explanation about the process being routine.

"Okay, you can wash up now. At the kitchen sink, please." He'd be able to see her in the kitchen from here. Not that he thought she would attempt to hide anything, but because . . . well, because that was what he'd do if it were anyone but her in this situation.

Not speaking, Kate marched into the kitchen, taking a good long time scrubbing her hands. He could hardly blame her for wanting to get rid of the blood.

She'd done the sensible thing in a situation that would have had many a civilian running mindlessly. That control of hers was standing her in good stead right now.

When she came back into the living room, he was on the phone.

The instant he hung up, she spoke, as if the words could barely be contained. "Was that the hospital? Is he . . . did he make it?"

A suspicious cop could look at her eagerness two ways—either she was innocent and genuinely concerned, or she was guilty and hoping Larry wouldn't name her.

"He made it to the hospital. The surgeon's with him now. And my officer."

"Good." Kate's relieved sigh sounded like the real thing. "He'll be under guard, won't he? The person who did this might come back."

"He'll be safe in the hospital." He pushed that aside impatiently. He gestured to a chair far enough removed from the spot where Larry had lain. "Tell me what happened from the time you left the farm. What time did you leave?"

Her face tightened. For a moment he thought she'd remain defiantly standing, but then she crossed to the chair and sat, very erect on the edge of the seat.

"I'm not sure. I went in the house with . . . with your family." For an instant she seemed to understand how difficult this was for him.

"Your mother insisted on giving me food to bring home—" She stopped, looking around. "I don't know what happened to it."

"Two pieces of pie on a plate," he said. "It was lying in the grass next to the walk."

Kate nodded. "I must have dropped it when I ran." She glanced at her watch. "I'd guess I left at about eight fifteen, but I'm not sure."

He'd already spoken to his parents. His mother had no idea, but Dad put the time at around eight fifteen, maybe five minutes either way at the most.

"Did you stop anywhere on your way back?"

Kate shook her head.

"So, figure ten to twelve minutes once you got going to get here."

"Or a bit longer. I don't know the roads as well as you do."

True enough. "Did you come straight inside?"

She looked slightly embarrassed. "I probably hesitated. Usually Mrs. Anderson has the back porch light on, but she didn't. I got out my keys with the penlight attached. The city is never totally dark," she said defensively.

In other words, she had taken what were probably normal precautions for her. "Right. When did you hear someone?"

Kate pressed her hand to her forehead. "I think not until I'd realized that the door was unlocked. I backed up—I was going to go to

Mrs. Anderson's, but it didn't look like she was home."

"You should have called me." He couldn't prevent the personal note from intruding.

"I knew you were at the fire." She shivered, rubbing her arms. "Anyway, I could hear someone in the bushes. Coming closer—I glanced back."

"Did you see him at all?"

"Just as a man-sized shadow." She glanced at him. "Run, hide, fight. That's what my stepfather always said. It was go toward him or come into the cottage, so I ran inside and locked the door."

"Did you turn the lights on?"

She shook her head. "The front drapes were open. I didn't want to be seen from outside. That's when I heard Larry make a noise and knew someone was in here with me."

Kate rubbed her arms again, hugging herself. He wanted to put his arms around her and knew he couldn't.

"And then?"

"I turned my penlight toward the noise and saw him. Larry, that is. And called you."

Her call had come in about thirty minutes after she'd left the farmhouse. He didn't see how she could possibly have had time to get in here, find Larry and hit him. But the questions had to be asked.

"We'll be trying to find someone who saw you pull in. That will narrow the time down still further." He thought that would be reassuring, but her eyes flashed in response.

"If you think I did this, then you don't know me at all."

"I don't think you attacked Larry," he said carefully, aware that he was treading the line between cop and man. "But if you came in and he attacked you, you'd have been justified in defending yourself."

"If it had happened that way, I would have. But it didn't. He was already lying on the floor, injured, when I came in." The words were firm. Not argumentative, just assured.

He switched ground. "Did you leave the door unlocked when you went out?"

"Certainly not. I've told you before—I'm careful about things like that. I remember turning the knob to double-check it."

"So how did Larry get in?"

She leaned her head on her hand for an instant, and the sign of weakness nearly knocked him off balance. But then her head came up.

"I told you someone had been in the cottage before, and you didn't believe me. I suppose Jason might have given Larry a key for some reason. Or he might have gotten hold of Jason's key and had a copy made. Or he could have walked in the back hallway of the bed-and-breakfast and lifted the key off the hook anytime Mrs. Anderson was occupied."

Too many choices, and all of them were perfectly logical. "Granted, getting a key wouldn't have been impossible. In any event, he was here, and so was someone else. He didn't hit himself on the back of the head."

"No." She pressed her lips together in the gesture he'd begun to realize meant she was determined not to let emotion show.

"You'll have to stay somewhere else for tonight, at least, so we can process the scene. Maybe my parents—"

"No." She snapped the word.

He couldn't help being relieved. His family was already too involved in this situation for his peace of mind.

"I can hear Mrs. Anderson out there now, giving Foster a hard time." He doubted very much that Foster could hold out against a determined Mrs. Anderson much longer. "She can give you a room in the house for tonight. Just pack up what you'll need for tonight and tomorrow, and I'll set it up with her."

For a moment Kate looked as if she'd like to argue the point. Then she shrugged and headed for the bedroom.

Just as well. He'd have had to insist, and that would have been uncomfortable, to say the least.

Who was he kidding? No matter what happened

from here on out, the events of the past few hours had changed his view. There was something still to be learned about Jason's life—and perhaps even death—or Larry Foust wouldn't be lying in the hospital.

Things had changed between him and Kate, as well. And he didn't have the least idea how he was going to handle that.

Everyone in town must have heard about the attack on Larry Foust, Kate decided as she walked into Blackburn House the next morning. And that he had been found in the cottage Kate was occupying. The only question left was: Did they think she'd done it?

She'd called the hospital as soon as she got up, but after asking if she were a relative, the response had been that the patient's condition could only be discussed with family. And the police, she assumed.

So, little as she'd wanted to talk to him, she'd called Mac. He'd sounded as reluctant as she was, but he did say that Larry was in stable condition in a medically induced coma to reduce chances of possible brain damage. He'd be of no help to the police for days, and perhaps not then.

Mac had also said he'd meet her at the cottage at one that afternoon. His tone hadn't allowed for argument. Well, she was past worrying about being alone with him, in any event.

Why did he want to talk to her there? Did he think being on the scene would make her confess? If so, he was doomed to disappointment.

As an alternative to brooding, Kate decided to go to work as usual. Anything was better than staying cooped up in the room, pleasant though it was.

When she passed the quilt shop, Allison came rushing out, followed more sedately by Sarah. Allison grabbed her hand. "We heard about it from Mac. What a thing to happen! Are you all right? Maybe you shouldn't be out yet."

Kate shrugged. "I'm fine. I wasn't hurt. As for being out—as long as I can handle people staring at me, it's better than staying in."

"That's certain sure." To Kate's surprise, Sarah gave her a quick hug. "If people want to talk they will. It always happens, but that doesn't change who you are."

"Thanks." Kate's throat was suddenly tight at the unexpected vote of support. Neither of them seemed to have doubts about her. "I appreciate it. I was afraid most people would be ready to ride me out of town on a rail after all the trouble I've stirred up."

"You're a newcomer. You couldn't stir up anything that wasn't already there to be uncovered," Sarah said firmly.

"Sarah's right, as she usually is," Allison said. She flashed a smile at her partner. "Why don't you join us for lunch? We're going over to the café around noon."

Sending a public message, in other words. "Maybe your future brother-in-law would rather you didn't show your support for me quite so visibly." Kate suspected Mac was already cursing the fate that had led her straight from his family's house to discovering Larry.

"Don't underestimate Mac." At the sight of a customer heading for the shop, Allison turned away. "We'll stop by for you when we're ready to leave."

"Sounds good. But I'll have to be home by one o'clock. I'm meeting with Mac then."

"No problem," Allison said. "We'll break a little early. Sarah's mother is coming in this morning, so she'll cover for us. See you later."

Feeling slightly better, Kate headed for the bookshop. At least Allison and Sarah didn't believe she'd brutally bludgeoned someone.

Emily looked up from the computer when Kate entered the bookshop, her expression somewhere between startled and dismayed. Planting a smile on her face, Kate approached the counter. "I hope I'm not late."

"What? Oh, no, not at all. I'm just surprised. After what happened . . ." Emily's pink cheeks deepened to rose. "I thought maybe you wouldn't feel up to coming in today."

"I'm better off working than sitting there

brooding about it." She hesitated, but Emily didn't say anything. This certainly wasn't the quick reassurance she'd had from Allison and Sarah. "Unless you don't want me here, that is."

"On, no, that's not it at all." Emily seemed to be making an effort to sound convincing. She nodded to the shelves Kate had been cleaning the previous day. "You can get on with that job. I've got to get some of the dead wood off the shelves, to make room for new releases. Although the minute I remove a book from the shelves, someone's sure to ask for it."

Emily always seemed torn, needing reassurance on the smallest decision regarding the shop.

"I'll get right on it." Kate tucked her bag on the shelf behind the counter and seized a cloth. Just keeping the shelves dust-free seemed a full-time job.

The area where she was working was out of sight of the front door. Had that been deliberate on Emily's part? She might not be eager to have such a controversial person on display in her shop.

If Emily felt that way, she'd have to come out and say so. Kate wasn't about to give up her access to Blackburn House for anything less. Not that it had provided her with much information so far.

Her thoughts reverted to that meeting with Mac this afternoon, as they'd done constantly since they'd spoken. Frustrated, she pulled a row of books from the shelf to dust behind them. She'd just begun to feel that Mac was cooperating with her. Now her involvement with the attack on Larry, even though she was innocent, would no doubt make that cooperation impossible.

Surely the fact that Larry had been attacked in the cottage proved that she was getting close to something, didn't it? It would focus Mac's attention on the drug angle, no doubt of it. Would he even follow up on the fact that Bart hadn't told him the whole story about firing Jason?

Her fingers clenched until the nails bit into her palms. If she didn't find anything—if she never knew what had happened to Jason—how was she going to live with that?

Her mind barely registered the jingle of the shop door until the snap of heels was followed by a sharp voice.

"Where is she? I know she's here, Emily. You get her out here right now!"

"Now, Ethel . . ." Emily's soft voice was immediately drowned by a louder one.

"Kate Beaumont! I'm not leaving until I see her."

Kate stepped down from the stool she'd been using to reach the upper shelves, and moved around the standing shelf between her and the front of the shop. "I'm Kate Beaumont. What can I do for you?"

The woman who swung to face her looked to

be in her forties. Thin and angular, she wore what seemed the uniform of the middle-aged in Laurel Ridge—stretch pants with a tunic-length top that masked whatever figure she had.

"You!" The woman strode toward her, anger twisting her face. "You did that to my baby. Why are you still walking around loose? You ought to be in jail."

"Now, Ethel . . ." Emily repeated ineffectually. She gave Kate a helpless look. "This is Ethel Foust. Larry's mother."

"You hurt my boy." She took a step closer, close enough that Kate could see the anguish behind the anger in her face.

"No, I didn't," she said quickly. "I just found him, that's all. I called for help."

"Liar! What was my Larry doing there, if you didn't lure him to that cottage?"

"I don't know." Kate tried to keep her voice even. No good would come of responding to anger with anger. "I wasn't there. He might have come by to talk to me about my brother." But if so, how did he get in?

"I don't believe you." She was shaking, her face contorted. "You—you . . ."

"*Ach*, Ethel, you're getting too upset." Kate hadn't heard Sarah come in, but she was there suddenly, her voice soothing as she put her arms around the distraught woman. "You have to be strong now, for Larry's sake, ain't so?"

Ethel Foust's face seemed to crumple. "My poor boy." Her voice caught on a sob.

Kate's heart twisted. The woman wouldn't believe it, but Kate knew exactly how she felt. She had been in the same place.

"You want to be with him. *Komm*, now." Sarah turned her toward the door. "Here is Allison, and she'll drive you to the hospital. You shouldn't drive yourself when you're so upset."

Allison hurried in, car keys swinging from her hand. "That's right." She took the woman's arm. "I'll take you."

All the fight seemed to have gone out of Ethel Foust. She sagged against Allison's supporting arm. "So kind," she murmured.

"We are praying for him," Sarah said. She darted a look at Kate as they went out the door, and her lips formed the word *sorry*.

"Oh, my goodness." Emily hurried around the counter to stand looking after them. "I never thought of such a thing. Poor Ethel. She's just not thinking straight, that's all. Are you all right?"

Kate nodded, but she was shaking inside. "I think I'd better leave. If you don't mind, that is."

"That's fine." Emily's response was quick. "Things will settle down in a day or two. You'll see."

Kate appreciated the optimism. But somehow she didn't think this situation was going to be resolved that easily.

CHAPTER TWELVE

It looked as if he'd finally found something Johnny Foster was good at, Mac decided. He'd assigned Foster the task of searching out a witness to confirm the time Kate arrived back at the cottage. Apparently considering that investigative job made him a detective pursuing truth on the mean streets, à la his favorite cop show, he'd diligently gone up one side of Main Street and down the other.

Mac gave a quick glance around before he headed back toward the cottage, not surprised to see that several people were openly staring. It was nearly one, and he wanted to remove the police tape before Kate got there.

Luckily, Foster's search had hit upon an unassailable witness—the Reverend Charles Wallace, pastor at the Baptist church a few doors down from the café. He'd been the last one out after a meeting and had checked the time as he'd locked the door. He'd noticed Kate's car pulling into the driveway of the bed-and-breakfast at a time that made it clearly impossible for Kate to have attacked Larry.

Even if she'd rushed in and hit him with no preliminary discussion, which was ridiculous, she still couldn't have hidden the weapon before

Mac arrived. Something approximately the size and shape of a baseball bat, according to the medical examiner.

He might be able to narrow it down once any fragments were isolated from the wound, but with the victim alive and undergoing medical treatment, the search was made more difficult. The man had actually sounded as if he'd regretted not having a dead body so he could check it out in his own methodical manner.

Reaching the cottage, Mac pulled off the crime scene tape on the door. They'd worked late, looking for any evidence, but the pickings had been slim. The assailant hadn't left any calling cards, as far as they could tell.

At least with Kate cleared, if not out of the picture, he could move ahead without the weight of suspecting someone for whom his feelings were anything but tepid. He opened the door with the key Mrs. Anderson had provided and stood looking around for a moment. Kate wasn't a suspect, but was she a potential victim? As long as he didn't know why Larry had been attacked, it was impossible to know.

The sound of steps on the walk had him turning. Kate didn't look as dazed as she had the previous night, but there was strain showing in the wrinkles between her brows and the lines around her mouth. Well, that wasn't surprising, was it?

Kate came to a stop when she reached him, glancing from him to the open door. "I see you've made yourself at home."

"We had to have a key last night." As usual, she'd made him feel off balance. "I'll return it to Mrs. Anderson."

"Why bother? It seems the immediate world can walk in and out with no problem." There was no mistaking the irritation in her voice. That wasn't surprising, either.

"I'm also going to tell Mrs. A. that she needs to have the lock changed. There seem to be too many keys around for comfort. And find a safer place to put them."

Kate gave a curt nod. She stared at the door for a moment, and he thought she squared her shoulders at the prospect of entering. "I suppose we'd better go in."

Mac followed her inside, not sure what to make of the mood she was in. Was she angry with circumstances, or with him?

"What's the idea of questioning me here?" She rounded on him as soon as the door was closed, leaving him with no doubt. "Do you expect me to confess because I'm back at the scene of the crime?"

"Just like before, I thought you'd prefer talking here to talking at the police station," he said mildly. "No ulterior motives, I promise."

For an instant she stared at him, and then her

anger seemed to deflate. "Sorry," she murmured. "I thought you were joining the ranks of those who think I attacked Larry."

The sense of her words sank in, and he frowned. "What do you mean? Has someone said that? Surely not Allison or Sarah or Emily?"

"Sorry," she said again. She rubbed her forehead. "They've been more supportive than I'd expect. After all, they barely know me, but they rallied around."

"Who, then?" He closed his hand over hers, holding it in a warm clasp. "Someone's upset you."

"Larry's mother." The lines around her mouth seemed to deepen. "She came to the bookshop looking for me. Not surprisingly, she blames me for what happened to her boy."

He raised an eyebrow. "Don't you mean her baby? That's usually how she reacts when anyone has the nerve to criticize Larry."

That forced a smile from her, which was his intent. "That attitude might explain a lot about him." She shook her head. "We shouldn't make light of it. He's badly injured, and I imagine she's just striking out blindly."

"That doesn't give her the right to throw accusations around. I'll speak to her."

"Not on my account," Kate said quickly. "She has enough to handle right now."

Kate was more generous than a lot of people

would have been. "I have to talk to her anyway, and I'll make sure she knows you couldn't possibly have injured Larry. You didn't have time."

Kate's golden-brown eyes lit with understanding. "You must have found someone to substantiate when I got back here."

"I put Foster to work on it right away. As it happened, the minister at the church across the street noticed your arrival just when he was locking up, and he knew what time it was when he left the building."

She nodded, turning away slightly. "At least now you don't have to waste time suspecting me." The words were tinged with ice. She was blaming him.

Mac's emotions surged, and he grabbed her wrists, spinning her to face him. "You know better than that." She did, didn't she? He tried to think past the pounding of his heart. "You do," he insisted.

Kate's eyes darkened, the brown seeming to overwhelm the gold. "Do I? Last night I thought . . ."

"Last night I was trying not to leave room for anyone to say I hadn't done my job. That I hadn't pursued every avenue because I was protecting you." He loosened his grip, letting his fingers move over the delicate skin on the inside of her wrists. "It was because I knew you didn't have anything to do with it. Not because I suspected you."

The tension went out of her all at once. "I imagined you believed . . ."

He shook her lightly. "Think again. I know you didn't have anything to do with the attack on Larry. We have to find out who did. And why."

"Okay." Her lips trembled on the edge of a smile. "I could think about that better if you let go of me."

"Same here," he admitted. He let go and took a couple of steps back. "Maybe this is a safe distance for a rational discussion. You think?"

"Could be." Kate seemed to prepare herself for action. "So, what comes next? Do you have any ideas about the attack on Larry? Any evidence?"

"Plenty of ideas. No proof, unfortunately. The assailant was careful enough to take the weapon with him."

And if he had been lurking in the yard when Kate came home, or perhaps had rushed to hide when he heard her car, he'd probably been ready to use the same weapon on her if he'd had a chance.

"No fingerprints?" She glanced with a bit of distaste at the film of dust left from Johnny's fingerprinting efforts.

"No. Either he didn't have to touch anything in here, or else he wore gloves."

For a moment he envied the heroes of those cop

shows Foster was so fond of. They could build an entire case on the evidence of a single hair. In real life it wasn't so easy—especially in a town of eight thousand residents with a police force the size of his.

"You're thinking of that person you suspect of being a drug dealer, aren't you?"

"He'll bear investigation, but I'm trying not to make quick assumptions." Still, no matter how he tried, logic led him to someone connected with both Larry and Jason, and a potential drug supplier was the obvious choice.

Frowning, Kate looked around the cottage as if assessing it as a crime scene. "You're sure you didn't find anything here that might lead you to the assailant?"

"No. We've been over everything. Just the prints we'd expect to find. Like I said, he either wore gloves or was careful not to touch anything."

Kate looked better for having something to focus on. "What about the weapon? Even though it's gone, did the doctors give you any idea of what to look for?"

"Something about the size and shape of a baseball bat. We may know more later if any fragments are recovered, but right now they're trying to keep Larry alive."

She shivered a little at the reminder. "What can I do to help you?"

He'd try to keep her concentrating. "I want to know if anything has been disturbed or taken from the cottage, and you're the best person to tell us that. I'd like for us to do a thorough search together, looking for any sign that someone has touched your belongings. Anything of value, or something that could have been used as the weapon."

"Right. Where do we start?"

There was a lot to be said for the toughness Kate showed, even if sometimes it got in the way. "The bedroom. Most thieves assume that's where you'd hide something valuable. There has to be a reason why Larry was here."

"And the other man?" She threw the question over her shoulder as she headed for the bedroom.

"Possibly they met here by design, but the assailant could have been following Larry, looking for a chance to attack him. Without knowing the reason, it's hard to tell." He gestured to the left side of the door. "Start here, and we'll work our way around the room clockwise. That way we don't miss anything."

Nodding, she moved to the bureau, its top liberally covered with fingerprint powder.

"Sorry." He blew it off the small lamp. "Foster gets a little excited when he's allowed to fingerprint something."

Kate didn't comment but went straight to work, pulling out the top drawer. It held an assortment of undergarments. She frowned. "Someone has been in here. But I suppose the police . . ."

Not just the police. *You,* she meant. *You searched my things.*

"Anything I looked at is exactly the way I found it." And, no, he hadn't allowed Foster to do that part of the search, but she didn't ask.

"Then someone else has been through here. I always arrange my drawers in the same way, no matter where I am." She shrugged. "Comes of moving around so much in recent years, I guess."

"Larry, most likely. But what did he expect to find?"

She pulled out the next drawer. "Maybe it was the other way around. Maybe the other person came first, started searching, and Larry interrupted him."

"I thought of that, but Larry did leave his prints on the dresser, so I think we can assume he was the searcher."

"I guess so. At least you have that much established, and when . . . if . . . he can be questioned, that evidence might help persuade him to loosen up on what he knows."

"Now you're thinking like a cop." He clamped his lips closed the instant the words were out, sure that was the last thing she'd want to hear.

But Kate, moving to the bedside table, didn't seem to take offense. Maybe she was too preoccupied with the search. She riffled through the book she'd left on the nightstand, then put it down.

She frowned, shoving a strand of hair behind her ear. "What was he searching for? What could he possibly think I have that might—" She stopped, looking up at him, eyes widening. "The journal. Jason's video journal."

Kate raced into the living room, with him right behind her, berating himself. It was the obvious thing. Why hadn't he thought of it? If Larry knew about the diary files, he might think Jason had left something that incriminated him.

Switching the computer on, she leaned over it, fists on the table, as if urging it to boot up faster. He stood close behind her, his gaze on the screen.

A few clicks took Kate to the file. Or rather, to where the file should be. It had been deleted.

Kate sagged, her pain palpable. The journal wasn't a source of information to her—it was a link to her dead brother.

She sucked in a breath, straightening, and her fingers flew over the keys. Mac realized what she was doing before the connection was made.

"An online backup?"

"Outsmarted him on this one, at least." The files appeared on the screen. "It's there. It's safe." Relief filled her voice. She turned to him, so close their bodies brushed with the movement, but Kate obviously wasn't even noticing that. "I didn't lose it."

"I'm glad." He took a careful step away from her, wary of anything that might send her guard up again. "For your sake, as well as mine."

"So now we know, don't we? Larry thinks there's something in Jason's diary that might incriminate him." She bit her lower lip in frustration. "What? I've been through it over and over."

"So we go over it again until we know. We have to find out what that is."

At least there was still an opportunity to learn the truth—and it was a truth he should have gone after a year ago.

By late afternoon, Kate was so restless that she'd taken to pacing around the small cottage—a singularly futile pursuit. Mac had left, promising to join her in looking through the journal later. She'd watched Jason's video diary until her eyes crossed, searching for something that had meaning for her.

It was all very well for Mac, busy pursuing the drug connection. That was something the police could do better than she could.

Despite the attack on Larry, she still wasn't convinced that the drug angle was the only thing to be discovered about Jason's death. Pausing in her pacing, she checked her email again. There was still no answer from her business reporter friend, although he'd promised to be in touch when he found something about Laurel Ridge Financial. If she didn't hear from him by tonight, she'd call him.

What else hadn't she done? She could try Lina again. The woman had seemed sympathetic, and she was more likely to be honest about Jason than Bart Gordon was. Or she could try Nikki. And there was Russell Sheldon. Was there any possibility that he could, or would, tell her more?

There was one obvious thing that she had been avoiding since she came to Laurel Ridge—the thing that Mac assumed she'd intended that first day when they crossed paths at the cemetery. She should visit the place where Jason had died.

Her throat grew tight at the idea. *There's nothing to be learned there at this point.* Her mind was quick with an excuse, and that decided her. Maybe there wasn't anything to find, but she owed it to Jason at least to see the place. She would not be cowardly about it. She'd go now, because the longer she waited to go to the spot, the harder it would be.

Getting up to the cemetery on top of the hill took less time than she'd like, but maybe that was a good thing. It gave her less time to regret what she was doing. She drove carefully between the two stone pillars that marked the entrance. A little farther on, the road widened to include a small graveled parking lot. Kate pulled in and got out.

The cemetery overlooked the town, the way cemeteries seemed to do in rural areas. She couldn't see the cottage from here, because it was hidden by trees, but the roof of the bed-and-breakfast was easy to pick out.

And the clock tower, reaching above the trees to proclaim its importance. She remembered what Mac had told her about those early town fathers, determined to prove the importance of their town. At least they had an architectural achievement to be proud of, even if it didn't represent what they'd wanted it to.

Kate looked across the cemetery, wondering where to begin. Maybe she should have taken Mac up on his offer to show her, but somehow she thought she'd better do this alone. If she was going to fall apart, she'd rather not have any witnesses.

Based on the newspaper photograph, Jason had been found in an older area of the cemetery, leaning against a worn stone. She'd been able to read the name on it, though. Elizabeth Bright. The dates had worn off, or perhaps they just didn't come through on the grainy newspaper photo.

"Afternoon. Can I help you find a grave site?"

An elderly man was kneeling next to a nearby grave. He'd obviously been weeding around the stone, but now he rose slowly to his feet.

"Thank you." She hesitated, not sure she

wanted to reveal what she was looking for to a stranger.

"You're Ms. Beaumont, aren't you?" He saved her the trouble. "I guess you're wanting to see where your brother . . . where he was found."

Kate discovered that she still wasn't used to having everyone in town, it seemed, know her business. The expectation of anonymity a city gave died hard. Swallowing her annoyance, she nodded. "Can you direct me?"

"Sure thing." He turned to point across the rounded curve of the hillside. "See where that clump of birch trees is? The old section of the cemetery is just on the other side of that. That's where he . . . where he was discovered."

Kate wasn't strong on identifying trees, but it was clear where he meant. The trunks of the birches were silvery against some darker green growth behind them.

"Thanks. I appreciate it."

"No problem." He turned back to his task, then paused and glanced back at her. "Sorry for your loss."

She nodded, throat tightening at the unexpected sympathy in the familiar words coming from a stranger. Then she struck off across the lawn between the headstones.

The afternoon sun slanted across the hillside, and below, in the town, the clock tower chimed the time. Almost automatically, she checked her watch against it. If she stayed here long enough, she'd be like the rest of Laurel Ridge, using the clock tower as her personal timekeeper.

The clump of trees seemed to grow taller as Kate approached them, and she felt a nervous chill slide down her spine. She glanced back. Maybe what she sensed was the man watching her, but he'd disappeared from view.

It was time she did this. She'd been avoiding it since she'd arrived in town, maybe trying to convince herself that Jason's death wasn't real. But avoiding the truth wouldn't bring him back.

The instant she stepped under the trees, she felt cold. The shadows were deep here, probably due more to the evergreens that grew among the birches. Pines, maybe? At least she could identify the shiny leaves of the rhododendron that grew under and around the trees.

Even here, the cemetery was obviously well cared for. She had no trouble walking between the trees, but the sense of isolation startled her. She couldn't even hear the sound of traffic from the street.

Was that what Jason had sought here? The isolation, so that he could do what he'd planned in privacy? If he'd just intended to get high, it would have made more sense to do so in the cottage. He'd come here with a darker purpose.

Pressing her lips together, Kate stepped out

of the belt of trees and into a cleared area. The gravestones immediately told her that this was the old part of the cemetery, even without looking at the dates. The stones themselves were weathered, some with the carving nearly worn away, some partially hidden by the lichen that attached itself to the stone.

And there it was. The stone she wanted was slightly tilted, as if it longed to give up the responsibility of standing erect. Elizabeth Bright, 1834–1854. A wave of pity went through her. Only twenty. Was that why Jason had picked this spot? Did he feel a kinship for someone else who'd died young?

There was nothing to see here. The grass around the stone was green and evenly cut. Still, she knelt next to the stone and put her hand on it. Cold at first, it slowly seemed to warm under the pressure of her hand.

Her throat was tight, and tears pressed against her eyelids. She had to blink rapidly to keep them back.

Why, Jason? Why did you do it? Didn't you realize there was still a life for you once you left here?

She'd thought, if only she found the person or event that pushed Jason into taking his life, she could be satisfied. Here, in the spot where he died, she saw the truth. She was desperately searching for someone else to blame so she didn't have to blame herself. But nothing could change the fact that she'd let her brother down.

I'm so sorry. I failed you. Forgive me.

There was no answer to that. There never would be, not in this world, anyway. Nothing would fill the hole left in her heart by Jason, or absolve her of responsibility. But there was still something to be done.

If she could help to find out the truth of who was bringing drugs in this town, targeting teenagers like the one Mac had told her about, she'd have done some good here. Maybe, in a small way, helping Jason's adopted home would give some meaning to Jason's life and death. So slowly she was hardly aware of it, the grief slid away, to be replaced by something else—a sense of being watched. Kate's mind flew to the man she'd spoken to in the cemetery. But surely he wouldn't follow her, wouldn't impose on her grief.

And he certainly wouldn't give her the sense that there was enmity in the gaze.

She sat back on her heels. *Don't go down any lonely roads,* Mac had said. He probably wouldn't approve of isolated spots in the cemetery, either.

Something brushed against a shrub, and a twig cracked in the belt of trees behind her back. She stiffened. Someone was there. It wasn't her imagination. And the very fact that the person didn't move again or speak meant danger.

Run. Hide. Fight. The three steps her stepfather had drilled into her lit in her mind like so many neon signs blinking at her. Moving slowly, casually, she picked up her bag from the ground, holding it by the strap. *Anything can be a weapon if you have to fight,* Tom's voice said. Ironic, that it should be Tom, and not Jason, that she'd found here.

Balancing on the balls of her feet, Kate rose, listening intently for any sound. The person in the bushes might only be watching, not attacking. If so, she didn't want to push them into attack mode. Nothing. Whoever it was, he or she wasn't moving toward her now.

She glanced around, carefully not looking in the direction of the sound. If she returned the way she'd come, she'd be walking right into him. But the rim of trees was thinner off to her left, and once she was in the open she'd be safe, wouldn't she? No one would attack her in broad daylight out in the open.

But even as she thought that, she realized it wasn't broad daylight any longer. The sun hung on the edge of the ridge, casting shadows around her. Once it dipped below the ridge, darkness would move in quickly. She needed to go, now.

As if she were saying goodbye, Kate patted the stone lightly with her fingers and moved off to the left, alert for the smallest sound. If she heard him coming—

She hadn't gone more than a few steps before she heard the sound she'd been listening for—someone brushing quickly through the undergrowth. Aiming at the spot where she could see lawn beyond the trees, Kate took off running, bag swinging in her hand.

No time to listen now, not when all she could hear was the rasp of her own breath and the pounding of her heart. She crashed through the final belt of trees and kept on running, veering when she spotted her car.

Finally Kate risked a glance over her shoulder. No one was there, but in the shadows under the trees, branches of rhododendron moved as if someone had just gone back through them.

If he didn't stop coming to the cottage in the evening to see Kate, the gossips would have them as good as married, Mac decided. But there was nothing lover-like in his attitude at the moment. He wanted an explanation from Kate, and he wasn't leaving until he'd gotten one.

Lights glowed behind the drawn drapes, so she was there. He rapped on the door, the sharp noise cutting the silence that enveloped this part of town in the evening.

A shadow moved across the rectangle of light. Then Kate's voice, separated from him only by the thickness of the door.

"Who is it?"

She was taking some precautions, at least.

"It's Mac. Open the door."

It seemed a long couple of minutes until she'd snapped back the dead bolt and opened up. He strode inside, knowing full well his anger was fueled by fear for her.

"What happened to scare you at the cemetery today?" He shot the question at her.

"I wasn't scared." Kate's reply was immediate. In sweatpants and a T-shirt, barefoot and with her hair loose on her shoulders, she looked young and vulnerable. And desirable. "Wait a minute. How did you know about that? Is this whole town spying on me?"

He'd like to assure her that no one was spying, but how did he know that was true?

"It's not spying to express concern for another person. It just so happens that Vern Maxwell saw you running to your car. Like a bat out of hell, according to him."

"So he called you to report? Is he one of your informants?" She walked across the small living room, putting some space between them.

He blew out an exasperated breath and clung to his patience. He didn't want to talk about Vern. He wanted to know what had made her run.

"Not exactly. Apparently you'd talked to him, and he told you where Jason was found. When he saw you bolt out of there, it worried him.

He stewed about it for a couple of hours and eventually decided I should know."

She faced him, chin up, as if daring him to push her.

"Come on, Kate. Don't make me work blindfolded. Tell me what happened."

At the change in his tone, she seemed to wilt, as if anger had been the only thing keeping her upright. "Sorry, I just . . ." She made an indeterminate gesture with her hand.

He moved closer. "You decided you wanted to see where Jason died. I would have taken you. You know that."

She pushed her hair back, exposing the delicate curve of her neck. "I just didn't want to be a coward about it. You can understand that, can't you?"

Unfortunately he could. The need to bear burdens alone—he suffered from that, too.

"Yes. But you didn't have to go alone." He moved again, so that he was within arm's reach. Jason's young face stared out at him from the computer screen. She'd been watching the recovered diary.

Kate blew out a long breath. "I guess I'm used to dealing with things on my own."

"That's a good quality except when it leads you into trouble. What happened?"

She shrugged, as if giving up. "Now that I look back at it, it hardly seems worth making a fuss about. I thought I sensed someone watching me."

"At the Elizabeth Bright stone, you mean?" An image formed in his mind—the old stones, the trees and shrubs that screened them off. A nice lonely spot.

"I suppose I was already feeling pretty emotional. And when I heard someone or something move behind me, I wanted to get out of there."

"That was the right thing to do." He wanted to touch her but wasn't sure he should.

"When I moved as if to leave, I thought I heard someone coming after me. So I ran." She shook her head. "Maybe it was my imagination."

"No."

She met his eyes, looking startled.

"Vern was worried enough to check the area. He found broken branches on the rhododendron bushes, as if someone had pushed through them. I went and had a look myself. I'd say someone did just that." He touched her arm gently. "Did you see anything at all?"

She shook her head again. "Nothing. Well, just a shadow. I can't even say if it was a man or woman." Her hands clenched. "It's so frustrating. Why would anyone come after me? I can understand some people not wanting me here, but who plans an attack in broad daylight?"

"At a guess, it wasn't planned." His fingers moved absently on her arm. "Somebody wanted to know what you were doing there and decided to take advantage of the isolated spot."

Just as Jason had apparently taken advantage of the isolation the night he died. And he was beginning to get some funny ideas about that death.

"Kate, tell me something." His hand tightened on her arm. "If Jason was staying clean, the way you think, what might he have done if someone tried to get him back into the drug scene?"

Her eyes widened as the import of the question penetrated. "I . . . I don't know, not for sure. You're thinking the dealer considered him a threat?"

"I'm wondering if it's possible."

"But what you're saying—that means his death might not have been suicide."

"Just a speculation, that's all," he said quickly. "There's not a shred of evidence of anyone else having been there with Jason, and I wouldn't know where to begin looking for any."

He could see how the idea rocked her, making him wish he hadn't spoken.

"If I could believe he didn't take his own life . . ." She let that trail off, a new vulnerability in her eyes.

"It's just a possibility," he said gently, not wanting her to build too much on something that was barely a theory. "Does it make so much difference?"

In answer she studied his face. "You've never lost someone close from suicide, have you?"

"No. But even so—"

"You can't imagine it, then. Suicide . . . the victim ends his or her pain, I guess. But for the survivors, the pain is just beginning. The questioning. The guilt. If only. That becomes your mantra. If only I'd done this or that. Or not done something else."

Her pain was palpable. He took her by the arms, searching for some way to ease it. "Kate, either way, you can't keep blaming yourself. It wasn't your fault."

"But it was." Her eyes were dark with pain. "You don't know."

"Tell me," he said. He drew her a little closer, hands gentle, fearing that the smallest misstep could hurt her even more.

She shook her head, but more from helplessness than from a refusal to speak. "It doesn't help. I've gone over it again and again."

"You tried to protect Jason. You were hardly more than a kid yourself." His heart hurt for her.

"Tom wanted Jason to go to the university. I was afraid a big school would be too much for him. That he'd be better off at a smaller school. Jason and I figured it all out. He was afraid of the pressure, of trying to keep up, of being lost in the crowd, so he was going to live with me and commute."

"I take it your stepfather got his way." He did his best to sound noncommittal.

"Oh, yes. Jason always wanted to please him, you see. When I objected, things really blew up between me and Tom. We both said more than we should have. Poor Jason. He couldn't stand seeing the two people he loved at odds. So he said he wanted to do as his father said." She put her hands to her face for a moment, as if she didn't want to see that scene again. "I was hurt and stupid. I reacted by walking away. Took a job in Baltimore, told myself that it was best. Maybe Tom was right. Maybe Jason needed a new beginning. Instead he found a refuge in prescription drugs."

Her voice seemed to die, and her lips quivered.

"You couldn't have done more than you did. You did your best for your brother." Even as he said the words, he knew they wouldn't comfort her.

Kate put her hands to her face again, and this time he saw the tears. With an inarticulate sound of pity, he drew her against him. Wrapping his arms around her, he held her while sobs racked her body.

"It's all right," he murmured. "You did what you could."

It wasn't enough. It was never enough.

Kate's face was pressed against his chest. He felt her tears soak through his uniform shirt and laid his cheek against the top of her head. What was it Mom said about helping people who'd lost someone? Sometimes all you could do was be there. Well, he was here, for whatever it was worth.

After several minutes the sobs lessened. Kate turned her head, her cheek against his chest. "Sorry," she murmured.

"Don't be," he said.

She drew back a little and managed a smile. "I got your shirt all wet."

He wiped a tear from her cheek with his thumb. "It'll dry." His hand moved, cupping her cheek. "Kate . . ."

Whatever he'd been going to say got lost when he looked into her tear-wet eyes. Slowly he lowered his face and found her lips with his.

Gentle at first. Comforting. That's all that was intended. But then her lips moved against his, inviting, welcoming, and passion took over.

He kissed her lips, her neck, the curve where her neck met her shoulder. Kate pressed against him, her hands moving on his back, drawing him closer, as if they couldn't possibly be near enough.

His imagination crossed the few feet to the bedroom, the welcoming bed—

And he seemed to hear a defense attorney in his head. *So you had sexual relations with this witness, Chief Whiting. How do you expect the jury to believe that your testimony is unbiased in this case?*

Groaning, he pulled back. Still holding her close with one hand, he pushed her hair back from her face with the other. "We have to stop."

She gave him a tantalizing smile. "We do?"

He held on to his sanity with an effort. "As long as there might be a case pending against someone in Jason's death or the attack on Larry, I can't risk tainting your testimony."

He saw her reluctant agreement. She pulled back slowly.

"Until the case is settled," he said, as if promising himself.

Something seemed to shutter her eyes. "When the case is settled, it will be time for me to leave."

He took a step back. "Maybe you could find a reason to stay."

"Maybe." But he could see in her eyes that she didn't believe it.

CHAPTER THIRTEEN

Kate leaned back on the sofa, holding a cold glass to her forehead. Her eyes were hot from the tears she'd shed, and her throat was still tight.

What had she been thinking, seeking comfort so readily from Mac? She never jumped into relationships, and she hardly knew him. But even as she thought the words, she realized it wasn't true.

Because of the circumstances that had brought them together, she knew more about him than she would in months of casual dating. They'd skipped right past the light, getting-to-know-you stage. She knew Mac at a bone-depth level— seeing his fierce integrity, his overwhelming sense of duty, even the family life that had made him who he was.

In a way, that made it more important to take her time, because nothing between them could be casual. It was either real or it was nothing.

Kate moved the cool glass to her cheeks, pressing it against first one and then the other. How embarrassing was it that Mac had had to be the one to pull back?

Her cell phone jingled, and her heart jumped. Mac? But a quick glance at the caller told her no. Morris Vail was returning her call, presumably with the results of his research into the financial partnership.

"Morris. I thought you'd never call." She could concentrate on this and keep thoughts of Mac at bay for a few moments, anyway.

"Hey, Kate. Listen, you gave me a tough job with looking into this Laurel Ridge Group."

She could picture him, leaning back in his swivel chair, one pair of glasses on top of his balding head and another probably perched on his nose.

"So it was hard. I knew if anyone could do it, you could. You have more contacts than anyone I know."

He chuckled. "That's right. Butter me up. I deserve it. I had to fish pretty deeply to come up with anything, but I finally found someone in the area who knows where the bodies are buried."

"I'll bet." He always knew someone.

She heard papers shuffling. Morris never kept his notes electronically, preferring dozens of slips of paper and countless sticky notes.

"Okay, here we go. Long-established family firm, excellent reputation, headed for years by Russell Sheldon, who's apparently above reproach. At least, that's how things were for a number of years."

"Until when?" All her senses went on alert.

"My sources couldn't pin it down, but it sounds as if things started to slip in the past couple of

268

years. Nothing solid, but the kind of vague rumors that would make the knowledgeable think twice about entrusting them with any investments."

At last, someone who wasn't singing the praises of Laurel Ridge Financial. "So do these rumors hint at incompetence or wrongdoing?"

"Take your choice." Kate could almost see him shrug. "It's impossible to know from the outside. It would take a serious look at the books. And when I say books, I mean records. They'll be digital, of course."

Her mind worked feverishly. Was this a break at last? She formed her next question carefully. "So if someone smart and competent had access to the records, would he spot it?"

Morris hesitated. "At a guess, and don't quote me on this, incompetence would show up in those circumstances."

"What about fraud?" If someone at the company had been lining his pockets at the firm's expense and Jason found out, that person would have a strong reason for wanting to be rid of him.

"That depends," he hedged.

"On what?"

"On how skilled the perpetrator was. And how smart the investigator was."

Jason was smart, all right. "But how could you go on hiding a thing like that?"

"Oh, it would come out eventually. You can only hide those missing funds so long. For instance, a full audit would turn it up. Whether a cursory look would tell anyone anything—well, that I don't know." She could almost hear his smile. "Not unless I could get a look myself, but I'm not breaking any laws, not even for a gorgeous girl like you."

"Now who's the flatterer?" She responded automatically, her mind busy with this new concept.

"Not flattery when it's true," he said. "But seriously, if you're thinking of investing, I'd go elsewhere."

"What do I have to invest?" she scoffed. "I'm working on a story, that's all." He didn't need to know the rest of it.

"I thought you inherited when your stepfather died. You could build up a nice little retirement fund with smart investing now."

"If I decide to, I'll talk to you first," she promised.

"See that you do. So, what are you doing with yourself these days? Anything new on the job front?"

"Not really." She was evading the subject, and he probably knew it.

"What about the freelancing you were doing? Given the way things are going with print publications, that might be a way to go, if you have a nest egg to keep you going until you start making some money."

"You might have something there." Kate rubbed

her forehead. What had happened lately to her early goals? When she'd finished her degree, she'd thought she was going out to change the world with her reporting.

Now—well, now, she'd be happy to right just one wrong.

Mac headed down the hospital corridor on Monday morning, trying to decide what he had so far in terms of actual facts. Unfortunately, it didn't seem to amount to a lot. Despite the DA's vocal determination, Mac couldn't say for sure that the assault on Larry had anything to do with drugs. Suspicion wasn't proof.

According to the doctor he'd finally nailed down this morning, Larry was conscious for short periods, but not saying anything of importance. Mac decided he'd rather decide for himself whether it was important or not.

He paused at the door to the hospital room. Ethel, in a padded chair to the left of the bed, seemed to be sleeping, head tilted and mouth agape. On the other side, one of his part-time patrolmen, George Danvers, in a less-comfortable chair, sat leafing through a copy of the *Pennsylvania Game News*.

Larry, the center figure in the tableau, was looking better than the last time Mac had seen him. His color was good, and he was breathing on his own. Aside from the fact that the curls on one side of his head had been replaced by a white bandage, he looked fairly normal.

Mac stepped into the room softly, but George dropped the magazine instantly, nodding when he saw who it was. Mac moved to him quietly.

"Has he said anything?"

"Just asked for his mother." George surveyed Larry's face dispassionately. "If you ask me, I'd say he's shamming—looking for sympathy and putting off any chance of questioning."

He wouldn't put it past Larry, but he couldn't push, not against the doctor's orders to the contrary. Not unless he wanted a case thrown out of court.

"Anyone try to come in who shouldn't?"

George shook his head. "Nobody but a couple of girls who graduated with him. His mother made short work of them."

"Well, stay alert. We still have no idea who assaulted him."

"Nobody will get past me without proper hospital credentials, believe me." George was comfortably confident—he'd lived long enough to have had several experiences of hospital routine, unlike Johnny Foster. That was the main reason Mac had assigned him.

He hadn't had much choice. Hospital security couldn't be everywhere at once. Still, he hated to think what it was doing to his department budget for overtime.

272

Mac's phone buzzcd, the sound jerking Ethel awake. She sat upright, frowning at the disturbance, and leaned over Larry protectively.

He could take a hint. Mac slipped out into the corridor before answering. The call was from the station, and he automatically went into business mode. "Whiting."

"It's me, Chief. I mean, Foster." Johnny made an effort to emulate Mac's tone, but excitement crept in. "I did it!"

"Did what?" The range of possibilities seemed endless.

"Found a photo of Ax Bolt."

Okay, the excitement was justified. Mac had felt hamstrung with nothing but a verbal description to go by.

"What? Where'd you find it?" He'd thought they'd exhausted all the possibilities.

"DMV," Foster declared.

He must be failing. He should have thought of that himself before he'd ventured on a search of police records.

"I just thought to myself, who would have a picture of me—"

Mac didn't want to listen to a blow-by-blow of Foster's thought processes.

"Send it to me now. And to hospital security. Right away."

"Will do."

"And, Foster, good work."

"Thanks, Chief."

In another minute he had the image on his phone. He studied it for a moment before heading back toward the room. Bolt had none of Larry's innocent choirboy looks. If he'd seen him, Mac would have remembered. Dark hair, long in the back but shaved at the sides, a gold stud earring and tattoos that extended up his neck. Yes, he'd have noticed.

Mac strode into the hospital room, feeling renewed energy. He showed George the image. "This is the guy we're looking for. You see him, you call in, right away. Don't try to tackle him yourself." He didn't want a fiftyish, overweight, out-of-shape part-timer going up against the person who'd put that dent in the back of Larry's head.

George nodded.

Ethel leaned across the narrow bed toward them. "What is it? Show me! It's evidence against that Kate Beaumont, isn't it?"

Mac clung to the shreds of his patience. "Ethel, I've already explained that Ms. Beaumont couldn't have attacked Larry. She didn't have time."

"So you say. Taken in by a pretty face, that's all. Let me see." She snatched at the phone, but Mac held it out of reach. He noticed what she apparently hadn't—that Larry had opened his eyes and was watching them.

"This is the person we think attacked your son."

He swung the camera screen in front of Larry's face. "What about it, Larry?"

There was no mistaking Larry's reaction. His eyes widened in fear, his face going white.

Then, with a quick sidelong glance at his mother, he collapsed back on the pillow, eyes closing.

"Now, look what you've done." Ethel reached for the call button. "Don't worry, baby. Mommy's here." She patted his face, crooning over him.

Mac exchanged glances with George. They both knew what they'd seen. "Sorry to leave you with the fallout," Mac murmured. "But I have to get moving on this."

George nodded, as Mac fled the room. There was someone else who had to see this photo right away, and that was Kate.

He drove down Main Street, wondering how far he dared push his suspicion of Bolt. Not as far as an arrest, certainly, but enough to bring him in for questioning. And enough to alert neighboring police departments. Someone must know where he might be found.

He was headed for Blackburn House, assuming Kate would have gone to work this morning, but before he reached the drive, he spotted her on the other side of the street, going into the Buttercup Café.

Pulling into the nearest space, he got out and crossed the street to follow her into the café.

Kate was already standing at the counter, waiting for her order. He joined her, exchanging greetings with the Amish girl who was working today—one of the many relatives of the owner.

Kate looked at him with raised eyebrows. "Time for a coffee break, Chief?"

He grinned, relieved that they seemed to be back on a friendly basis. "I was about to ask you the same thing." He gestured toward the crullers the girl was putting into a box.

"Emily decided we deserved something special today, so she asked Allison and Sarah to join us for coffee."

"Who's going to watch the shops?" he asked.

"Apparently Monday is quiet enough to prop a sign on the door and take a break." If she disapproved, he couldn't tell it from her expression.

He studied her, wondering. Did she regret having confided in him about her guilt over Jason's death? He'd never really thought before about how much suicide impacted the survivors. How did a person get over it?

Maybe in the same way he got over his grief in a situation where he hadn't been able to save someone. Never getting over it, just learning to live with it. He'd been trying that since he'd come back from Afghanistan, and it was still a struggle every day. To say nothing of the nights, when innocent faces haunted his dreams.

Her order was ready then, and he waited while she paid and then he picked up the container holding the coffees. "I'll take this one."

Kate gave him a questioning look, but she didn't protest. As soon as they'd reached the sidewalk, though, she stopped, frowning. "What is it? Is something wrong?"

He grinned. "You read me pretty well, don't you? No, not wrong, but something I need to show you." He nodded to the bench in front of the café. "Let's have a seat for a minute. The coffee won't get cold that fast."

For a moment he thought she'd object, but then she went to sit on the bench, the box perched on her lap. He joined her, pulling out his phone.

"We finally found a picture of Ax Bolt. I thought you'd better see it." He passed the phone to her.

Shielding the screen with her hand, Kate peered intently at the image and then shook her head. "I'm sure I've never seen him before. I don't think he was at the Lamplight that night, if that's what you're wondering."

He frowned absently down the street, barely noticing the gold of the leaves. "Not exactly. It would give me a little more to go on if you'd seen him, but I didn't really expect it. Larry had a bit more spectacular reaction to it."

"Larry?" She swung toward him. "You mean he's come around? Is he talking?"

"No, and neither the doctor nor his doting mother will allow me to question him. But I did have a chance to flash the photo in front of him. He looked terrified. Then he faked a faint so I couldn't press him. Still, it's something."

Kate nodded. "It certainly shows how he feels about the man, if nothing else."

"And you can take a lesson from his fear. Be aware. If you spot Bolt, don't try to speak to him. Just give him a wide berth and call me. Here, I'll send the photo to your cell phone."

He clicked to send the image on to her.

"Don't worry. I won't forget that face. And I won't try to be a hero, I promise." Her smile seemed distracted.

"What is it?" It was his turn to read her expression.

"I know you want to stop the drug traffic. But are you forgetting about the fact that Bart didn't tell you the whole story about Jason's departure that last day?"

"Not forgetting, no." His reply was cautious. "I can pursue it, but I know pretty much what he'll say—that he didn't want to blacken Jason's reputation when he was dead. And Lina would agree. Don't forget, as much as she does to keep that place going, she's not a partner. She can be fired."

"They were trying to protect themselves," she snapped. His caution always seemed to infuriate her, but he wasn't going to go off half-cocked and either ruin a possible case or alienate his neighbors.

"Maybe so, but that's nothing I can prove. And it's not illegal, even so."

"Lying to the police . . ." she began.

He put his hand over hers where it lay between them on the bench and felt the instant connection. "I don't think I can make a case out of that, Kate. Not without more."

"And what if I have more?" Her golden-brown eyes held a challenge.

"Then I want to hear it," he said instantly. "Or you'll be the one who's not cooperating with police, remember?" he added, tone light.

Her face relaxed in a smile. "I'm a reporter. I could claim I didn't have to reveal my source, but I intend to tell you." She glanced down at their clasped hands. "I heard from a business reporter friend of mine. I'd asked him to dig up anything he could about Laurel Ridge Financial Group."

Mac couldn't imagine that there'd be anything derogatory, but he nodded.

"According to his sources, the firm had a solid reputation up until the last couple of years. Since then, rumors have been circulating. Very vague ones, apparently, but he says they hint at either incompetence or wrongdoing."

Mac frowned, assessing her words. "It's a straw in the wind, but not much to go on."

"I guess not," she admitted. "But on the strength of it, he said if I had anything to invest, it shouldn't be there." Kate gave him a questioning look. "You're going to tell me it's not enough to base an investigation on."

"You already know that. But . . ." He hesitated, trying to work his way through the maze of possibilities. "You think that if Jason happened on to some information that would expose the problem, someone might have wanted him out of the firm."

"Or out of the way." Now it was her turn to pause. "I keep thinking about what Mr. Sheldon said. That something was not Jason's fault."

Mac came to a reluctant conclusion. "There's only one thing I can do at this point. Talk to both Bart and Lina. Push them on the fact that they didn't tell me what they should have in the wake of Jason's death."

"That's all?" Kate pulled her hand free, turning to face him. "What about the rumors about the company? What about what Sheldon said? You can't just give them an easy out."

Keeping his temper under control had become a lot harder since Kate's arrival in Laurel Ridge. "I'm not. But I'm also not accusing thcm of financial malfeasance on the basis of rumors. Or giving away everything I know, just in case one or both of them actually has been cooking the books."

"Still protecting your town?" There was a bite to her voice.

"I'm doing my job the best way I know. Don't make it harder by charging in and stirring things up before I have a chance to make some private inquiries of my own."

Kate's jaw hardened. Her eyes looked stormy. But finally she jerked a nod. Then she got up, gathered her belongings, and strode off without another word.

Mac watched her go, torn between his longing to help her and his determination not to make a misstep that might keep him from ever learning the truth. She thought he was too cautious. Well, he'd just have to live with that, wouldn't he?

Kate headed into the bookshop, trying to ensure that she had a pleasant expression on her face. They were meeting in the bookshop because Emily already had a cozy corner with some comfortable chairs for reading or for the book club she hoped to start.

Maybe she'd been a bit unreasonable. Mac was doing his job, after all. But the drive inside her to know the truth grew stronger every day. How would she bear it if she never knew?

"Coffee and crullers," Allison exclaimed as she opened the box and distributed crullers and napkins. "If I'm not careful, I'll be too big for my wedding dress."

"As busy as you are, I'm sure you run off the calories," Emily said, helping herself to the coffee with cream. "Thanks so much for picking up the order, Kate." She beamed at the three of them. "It's so nice of you young things to make me feel part of the group."

"*Ach*, Emily, you're only as old as your heart feels, and you'll always be young at heart." Sarah reached across to pat her hand.

"Sarah has a saying for every occasion," Allison said. "Now, let's get down to the serious stuff. Is there any news about who attacked Larry in the cottage?"

Kate stopped to consider before she spoke, knowing that some things were better not broadcasted. On the other hand, some were. "Mac has a photo of the man he thinks might have been involved. I haven't ever seen him, but he's hoping it will lead him to the man." She brought the photo up on her phone and passed it to Emily. "Let Mac know if you spot him in Laurel Ridge."

Emily took one look and shuddered. "He looks like a hoodlum if ever I saw one."

Allison's lips twitched a little, and Kate suspected she was thinking it was very unlikely Emily had ever seen what she called a hoodlum. She took the phone.

"A few too many tattoos, I'd say. If I'd seen him in Laurel Ridge, I'd remember."

Sarah took it in her turn and studied the face with serious intention. It seemed unlikely that the Amish woman would have run across someone like Bolt, but . . .

"You know, I think I've seen him somewhere," Sarah said, her forehead puckering. "I just can't think where."

"I doubt he was at the last barn-raising," Allison teased. "Where have you been hanging out to see a character like that?"

Sarah shook her head, ignoring Allison's teasing question. "No, I'm not sure. But it will come to me." She handed the phone back to Kate.

"Well, wherever he is, Mac won't give up until he locates him," Allison said. "I've never known anyone with greater determination."

"He certainly has a strong sense of responsibility to this town." Kate made an effort not to let the words sound critical.

"You should have known him when he was young," Sarah said. "He was a mischief-maker if ever there was one. He always had to test the rules, and he just grinned when he got caught."

"Nick says the military really sobered him up," Allison said.

She hadn't realized Mac had been in the military, but she should have guessed it. "What service was he in?"

"Marines. He served in Iraq and Afghanistan. Nick says whatever he experienced there made him more protective. Gave him a deep sense of duty."

Kate nodded. She'd known people for whom serving had had that effect. Some returning vets could shake off their experiences, but she'd guess Mac was not one who could.

"I've got it," Sarah said suddenly. "I know where I saw him—the man in the picture, I mean."

"Are you sure? Where?" Allison grabbed her partner's arm.

"It was that day I dropped off the order for Melody Andrews on my way home from work. Remember? What day was it? I can look in the book . . ."

"No need," Allison said. "I remember. It was the day Larry was attacked."

For a moment they all stared at each other. Kate recovered her senses first. "This Melody Andrews—where does she live? And what time was it?"

"That's just it. She lives in the same block as Larry Foust and his mother. And it would have been after five when Sarah was there. We need to tell Mac." Allison turned to Sarah. "You're sure? What was he doing?"

"Just . . . just walking toward the Foust place," Sarah said, but her cheeks grew pink.

Allison's eyes snapped. "He said something offensive to you, didn't he?"

Sarah shrugged. "It doesn't matter. I've forgotten it already."

"Wish I'd been there. I'd have given him something for his smart mouth." Allison's hands tightened into fists, and she looked ready to take on all comers.

"He may live to regret it," Kate reminded her. "He called attention to himself. And Sarah seeing him there ties him to Larry within hours of the attack."

Her mind was spinning. Bolt might have been on his way to meet Larry, with the intent of breaking into the cottage. Or he might have followed him there. Either way, it was a link.

CHAPTER FOURTEEN

Kate slit open the newly arrived box of books that Emily had asked her to unpack. The storeroom at Blackburn House seemed to be divided into sections—unmarked, but defined nonetheless. In one corner, boxes of fabrics were stacked on shelves, obviously belonging to the quilt shop. In another area, bins held various kinds of hardware, most likely from the cabinetry business.

Emily claimed to have been sorting out the mass of old stock left by the previous owner of the bookstore, but judging by the number of boxes left in her area, she hadn't been making much progress.

The relatively mindless choice of unpacking was probably all Kate was suited for at the moment. Her thoughts skipped from one issue to another like a water bug skittering on a pond.

Mac had speculated as to what might have happened if Jason had threatened to expose a dealer but he'd insisted it was just that, speculation. With no physical evidence, convicting anyone of killing Jason would be impossible, unless someone talked. With the injection of Ax Bolt into the picture, that was becoming more and more likely.

Her initial reaction to the possibility that Jason

had been murdered had been, she was ashamed to admit, a sense of relief that she hadn't been responsible. She'd come here wanting someone, anyone else to blame, so she didn't have to blame herself. But she'd known, those moments at the cemetery, that there was no escaping her own responsibility even if someone else was involved in Jason's death.

The police report had indicated that there were no marks of violence on Jason. So how could someone like Bolt have persuaded him to take anything?

Almost against her will, Kate found herself picturing the scene. If he'd been drugged without his knowledge, it could have been done. Someone—Bolt, perhaps—getting him to the cemetery. Leaning him against the stone, pouring the rest of the alcohol and drugs down his throat.

Jason would have been helpless, alone in the dark, perhaps able to know what was happening to him, crying out in his mind for her . . .

Kate bit her lip, hard, forcing the image out of her head. Reliving his death made her weak when she had to be strong.

The storeroom door creaked open, setting her nerves jumping. Gripping a heavy hardback in one hand, she straightened. Then she dropped it into the box at the sight of Mac's tall form.

"You talked to Sarah?" She skirted the box she'd been working on and moved toward him.

"Hello to you, too." Mac had a warm smile for her before turning serious. "Yes, I heard what Sarah had to say."

"And?"

"And it goes a long way to suggesting Bolt's involvement with Larry."

She nodded. "That's what I thought. He could have followed Larry to the cottage. Or they might have gone together and then had a falling-out over something."

"Bolt might have thought Larry was more of a handicap than an asset." Mac leaned against a stack of boxes. "I'd never get the DA to cooperate in opening your brother's case again, but with the possibility of a prosecution in a current case, he's on board. I talked to the drug task force people from the state police. They have assets I can only dream of. With them looking for Bolt, it's only a matter of time."

"Unless he's left the area altogether," she said. "I would."

He studied her face for a moment. "I'd feel easier in my mind if I knew he wasn't around to chase after you."

"I'm not afraid."

At his skeptical gaze, she shrugged. "All right. Only a fool wouldn't be afraid of someone who killed so readily. But if Bolt attacked Larry, he certainly wouldn't hang around."

"Be careful anyway," Mac said. He straightened.

"Speaking of hanging around, as much as I'd like to hang around here, I'm on my way to have a chat with Bart about a little matter of not telling the police the whole story."

"I was afraid you'd forget that, now that Bolt was occupying your attention."

"I'm not ignoring any possibilities. That's my job."

That oversize sense of responsibility of his came to the fore again. Kate thought about what Sarah and Allison had said about his service in the military. About how it had changed him.

Mac raised an eyebrow. "What? You're looking at me as if you haven't seen me before."

"Not that. But Allison mentioned that you'd been in the military, and I realized I should have known that from the beginning."

"Carry the marks of it, do I? Well, maybe so. Being a marine affects a person for life."

"Why did you join up? Patriotism?"

"Nothing so noble, I'm afraid." He shrugged. "I was a restless kid, not willing to settle down in Laurel Ridge for the rest of my life. I wanted adventure."

"At a guess, I'd say you found it."

"Yes." He sobered, and his eyes darkened with pain so intense that it seemed to reach out and grab her heart. She longed to reach out to comfort him, but she wasn't sure it would be welcome.

He turned away, and the opportunity, if it had existed, vanished. "I'd best get going. By the way, I think I've found the right gamer to help us interpret Jason's diary. I'll bring her over to the cottage later if that's okay."

"She?" Kate was sure she showed her surprise. "Somehow I was expecting a teenage boy."

He grinned. "Don't be sexist, Kate."

Before she could respond, he'd gone out, closing the door behind him.

Mac's smile faded rapidly as he headed up the stairs to the second floor offices. Bart was always a bit tricky to talk with, especially when it was something he didn't want to hear. He got huffy, stood on his dignity and generally made a nuisance of himself on every town committee he'd ever served with.

With Russ Sheldon's retirement, Bart was the power running Laurel Ridge Financial Group, and the opinions Kate had passed on from her reporter friend weren't reassuring. A lot of people in town had their investments with the firm, and any hint that it might be unstable would rock them to the core.

Not his dad and mother, though. Dad always joked that he was worth nothing more than the cabinetry business and the farm, and that if he ever reached the point that he had any left over, he'd take Mom on a trip around the world. Since his mother had no desire to go anywhere, that didn't seem likely to happen.

Too soon he'd reached the door. He paused, remembering that first day when he'd seen Kate's face reflected in the glass window of the real estate business next door. A lot had changed since then—and he wasn't sure he was ready for some of those changes. He liked his life the way it was, maintaining a careful balance between the grief and guilt of the past and the duties of the present. Kate made him feel as if there was something missing.

Nikki had spotted him standing outside the door and was clearly wondering what he was doing. Shoving his mind back into gear, he went in.

"Hi, Chief Whiting." She closed the top drawer of her desk on the magazine she'd been reading and gave him her best receptionist smile. "What can I do for you?"

That reminded him that he ought to hear Nikki's account of what had happened to Jason that last day. But not here if he wanted her to be frank.

"I'd like to see Bart if he's not busy. I don't want to interrupt him if he's with a client."

"No, not a person in all morning." She gave him a conspiratorial grin as she pressed a button on the phone. "He's probably practicing his putting. He has one of those—" She cut off to turn her attention to the phone. "Chief Whiting is here to see you, Mr. Gordon."

She nodded to Mac, jerking her head toward the door. "You can go right in."

Mac suppressed a smile as he headed for the door. He could imagine Bart's reaction if he heard Nikki talking about his putting practice. Still, Laurel Ridge didn't have that many young women looking for receptionist jobs. The cream of every high school class went on to college, and many of them just kept on going afterward. On to bigger things, if not necessarily better.

Bart opened the door before he reached it, extending a hand with his professional smile. "I didn't expect to see you, Mac. I thought you'd be too busy tracking down drug dealers."

"What makes you think that?" He ought to know. Rumors spread faster than a cold in the head.

"Talk." Bart spread his hands expressively. "It's all over town that Larry Foust was attacked because of his involvement in drugs."

"I'd be careful about rumors. Ethel might sue if she heard."

Bart was shaking his head as he led the way to the chairs on either side of the large mahogany desk. Other than the computer, the desk surface was completely clear.

Mac mentally contrasted it with his battered

and scarred desk, piled high with the steadily increasing flow of forms to be filled out. Either Bart was extremely efficient, or he kept his work confined to the computer. Somehow Mac had never found that possible.

"If Ethel hadn't spoiled that boy so thoroughly, he might have amounted to something." Bart spoke with the confidence of one who had no children. "Of course the other question in everyone's mind is, what was Larry doing in the Beaumont woman's cottage at that hour of the night?"

"The police would like an answer to that one, as well. Since Ms. Beaumont was out that evening, he didn't come to see her."

Bart's head came up alertly. "Was anything missing?"

"I'm afraid I can't divulge matters pertaining to an ongoing investigation." Not only was that true, it also allowed him to keep a few secrets, at least.

Had the person who'd deleted Jason's file made a copy of it first? And if so, what might it tell him that it hadn't told Kate?

"No, no, of course not." Bart leaned back in his leather chair. "Well, tell me what I can do for you."

Mac made a point of getting out his notebook and pen. "A few little things have come up in regard to the death of Jason Reilley. You'll understand that recent events have made it necessary to take another look at the case."

"I don't understand anything of the kind." Bart sat upright in a hurry. "Just because that Beaumont woman has been talking wildly . . ."

"More to the point is where Jason got the drugs that ended his life." And if Bart didn't stop referring to Kate as *that Beaumont woman,* Mac wouldn't be answerable for the consequences.

Bart seemed to swallow his defensiveness. "Well, of course you want to know that, but I thought you'd looked into it thoroughly at the time."

"That's where Ms. Beaumont's presence has been very helpful. She has access to a bit more information than we did about her brother's life here." He watched a wary look slide across Bart's face.

"Is Larry Foust somehow involved in that?" Bart waved his hand. "Never mind. I'm sure you can't divulge that information."

"Thank you for understanding." So far, this conversation had been relatively amicable, but it was about to get rocky. "Now, according to my notes at the time, you said that nothing unusual had happened at work that might havc upset Reilley. But you recently admitted that he'd been fired. Why was he fired?"

"I don't feel comfortable discussing personnel matters. That's private. You understand." Bart was outwardly calm, but his fingers twitched a little. As if becoming aware of that, he pressed his hand firmly against the desktop.

Mac leaned forward into Bart's space. "That won't do, not when we're looking into what might be a capital crime. If what you say has no bearing on the case, I'll be happy to forget it, but I have to know."

He watched in fascination as Bart's face paled and then grew red. Was he going to try to bluff it out?

"You can't force me to talk to you about company business."

"No one is requesting access to your client files." Although he'd love to know what a private audit might show. How reliable was that source of Kate's? "We can either have a quiet discussion about it here in the privacy of your office, or I'll have to ask you to come in and make a formal statement."

Bart swallowed visibly and seemed to do some fierce concentrating. "Well, I suppose if you must know, the truth of it is that we had to let the boy go for . . . well, for laxity in his work. A firm like ours can't tolerate any laxity, you know."

"Odd, wasn't it, that it took the better part of three months for this laxity to show up?" He didn't ease off on the intensity of his stare.

Bart moved restlessly in his chair, glancing around as if for inspiration. "His internship would have been ending in a few weeks anyway, so it wasn't a big deal. Certainly not something he'd kill himself over."

"Why?" Mac shot the word at him, tired of dancing around the issue.

"It seemed there were some issues relating to the records of some accounts." Bart picked his way carefully. "I'm not accusing Reilley of any malfeasance, you understand. We've determined that no funds were missing, but we have to be able to rely on the accounts being kept accurately."

"So you fired him because he made a mistake in accounting, in other words."

Bart glared at him. "Not just a simple mistake. It took days to go back through all the records and make sure they were correct. We just can't have that sort of thing. Laurel Ridge Financial Group has always had a spotless reputation."

Mac shifted ground. "How did Reilley react when you accused him?"

"He denied doing it, of course. What else would you expect?" Bart's color deepened dangerously. "I should never have taken a chance on someone like him. I let myself be persuaded as a favor to a friend, and look what happened. And now you're raking it all up again."

"I'm doing my job." Mac tried easing off a little. "Did Russ Sheldon agree with firing Jason Reilley?"

"Russ?" That startled him. Unpleasantly. His gaze shifted away from Mac's. "I'm not even sure Russ knew what was going on. That was when he'd started to fail mentally, and he retired shortly after that."

"And Lina Oberlin? Did she agree?"

"Lina is not a partner. It's not her business to agree or disagree. However, I can tell you that she was completely in accord with my decision." His voice gained confidence. Apparently he felt he was back on solid ground.

"So if you're quite sure that firing him was justified, why didn't you mention it when I questioned you at the time?"

Bart stiffened. "I saw no reason to bring it up. Why upset the family even more by letting them know he'd failed at his internship?"

"Very thoughtful of you."

"Well, it seemed the right thing to do." Bart was sublimely unaware of any sarcasm.

"And you have to be careful of the firm's reputation, don't you? Were there any repercussions in that area? Any chatter going around about mistakes being made in clients' accounts?"

"Certainly not!" Bart shot to his feet. "If you're accusing the firm . . ."

"Just asking what seemed a logical question," Mac said mildly. "Obviously if people got hold of that kind of idea, it would be bad for you."

Bart leaned forward, hands planted on the desk,

but before he could speak, the side door opened. "Bart, is—" Lina broke off. "I'm so sorry. I didn't realize you had anyone with you."

"The chief was just leaving." Bart took a step back from the desk.

"Not just yet. I have a question for Lina before I go." He rose casually, turning toward her. "I understand Jason Reilley was fired that last day he worked here. Why is it you didn't mention that when you were asked if anything unusual had happened?"

"I'm afraid that was my fault, Chief Whiting," she said smoothly. "You see, Mr. Sheldon had been so upset about the suggestion of error by the firm and the need to fire the boy that really, we were afraid for his health. So I suggested we not mention anything about the firing. It would be easier on that poor boy's family, of course, but my main concern was Mr. Sheldon. We didn't want to give him or anyone else the impression that he'd been responsible for Jason's overdose."

"So firing him was Russ Sheldon's idea? If so, I don't see how withholding the information from the police would help him."

Mac didn't believe it for a minute. He thought Lina was too concerned with being the perfect assistant, keeping her boss's reputation spotless.

She glanced quickly from him to Bart, as if looking for cues. "I didn't say that. I think all of us agreed that the boy would have to go, but Mr. Sheldon really took it to heart. And, honestly, as forgetful as he was getting, we thought he wouldn't remember it a week later, anyway."

A week later, Russ Sheldon was no longer associated with the firm his family had founded. What, if anything, did that have to do with it? Mac had to admit he hadn't taken Kate's suspicions of the firm seriously. His fault. Maybe he knew the people of Laurel Ridge too well to look at them objectively.

He'd put Bart's over-the-top attitude down to his need to keep the firm as spotless as it had been when Sheldon was at the helm. Now he was beginning to wonder what was actually behind it—concern about the firm? Or concern that his actions might be culpable in Jason's death?

Kate was having second thoughts as the time approached for Mac to show up with this teenager he'd found to help decipher Jason's messages. Or maybe second or third thoughts. She'd begun to think of Jason's diary as a private connection between them. It had been difficult enough to share it with Mac. Why would she want some unknown teenager to have access to it?

She roamed to the windows and then stopped. That was odd. She could see the lights on in the bookshop. Why would Emily be there so long after closing time?

Picking up the phone, she rang the shop. Emily answered at once.

"Emily, it's Kate. I saw the lights were still on. Is something wrong?"

"No, no, nothing like that. I just thought I'd stay a while after closing to catch up on some orders."

"Do you need any help?" If she had to go to the shop, it would be a good excuse to get out of meeting with Mac and his find.

"No, I'm almost finished. I'll be out of here in a few minutes, so don't you bother. I'll see you tomorrow."

Kate hung up. Well, that excuse was gone. She ought to just call Mac and tell him she'd changed her mind, but a glance out the window told her it was already too late. She glimpsed movement, followed by Mac's now-familiar knock on the door.

Trying to find a polite way to turn down the young woman's services, she went to the door. And couldn't help staring when she got a look at the video gaming expert Mac had found. With her long blond hair, designer jeans and sparkling T-shirt, she looked more like a cheerleader than a nerd.

Recovering her senses, she stepped back and gestured them in.

"Kate, this is Kristie Paxton, the expert I told you about."

The teen had an engaging grin that showed off colorful braces on her teeth. "I wouldn't say expert. But if you need to know anything about fantasy gaming, I'm your girl."

"That is what we're looking for." Kate sought for words. "But I'm not sure . . ."

"Hey, listen, Mac already explained to me. This is strictly top secret. I watch the tapes, interpret any mentions of fantasy games, and then forget everything I saw and heard. No problem."

Kate realized that Mac was watching her with sympathy. At least he understood how hard this was for her, whether he thought it was reasonable or not. Somehow that helped her decide to give the girl a chance.

"That is what we need. Some of the references I can understand, if they come from fiction, but the games are beyond me."

Kristie nodded, her hair moving like a ripple of silk. "What games was he into?"

"I don't even know that. If this is hopeless . . ."

"I didn't say that. It would just be easier if I knew what he was into, but I'll figure it out. You want me to give it a try?"

Kate took a breath and nodded. "Okay." She moved to the computer, trying to repress any lingering doubts. "Let me play a sample of the diary for you, so you'll understand what we're after."

As always, the sight of Jason's face on the

screen wrenched at Kate's heart. She deliberately picked a segment that was fairly innocuous, recorded shortly after Jason had come to Laurel Ridge.

"My brother used fantasy as a kind of code, comparing the people he met to the characters in some of the books he enjoyed. I suppose he thought that if anyone ever saw it, they wouldn't understand."

"Privacy. I get it." Kristie bounced into the chair in front of the computer. "Nobody wants someone else looking at their private notes. Or emails." She grinned. "A lot of people learned that the hard way."

Kate nodded, thinking of some of the more spectacular stories to hit the newspapers in recent years.

Kristie shifted a small backpack to the floor and pulled out a notebook, pen and a pair of top-of-the-line earphones. "Okay, I'm ready. Let's have a look."

With an inner pang, Kate pressed the key to start the playback. For a moment she stood staring at Kristie, watching the expressions that flitted across the girl's face and the movement of her pen when she jotted something down. Then, knowing how annoyed she felt when someone looked over her shoulder while she worked, she stepped away.

Mac watched her face for a moment. "Okay?"

"Okay." She managed a smile. "You were right. This is the only way to know what Jason meant. As long as there's a possibility that the key to his death is in those diaries, I have to do whatever it takes."

"Good. And you can trust Kristie. I've known her since before she was born."

"Before?" She raised her eyebrows. "Are you trying to tell me something?"

"Only that her dad used to babysit us when he was in high school, and her mother is my second cousin." He grinned. "Frank's the ultimate jock, and Peggy's a sweetheart, but how they produced a kid as off-the-charts bright as Kristie is a mystery to me."

Kristie glanced at him. "I heard that."

"Keep your mind on . . ." He began, but stopped when he saw her frown with concentration and play back a segment of the tape again. He turned to Kate again. "Is that coffee I smell?"

"Coming right up." Maybe he was just trying to distract her, but she'd been brewing her after-supper cup, anyway.

Mac followed her into the kitchen. She pushed a mug toward him and indicated the sugar bowl. "If you need milk, there's some skim in the fridge."

"Black is fine." He lifted the mug to his lips, leaning back against the counter. Kate had seen him do that enough times that it no longer fooled her. He was never as relaxed as he seemed.

She poured a cup for herself, stirring sugar into it with a little unnecessary vigor. "Are you going to tell me how it went with Bart Gordon today?"

"About the way I expected. He and Lina both had a string of reasonable answers as to why they hadn't initially mentioned that Jason had been fired." His already firm lips tightened. "A few too many, I thought."

"Did you ask them why they let Jason go?"

He hesitated, eyeing her in a way that made her steel herself for the answer. "Bart told me that some problems had turned up in the account records. Nothing missing, you understand, but apparently a jumble of incorrect entries."

"And they blamed that on Jason?" She straightened, ready to take her ire out on anyone in the line of fire.

"That was the implication." Nothing changed about his relaxed posture. Flaying him with her anger would not only be unfair, it would also be useless. He'd stand against it like a rock battered by waves.

"Listen, you know how you said that Kristie was off-the-charts bright? Well, that's how Jason was. He couldn't possibly have fumbled the accounts. He trusted figures—he always said they didn't lie. He could do that sort of work in his sleep."

"Anybody could have an off day," Mac began, but she shook her head.

"Not Jason. Not about that."

Mac studied her face and nodded. "Okay, then that makes it look as if someone else did."

"Who?" She set the mug down with a thud.

"Much as it goes against the grain to suggest it, I'm wondering about Russ Sheldon. Bart and Lina both seemed very eager to protect him, so much so that it made me wonder why. If he did it . . ."

"If he did it, why would they blame Jason? Why not just keep quiet and encourage Sheldon to retire?"

"That I can't answer," he said. "But I'd like to know."

Before she could speak, Kristie popped into the kitchen. "Okay, I went through the first one." She held a notebook out to Kate. "Nothing unusual there." She grinned. "I liked the reference to Mrs. Anderson, though."

Kate tried to suppress a smile and failed. "It's spot-on, isn't it?"

Mac sighed and put down his coffee. "You two going to let me in on the secret?"

"You wouldn't understand, Mac," Kristie said, patting his arm. "You're too mundane."

He gave her a quick hug, apparently accepting the comment.

Kristie glanced at Kate. "If you'd let me copy

the files to a flash drive, I could get this done faster. I promise no one would ever get access to them from me. But it's up to you."

Kristie looked so earnest that turning her down would be like hitting a puppy. Besides, she'd already seen them now. Kate nodded.

"Okay. I'll just be a sec." Kristie dashed off.

"You really can trust her, you know," Mac said.

Kate managed a smile. "Jason would tell me I'm being too possessive. And I'd always promise to do better, but I never would."

"It's tough to let go." He clasped her hand in a sympathetic grip.

"You ready, Mac?" Kristie sang out from the other room.

Mac released her slowly, his fingers caressing her palm. "I have to take her home. Do you want me to come back afterward?"

The strength of her longing to say yes almost frightened her. Giving in to the feelings she had for Mac would be dangerous.

"Better not." There was a world of regret in the words.

He nodded. "You're right. Not yet." His fingertips trailed up her arm, leaving fire in their wake. "I'll call you."

Naturally, Kate was even more restless after Mac and Kristie left. Pacing was getting her nowhere, but she couldn't seem to stop.

A relationship with Mac was impossible.

She'd told herself that from the beginning. Their lives were too different—they wanted different things—he was a cop—

But the longing wouldn't be stilled.

She glanced out the side window toward Blackburn House and came to a stop. That was odd. The light in the bookshop was still on. Surely Emily would have finished by now. It was dark outside, and she'd told Kate several times how much she hated to drive at night.

Even as Kate watched, the light went off. And then the hall light, leaving the building in darkness.

That wasn't right. She'd been here long enough to know that the hall light was left on all night. Kate picked up her cell phone, but before she could do anything it rang. She checked—it was the bookshop number.

"Emily? Is something wrong? What's happening?"

Nothing. Silence filled the line.

"Emily!" She raised her voice. No answer. And then, after a long moment, a dial tone.

Kate punched Mac's number, already heading for the door.

Mac picked up immediately. "Changed your mind about my coming over?" His warm tones seemed to wrap around her.

"There's something wrong at Blackburn House." She yanked the door open and ran out, leaving it wide behind her so that the light spilled out, illuminating part of the yard. "Emily was there processing some new orders. Both the shop light and the hall light went off, and then I had a call from the shop number, but no one was there."

"I'll check it out," he said instantly. "Might be just a fuse. That wiring is nearly as old as the house."

"Emily's alone." She'd reached the path through the shrubbery and had to use the light from the cell phone to make her way through. "I'm going over. Even if it's nothing, she'll be afraid."

She hadn't known Emily long, but she'd already heard about some of the many fears she had, and top among them was the dark.

"Don't." Mac's tone made it an order. "Go back inside and lock the door. I'll let you know when I've checked."

If there was anything Kate hated, it was someone giving her orders she had no intention of obeying. "I have a key to the side door. I'm going in." She ended the call.

Luckily Emily had trusted her with the key to the side door for those days when she opened the shop, saying that the janitor couldn't be relied on to have it unlocked on time. Kate ran across the side lawn, crossed the driveway and hurried to the door.

She fumbled with the lock, imagining how Mac

was fuming. He ought to know better than to bark orders at her.

The lock finally turned, and she pushed the door open. Ahead of her to the right, the cellar steps led down, and to the left, another flight led up to the first floor. Both were pitch-dark.

Kate groped for a switch beside the door. She'd seen one there, hadn't she? Her fingers touched it, and she pressed.

Nothing. Maybe Mac was right about a fuse. "Emily?" She shone what little light she had up the flight of stairs. "Are you there?"

Nothing again. She imagined Emily tripping, falling in the sudden darkness, those birdlike bones snapping. She stepped forward.

She sensed, rather than saw, movement behind her. Dodged to the side. The blow that could have hit the back of her head glanced against her shoulder instead.

Gasping and blinded by the pain, Kate reached for the wall, trying to keep from falling. Someone was there—someone who meant harm . . .

Hands struck her from behind. She went sprawling, reaching vainly for something to stop her fall, and tumbled down into darkness.

CHAPTER FIFTEEN

Muttering under his breath, Mac spun the wheel, making an illegal U-turn on a deserted Main Street, and hit the siren. Chances were good it was nothing—a blown fuse or some glitch in the wiring. But with Emily alone in a dark building, it could have serious consequences.

And with Larry's assailant still on the loose, it might well be something more intentional. Either way, he wasn't taking any chances.

Why couldn't Kate be content with reporting it? He might have known she'd disregard his warning. A more stubborn woman he had yet to meet.

He spun into the driveway at Blackburn House, his heart thudding in his chest and his adrenaline pumping. If Kate had gone in the side door, chances were good she'd have left it unlocked.

He jumped out and charged to the door. Locked. Hard to believe that Kate had actually changed her mind and done what he told her and stayed away. Switching on his powerful flashlight, he peered through the window. His heart sped into overdrive. Kate's cell phone lay on the floor.

In a swift movement, Mac broke the glass with his torch, reaching through to flip the dead bolt on the door. How many times had he recommended to merchants that plate glass on doors be replaced with fortified glass? Just as well no one had listened.

He barreled in and then stopped. Stop and think. Don't run off half-cocked. He sent the beam of his flashlight up the stairs. All was quiet and still. Swiveling, he directed the beam to the cellar stairs. Its light caught a huddled figure halfway down.

Taking the steps two at a time, Mac reached her in seconds. His heart was thumping in his ears as he bent over her. "Kate." Urgency filled his voice, and he was afraid to touch her until he knew how badly she was hurt.

Kate's head turned, hair falling away from her face, and her eyelids fluttered. "What . . . what . . ." She attempted to move, and the words ended in a moan.

Calling for EMTs, he smoothed her hair back from her face. "Easy, don't try to move."

Of course she did, shifting her body and then gasping with pain.

"Don't you ever listen?" he murmured, running his hands over her head, looking for signs of injury. "Without moving, tell me where it hurts."

Kate's eyes came fully open, and she squinted against the light. "My head." She turned her face slightly so that he could see the red mark already rising into a lump on the right side of her forehead.

"EMTs will be here in a few minutes and check you out. Anything else?"

"Shoulder." She made a small movement with her right hand toward her left shoulder, and he realized that her left arm hung limply at her side. "Don't touch it."

"I won't," he said, relieved that she was awake and coherent. "Will you promise me to stay still while I check on Emily?"

"Emily." Alarm filled her voice. "I have to see . . ."

"You don't have to do anything. Just stay put until I get back." He stood, then realized he'd have to leave her in the dark while he looked for the elderly woman. One man wasn't enough for this game. "I'll be as quick as I can. Help will be here soon."

"Go." She gestured faintly with her fingers. "I'm okay." She leaned her head against the wall.

He sped up the stairs, hitting every light switch he came to along the way without success while he called for backup. How had Kate ended up halfway down those cellar stairs? Had she missed her way in the dark? Tripped on something?

The blackness was intense in the hallway, not even enough light seeping in to allow him to spot the bookstore if he hadn't had his torch. He swung it around as he went, but the hallway was empty and the bookstore dark.

He tried the door, calling Emily's name. It

swung open, but there was no answer to his hail. It only took him a few minutes to scan the whole bookshop. No one was there. If Emily had left—but surely then the door would have been locked.

The wail of a siren sent him racing back to the side door. *Show the paramedics to Kate, make sure she was safe.* That came first.

Then he'd get some lights on and do a thorough search of the building. For Emily or for an intruder.

Kate's face turned toward him as soon as she saw the light. She was white, but her eyes were alert. "Did you find Emily?"

"No sign of her. She probably already found her way out."

Kate frowned, moving her head slightly. "Why did she call me? Why wasn't she there when I answered?"

He clasped her hand. "I don't know, but I'll find out. All you have to do is relax and let the paramedics take care of you. Can you handle it?"

A faint smile curved her lips. "I'm not very good at that."

"Try." He looked up as someone came through the side door, flashlights blazing. "Down here."

He gave Kate a lingering look before moving to give the paramedics space. "I'll come and tell you as soon as I find Emily. I promise."

Now he'd better take his own advice and concentrate on the next task, letting the paramedics do their thing. Swinging around, he headed down the steps to the cellar. If he remembered correctly, the circuit boxes were at the bottom of the stairs.

Sure enough, it was where he thought, and a moment's examination was all it took to see what the problem was. Everything had been turned off by the simple expedient of throwing the main switch.

An accident? It could happen, but somehow he doubted it. Using the edge of the flashlight, he pushed the switch back into the on position. The stairway light came on instantly.

He stood for a moment, frowning. The box would have to be fingerprinted, of course. Who knew where it was located? And more to the point, how had they gotten in?

By the time Mac reached Kate, the paramedics were preparing her for transport.

"Didn't I tell you you have to stop giving us so much business?" Mike Callahan said.

Having heard that refrain before, Mac ignored it. "How is she?"

"Doesn't look too bad, but we'll let the doctor make that decision. He doesn't like it when we tramp on his territory."

"Do me a favor and don't let her leave the hospital until I'm there," Mac said.

"Stop saying *she*. I'm right here." Kate sounded more like herself.

He bent over her, giving a hand as the two

paramedics lifted the gurney up the steps. "I know. So I'll tell you the same thing. Don't leave there until I come for you. Police orders," he added, before she could argue.

Kate was still protesting when they wheeled her out the door, but he didn't stay to listen. Mike had handled more recalcitrant patients than Kate. And he had a building to search.

Fortunately, Foster showed up before he'd gotten back to the bookshop.

"Breaking and entering?" he asked hopefully.

"I did the breaking," Mac said. "Come into the bookshop. I need to make a call before we start searching."

Emily's home phone number was posted beside the phone, presumably for the use of anyone helping in the shop. He dialed it on his cell phone and waited. If she wasn't there—

"Hello?" Emily answered on the third ring.

"Emily, this is Mac. Is everything all right?"

"All right?" She began to twitter. "What do you mean? Why wouldn't I be all right? What's wrong?"

"Nothing." There was little point in telling her about Kate now. "The lights were off in Blackburn House, so I'm here checking it out. When did you leave?"

"Well, I don't exactly know. But I was home by seven thirty, because I watched my favorite quiz show. Why?"

315

"Did you lock up when you left?" So Emily would have been out of the building well before that call was made from the shop phone.

"Of course I did." She was indignant. "The shop door and the side door, like always. Are you sure there's nothing wrong in the shop?"

"It's fine." The shop was fine, but Kate wasn't. "Have a good night." He clicked off his cell phone before she could ask anything else and stood for a moment, frowning.

Emily had left the building before seven thirty, locking everything behind her. So who had dialed Kate's phone from the bookshop? And who had been playing games with the lights?

It looked as if whatever this incident was, it had been aimed right at Kate.

The last thing Kate wanted to be doing was sitting on an exam table in a curtained cubicle, waiting for X-ray results. She wanted out. And she wanted to know what had happened to Emily. She felt helpless without her cell phone.

For the third or fourth time, she did a mental inventory of the contents of her cubicle—one bed, one side table and one digital readout, probably registering her blood pressure, which no doubt was getting higher the longer she waited for information.

If Emily had been hurt, it was her fault. She should have insisted Emily leave this evening's chores to her. But she'd been listening intently since she'd been in the cubicle, and she hadn't heard the stir that surely would have accompanied someone else coming into the small ER.

The curtain quivered. She straightened, paying the cost in a stab of pain. But it wasn't the doctor—young and ridiculously cheerful. Mac walked in on her.

Kate grabbed the sheet, pulling it up and trying to ignore another spasm of pain. "What are you doing? You can't just walk into the treatment area."

"Professional courtesy," he said, studying her as if memorizing her features. "The ER staff always calls me when they'd got an unruly drunk to deal with. So the doc is returning the favor. He says you'll live."

She glared at him. "Just tell me about Emily. Is she all right?"

"Fine," he said quickly. "She's fine, I promise. I talked to her. She had gone home much earlier."

"But . . ." Kate stared at him blankly, trying to force her brain to work. "How can that be? Who called me from the bookstore, then?"

"A good question." He started to lean against the exam table and then seemed to think the better of it, contenting himself with resting a hand on the top. "It wasn't Emily. You're sure it was the bookshop number?"

"Of course. You can check my cell phone."

She rubbed her forehead. She'd had it when she reached Blackburn House. "I don't know . . ."

"I have it." He pulled it from his pocket and handed it to her. "It was lying on the floor of the landing. Did you drop it when you fell?"

"When I was pushed," she corrected.

His eyes grew very hard. "Wait. Go through it from the beginning, okay?"

Kate tried to focus. "I had noticed the light on in the bookshop earlier—before you and Kristie arrived. I called to see if Emily needed some help, but she said no. I had the impression she didn't intend to be there very long."

Mac nodded. "Emily doesn't usually drive after dark."

"So she told me. That's why I was surprised when I saw the bookshop light was still on after you left." Her skin warmed at the thought of his offer to come back. "Before I could do anything about it, it went off. But then the hall light went off, as well."

"That's normally left on all the time," he commented.

"Right." She pressed her fingers to her forehead. "I think . . . I was going to call the shop, but before I could, my cell rang. Like I said, it was the shop number."

Even though Mac hadn't asked to see it, Kate pulled up the call log, clearly showing the call from the shop. "See?"

"I didn't doubt you, Kate." His smile nearly undermined her.

"Well, anyway, there was no one on the other end of the call. I was afraid for Emily, so I called you. And I headed over to Blackburn House."

"Despite my telling you not to."

She frowned. Was it really so hard for him to understand? "Emily could have been hurt."

"And you couldn't sit by and do nothing."

She wasn't sure whether that was a statement on her character or a sarcastic comment on her impatience. Maybe it was best to let it go. She felt too rocky to argue.

"Did you see anyone or hear anyone on your way over?"

Kate shook her head and gasped when the unwary movement sent a spasm of pain through her shoulder like a knife.

"Kate?" Mac clasped her hands warmly. "Is it your shoulder?"

She nodded. "They're waiting for the X-rays."

"Let me see." Before she could say no, he peeled back the sheet and the hospital gown, its print faded almost to invisibility by many washings. At the sight of her shoulder, he gasped audibly. "Did you hit this when you fell?"

"No." She wasn't going to risk shaking her head again. "Someone hit me."

Mac was so close she heard his breath hiss. He touched her shoulder briefly, a featherlight brush

319

of the fingertips. She looked up, meeting his eyes, and his expression of concern and caring and desire nearly undid her. Her lips trembled, and she found herself focusing on his mouth, tracing the firm arc. She felt as if she were melting.

The curtain rattled on its rings as the doctor shoved it back, breaking the moment. "Well, let's see what we have here." He slid his glasses up his nose with one finger while he stared at the clipboard in his hands. "Nothing broken, you'll be happy to hear. That's the good news." His cheerful smile took in both of them.

"So, what's the bad news?" Mac asked the question for her.

"The bad news is that it's going to hurt like the very devil for a few days." There was sympathy behind his brisk manner. "I'm going to insist on a sling, so you won't try to use that arm at all. And I'll be giving you pain medication—an injection first and then pills." He hesitated. "You probably shouldn't be alone tonight. Do you have a friend who can stay with you?"

Now Mac answered. "I'll make sure she's not alone."

Kate glared at him without noticeable effect.

"Good. I'll send a nurse in to help you dress while I deal with the meds. Mac, you're not going to be welcome in here for a few minutes."

"I'll wait in the hall. I have some calls to make."

To check on the progress of the investigation, no doubt. He probably wanted to be there, not here. "If you need to leave," she began.

"I'm taking you home," he said, and shouldered his way between the curtains.

Mac pulled out his cell phone, earning a glare from a passing nurse. Taking the hint, he walked out from between the row of cubicles and into a corner of the empty waiting room. He called Foster.

"Chief." Foster sounded harassed. "We got through the whole building. Your brother showed up to help. Nobody here, and no signs of any disturbance."

"Good." His mind churned as he tried to prioritize the remaining tasks. Some things would have to wait until daylight, but he had to have the crucial areas fingerprinted before anyone showed up with a legitimate reason for entry. "You kept anyone from touching the area of the side door and the bookshop, right?"

"Sure thing. I roped them off with tape first thing."

Mac could imagine. There was little Johnny Foster liked better than a chance to put up crime scene tape.

"Okay, then, I want you to go ahead and fingerprint the side door, the wall areas on either side of the door where someone might have touched, and the bookshop door. We know he touched the shop telephone and the surrounding counter, so do DNA swabs before you fingerprint there."

Although, as long as it took the state police lab to get back with DNA results, he might expect to see them by Christmas.

"Will do." Foster sounded eager to get at it. "Then what?"

"Then get the results out to the lab ASAP."

Mac clenched his teeth. Did he really want to trust Foster where important evidence was concerned? He itched to do it himself, but he wasn't about to leave Kate alone and unprotected.

"Listen, I'll be bringing Ms. Beaumont back to the cottage as soon as the doctor releases her. Keep in touch every step of the way. When you've finished, board up that window where I broke in. Got that?"

"Right, Chief. I'll report back on the finger-printing."

Chances were good all the prints would belong to people who had every reason for being in Blackburn House. Whoever they were dealing with, he wouldn't be dumb enough to leave his prints on the phone. Still, if it had been wiped off, that was evidence—negative, maybe, but evidence of intent.

As he clicked off, Mac spotted the doctor and pulled him aside for a little private chat. "What did you make of Ms. Beaumont's injuries, Doc?"

"Assorted bumps and bruises from the fall. The head injury is the worst of those, and I don't see any sign of concussion. As for the shoulder—well, she didn't get that falling."

"No, I didn't think so." Mac's tone was grim. He'd be finding the person who had set a trap for Kate before the guy had a chance to try anything else.

"She said she was hit by someone behind her." The doctor pushed his glasses up. "I can't prove it, but I'd guess the assailant was aiming for the back of her head. She moved, and it turned into a glancing blow to the shoulder."

"And if he had hit the back of her head full-on?"

"Then we'd be talking about a fractured skull. Strictly off the record, of course."

"Of course."

So he'd have plenty of charges to bring against the assailant when he found him. Which he would.

"Any guesses as to what the weapon was?" They still hadn't found the weapon used on Larry, and that fact frustrated him.

The doctor shrugged. "The proverbial blunt instrument."

"The same one that was used on Larry Foust?" He snapped the question, desperate for something concrete to build a case on.

Another shrug. "Could be." He frowned. "But

I have a feeling this one had more of an edge to it. There's a straight line abrasion that might indicate something with a corner. Like a two-by-two, for instance. I didn't see that with the other injury." He spread his hands. "Afraid that's all I can say. We don't see that many assaults, and those we do are usually the result of fists."

The door swung open, and a nurse beckoned to Mac. "She's all ready to go. Pull your car up to the entrance, and I'll bring her out."

"Yes, ma'am." Harriet Longenberger had been a fixture in the ER for twenty years or more, and even the doctors, invariably younger, snapped to when she spoke. "Right away."

He wanted to check on Foster's progress, but that could wait until he'd gotten Kate back to the house. Tomorrow they'd be doing a marathon of fingerprinting to eliminate the prints of anyone who belonged in Blackburn House. And he suspected that the net result would be no help at all.

Mac had just enough time to pull the car up and jump out and open the passenger door before Kate, confined to a wheelchair and looking annoyed about it, was wheeled up.

"I can get in myself," she began, but before she could go on, Harriet had seized Kate's good arm and was guiding her into the seat, leaving Mac with nothing to do.

"You have your instructions." Harriet nodded to the papers Kate clutched in her right hand. "Follow them."

Most people quickly got used to being treated like a six-year-old by Harriet. Kate nodded meekly enough. Or maybe she just wanted to get out of there.

Mac slid behind the wheel and pulled out slowly, mindful of potholes.

"I'm not made of glass," Kate said.

"I'm well aware of that," he replied, and smiled when her gaze slid away from his. "But if Harriet is watching us, I'll hear from her if she thinks I'm going too fast."

That earned a slight smile from Kate. "I never realized that being police chief in a small town was such a dangerous undertaking."

"I got acquainted with Harriet when I fell out of the apple tree and broke my wrist when I was six. She gave me a lecture with my cast."

But Kate leaned her head back, eyes drifting shut. Maybe the shot the doctor had promised was taking effect. If so, he might be able to get her settled for the night without interminable arguments.

First, though, he wanted to be sure she'd told him everything she remembered from the attack. "Tell me about the call again."

"I already did." She didn't bother to lift her head from the headrest.

"Did the party stay on the line at all? Could you hear any noise?"

Her forehead wrinkled. "I think the line stayed open for just a minute or two. I said Emily's name, but I didn't get an answer. And I didn't hear anything else except the dial tone."

"So whoever it was, he took the precaution of hanging up the phone before getting into position to attack you. But how did he know you'd come to the side door?"

"I always do, ever since Mrs. Anderson told me about the shortcut."

"So if he's been watching you, he'd know."

Kate made a small, involuntary movement. "I don't like the idea of someone watching me."

"No. It's not pleasant. But whoever he is, he must think you're a threat to him."

"How? Why?" Her voice rose. "I don't know enough to be a threat to anyone."

"You could have been killed tonight." He hated saying the words, but she had to be aware of the danger. "You must have sensed something when you were about to be hit, or you wouldn't have moved. What was it? What made you turn?"

Kate frowned and then rubbed the lines between her eyebrows with her fingers. "I'm not sure. I don't think I heard anything—just sort of sensed someone behind me."

"Man? Woman? What was your first instinctive response?"

"I don't know, I tell you. I suppose I think it's a man, but only because a man seems more likely. If it's this guy Bolt . . ."

"Bolt might have a reason for attacking Larry, if he thought Larry was giving him up to the cops. But I can't think why he'd go after you."

She didn't respond, and a glance told him that her eyes had drifted shut again. There was no point in asking more anyway, he supposed. Kate couldn't tell him what she didn't know.

He turned into the driveway, slowing as the tires crunched gravel, and Kate's eyes opened at the sound.

"Thanks for driving me home." She began what was obviously going to be a dismissal.

"I'm staying," he said in a tone that he hoped left no doubt.

"No, you're not." She pushed the door open with her right hand and then gasped at the effort.

"You can't be alone. Doctor's orders, remember? I'll stretch out on the sofa. I'm not leaving you tonight." He got out, coming around the car to help her get out.

Kate tried to pull away, but he put his arm around her waist, avoiding her injured shoulder, and supported her as they walked to the wide-open door.

"You extending an invitation to burglars?"

"I forgot I left it open. For the light, when I ran over to Blackburn House."

Parking her in the wicker chair on the porch, he checked the cottage quickly and found no sign of disturbance. "Okay, let's get you . . ."

He stopped, because Kate had fallen asleep, slumped uncomfortably in the chair. Mac lifted her gently and carried her inside. Once there, he hesitated for a moment and then went on through to the bedroom, lowering her on to the bed.

As Kate's head touched the pillow, her eyes flickered and opened. Her breath caught at his nearness.

"It's all right," he said, his voice husky despite his effort to sound normal. Looking down at her lying on the bed was enough to test the resolve of a saint. "You feel asleep. I carried you in."

"Thank you." Her voice was hardly more than a whisper. "I'll be okay now. You can leave." But he saw the same desire in her eyes that he knew was in his.

No. In addition to all the other reasons why it would be wrong, he couldn't possibly take advantage of Kate when her guard was down. When . . . if . . . something happened between them, it had to be because the time was right. Because they both wanted it, and they were both frcc to make the choice.

"I'll be in the next room. All you have to do is call out and I'll be here."

She nodded. He should go. But he couldn't. Not yet.

Slowly, giving her every chance to draw back, he brushed her lips with his. Hers opened in response, and a little sigh escaped her. He drew in the scent of her, the feel of her lips, the sound of her breathing. He'd never wanted a woman like this in his life.

He cupped her face in his hands and kissed her again lightly. "Remember. Just shout if you need me."

And then he straightened and beat it out of the bedroom before he could break all the rules and most of his own resolutions.

CHAPTER SIXTEEN

Mac had checked in with Foster several times and finally told the kid to lock up and go home. There was nothing else that could be done tonight. Tomorrow they'd move on with the business of getting fingerprints for comparison. He could just imagine how some of Blackburn House's residents would feel about being fingerprinted.

Finally, leaving one of the shaded table lamps on to provide a dim light, he stretched out on a sofa that was too short to accommodate his six-foot frame. After a few minutes of staring at the ceiling, he drifted into a light doze.

Jolting awake at a slight sound, Mac swung to his feet in a quick movement, heart pumping. What . . . ?

It came again—a kind of strangled choking sound from the bedroom. He pounded across the room and thrust the door open, gaze probing the semidarkness.

Kate sat straight up in bed, hair ruffled around her face, her eyes wide and staring. He switched on the small lamp on the dresser, gaze sweeping the room for signs of an intruder. Nothing. The room was just as he'd left it. He checked the bathroom and closet—nothing. They were clear. No indication anyone had been here.

But still Kate stared, as if she saw something he didn't. It took a moment for Mac to realize that her gaze was dark and unfocused. She wasn't looking at something in the room. She was staring at some image that existed in her own mind.

He approached the bed with care. "Kate." He said her name quietly, afraid of jarring her. "It's okay. Wake up. You're safe."

Easing himself on to the edge of the bed, he touched her right hand gently. Slowly, very slowly, her eyes blinked. She turned to look at him, gaze focusing on his face.

Mac smiled in relief. "There you are. For a minute there, you looked as if you weren't home."

"I . . . I'm all right." She lifted her right hand and thrust the tangled mass of honey-colored hair away from her face. "Sorry." She took a deep breath, as if she'd forgotten to breathe for a moment. "I'm awake now. Did I . . . did I say anything?"

"No." He possessed her hand again, holding it between both of his. "You sounded as if you were choking. About scared the life out of me."

"You don't look scared."

It was the sort of retort he expected from her, but somehow lacking the usual bite.

"Bad dreams?"

She made a face. "You could say that." She stirred. "What time is it?"

He checked his watch. "Just about 3:00 a.m." That dead hour of the night, when vulnerable minds were prey to dark dreams. He knew all about that. In his nightmares he was always back in Afghanistan, clawing helplessly at the rubble of what had once been a loving home.

Kate shoved back the quilt he'd pulled over her. "I'd better get up. I can't just go back to sleep."

Again, he knew the feeling—that fear that if he slipped back into dreams too quickly, the bad memories would take over again. "How about a cup of tea?" He stood back and put a steadying hand under her right arm to help her up. "That's my mother's remedy for night terrors."

"Good idea. I'll meet you in the kitchen."

Obviously she wanted a few minutes of privacy, so Mac headed for the kitchen. After a brief search he located a teakettle, and by the time she came to join him he had the water boiling and the mugs ready.

Kate looked as if she'd splashed water on her face and run a brush through her hair. She was pale and crumpled, but he found just looking at her filled him with tenderness.

"All ready," he said. "Sugar?"

"One, please." She dragged a chair out before he could do it for her and sat down. "Thanks."

"All part of the service," he said, trying for a cheerful note. The shadows under her eyes were like dark stains on her fair skin, making him want to soothe them away.

He set the cup down in front of her and took the chair on her right, mindful of her painful shoulder. "I think I can guess what your nightmare was. Or maybe is."

Kate's eyes met his. "Yes, I guess you can. Jason, alone in the cemetery. Usually I'm trying to reach him, but I can't. At least, not in time."

Her hand lay on the table between them, and he clasped it warmly. "It fades. It never goes away, but it fades."

She pulled her hand away. "How would you know?" The bitterness filled her voice.

Mac stared down into his cup, as if he could read the future in its dark depths. Or maybe the past. He was going to tell her what he never told anyone. He had to. She'd come along when he had stopped even looking for someone, and her pain had made him aware of the empty place in his heart. Even if nothing came of their relationship, she deserved to understand.

"I did two tours in the Middle East—one in Iraq, one in Afghanistan." He tried to keep his tone easy, but he could sense the sudden still intensity with which she watched him. "It was toward the end of my second tour. We were working with Afghani tribesmen—fierce fighters, most of them. They were trying to reclaim their land. Had been for a long time."

He gave her a brief glance, and she nodded, her face grave and set.

"There was one village in particular—it had been hit by both sides, it seemed like. The middle of a war zone is no place to be safe. But they went right on living their lives, raising their kids, and I guess waiting for it to be over. Friendly to Americans, too. Inviting us to supper, even though they had little enough."

He swallowed hard, not wanting to go on but knowing he had to. "There was a family I got to know—mother, grandfather, a couple of young girls, a boy of about six or seven. Cute kid— smart, lively, always trying to pick up English words. Ahmed. I didn't have much to spare, but I gave him a little penknife I used to carry on my key chain. He was proud as can be of that."

His voice choked suddenly, and he had to stop. Kate put her hand over his, her fingers tightening.

"We got ordered out, of course. Ahmed was upset, sure I was going to get killed and he'd never see me again. I told him I'd be careful. Told him we were going to chase the bad guys away so he could sleep safely in his bed. He believed me." He held her hand as if it were a lifeline. "We were gone two days, searching and not finding the enemy. And during those two days, they attacked the village. When I got back . . . the house was flattened. The room where Ahmed's mother had served us stew, where the grandfather had smoked his pipe and told stories . . . everything gone."

He had to press his hands against his eyes for a moment before he could go on. "We helped the villagers dig it out. We found Ahmed under a collapsed wall with one of his sisters. Looked like she'd tried to shelter him. He was holding that penknife in his hand."

Mac swallowed against the painful constriction in his throat. His eyes burned with the tears he wouldn't shed.

"You can't blame yourself." Kate's voice was soft. Distressed. "You couldn't have done anything else."

"I told him he'd be safe." His fingers tightened on hers. "I let him down."

"The people who attacked were responsible for his death, not you." She was silent for a moment, as if processing her own words. "Why did you tell me?"

"I think you know," he said. "We're alike, you and I. We're both fighting battles that can't be won, because they're over."

He ventured to look at her, but her head was down, her loosened hair swinging to hide her face. She was very still. Finally she took a deep breath.

"Maybe you're right. I think I'm too tired to know." She rubbed her forehead. "But I don't think I need that tea after all."

Kate stood, her hand on his shoulder for balance. With a quick movement, she bent and dropped a light kiss on his lips. "Good night, Mac. And thank you."

Although Mac's story had hardly been a soothing bedtime tale, Kate slept soundly the rest of the night. Maybe bringing their pain out into the open was good for both of them. Maybe she slept because of knowing Mac was just on the other side of the bedroom door, ready to jump into action. Whatever it was, she'd slept better than she'd have dreamed possible.

She woke to the sound of Mrs. Anderson's voice in the living room. She was lamenting the fact that she'd been out the previous night and hadn't been there to help. Mac sounded as if he were trying to stem the tide of her self-recriminations. He wasn't succeeding.

Dragging herself out of bed, Kate shoved her feet into slippers and padded to the door. She'd better go to his rescue.

"Kate!" Mrs. Anderson rushed to her the instant she heard the bedroom door. "My dear, how are you? I'm so sorry I wasn't here last night. If only I had been, you could have come to me. Why did it have to happen on the one night of the month I'm always out at my card club? I just feel so guilty."

Kate saw Mac's head come up at the mention of

Mrs. A.'s schedule. He was thinking exactly what she was. Had someone known that the bed-and-breakfast would be empty last night and planned accordingly?

"Now, I'm going right over and fixing breakfast for you, and I'll bring it here. You just relax, and I'll be back with it in a few minutes. I have an egg casserole all ready to come out of the oven."

"That sounds wonderful." Kate discovered that she was ravenous. Besides, agreeing would at least get Mrs. Anderson out of the way so she could have a word with Mac.

When Mrs. A. had bustled off to her kitchen, Kate raised her eyebrows at Mac. "So, did someone know about Mrs. Anderson's card club night?"

His lips quirked. "It wouldn't be difficult to find that out, I'm sure. Although I can't picture someone like Ax Bolt knowing or caring."

Obviously Mac was still fixated on the drug aspect. She could understand that, and certainly someone like Bolt sounded likely to resort to violence.

"Why would Bolt attack me? I don't know anything about him."

"True, but he may not realize that. He may think Jason confided in you." He stepped closer, reaching out to trace the line of her cheek with one finger. "Never mind about that for the moment. Mrs. A. will be back before we can blink. How are you?"

"Better for the sleep." She tried to move her shoulder and instantly regretted it. "Stiff. Sore."

"Taking it easy today may help. Don't forget that the pills the doctor ordered are on the kitchen counter."

"I won't." She studied his face, bristly with the night's growth of beard, eyes dark with concern for her. He looked tough. Dangerous. And so close she couldn't take a breath without inhaling the scent of him.

"Kate." His voice had deepened, roughened, and his gaze was so intent it warmed her skin.

"Here we are." The door rattled as Mrs. Anderson pushed it open with the tray she carried.

"What did I tell you?" Mac grinned.

"A good hot breakfast will make you feel much better." Mrs. A. carried the tray to the kitchen table. "And then I'll help you get washed up and dressed. It's not easy to do with your arm in a sling. I know that—did I tell you about the time I broke my wrist? I fell on an icy sidewalk."

"I remember," Mac said. "I have to go," he murmured to Kate. "It'll take some pushing to get the tests moved to the top of the list for processing. Still, if the DA thinks there's a drug connection, he'll move it along."

"There may not be," she said quickly. "You haven't forgotten . . ."

"I haven't forgotten anything." His voice was low, and his look scorched her skin. "I'll check back with you later. Meanwhile, stay in, rest and keep the dead bolt on. Okay?"

"Okay." She hurt too much to argue the point.

"Good girl." He grinned as he said it, as if he knew it would make her mad. "Take care."

The next half hour was spent eating under Mrs. Anderson's supervision and answering her many questions as briefly as possible. Finally she took refuge in claiming that the police didn't want her to discuss it with anyone. Mac hadn't actually told her that, but she felt sure he'd agree, especially if faced with this barrage of questions.

Kate was truly thankful for the woman's determination when it came to getting cleaned up and dressed. She hadn't realized how incapacitating it was to have one arm in a sling. Mrs. Anderson, having been through it herself—Kate heard the story of slipping on the ice three more times—seemed to know just what to do.

Even so, by the time they'd finished, she was exhausted and only too glad to stretch out on the sofa. After Kate promised to call immediately if she needed anything, Mrs. A. departed, leaving restful silence in her wake.

Kate smoothed her hand over the sofa, thinking of Mac. He'd have been too tall to get much rest on it, but she didn't suppose he'd have rested much, anyway. He'd been on guard, determined to keep her safe from all the things that go bump in the night. She smiled, remembering how she used to make that promise to Jason when she put him to bed.

Mac had opened up to her last night, moved by her pain to share his own private nightmares. She knew instinctively that he didn't talk about it often, if at all. That fact that he told her meant . . . well, among other things it meant that he recognized the bond between them.

It was a bond that both thrilled and dismayed her. She'd be leaving soon, and she knew now that Mac wouldn't leave Laurel Ridge. This town was his atonement for what had happened in Afghanistan. He hadn't been able to save Ahmed and his people, but he'd transferred that pain into dedication to his town and its residents. Everyone in Laurel Ridge was part of his responsibility, and he wouldn't let them down.

So while he stayed here, the guardian of this place, she would go . . . where? She didn't have a job. She didn't even have any viable lead. It had begun to look as if she'd have to find some other venue for her work than the dwindling pages of a big-city newspaper.

A wry smile crossed her face. She had fallen between the golden age of newspapers and the rise of all the other ways in which people currently found their news. But no matter where she got a job, it was hardly likely to be in this small town.

She was still mulling over the possibilities when someone tapped at the door. It opened a crack, and she belatedly remembered her promise to Mac to keep the dead bolt on.

"Hi, Kate. Okay if I come in?" Not waiting for a response, Allison entered, carrying a large basket, with which she gestured. "Enough food for a small army, courtesy of my future mother-in-law. And from Sarah, as well. And both of them said that anything you need, just call."

"It's kind of them. And a little overwhelming." She started to get up, but Allison waved her back.

"Relax. No need to get up, and I can only stay a few minutes. This would be the day we advertised all our Christmas fabrics, and we're swamped." She smiled. "Well, as swamped as anyone can be in a town of eight thousand people."

Allison rattled around in the kitchen for a few minutes and then reappeared. "There's a chicken pot pie you can heat up for your supper. And a quart of chicken soup and one of beef vegetable, canned by Ellen. And various assorted desserts. Apparently they think being injured makes you hungry."

Kate shook her head, gesturing to the chair opposite her. "As I said, overwhelming."

Allison settled herself in the chair, looking as

341

sleek and pulled together as if she were posing for a layout in *Country Living*. "I know what you mean. That was my reaction when I first came to Laurel Ridge. But people here look out for each other. I'd never lived in a small town before." She smiled. "And now I'm settling down here for life."

"No downsides?" she asked.

Allison grinned. "Well, you do have to get used to everyone wanting to know your business. And the gossip flies faster than you'd believe. By the time something appears in the paper, everyone knows it already."

"I hate to think what they're saying about me." Kate could imagine the talk.

"Not as bad as you might suppose. Being approved by the Whitings means something in Laurel Ridge."

Kate didn't know what to say to that, but Allison didn't seem to expect an answer.

"Mac comes across as a tough guy," Allison went on, and Kate didn't think the comment was as random as it sounded.

"He's a cop. I suppose he has to." Kate's thoughts flickered to her late stepfather, only to discover that some of her anger with him seemed to have dissipated. Before she could assess that, Allison was continuing.

"But Mac has a tender heart under that tough exterior. I'd hate to see him get hurt."

So Allison thought she needed a warning, did she? Well, she might be a bit too late.

"I'd hate that, too. But sometimes it can't be avoided." She met Allison's gaze and hoped the woman understood.

Getting hurt was the flip side of caring, and she expected both she and Mac might fall victim to it.

Allison studied her face a moment longer, and then she gave a nod, apparently satisfied. "Well, I'd better get back to the shop. Remember, if you need anything . . ."

"I'll call," Kate said, but she suspected she wouldn't. She was used to taking care of herself. Laurel Ridge had nibbled away at that independence, but she'd better grasp it back before anyone else got hurt.

Mac hung up the phone after calling the lab and extracting a promise that they'd get to his samples soonest. He had too much experience to expect that to happen in the near future.

He had to force himself to sit still and think things through. Urgency pushed at him—the need to do something, anything, that would resolve this problem and keep Kate safe. There was no point in rushing off half-cocked. Unfortunately, he couldn't approach keeping Kate safe with the same protective attitude he had toward everyone else in this town. His feelings about her were way too complicated and primal for that.

Marge buzzed through from the outer office. "Sheila called from Russell Sheldon's house while you were on the phone. She says he wants to see you right away. Can I tell her you'll be right over?"

Mac hesitated. He wanted to talk to everyone involved in Blackburn House himself, not leave it in Johnny's inexperienced hands. But there was always the possibility that Russ remembered something about Jason—something important to resolving the riddle of his death.

He blew out a frustrated breath, hoping this wouldn't be a wild-goose chase. "Okay. Tell her I'm on my way."

When he reached the house, Sheila was waiting to open the door for him. "Hey, Sheila. Is something wrong?"

"I guess not." She sounded unsure, and her good-natured face was troubled. "He seems pretty much with it today, but he's got a bee in his bonnet about seeing you. It was all I could do to keep him from walking down to the station." She sent a furtive glance toward the living room. "You know he'd get lost if he tried to do that, but hc's determined."

"It's okay. I'll talk to him." He patted her arm reassuringly. "It'll be okay."

But when he reached the archway to the living room, he wasn't so sure. Using a cane to help,

Russ Sheldon was thumping his way across the room. Ruffy, apparently knowing his master was upset, whined plaintively, tail and ears down.

"There you are at last." Russ shot the words at him in a tone Mac didn't remember ever hearing from him before. Russ had always been the perfect gentleman, even when things were not going according to plan.

"Sorry I didn't get here more quickly." Mac took his arm and guided him toward his usual chair. "Let's sit down, and you can tell me all about whatever is troubling you."

Russ shook off his arm. "I can sit myself." Then, seeming to hear his temper, Russ shook his head, looking sheepish. "Sorry. Not your fault. I'm just so angry with myself that I didn't tell you before."

"So you'll tell me now." Mac kept his voice calm and easy, despite the questions that raged through him. "I'm right here."

For a moment Russ stared down at the Oriental carpet. Then he shook his head. "Not your fault," he said again. "It's a terrible thing to feel your mind failing." Russ raised his head to look at Mac. "That's why I wanted to talk right away, while it's still clear in my mind."

Mac felt a twinge of pity and knew it would be unwelcome. Russ Sheldon was a proud man. He didn't invite sympathy, let alone pity. For a moment he had an insight into what it must be like to know that your thoughts and memories, the very essence of yourself, was slipping away.

Russ reached out a hand to the dog, and Ruffy pressed his head against the hand with a soft whine.

"You came here before, asking about Jason. You and that girl—his sister."

"That's right. She wants to know why he killed himself."

The old man's lips quivered slightly, and he pressed them together. "You know that there were problems with the accounts, don't you?"

Mac nodded. "You said something about it, and I got the story out of Bart. How someone had messed up the account records, and they thought it was Jason." He studied the man's face. "You told us something was your fault. Was that what you meant?" He should have taken Russ's words more seriously at the time, but he'd known someone as conscientious as Russ always would think any problem was his fault.

Tears welled in Sheldon's eyes. "My fault. It wasn't just a mix-up. Money was missing."

Mac zeroed in on him, startled. "No one has even come close to suggesting that."

"It's truc," Sheldon insisted. "I know it's true. And I know that boy—Jason—he wasn't to blame."

Bart hadn't even hinted at malfeasance. The thought shot through him, upsetting all his assumptions. "Bart told me that it was just a matter of messing up some of the accounts."

"Money was missing." Russell insisted. "I know. Bart wanted to cover it up. He said we'd get in trouble with the authorities if it became known. It would ruin the business."

That made sense. He could hear Bart saying just that. He wouldn't want a scandal, not even . . .

"What happened? Did Bart make up the difference with his own money?"

"We did it between the two of us. I couldn't let Bart bear the cost himself." He shook his head. "That's not the important thing. The important thing is that Bart blamed Jason. He was so sure. Nothing had happened until Jason came to work with us, he said, so it had to be Jason."

Mac tried to wrap his head around it. "Surely an intern didn't have that kind of access to funds, did he?"

"That's what I said. I kept saying it and saying it, but Bart didn't listen. He was so sure."

"Did he accuse Jason to his face?" The versions he'd heard about that last day certainly hadn't included this. If it was true, Bart had lied to him. Or at least, omitted a good part of the truth.

"He called Jason in. Said he knew what Jason had done. That he had to go that minute. The boy tried to defend himself, but Bart wouldn't listen to a word." Tears welled in Russ's eyes.

"It wasn't fair. It wasn't right. But once Bart gets an idea in his head, nothing can budge him. He won't listen to anyone."

"So when Jason Reilley left the office that day, he had been accused of theft. Did Bart intend to prosecute?"

"No, no, he wouldn't do that. The publicity would kill the firm. He told Jason he wouldn't go to the authorities, but he said he'd make sure Jason never got another job in the field." Russ lifted a trembling hand to his face to wipe at the tears, and Ruffy whined, pressing against his knee.

"Did you speak up for Jason?" It was probably a cruel question to put, but Mac had to know all of it. The truth, for once.

"I tried. God help me, I did try. But not—not hard enough. It wasn't Jason. I know it wasn't." He was shaking now, his face white.

"Easy." Mac put a hand on Russ's arm. "Take it easy. No one is blaming you."

"I am." Sobs racked his body, so that his words were barely comprehensible. "I'm to blame. Jason didn't do it. It must have been me."

Sheila, hearing the upset, hurried into the room, putting her arms around the old man's shoulders. "Here, now. You don't want to go getting all upset."

He turned to her like a child seeking sympathy. "I did it. I'm guilty."

Sheila's gaze met Mac's, and she shook her head. "Now, Russell, you know that's not so. You wouldn't steal from your own firm." Obviously she'd been listening from the hallway.

"My fault," he managed between sobs. "My fault. There's no one else. It must be me."

"Hush, now, hush. You don't want me to have to call the doctor, do you? Everything's going to be all right. Mac will take care of it." Her gaze challenged Mac.

"I'll take care of it," he echoed. "It's all right." He got up, mind spinning.

How much of that was true, and how much the ramblings of someone whose mind was going? Upset by Jason's death, Russ might well have brooded on it until convinced he'd caused it.

Mac didn't know. And until he was sure, how could he tell Kate that Russ thought he'd stolen from the firm? She'd insist on confronting him, and the damage that might do to Russ . . . Well, he just couldn't risk it. Not until he was sure this wasn't a figment of Russ's imagination.

He was letting Kate down, reneging on his agreement to share information. Whatever he did, someone was going to get hurt. All he could do was find the truth, and let the chips fall where they may.

CHAPTER SEVENTEEN

When she couldn't stand the solitude any longer, Kate ventured out onto the porch. It was cooler today, with a chill in the air that reminded her it was fall. Time was passing.

She'd come here in hope of laying to rest her burden of grief and guilt. Unfortunately, what she'd found out was that no matter what answers turned up, she'd never be able to deny her responsibility for Jason. She wouldn't want to.

Knowing the people he'd met here, seeing the place where he'd died—none of that was as important as the Jason she carried in her heart.

Was she any nearer to finding the answers that had brought her to Laurel Ridge? It didn't seem so, but maybe that was the pain talking.

Giving in to depression wouldn't help. She'd be better off doing something, even if it led nowhere. She'd go over to Blackburn House—take a look at the scene of her misadventure in the daylight. Maybe something would come back to her. Or one of the people there might remember anything odd that had happened yesterday. Surely, if Ax Bolt had been in the building to plan a trap for her, someone would have noticed him. The most trivial incident would be better than what she had now.

Moving cautiously, she headed for the path through the shrubbery. She'd come this way last night, rushing and frightened for Emily. Running right into a trap that had been set for her.

Kate spotted a few broken twigs. She'd probably done that in her hurry. There was the root she'd stumbled on, nearly falling. She stepped over it carefully, mindful of how the slightest jolt sent the pain ricocheting through her shoulder.

If she hadn't gone rushing off, would Mac have caught the person playing tricks in the building? Somehow she didn't think it would have been that easy. There were too many hiding places, too many ways out of the old place. The person they sought was too clever to be caught so easily.

Why? She came back to the primary question again. Why would someone want to harm her? It wasn't as if she'd discovered anything. She didn't have a clue to the person who'd attacked her. The person who'd probably, in some way, led Jason to his death.

Kate came out into the open by the driveway with clenched fists. Who? Why? This was more frustrating than knowing nothing at all.

The yellow crime scene tape still adorned the outside of the side door, so it didn't look as if she could retrace her steps that far. She headed around the building toward the front door. She needed to do something.

The police had the search for Bolt well in hand, and there was nothing she could do that they couldn't do better. If Jason had died because he knew too much about drugs coming into town, Mac would find out.

But if someone else was involved, either because of drugs or for some other reason, it was possible that person would make a slip talking to her. A slim hope, she supposed, but better than sitting and brooding.

Not all lies indicated guilt. Some people just had to embroider what they knew, trying to appear important. Others were careful to present themselves in the best possible light. She'd dealt with both types as a reporter. It shouldn't be difficult to tell the difference, not if she listened as a reporter instead of as a grieving sister.

She'd nearly forgotten how imposing Blackburn House was from the front. The Italianate mansion must have been quite something when it was the most important house in town. Even now, its graceful lines and balanced exterior gave an air of dignity to the housing of shops and businesses.

Maybe the best place to start was with Nikki. Maybe, since Larry's injury and the focus on Ax Bolt, she'd be more forthcoming about her relationship with Jason. And Jason's relationship with his job. She could slip back to the bookshop and call her from there on the chance she could get out this afternoon.

Little though she would have imagined it a few weeks ago, she'd begun to care about this town. These were good people, by and large, and they didn't deserve either drug dealers or untrustworthy investment brokers.

No sooner had Kate entered the front hall than she realized that the idea of "slipping" anywhere without being seen was absurd. Sarah spotted her first and came hurrying from the quilt shop, calling to Allison. And Nick Whiting came out of the cabinetry showroom, leaving a pair of customers staring at what looked like samples.

"Hey, how are you?" Nick reached her first with the long, purposeful stride that reminded her of his brother.

"Shouldn't you be resting?" Sarah's expression was anxious.

"Of course she should." Allison shook her head at Kate. "Mac is right. You're stubborn."

Nick grinned. "If that isn't the pot calling the kettle black, I don't know what is."

"If you're implying I'm stubborn . . ." Allison began.

Sarah interrupted by putting her arm around Kate's waist. "Won't you come in the shop and sit for a bit? I'll fix you a cup of tea."

Their kindness was not only overwhelming, it was nearly suffocating. If she were on a city street, she could collapse in pain and everyone would walk on by.

"That's kind of you." She disengaged herself firmly. "But I must go and see Emily. She called earlier, sounding so upset that I thought she'd like to see for herself that I'm all right."

Sarah still looked concerned, but she nodded. "*Ja*, that's what it will take with Emily for sure. But if you need to rest afterward, you'll come to us, ain't so?"

Irrationally touched, Kate had no choice but to agree. "I will. Thanks."

Allison insisted on walking with her back to the bookshop, just to be sure she was all right. "Mac would kill me if I let something happen to you," she said, half laughing, half serious.

"Mac worries too much."

"Not without reason," Allison said. She gave Kate's hand a squeeze, and they parted at the door.

Of course Emily rushed at her but stopped short of an embrace. "I don't want to hurt your poor shoulder. I'm so upset about it. Mac told me you thought I was in the building when the lights went out and that's why you came rushing over and got hurt. Oh, my goodness, I can't tell you how sorry I am. If only . . ."

"It wasn't your fault." Kate put her good arm around Emily and gave her a hug. Amazing, how people instantly assumed the burden of guilt. "I should have been more careful."

And she was careful now, not sure what Mac might have told Emily. From her comments, it sounded as if Mac let her believe it was an accident, which might be the best thing.

Emily dabbed at her eyes. "Well, you surely didn't think you had to come in to work today."

"No, I didn't intend to. I just felt like stretching my legs, and I thought I'd show you that I'm okay." Although actually, her shoulder was starting to ache right up to her back teeth. "Is it okay if I use the phone? I just thought of a call I should make."

"Of course, of course." Emily waved to the phone. "When I came in, there was powdery stuff all over it. I don't know what Mac was thinking about to leave it that way. But it's all cleaned up now. I'll just take care of some things in the back room as long as you're here, but you call me if a customer comes in."

Kate nodded, assuming that was Emily's way of giving her some privacy while she used the phone. And really, she could use it, given the difficulty she was likely to have getting Nikki to meet her again.

Simple enough to call the office number and ask if she was alone. At Nikki's cautious agreement, the job began in earnest.

"I have to see you again." No point in beating around the bush. "We need to talk."

"You shouldn't have called me at work." Nikki

sounded as if she were looking over her shoulder as she talked.

"How else was I going to get hold of you? Anyway, they can't know who you're talking to. Just don't mention my name."

"I know a better way," Nikki said. "I'll just hang up."

"Don't." She thought fast. "I suppose you heard what happened to me last night."

"I heard you had an accident."

"It wasn't an accident. Any more than what happened to Larry was an accident. I'm getting too close to something. That's why I need to talk to you again. You can help me figure out what."

"No." The word came quickly. "It's dangerous to be around you. Besides, if Mr. Gordon found out . . ."

"He won't. We'll meet someplace he'd never go. Out in public, so it's safe. Come on, Nikki. You were Jason's friend. Don't you want to help him?"

She sensed hesitation in Nikki's silence.

"Listen, meet me the same place as last time. Around eight. No one at the office will suspect a thing." She didn't wait for agreement. "I'll see you then." She hung up quickly before Nikki could find any other arguments.

She barely had time to look up before she saw Lina Oberlin entering the shop. For an instant she thought Lina had somehow found out about her call, but sheer common sense asserted itself. Lina couldn't possibly know.

Lina started toward her, a smile pinned to her face. "Kate, I'm so happy to see you out and about. Some of the rumors have you lying in the hospital unconscious."

"Rumors always exaggerate. I'm a little sore from falling down the stairs, but otherwise fine."

Setting her bag on the counter, Lina studied Kate as if looking for damage. "I must say, you look better than I expected. Just a little pale. Is that a bruise on your head? Are the doctors sure you don't have a concussion?"

"Positive." Kate brushed a strand of hair across the angry-looking bruise. "I've always been told I have a hard head, and I guess that's true."

Lina's visit to check up on her was a bit surprising, since Kate hadn't seen her since the day she'd stopped by the cottage to chat. Maybe Bart had sent her, hoping for news that she was leaving town?

"In this case, it must be an advantage. But what happened? I heard you interrupted a burglar."

How much did the woman actually know? If Mac was downplaying the attack on her, he probably had a reason.

"I'm not sure of anything." Maybe her fall would excuse anything she might seem to have forgotten. "I came over because I saw all the lights go off in the building. I guess I must have fallen in the dark."

"That's not surprising. I was in the building once when the power went off, and I couldn't see a thing. I had to grope my way out. You're lucky it wasn't worse. But nothing was disturbed in our offices. Was anything taken down here?"

"Not that I know of. I suppose I might have made enough noise to scare someone away. Or it could have been an electrical fault."

"That's just what I was telling Bart. It could have happened to any of us." Her expression seemed to say she was suppressing Bart's opinion.

"Let me guess," Kate said. "He thinks it serves me right for poking around."

Lina gave a wry smile. "Something like that. You have to understand that he's worried about the business. The past few years haven't been easy." She shook her head. "Sometimes he talks about throwing it all over and retiring to a Caribbean island, but I don't know how he'd afford to do that."

She was about to say that she thought Bart would rather be a big frog in a little pond, but decided that wouldn't be tactful.

Lina picked up her bag as if preparing to leave, half turned and then stopped. "I . . . I suppose you know from Mac Whiting that Bart fired your brother."

"Yes." She waited, suspecting there was more to come.

"I just wanted to say that I'm sorry I couldn't tell you the whole story when I spoke with you before. Bart was so determined not to let anything out that might reflect badly on him, and I need my job. He's not one to forgive and forget if he thinks someone has betrayed his trust."

Kate would like to believe she wouldn't knuckle under to a boss like that, but what did she know about Lina's circumstances? So she just nodded.

Lina, apparently satisfied, left more quickly than she'd come in, leaving Kate wondering what her real purpose had been. Trying to absolve herself of any blame for Jason's death? Clearing her own conscience? She wasn't sure.

But the things Lina had let fall about Bart's financial troubles were interesting. Everyone seemed to assume any problems with the firm had been due to Russell Sheldon's failing mental powers. Was it possible that it was Bart who couldn't live up to the reputation Sheldon had built for the firm?

And if so, might he have been responsible for the errors he'd blamed on Jason?

She'd like to talk it over with Mac, but she hadn't heard a word from him since this morning. Toying with the idea of calling him, Kate pulled out her phone and felt that familiar curl of warmth in her stomach at the thought of hearing his voice.

She shoved her phone out of sight. Things were tangled enough between them without her chasing him down when he was working. And what exactly was she going to do about that?

Mac still hadn't figured out a way to look into that worrying claim Russ had made. He could never get an audit of the business ordered on that basis. He could try to talk to some of the investors, but he'd have to choose carefully if he didn't want the news getting right back to Bart.

The search for Ax Bolt seemed more urgent. He'd had a call from a nearby force, saying rumors indicated Bolt was back in Laurel Ridge. What he needed was a lead on where to look for him. So he headed to the hospital to see if he could get anything new out of Larry Foust.

According to his sources, Larry was nearly back to normal, but he'd conned the doctors into keeping him another day or two. Maybe he felt safer there.

Larry seemed to have known Bolt as well as anyone he'd found, and Mac intended to get it out of him. Even if hc had to bulldoze his way past Larry's anxious mother.

But when he opened the door to the room, Ethel wasn't in evidence. Instead, Larry was sitting up in bed, trying unsuccessfully, it seemed, to kiss the nurse's aide. She swatted him away with an experienced hand. When she saw Mac, she looked relieved.

"He's all yours, Chief. I'm done. He can give himself a back rub from now on."

"Sounds like a good plan," Mac said. He approached the bed but waited until she was out of the room.

Larry pulled the sheet up, looking apprehensive, and pushed himself back on the pillow. "I can't talk now. I'm too sick."

"Not according to your doctor," Mac said.

Larry made a dive for the call button, but Mac grabbed it and tossed it out of reach.

"I don't think so. Let's just have a nice, quiet chat, you and me."

"You can't talk to me without my mother here." Larry was beginning to look panicky.

"Forget it, Larry. You're not a minor, much as you act like one. You can talk to me here and now, or I'll take you in for questioning. Then word would really get around," he added, guessing that was what Larry feared most.

"I don't have to say anything." Folding his lips, he tried to look resolute and only succeeded in looking like the spoiled brat he was.

"That's your right," Mac agreed. "But then I might have to let folks think you had. How would your buddy Ax Bolt feel about that?"

Larry paled. "You can't do that. You don't

know him—he might do anything. He already—"

"He already beat you up once, right? Why? Because he thought you'd said something about him to Kate Beaumont?"

It was a shot in the dark, but it seemed to work.

"No! No, I never . . . He never . . ." Larry buried his face in his hands.

"Look, nobody can blame you for being scared of him. He's bad news. Won't you be better off if we put him away for a nice long stretch?"

"I wish I was dead," Larry muttered into his hands.

"You might be if you don't help us put him away. Come on, talk. Tell me where he hangs out when he's in town."

"He crashes sometimes with some guys in a house down at the end of Miller Street."

"The place that looks ready for the bulldozer?" He knew the house. He'd suspected the residents of dealing, but he hadn't caught them at it. Not yet.

Larry nodded, seeming a little calmer now that he'd started. "Phil's Roadhouse. He's there sometimes. And he shows up at the Lamplight once in a while."

"Anyplacc clse? Any way you contact him?"

"I don't know any more. I swear it. Just promise me he'll never know I'm the one who told you. Promise!"

Mac suspected he wasn't doing a very good job

of hiding his opinion of the kid. "He won't hear it from me." He tossed the call button back on the bed. "You might try behaving like a decent human being for once in your life."

He stalked out, already setting up a plan of action. He'd put Foster on to keep an unobtrusive eye on the house on Miller Street. Come to think of it, George would probably do a better job of being unobtrusive. He'd need Johnny himself later on. If Bolt was in town, he wouldn't appear at either of the other hangouts until well after dark.

Mac could pick up Bolt for the assault on Larry, at least. And that would give them a chance to dig for more evidence. The attacks on both Larry and Kate might well be classified as attempted murder, in which case Bolt would be going away for a good long time.

By the time she reached the cottage again, Kate was too tired even to think. Exhaustion had swept over her as sudden and fierce as a tidal wave. Maybe the doctor had meant it when he'd told her to take it easy for a few days. She collapsed on the sofa, not even willing to walk the few extra feet to the bedroom.

The persistent ringing of her cell phone finally penetrated, bringing her reluctantly awake. She dived for the phone, lying on the floor next to the sofa, trying to orient herself.

"Hello?" She blinked, rubbing her eyes.

"Kate, are you okay?" Mac's voice was sharp with concern.

She swung her feet to the floor. "Fine. Sorry if I sound foggy. I'd fallen asleep."

"Too bad I couldn't wake you in person." His voice deepened. "Sorry."

Kate pushed away the image that brought to her mind. "Any news?"

"A couple of things. Kristie called. She's gone through the tapes and wants to talk to you about what she found. Okay if she comes over now?"

"Yes, of course." Kate ran her fingers through her tangled hair. "Are you coming over?"

"Can't. A couple of leads to Bolt have surfaced, and I need to follow up. You can fill me in later. Listen, about tonight . . ."

"I'm fine on my own," she said quickly. "No dizziness, no blurred vision, just tired. I don't need a babysitter." And if he came, they'd be together in that shared intimacy that was bound to lead to more. He shouldn't, because of the case. And she shouldn't, because . . . well, because she was leaving, wasn't she?

"You're probably right. There's too much at stake to let things between us get out of control. But I'll check in with you later if I can, okay?"

"Okay." Now was the moment when she should tell him she'd arranged to meet Nikki. But if she did, he'd only object, and she didn't have the energy for an argument. She'd rather act first and apologize later.

When he'd hung up, Kate splashed some water on her face and made a few necessary repairs. She'd barely run a brush through her hair when she heard the doorbell. Kristie must have been on her way even before Mac called.

She hurried to the door to let Kristie in. The girl looked her over as she entered.

"I heard you'd had an accident. Wow."

Kate fluffed her hair over the by-now-spectacular bruise that she suspected was going to turn into a black eye. "Not as bad as it looks," she lied. "What do you have for me?"

Kristie dumped her backpack on the floor next to the sofa and burrowed into it. "Here's the flash drive back, like I promised." She waved a folder. "I didn't do a transcription of the whole thing, but I separated the references by his individual recordings."

Kate took the folder, flipping it open. It didn't take more than a glance at the first page to see that Kristie more than lived up to Mac's recommendation.

"This is excellent work." She leafed through it. "I didn't dream you'd be able to identify so many references."

"Once a fantasy geek, always a fantasy geek." Kristie grinned. "I didn't run across anything I didn't either know or could find out by some quick research." She hesitated. "We had the same taste in games and fiction. Makes me wish I'd known him."

Kate nodded, her throat suddenly tight.

" 'Course I didn't know who he meant—well, most of the time." Kristie hurried on, as if embarrassed by the moment of emotion. "But I figured if you knew what each character was like, you'd be able to make a pretty good guess."

"What about that one character he mentions toward the end? Baldicer, I think it was."

Kristie nodded. "He was kind of cagey about that—almost like he wasn't sure and didn't want to commit himself, you know? But in the fantasy series where Baldicer appears, he's a shape-shifter, able to take on different forms. He also switches from one side to the other, always with his own gain in mind. You know?"

"I see." She didn't, not entirely, but knowing this much was a good step to understanding. "I can't wait to go through the journal again with your notes in front of me."

Kristie rose, gathering up her backpack and slinging it over her shoulder. "I hope it helps."

"Wait a second." Kate grabbed her bag. "You have to let me give you something for your time."

"No, no." Kristie looked horrified at the suggestion. "I don't want anything. My folks would kill me if I took money for helping. And I don't know what Mac would say." She scurried to the door. "Good luck. Let me know if you run into anything you don't get, okay?"

She was gone before Kate could protest again.

Kate sat for a moment, staring at the printed pages. It would have been easier for her if she'd been able to pay Kristie. Why?

Because she didn't want to accept help from anyone. If she paid, it was like employing a professional to do what she couldn't.

That didn't seem as admirable as she'd thought. Was there something wrong with a person who couldn't accept the generosity of others? She had a feeling that Mac, at least, would think so.

CHAPTER EIGHTEEN

Kate reached the Lamplight before Nikki. Nodding to Pete behind the bar, she snagged a table for two near the back wall. With the jukebox blaring, it was unlikely anyone would be able to hear them talking. Assuming, that is, that Nikki actually showed up.

Well, Nikki or not, she'd made a little progress this afternoon with the help of Kristie's explanations. It hadn't taken much imagination to identify Russell Sheldon as the King, and Kristie had added a brief explanation of the plot of a popular game which had a courtier killing the aged king in order to take his throne. A reference to Bart? It sounded so. From what Jason said, he believed Sheldon was being pushed into a retirement he didn't want.

Had anything other than pushing gone on? Maybe Bart had just been lucky that the course of Sheldon's illness seemed to accelerate.

The shape-shifter references had been harder to track down, mainly because it wasn't clear whether the character belonged to his office life or his personal life. Larry? She could imagine Larry playing both sides. Or could he have referred to Nikki? She certainly seemed to have her eyes open for any chance of furthering her own ambitions.

Her thoughts had reached that point when she spotted Nikki herself, weaving her way through the occupied tables toward her. The tavern had been filling up steadily, but mostly in the bar area, where it was smoky and noisy.

Nikki plunked herself down in a chair. "Whew! Just in time. I need a beer." Before Kate could speak, she was waving a server over. "You don't mind, do you? If you don't grab someone fast, they forget about you."

"Good idea. You want something to eat? A sandwich or an appetizer?"

"Let's get some wings to share." The server was there, so Nikki ordered, adding nachos to the wings. Apparently if someone else was buying, she was hungry.

Kate passed on the beer, ordering a soft drink instead. If she had to take one of the pain pills to sleep tonight, she didn't want any alcohol in her system.

Once the server left to put their order in, Kate focused on Nikki. "You look like it's been one of those days," she commented.

"So do you," Nikki said.

"But I have a good excuse," she said, smiling. "I fell down the stairs."

"Yeah, I heard." Nikki eyed her curiously. "That all there was to it?"

Kate shrugged. "Apparently it was a false alarm about a burglar in the building." No burglar, just someone intent on harming her. "What about you?"

Nikki consulted her face in a pocket mirror before answering. "Boring, as usual. Until late this afternoon. Then everything blew up."

"What happened?"

"Mr. Sheldon called. He hardly ever uses the phone anymore, from what I heard, but it was him, sure enough. He wanted to talk to Bart, and he wasn't taking no for an answer."

Kate's attention sharpened still more. "Why do you say that? Didn't Bart want to talk to him?"

Nikki shrugged. "Didn't act like it. He tried to say he was too busy, and Mr. Sheldon told me to interrupt him. So I told Bart he'd better take it."

"What did they say?"

"You think I'd listen?" Nikki grinned. "I tried. But Bart came to the door and glared at me, so I had to hang up. I could tell he didn't want anyone else to hear."

"How much *did* you manage to hear?"

"Mr. Sheldon said he'd talked to the chief. Said he wasn't going to put up with having Jason blamed for something he didn't do. Said Jason was innocent, and everyone should know it."

Kate sucked in a breath, hardly able to take in what she was hearing. "Let me get this straight. Sheldon said he'd already talked to Mac?"

"I think so. Yeah, I'm sure that's what he said."

If Mac had known about this, if he'd known and hadn't told her . . .

She forced herself to set that aside for the moment. "What did Bart do next?"

"Came storming out of his office, swearing like a crazy person. He charged out the door without a word to anyone." Nikki leaned back, pleased with the effect of her words.

Kate paused, considering. "How did Lina react to that?"

"I don't think she liked it much, but she knows when Bart's in that kind of mood, there's no talking to him."

"You think he was going to see Mr. Sheldon?"

"Maybe." She seemed a little doubtful. "He didn't say he was."

Kate looked down, turning her glass and watching the wet circles form on the scarred table top. "Did you ever get the feeling that Bart wanted to push Mr. Sheldon out of the business?"

"I don't know about pushed." Nikki seemed to develop some belated caution. "I'd guess he wanted to take over, all right. He'd say things sometimes about Mr. Sheldon being too conservative. He wanted to move investments faster, he said, to take advantage of the market."

Thinking of the courtly old gentleman, Kate could imagine what Sheldon thought of that.

"You know, the person Mr. Sheldon really trusted for advice was Lina," Nikki said. "He always said she knew as much about the business as he did."

Kate nodded. That was her impression of the office dynamic as well, both from what she'd observed and what Jason had said. The office manager often was the linchpin that held the place together.

Their food arrived then. Kate let Nikki help herself. Her own mind was too busy for eating.

"What do you think it meant? What Mr. Sheldon said about Jason being innocent?"

Nikki shrugged. "Dunno. But he sure sounded determined about it. You should talk to him yourself."

"I will." That was a promise. She glanced at her watch, realizing it was already too late for calling on Sheldon. He was probably in bed already. But soon.

As for Mac, and whatever he knew that he hadn't told her—the only thing to do was to ask him. She shouldn't start blaming him without the facts. But there was a cold lump in the pit of her stomach that told her she wasn't going to like the answers.

A sudden change in the level of chatter in the room had her looking up. Mac stood just inside the door, flanked by Foster and another of his part-timers. His gaze scanned the space, and when it reached her it paused for a fraction of a second.

Even from across the room she could see his jaw tighten. Then he continued his survey of the place. He wasn't here for her. He was here in pursuit of someone, and she was right in the middle of it.

He might have known that Kate wouldn't stay quietly at home where she belonged. She should have told him she was meeting with Nikki tonight. Now she'd put herself right in the middle of his arrest.

Not that he expected Bolt to cause any trouble. He'd outfoxed the system enough times that Mac wouldn't doubt he could do it again. If Mac had a choice, he wouldn't be doing this in a crowded room, most especially with Kate here. But Bolt had eluded him for too long, and Mac wasn't taking a chance that he'd do it again.

The roar of talk, which had died down a little when he came in, reasserted itself. Mac had spotted Bolt, leaning against the end of the bar. He acted as if he hadn't noticed them, but he was casting surreptitious glances at the mirror.

A slight gesture of Mac's hand had the two patrolmen separating, working their way casually toward either end of the bar. Mac headed toward the bar, nodding to Pete.

Pete, seeming to sense something, sidled toward

the spot under the bar where Mac knew he kept the small baseball bat his kid had outgrown. He always said it was the ideal size to discourage the rowdy without seriously injuring anyone.

Mac shook his head slightly, and Pete eased off, though his hand lingered near the bat. Mac would prefer to do this without the need for baseball bats or any other weapons. A nice, clean, uncomplicated pickup was all he wanted—all that was usually necessary in Laurel Ridge, barring the occasional combative drunk.

When he got about eight feet from the man, he said his name. "Ax Bolt?"

Bolt turned slowly, his narrow face insolent. "Who wants to know?"

"Police. We'd like to have a word."

Bolt shrugged, turning back toward the beer on the bar. "So talk all you want. I got nothing to hide."

"Not here." Mac took a step closer even as the men standing next to Bolt moved away, as if advertising the fact that they weren't with him. "Let's step outside."

"Hey, you can let a man finish his beer, can't you?" Bolt reached for the bottle. "What's it all about, anyhow?"

"Your buddy, Larry Foust, ran into a little trouble."

"Not my business. I hardly know the guy."

Bolt's voice sounded casual, but his hand moved toward the neck of the bottle.

"Then our talk won't take long." Mac moved a step nearer even as the patrolmen closed in from either side. The usual tavern noise had ceased, as those at the bar found a reason to back away. "Let's go."

Bolt grabbed the bottle. Whirled toward him, slamming the bottom of the bottle against the bar. He swung the jagged edges toward Mac, beer splashing.

Mac gave an elaborate sigh. "Now, what did you want to go and do that for?"

"Stay away from me!" Bolt swung the bottle in an arc that included the two patrolmen.

"What good is this going to do?" Mac kept his voice casual. Easy. Nothing would be gained by escalating the situation. "You know this will just make things worse. Even if you get out of here, I'll have to put out an alert on you, and half the police in the county will be looking for you for resisting arrest. You can't win that way."

"You move over there." Bolt gestured to the left with the bottle.

In answer, Mac pulled out his handcuffs. "No, I'm not going to do that. You just drop the bottle and keep your hands where I can see them. Come on now. Don't make a bad situation worse by overreacting."

The room seemed frozen, as if the crowd held

its collective breath. Mac kept his gaze focused on Bolt's face, but from the corner of his eye he caught Foster edge closer, saw Pete's hand emerge holding the bat.

Mac waited. And saw the exact moment when Bolt decided not to fight. Slowly, both hands visible, he put the bottle on the bar.

"Good decision." Mac stepped forward, and the other two closed in. In a moment Bolt was handcuffed.

Some of his bravado came back as they moved toward the door, and Foster began to read him his rights. "Forget it. I've heard it all before. Whatever happened to Foust, I didn't have anything to do with it. And you can't prove any different."

"We'll see about that." Foster propelled him through the door.

Mac did a quick mental list of all that had to be done—find Bolt's vehicle, for one thing. Notify the DA, in case he wanted to sit in on the questioning. And do a detailed search of the place where Bolt had been staying.

Not enough staff for all that had to be done, but they'd manage. He wanted Laurel Ridge's problems kept right here, under his control. He'd deal with them, like always.

As for Kate . . . well, he was going to have more than a few words to say to her about tonight, but not now. If he could get the truth out of Bolt, it might be that Kate's problem would be resolved, or at least as much as it was ever likely to be. That was the thing she'd have trouble accepting, he knew. Even if she found the truth, it wouldn't be enough to take away the pain.

When the door closed behind Mac and his prisoner, Kate realized she'd been barely breathing throughout the encounter. She sucked in a breath and ran the palms of her hands down her pant legs. Despite everything that had happened since she'd come to Laurel Ridge, she'd never really imagined Mac putting his life on the line in the course of his work.

She'd often thought that in Philly, of course—every time Tom was late coming home she'd wondered. But not here. It left her without words.

Not so with Nikki.

"Wow! I never saw an actual arrest before. Did you? I didn't know what to do. What if that creep had had a gun? What if he cut somebody with that bottle? Mac could have been killed, right?"

"Don't!" The force of her response startled her. "I mean, I'm sure he had everything under control."

That seemed to be what Mac wanted in every area of his life. Control. She understood why, at least in part. He'd seen the innocent die because a situation went out of control. Not that it had been his fault, but no one would ever convince him of that.

Nikki, finding Kate nonresponsive, turned to the next table and was soon involved in marveling about what had happened with someone else, leaving Kate prey to her own thoughts.

What was Bolt's arrest going to mean? Did Mac have some evidence implicating him in the attack on Larry? Or the one on her? She came back up against the question that haunted her. Why?

If Bolt had supplied the pills Jason had taken, he might have been afraid Larry had ratted on him. He might think she had some evidence from Jason of where he'd gotten the pills.

But even so, that was just *what,* not *why.* The motive was still an open question. Unless Mac's idea had been on target. If Jason had threatened to blow the whistle of Bolt's drug operation, Bolt might have been frightened enough to kill him.

No marks of violence on Jason's body, she reminded herself. How would someone like Ax Bolt be able to persuade Jason to take an overdose? She couldn't imagine them sitting down together for a friendly drink in the cemetery. That seemed a strong argument against murder, at least by Bolt.

She came back to her conviction about Jason's death. If he had taken his own life, it must relate to what had happened at the office. Murder or suicide? Which?

She abruptly reclaimed Nikki's attention by grabbing her arm.

"Tell me again exactly what was said today by Mr. Sheldon and by Bart Gordon."

Nikki obviously found the current drama far more interesting. "I already told you everything."

"So tell me again. You might remember something else."

Nikki gave an elaborate sigh and apparently decided to humor her. Unfortunately, she didn't add much of anything to the story, just repeating what she'd already said. Mr. Sheldon was insistent on talking to Bart, Bart tried to avoid him, and the bit about Sheldon saying he'd told the chief that Jason was innocent.

Innocent of what? And how did Mr. Sheldon know? If it was true he'd been failing in those last months, would he have even noticed?

Kate rubbed her temples. A headache was building, fueled by the incessant noise and the cigarette smoke. She felt as if it throbbed in time with the beat coming from the jukebox.

Why hadn't Mac told her? It was always possible that the whole episode was a figment of the elderly man's imagination, she supposed. He might not have even talked to Mac, or it might have been so garbled Mac hadn't understood.

One thing was sure—she had to straighten it out, which meant she had to talk to Mr. Sheldon again, no matter who stood in her way.

"Ms. Beaumont?"

Kate looked up to find the young patrolman, Foster, looking down at her, still a bit flushed from the excitement of the arrest.

"Yes?"

Before he could answer, two burly characters who'd been propping up the bar all evening were pounding him on the back, congratulating him for his efforts and insisting on buying him a drink.

Foster, red with embarrassment, succeeded in shaking them off after several attempts. "Sorry about that." Even the tips of his ears were red when he turned back to Kate. "The chief sent me to see you safely home."

She might have known. "That's not necessary. I have my own car." Her smile seemed to further complicate his embarrassment.

"Sorry," he said again. "But it's the chief's orders. I'm to follow you home and check the cottage for you."

He would obviously not take no for an answer. She shrugged, laying a bill on the table to cover their tab.

"Thanks, Nikki. I didn't intend so much excitement, but I'm glad we had a chance to talk again."

"Anytime." Nikki was already turning back to her interrupted conversation, the presence of Foster at their table apparently giving her something else to talk about.

Kate rose. "Maybe we should go before anyone else tries to buy you a drink."

"Good idea." He looked relieved. "My patrol car's right outside. I'll walk you to yours."

Again, she didn't think it necessary, but arguing was pointless. Assuming Bolt was the author of everything that had happened here, she was in no danger with him locked up. But Mac no doubt believed in going the extra mile.

Kate drove back down Main Street to the place that, oddly enough, had started to feel like home. When she pulled in the driveway, Foster was right behind her, and as they approached the door, he took the key out of her hand.

"Stay back, please, ma'am. Just until I tell you it's clear."

Everything was just as she'd left it, and Mrs. A. was already peering out her back window and waving, but Kate nodded agreement. She waited patiently as lights went on in kitchen, bedroom and bath. Then Foster came back to the door.

"All clear." He handed her the keys as she stepped inside.

"Thank you. That makes me feel very safe."

He flushed again. "No wonder if you're upset, after everything that's happened. But we've got Bolt safe under lock and key now. Just sorry you had to see it."

"I'm glad I did." She looked at him speculatively, wondering how much he'd be willing to say about Mac. "I was surprised at how calm everyone was. In the city, there would have been sirens wailing and guns drawn."

Foster shook his head. "Not on Chief Whiting's watch. He says anytime you have to draw your weapon, it's like an admission of failure that you couldn't do it any other way."

"That seems like a unique attitude for a police officer."

"Chief says we have to remember we're peace officers. He says you don't draw your weapon unless it's the only option, and then you have to be prepared to use it."

Foster obviously had a case of hero worship for Mac. "Have you ever seen him draw a weapon?"

"Just once since I've been on the force." He seemed to withdraw a little, as if thinking he'd been indiscreet. "I'll say good-night, Ms. Beaumont. You be sure to lock up now."

"I will. And thanks."

Foster nodded, stepping outside. He waited until she turned the dead bolt, and then she heard his footsteps receding.

Kate wandered to the kitchen, restless. How long until she could talk to Mac? She glanced at the clock. It wasn't all that late, but he'd be busy. Not soon, she supposed. And Sheldon? Maybe in the morning.

Rubbing her temples again, Kate decided some

caffeine was in order. She started some coffee, then downed a couple of aspirin.

Kate had no sooner swallowed a mouthful of coffee than her cell phone rang. Frowning at the unknown number, she answered.

"Kate Beaumont here."

"Kate, I'm sure glad I had the right number. This is Sheila. You know—Mr. Sheldon's caregiver."

"Yes, of course I remember who you are, Sheila. Is something wrong?"

"Well, yeah. I'm at the hospital. I had to bring Mr. Sheldon in earlier this evening."

"Why? What happened?" Surely he hadn't been attacked, as well.

"He had a bit of a fall. Nothing serious, the doc says. They want to keep him, though, because he's really agitated, and they don't know why."

"I'm so sorry." Sorry for herself, too. Given the state of his health, Mr. Sheldon might not be able to tell her whatever it was he'd told Bart.

"That's really why I'm calling. He keeps asking for you. We can't get him to settle down. He insists he has to tell you something. So I figured, if you came in and talked to him, maybe then he'd relax and go to sleep. If you're willing, I mean."

"Of course I will," she said quickly. She glanced at the clock. A little after nine. "But will they let me in this late?"

"I talked to the nurse. She said it's okay. I guess she wants him to settle down as much as I do. We're in the Special Care Unit, third floor, room 320. Just come right up. If anyone stops you, say the nurse asked for you to come. Okay?"

"Wait, before you hang up. I'll come right away, but what happened? What got him so upset to begin with?"

Sheila hesitated for a moment. "I guess it's okay to tell you. Bart Gordon came over. I guess Mr. Sheldon called him, but I didn't hear it. I was in the kitchen," she added hurriedly, lest Kate think she was slacking off. "Anyway, Gordon was in a rare taking. Upset and demanding to see Mr. Sheldon. I had half a mind to turn him away, but Mr. Sheldon heard him and insisted he come in."

"Did you hear what they said to each other?"

"No." She sounded as if she regretted it. "But they went at it hammer and tongs for about fifteen minutes before Gordon slammed out. That was when Mr. Sheldon was so agitated. I knew I should have kept Gordon out."

"I don't see how you could have stopped him." She grabbed her bag and her keys. "Listen, I'm on my way. I'll be there in a few minutes. Maybe, when he's told me what he wants to say, Mr. Sheldon will feel better."

Maybe. She hurried out, locking the door. And maybe she'd feel worse. Maybe she was reaching the heart of what had caused Jason's death.

CHAPTER NINETEEN

The hospital was quiet at this hour of the evening. Kate expected to be challenged when she came in, but the woman at the desk just smiled when Kate headed toward the elevator.

It was only when she reached the Special Care Unit that anyone spoke to her. An RN came hurrying to greet her, as if she'd been watching for Kate.

"Are you Ms. Beaumont?" At Kate's nod, the woman hurried her down the hallway. "I certainly hope you can calm down the patient. He's been upset and agitated since he arrived, and he hasn't let us give him anything to help him sleep."

"I'll try," Kate promised, with an inward quake at the responsibility thrust on her.

"He has something he's determined to tell you." A very human curiosity peeked through the woman's cool professional facade. "We're hoping getting it off his chest will quiet him." She paused, one hand on the door to the room, beyond which a voice could be heard. "You do realize that with his mental condition, what he says may not make much sense."

"Should I ask him questions?" Kate was beginning to get as impatient as Sheldon sounded.

"If you want. But just let him feel that he's getting through to you. That should help."

She pushed the door open, and Kate followed her into the hospital room.

Mr. Sheldon was in the first bed near the door, with Sheila sitting beside him and attempting to hold his hand. He flung it out, banging it against the metal bed rail, and Kate winced. That must have hurt.

"Here's the person you've been asking for." The nurse spoke in such a cheerful voice that it set Kate's nerves on edge. "You can talk to Ms. Beaumont, and then I'm sure you'll feel better."

Sheldon sat up, peering at Kate suspiciously. Then, apparently satisfied, he nodded. "You two go out. We want some privacy."

Given the imperial tone, it was a good thing there was nobody in the other bed, or Sheldon would probably have wanted the roommate out, as well. She sent an apologetic glance toward Sheila.

But Sheila nodded, her round, ruddy face relieved. She got up quickly. "Here, Kate, have my chair. I'll just go out in the hall and stretch my legs."

As Kate sat, the nurse twitched, unnecessarily, it seemed, at the bedcovers. Then she followed Sheila out into the hall with what looked like a warning glance at Kate.

"I'm so sorry to hear about your accident.

386

I wouldn't have intruded, but Sheila said you wanted to see me."

"You came. They said I shouldn't bother you." The figure in the bed was a far cry from the courtly, well-dressed gentleman Kate had met in his home. He seemed wizened in the faded print of the hospital gown, and his white hair was ruffled.

"It's no bother at all. You wanted to tell me something. Is it about my brother?" She couldn't help the eagerness in her voice.

Sheldon clasped Kate's hand in a hard grip. "Jason." He closed his eyes for a moment. "He was a fine boy. Smart, honest. A hard worker. Don't believe anyone who tells you otherwise."

"I never have." She managed a smile. "After all, I knew him better than anyone did."

Sheldon nodded. "He talked about you sometimes. His clever big sister. He said you always took care of him."

"I tried." Her throat grew thick. But when it had counted, she'd failed.

"Don't blame yourself for what happened. You're not to blame." His grip tightened painfully. "It was our fault. My fault."

"I'm sure you didn't—" she began, but he cut her off.

"Bart said some of the client files were a mess. He said money was unaccounted for. He thought Jason was to blame."

"No!" The very idea was repellent. "Jason wouldn't steal."

The old man didn't seem to hear her. His eyes were wide and a little frightening in their intensity. "Bart accused Jason of embezzlement. He wouldn't listen to any defense. Lina tried to correct him, but he was determined. He thought he knew it all. But he didn't. He didn't."

Sheldon's chin quivered. Tears started in his eyes. He looked like a hurt child. "It wasn't Jason. It was me."

Kate could only stare at him. "You? But why?"

"My mind." He pressed his clenched fists to his head. "It's not working right anymore. I muddle things. But Bart Gordon was so sure. He told Jason he was fired—said he'd make sure no company would hire him. Sent him away."

And Jason, seeing nothing but failure in his future, had succumbed to a way out of his pain. Whether he'd intended to or not, he'd taken his own life. But . . .

"You said Bart thought there was money missing. No matter how muddled you were, you wouldn't steal from the company you'd built."

Tears were streaming down his face now, and his lips trembled. Her heart twisted, but she had to know all of it, once and for all.

"That's what Chief Whiting said when I told him. But how do I know what I would do when I can't make my mind work?" He hit his knuckles against his head.

Kate grasped his hands, holding them in hers. "It's all right. It was probably all a mistake." It was the only thing she could say that might comfort him a little.

But what was going to comfort her? Jason had been driven to his death by false accusations. Mac had known the truth, and he hadn't told her.

She'd not only lost her brother. She'd lost the man she might be beginning to love.

It wasn't until the next afternoon that Mac managed to take a breath and get away from the station. Bolt had done the smart thing and remained silent, only speaking to ask for a lawyer.

But once his car had been searched and the evidence began to roll in, he'd looked increasingly uneasy. Finally he'd consulted his attorney and agreed to a plea bargain. He'd give them the information they wanted in exchange for a break on the charges. Once the DA was satisfied, he'd headed off to his office, exultant at having something positive on his record.

In the meantime, Mac could shift his attention to something else. Or rather, someone else. He wanted to talk to Kate about what had happened with Bolt. And incidentally, find out what she'd been doing at the Lamplight last night.

He took a chance that she'd be at the cottage, rather than going in to work today. Sure enough, Kate opened the door to his knock. She'd shed the sling but held her arm a bit awkwardly, as if any unwary movement might cause pain.

"Mac." She didn't seem overjoyed to see him. "Come in. I wanted a word with you."

"I've been tied up with the case against Bolt." He walked inside. "I see you're doing without the sling. Are you sure that's a good idea?"

She gave a slight shrug and then winced. "The doctor said I could start moving it more today. But I'm not attempting to haul any boxes of books around just yet."

Barefoot, in jeans and a loose shirt, she looked as if she might have been resting, but he saw that the computer was on, with Jason's face frozen on the screen.

He nodded toward it. "Kristie's notes—are they helping?"

"Yes. She did a good job." Kate's fingers hesitated over the keys, and then she clicked the file closed. She turned to face him. "Has Bolt admitted to anything?"

"He's too much an old hand at this game to admit to anything until he saw a chance to make a trade. But we have the evidence to put him away on drug charges as well as the attack on Larry. His car trunk looked like a pharmacy warehouse, and the baseball bat he used on Larry had enough trace evidence to convince a jury. So he decided to cooperate in exchange for some consideration from the DA."

"What about Jason? Does he admit to supplying him with the drugs?" Her fists clenched until the knuckles were white. Obviously this was the only important factor to her. She hadn't even asked about the attack on herself.

"No. He denies it." He hated disappointing her—hated not being able to give her the answers she so desperately needed.

Anger flared in her eyes. "But . . . if he confessed to the rest, why would he hold back on that?"

He leaned against the back of the sofa, trying for a casualness he didn't feel. "I wish I knew. It's possible he's afraid of even more serious charges being brought if he supplied the instrument of Jason's death. Or it might just be true."

"Then where . . ." Kate stopped, shoving her hair back with a frustrated gesture. "I suppose I'll have to be satisfied with less than the full story."

"You haven't even asked about either of the attacks on you."

She rubbed her shoulder. "I haven't forgotten. It just . . . doesn't seem to matter so much."

"It matters to me. We questioned him thoroughly about both incidents, but he insists he wasn't involved. He claims Larry's been moving a few pills for him, and Larry tried to run you down that night at the Lamplight. Says Larry was scared out of his wits when you started asking questions." Bolt hadn't put it quite that way, but Mac saw no reason to quote him.

"But why?" She seemed honestly puzzled. "How was I a threat to Larry? And we know he can't have attacked me at Blackburn House, because he was in the hospital."

"It didn't make much sense to me, either, until Bolt said that Larry was afraid Jason might have said something about Larry pushing pills on his video journal." At her startled gaze, he nodded. "Yeah, Bolt says Larry knew all about the journal. Apparently Jason didn't make a secret of it."

"So anyone could have known."

He nodded. "But the laptop with the diary on it disappeared when the place was cleared out. His father had packed everything up and taken it even before the funeral. It wasn't accessible until you came back to Laurel Ridge."

"Larry must have been the one to wipe my computer then."

"That's what I figure. He's being released from the hospital tomorrow, and he'll be coming straight to the station to make a statement. Not even his doting mother can protect him this time."

Kate nodded, looking down at the photograph of Jason that stood next to the computer. It almost seemed she'd lost interest in both Bolt and Larry, and he didn't understand it.

"Look, this is good news, isn't it? So, what's wrong?" He moved closer, wanting to pull her around to face him but afraid of her reaction. "You're holding out on me, Kate. What is it?"

Her head came up at that. "I'm holding out on you? Don't you have that the wrong way around?"

"What are you talking about?" he demanded.

"Russell Sheldon." She said the name with heavy emphasis, her eyes hard as ice. "I had a call last night from Sheila. He's in the hospital. Did you even know that? But he wouldn't rest until he'd talked to me. Maybe he didn't trust you to let me in on what he'd told you. He'd have been right, wouldn't he?"

"Look, Kate, I don't know what he told you, but . . ." She'd found out, and in the worst possible way.

"He told me what he'd told you. That Bart Gordon accused my brother of theft. He threatened to ruin his future. And he did, didn't he? Because after that, Jason didn't have a future."

Mac took a breath, struggling to keep his voice even. "Look, I admit, Russ did tell me that story. He also claimed that Jason was innocent and that he'd done it."

"You should have told me!" She flung the words at him.

"You know as well as I do that Russ's mind can't be relied on. His senility could be prompting him to come up with all kinds of things. And as for believing that he'd steal from his own company—well, that's downright crazy."

"Obviously. Since he's a pillar of the Laurel Ridge community, he couldn't possibly be guilty of anything. Not if there's a handy outsider to blame."

Her words were laced with a bitterness that scoured his soul. Mac saw every bit of the relationship that had begun between them crumple into dust at his feet.

"I don't blame Jason. I'm not even sure there ever was any money missing from the accounts. You've seen enough of him to know that Bart's the type to blame first and find out the facts later, if at all."

"So you're taking the easy way out. Ignore the whole thing. After all, Jason's dead now, so what difference does it make? Well, it makes a difference to me! It makes a difference to that badge you wear that's supposedly represents justice. Where is Jason's justice?"

Mac's jaw hardened. "I've been trying to find out the truth. But not by running off half-cocked throwing accusations at people. I'll investigate Russ's claims, no matter who is involved. The law doesn't play favorites."

"It looks like it to me. It looks like you're doing

what you always do. Protecting your town and your people, no matter who else gets hurt."

Her anger hadn't abated in the least, and his own flamed to meet it.

"At least I'm not trying to find someone else to blame to make up for my own failures."

He stopped, appalled that he'd lost control of himself. But Kate didn't flinch.

"Get out." She spoke quietly. "Just get out. I came here to do a job, and I'm going to do it. Alone. I don't need your help, and I don't want it."

They'd left themselves with nothing else to say, it seemed. Mac turned and walked away.

Kate spent most of the night wondering if it was time to give up and leave Laurel Ridge. She'd put on a show of bravado with Mac, but the truth was that there seemed little else she could do.

Bolt was in police hands. They'd find out what they could, but obviously the DA would be interested in putting Bolt away, not in satisfying her need to know why Jason had done what he'd done. And Larry was in a similar state. She didn't cherish any belief that she'd be able to question him before the police did. Probably, like Bolt, he'd say whatever he could to get the least sentence for himself.

Russ Sheldon—well, she believed that what he'd told her was true, but there was no way she could think of to prove it. Bart Gordon would deny everything, not wanting it known that he'd driven Jason to suicide.

She'd thought, when she'd started this quest, that just knowing the circumstances would be enough to lift the burden of pain and responsibility she carried. She'd been wrong.

The truth was that Jason, facing the biggest disappointment of his life, hadn't turned to her. It was almost more than she could bear to think of the pain he'd been in, seeing his future ruined. Always before, she could count on a call when he was in trouble. Not this time.

Why, Jason, why? Why didn't you call and talk to me about it?

She could have helped. She'd have gladly fought the battle with him, insisting on an audit and an outside investigation to find out exactly who had been responsible for the problems at the financial group. Jason must have known she'd have left no stone unturned to defend him.

But he hadn't called. Had he thought she didn't care? That the fact that she hadn't been around all summer meant that she was relieved of the responsibility for him? It tore at her heart, and knowing the circumstances hadn't really helped at all.

As for Mac—she couldn't so much as think of Mac without feeling a fresh surge of pain. She wasn't sure how he'd come to mean so much to her in the short time they'd been together. He ought to have no place in her heart.

But he did. And he'd shattered her by his actions. He'd been so intent on protecting his own that he'd ignored her needs. The only thing left was to forget about him, but she suspected it was going to take a long, long time to do that.

In the end, though, she couldn't bring herself to leave. She showered and dressed, avoiding looking at the ugly purple-and-yellow bruise on her shoulder, and headed for Blackburn House. If there was anything new to learn, she'd be far more likely to hear about it there.

Emily twittered at her arrival. "Kate, I'm sure you shouldn't come back to work so soon. What if you make your shoulder worse? I'd never forgive myself."

"I'll take it easy, I promise." She gave Emily a reassuring smile. "At least I can wait on customers for you, even if I can't do any shelving or cleaning. Besides, I'll go crazy, stuck in the cottage with nothing to do."

"Well, if you're sure . . ." Emily's face brightened. "I suppose you know all about the arrest. It's the biggest thing that's happened here in the past month, I do believe. Not that anyone actually knew this criminal."

"Bolt." She supplied the name. "Ax Bolt."

Emily shivered. "Horrid name for a horrid

person. We're all better off with him behind bars." She leaned a little closer. "Do they think he had anything to do with the funny business here? Maybe he was trying to break in to get money for more drugs."

"From what I've heard, I think he was a big enough dealer that he didn't need to do that." She suspected Emily would enjoy the vicarious thrill of thinking a vicious criminal had tried to rob her store—at least, now that the criminal was safely locked up.

Emily shook her head, white curls bouncing. "You never can tell what people like that will do. At least Mac caught him. I knew we could depend on Mac to keep us safe."

"Yes." The word tasted bitter on her tongue.

Apparently deciding Kate was a poor source of information, Emily slid from behind the counter. "Since you can take care of any customers, I believe I'll go over to the Buttercup for some coffee. I'm sure there's a lot of chatter going on there."

Kate nodded. As long as the chatter wasn't about her, she didn't really care. "I'll be here. Take as long as you want."

The bookshop was oppressively silent once Emily had left. Kate checked the computer for messages and found herself staring absently at the phone. Someone had stood here, where she was standing, and picked up the phone to call her. To lure her into the building. Whoever he or she was, they'd left no trace behind.

"Kate?"

She looked up at the sound of her name to see that Lina had just come in.

"Yes, I'm here." She gave a mechanical smile. "I guess I was just spaced out for a second. How may I help you, Lina?"

Lina approached the counter. "To tell you the truth, I haven't had much time for reading lately. I was on my way to the post office when I saw you here, so I thought I'd pop in and see how you are."

Someone else who was curious, Kate supposed. Well, she had a bit of curiosity of her own to satisfy. What did Lina know about the accusations of theft against Jason? She had to know something. She'd been there at the time, according to Nikki.

"It's nice of you to stop by," she said automatically, trying to think how to put the questions she wanted to ask.

But Lina forestalled her. "You know that Mr. Sheldon is in the hospital. I understand he asked to see you. I think I can guess why."

"He was feeling burdened by a secret he'd been keeping about my brother." Kate looked into Lina's eyes, hoping to read the truth there. "A secret I believe you know."

Lina glanced away for a moment. "I'm sorry.

I wish I could have said something earlier. But you have to understand—I need my job. I hoped just telling you that Jason had been fired would be enough to help you. I could never get another position that pays nearly as much. Not at my age, here in Laurel Ridge."

The woman looked so distraught that Kate's anger seeped away. She'd never been in that position, so what right did she have to judge? She was young and well educated, she had enough money to live on, thanks to her stepfather, and she could always find a job, even if it wasn't the reporting job of her dreams.

But Lina, plain, middle-aged and trapped by circumstance—well, she wasn't so lucky.

"I understand," she said finally. "But now that I already know, won't you tell me about it from your perspective?"

A rattle at the door interrupted them, and a moment later the bell over the door rang as a couple of women came in, chattering about their purchases at the quilt shop.

Lina gave her a haunted look. "Not here. I can't. Bart can't know I talked to you."

"We could meet someplace after work. Or I'll take you to supper . . ." She let that trail off because Lina was already shaking her head.

"I can't. I won't be free until fairly late this evening. Suppose I come to your place—say, around nine o'clock? Is that all right?"

Kate would like to make it earlier, but she didn't have much choice. "Great. I'll expect you at nine." As Lina turned away, she added, "Thanks. I appreciate it."

Lina leaned closer, glancing around, apparently to be sure no one could overhear. "Don't say anything about it, all right? I don't want word getting back to Bart."

Lina turned and scurried out of the shop, as if afraid someone would spot her and report to her boss.

Kate would have liked time to mull over Lina's sudden capitulation, but she didn't have it. By the time she'd finished with the two women, who'd seemed to expect her to remember the author of a book they'd once read that they'd really enjoyed, and if only she could tell them, they'd be sure to buy another by her.

By dint of considerable questioning, Kate was able to narrow down the possibilities to a few female cozy mystery authors, and she finally had them browsing contentedly through the shelves.

She headed back to the register, shaking her head. She had no doubt that Emily would have been able to pull the answer out of her brain, because Emily seemed to have all her customers' preferences memorized. Kate wasn't so skilled.

She cast a brief glance at the fantasy section as she passed it. Jason was the only person whose reading tastes she'd ever known well enough to guide, and even Jason had eventually moved beyond her, finding a score of favorite authors and games she knew nothing about.

That reminded her she wanted to go through Jason's journal again with Kristie's notes in front of her. She might see something she'd missed. She ought to be able to do that before Lina came over. If only he'd recorded something that final day . . .

Once again, the sound of the bell interrupted her thoughts, and maybe in this instance that was just as well. Allison came toward her, every hair casually in place as always.

"Kate, hi. I'm glad to see you could give up the sling. But are you sure that was wise?"

"I'm fine." The response was a bit short, but she was beginning to tire of sympathy.

"Good." Allison didn't seem to take offense. "I won't take up much of your time, but I did wonder if you'd like to come over this evening. My apartment is right upstairs, you know, so we're neighbors. I have some nice white wine, and we can settle down to a bit of girl talk. And absolutely no need to say anything about my future brother-in-law."

Kate blinked. "Has he been talking?"

"Not at all," Allison said. "And I mean that literally. But when his jaw turns to rock at the mention of your name, and you about bite my head off for a simple question, oddly enough I begin to think something went wrong between you two."

Kate's thoughts flickered back to Allison saying she hoped Kate wasn't going to hurt Mac. That he had a tender heart. Well, as far as she could see, his heart wasn't at all affected, and she was the one who'd been hurt.

"I'm sorry, but I . . ."

"Listen, I meant what I said. Absolutely no talk about Mac. Just a chance to relax. You've had a rough couple of weeks."

"Thanks. But honestly, I can't. Lina Oberlin is stopping by to see me this evening, so I'll have to stay in and wait for her." As soon as the words were out of her mouth, she remembered Lina's insistence that no one know. Well, it was too late now. And Allison surely had more interesting things to talk about than what Lina was doing.

"Lina? Well, I venture to say you'd have more fun with me, but if you can't, you can't. Just give me a call if anything changes." She pulled a card from the pocket of her bag. "There's my number."

Kate took it. As far as she could see, Allison was genuine, but she wasn't sure a tête-à-tête with her was a good idea. She was bound to take Mac's side, and an evening spent avoiding the thing that was occupying her mind would be doomed to failure.

"Another time, all right?" Allison flashed her a smile.

She nodded. That was vague enough, and she doubted it would happen. Whatever Lina had to offer, she didn't think it would make a difference. It was time she was moving on, leaving Laurel Ridge and all its painful memories behind like the bad dreams of childhood.

Someday, maybe, she'd be able to think of it without this crushing sense of failure.

CHAPTER TWENTY

Kate turned back to the video diary and Kristie's notes that evening, trying to read something new into them. But if Jason was trying to tell her something, she didn't know what it was. Finally she closed the file, running her hands through her hair to pull it back, as if that would help her think. It didn't.

She found she was doodling on the pad where she'd jotted some notes, sketching in a row of tombstones. She nearly scribbled over them but stopped, frowning.

Why the cemetery? If Jason had simply wanted to take some pills to blank out his pain, why hadn't he done it here? It seemed so improbable of him to wander into a dark cemetery.

He might have been out walking, of course. That wasn't his usual reaction to stress, but it could have happened. His car had been found here at the cottage, on the gravel strip where her own was now parked.

Idly she sketched a dragon coiling around the tombstones. And what had happened to the dragon charm? She couldn't believe he'd have thrown it away. It had been important to him, hadn't it?

Her fingers tightened on the pen, leaving a

jagged mark on the paper. She'd read up on suicide in the aftermath of Jason's death, trying to convince herself it had been an accident. One comment sprang into her mind—the fact that sometimes a young person contemplating suicide might give away things that were important to him.

Kate felt as if she'd been struck in the stomach. She sucked in a breath. Was that it? Had he given the dragon charm to someone, divesting himself of the links to his past life?

It hurt too much to linger on the thought. But in a way, suicide explained other things—like the fact that Jason had left the cottage that night. He wouldn't have wanted Mrs. Anderson to be the one to find him. One last chivalrous gesture from the boy who'd wanted to be a hero.

Fortunately, there was a knock on the door before she could slide into her own depressed state. Lina came in, apologizing.

"I'm so sorry I couldn't get here any earlier. I was held up at a meeting that I thought would never end." She set the shopping bag she carried on the coffee table. "I hope you don't mind, but I barely had time to grab a snack. I thought wc could share a glass of wine and some crackers."

"That's fine." She didn't want wine—she wanted answers. Or maybe reassurance. But it would be rude to say so.

"I have an opener right here, if you can supply the glasses. Then we can settle down and talk." Lina seemed unusually gracious, as if she were the hostess, entertaining a friend in her home.

"I'll get them."

Kate headed for the kitchen and reached up to take two wineglasses from the top shelf, mentally calculating how long it had been since she'd taken one of the pain pills the doctor had given her. This morning, wasn't it? Certainly not more recently, so that would be all right. Maybe the wine wasn't a bad idea. It might help her sleep. She hadn't had a restful night in what seemed like a week.

"That's just what we need." Lina deftly pulled the cork. Kate saw, to her relief, that the bottle was a nice Merlot rather than something she'd have to choke down.

Lina poured the glasses, sliding one in front of Kate. Rummaging in her bag again, she pulled out a package of thin crackers and a wedge of Brie. She hesitated, looking at the cheese.

"I thought I'd brought everything, but I seem to have forgotten a knife. Do you mind?"

Kate got up again, wondering if this was really worth it. She could claim she didn't want any cheese, but she could hardly deny Lina the implement to cut it.

Finally they were settled, one on either side of the coffee table. Kate took a cautious sip of the wine and felt it warm her. "Now, about what happened at the office . . ." she began.

"I wish I had told you before," Lina said quickly. "Really, I do. But it would have cost me my job."

"I understand." Hadn't they said all this already? She sipped again, leaning back against the cushions.

Lina gave her a stilted smile. "I know what you're thinking. If it had been you, you wouldn't have hesitated. But you don't understand my situation. I'd never get another job that pays so well in Laurel Ridge. I'd be lucky to find anything, especially if Bart said I'd let out private information. And he would."

"Please, believe me. I'm not blaming you." Just get on with it.

"My mother's in a nursing home here, you see," Lina went on, studying Kate intently as if to be sure she was listening. "It would kill her to be moved now, and if I lost my job, I couldn't have paid the fees. It's all very well for you young women and your careers. You have choices. But I don't."

If she had to listen to Lina's self-justifications much longer, she'd need more wine. Kate took a hefty swallow.

"About Jason's last days at the business . . ."

"Yes, well, I did notice that Jason seemed upset. For that matter, Mr. Sheldon did, as well.

No one told me why, of course. When you're just the office manager, they don't take you into their confidence."

Kate struggled to look sympathetic. "But you did know about it that last day, isn't that right? You were called in on that meeting the partners had with Jason."

"I suppose they—or Bart, at least—wanted a witness to what happened. So that they couldn't be accused of firing Jason unjustly. Bart was very sensitive to things like that. Why, he kept a completely inept receptionist on for months, just because he feared she'd say she was fired because she was a woman." Lina sniffed. "She was fired because she couldn't take a simple message, that was why."

"About that last day," Kate repeated. If the woman kept on being this discursive, Kate would be asleep before they got to the subject. Those sleepless nights seemed to be catching up to her.

"Apparently Jason said he'd found some irregularities in some of the accounts. He went to Mr. Sheldon about it, and they looked at the files together." She paused. "Well, I think by then Mr. Sheldon wasn't really able to discern what was going on with the accounts. So he took the problem to Bart."

"And Bart blew his top, I gather." Kate reached for a cracker. If she were going to drink wine, she'd better have something with it. She couldn't possibly be getting light-headed on one little glass, could she?

"That's Bart's way, you see." Lina touched her lips to the glass and then set it down. "He couldn't handle the idea that the firm had done anything wrong. Jason was the only person, other than the partners, who had access to the accounts, so he must have done it."

Kate frowned, trying to concentrate. "But you must have access as well, don't you?"

"Well, of course. But only so I can prepare statements and that sort of thing. I don't make any decisions." She shook her head, her gaze intent on Kate's face. "Bart took a look himself and jumped to the conclusion that Jason had been skimming from the accounts. It was a terrible scene, terrible. Bart kept making threats, like he always does. Poor Jason just got whiter and whiter."

"What about . . . about Mr. Sheldon?" She shook her head, and it felt as if it would wobble right off. "Sorry. I can't seem to think . . ."

"Have a little more wine." Lina leaned over to refill her glass. "That will help."

"I don't think . . ." The words tapered off, and she struggled to rouse herself. "Was there really money missing from the accounts?"

"No, there wasn't. To tell the truth, I think the whole thing was a mix-up caused by Mr. Sheldon. He's not to blame. He'd just been losing his grip. But by the time we knew, it was too late."

410

Too late. The words echoed in Kate's mind, repeating themselves over and over. Lina leaned over her, her eyes sharp. She looked like a ferret . . . beady eyes, sharp teeth . . . Kate found she was giggling at the thought. She tried to stop, but she couldn't.

"I'm afraid you're just the teeniest bit drunk." Lina began putting the cheese and crackers back in her bag. "I'll just tidy up a bit, and then I'll take you outside for some air."

Kate tried to protest, but she couldn't seem to get the words out. Lina bustled around like a neat freak, taking the glasses and knife to the kitchen and then wiping the table off thoroughly.

"Don't need . . ." She managed to get out, and then lost the thread.

"I like to leave everything neat. There, now." Lina looked at her work with satisfaction. "No one would know anyone had been here."

She put an arm around Kate, hoisting her to her feet. "Come on. We'll go outside. A little fresh air will sober you up."

In the dim recesses of her mind, something was crying out. *Danger. This isn't right. Stop.*

Lina guided her a step away from the sofa. "That's right. Just come along with me."

Kate reached out, managing to get her fingers on her cell phone. Something . . . something she needed to do . . . someone to call. Mac. She had to call Mac.

Lina brushed the cell phone from her nerveless fingers. "Right now, let's get you out in the air."

Her legs didn't seem to have any choice but to obey. Kate stumbled out into the dark.

Lina was carrying the wine bottle in her other hand. Funny. Did she want another drink? Kate would ask, but she couldn't seem to form the words.

Lina kicked the door closed behind them. They wobbled across the lawn. She'd been wrong. The air wasn't helping.

"Go back . . ." she muttered.

"We'll just go for a little ride," Lina said. "That's what you need."

Kate stumbled, falling against the car parked in the drive. She was vaguely aware of the door opening, of falling into the seat, of tumbling into darkness.

Mac realized how late it was, but somehow he couldn't seem to leave the office. He'd gone through the transcripts of Bolt's statement and Larry's statement again and again, sieving the words for any hint of evidence.

They were blaming each other, of course. He was inclined to believe that Larry, in a panic, had driven his car at Kate in the Lamplight parking lot, and he'd probably been responsible for the dragon symbols that had dogged her. If he'd known Jason well enough to know about the journal, he'd have known the symbolism of the dragon, too.

And the evidence alone was enough to convict Bolt of the attack on Larry, in addition to drug dealing.

But what about luring Kate into Blackburn House? And who had supplied the drugs that ended Jason's life? Nothing he'd learned seemed to fit as an answer to those two questions. It was like constructing a jigsaw puzzle with a missing piece.

Mac pulled out his phone and stared at it. Kate wouldn't want to hear from him, he supposed. But her persistence had led them a long way toward exposing a drug connection in his town, and he was grateful. He shouldn't have been so angry about her reaction to his withholding the story Russ Sheldon told him.

As for her accusation that all he cared about was guarding his town—well, there was some truth to that. But he didn't care for Laurel Ridge as much as or in the same way as he cared for Kate.

Now that he'd actually formed the words, if just in his mind, Mac had to look at the truth. He'd only known Kate for weeks, but he had fallen hard and fast in a way he never had before. He knew her better in a couple of weeks than he knew some people he'd known all their lives.

And he didn't think she'd ever give him a chance to tell her so.

Making a sudden decision, he hit her number. He owed it to her to tell her where the case stood against Larry after today's interview. And try to apologize for what he'd said to her.

The phone rang several times and then went to voice mail. He clicked off without leaving a message and sat frowning. Maybe she'd seen who was calling and hadn't wanted to answer. Maybe.

His phone rang in his hand. Allison. He answered quickly.

"Hey, Allison. What's wrong?"

"I might call you just to chat," she said.

"You might, but I don't think you did."

"No, I guess I didn't. Mac, do you know where Kate is?" She sounded troubled.

"I thought she was at home. Why?" He sat up straight, coming to attention.

"I'd suggested we get together tonight, but she said Lina Oberlin was coming over. I just looked out my window—you know, the one that overlooks the side yard?"

"I know." It also overlooked Mrs. Anderson's backyard and the cottage.

"Kate's car is there, and every light in the place is on, but I don't think she's there. Usually if the drapes are open I can see her moving around, but there's nothing. Maybe I'm making a fuss over nothing, but it just seems odd."

"Did you notice Lina come?" He was getting up as he spoke, heading for the door.

414

"I happened to see the car in the driveway. I'm not spying on my neighbors, but I've been worried about Kate. Lina's car is gone now, but Kate's is still there. I think I'll go over and check . . ."

"Don't. I'm on my way. I'll let you know."

He clicked off before she could respond and tried Kate's number again. Nothing. He was filled with a probably ridiculous level of concern.

Lina had been there, presumably to talk about what happened to Jason. What if she'd said something that made Kate want to confront Bart Gordon? That could have unpleasant consequences, but not serious enough to account for the level of worry he felt.

When he reached the cottage and jumped out, he found Allison standing in the yard, arms wrapped around herself.

"I told you to stay home."

"I'm not good at following orders, just like Kate. I knocked and rang the bell, but there was no answer."

"The Whiting boys have a way of falling for stubborn women," he muttered, striding to the door.

"I heard that," Allison said, right behind him.

He rapped loudly. He could see what had bothered Allison. Lights were on in every room, all the curtains open, and no one was visible. He rapped again and then tried the knob.

The door wasn't locked. He opened it and paused, halfway in. "Kate? Are you here?"

No answer, and all his instincts were telling him something was wrong. He strode inside, calling her name again. Then he made a quick circuit of the rooms. Nothing. A couple of wineglasses stood in the dish drainer, still wet.

He headed back to the living room, where Allison stood looking as if she needed something to do.

"What's going on? Where did she go?" Worry sharpened her tone.

"Allison, look up Lina Oberlin's number in the phone book and call her, will you? If she's home, find out when she left here."

Nodding, Allison pulled the phone book out from under the landline phone on the end of the table. Mac prowled around the living room, looking, not touching.

Kate's cell phone lay on the floor. Her bag was on the sofa, her keys lying on top of it. The silver dragon seemed to look at him. Reproaching him for his failure. Warning him.

He moved to the table, where Allison had dialed the number. She listened for a moment and then held the phone out so he could hear. It rang over and over, and he could picture it ringing in an empty house.

His gaze fell on papers lying next to the computer. It looked as if Kate had been watching the tapes again. Kristie's notes lay open beside it. On top of the Kristie's report was a pad, with several of the obscure references jotted on it.

Below the notes, a small row of tombstones stood, a dragon coiled around them.

Mac spun, heading for the door.

"Mac, wait! Where are you going?" Allison followed him, hurrying to keep up. "Let me go with you."

He hesitated a moment, then nodded. Allison would be another pair of eyes, at least.

They ran to the police car and slid in. "Where are we going?" Allison asked.

"Following a hunch." Quickly he rang Foster. If they ended up searching the cemetery, he needed more people.

If. It was crazy. How would Kate have gotten there? Surely she hadn't set out to walk half a mile in the dark. Not a city girl like her.

But it wasn't just a hunch, it was instinct— instinct that said he'd find Kate where they'd found her brother.

Someone was shaking her, pulling at her. Kate struggled to wake up—to find out what the urgent person wanted.

"Come on, I can't carry you." The voice sounded annoyed. "You can stand up if you try. I'll help you."

Better to make the effort than let the person

keep on shaking her. Kate found she had her feet on a gravel surface. The driveway? Was she home? She pushed herself up and felt an arm go around her.

"That's right. Had to park out here on the gravel where my tires won't leave a trace. That's why we have to walk so far."

The words didn't make sense to Kate. Of course they wouldn't drive on Mrs. Anderson's nice lawn. She'd be furious if it was torn up. She managed to put one foot in front of the other. She could walk to the house.

"Better. You're doing better." The voice had become a little breathless, hadn't it? "Right this way."

"Silly," she said, pleased she'd gotten the word out. Naturally she knew the way into the house.

"Silly, is it? Well, that's okay. We'll be silly. A little farther now."

Kate stumbled on, finding it harder and harder. "Tired," she muttered.

"You'll be able to rest soon. Rest for a long, long time."

It was a woman with her, Kate realized. Who? She couldn't seem to think. She could only follow the pressure of the arm, leading her on.

"Good thing it's been so dry. We won't leave any tracks in the grass. Keep going now, through the bushes."

A branch hit Kate in the face, rousing her

slightly. She tried to pull back, but the woman's grip was iron.

"Just a little farther. There now."

They were on smooth grass again. Kate forced her sluggish wits to work. Where were they? Not at the cottage. She tried to lift her head. It was so heavy, but she kept forcing it. Trees. A tower. Tower with a face, looking at her. The moon— full, so big, too big. What was it doing so close?

She cringed away from it, and the supporting hands lowered her to the grass. Damp, chilly. She didn't like it. But she leaned back, too sleepy to get up. Something hard and cold behind her back. She'd just rest for a moment, and then she'd leave.

Her fingers were forced to close around a bottle. "You have a drink. That will make you feel better."

A face loomed over her, looking bigger and bigger, growing until it was the size of the moon. The bottle was pressed to her lips.

"Drink," the voice commanded.

Kate tried to shake her head, to get away from the pressure of the bottle. She put a hand behind her to push against the chair and knew that it wasn't a chair. Stone, cold as death.

She was in the cemetery, in the place where Jason died.

Jason seemed to fill her mind, as young and alive as he was the last time they'd been together.

Run, Kate, run. You have to get away from her. It's Baldicer. She's evil. Get away.

Jason's face, Jason's voice, so clear that they compelled her vision to clear, too. She saw the row of rounded tombstones, the full moon shining down with its cold light, the figure that bent over her, forcing the bottle against her lips—

"No!" She lunged out, shoving with all her strength. Surprised, the woman fell backward. Kate struggled, trying to get to her feet, trying to cry out, but the woman was on her, knocking her to the ground again, coming at her. She'd never be able to tell the truth about Jason, never be able to tell Mac what she felt . . .

Lights pierced the darkness, voices calling out. Then strong arms going around her, Mac's voice telling her to be still. Her vision cleared a little, just enough to make out his face.

"Thank goodness you came." Lina said. "I found her trying to kill herself, just like her brother did."

Kate braced herself against Mac's arm. "Liar," she said, and then she slumped against him.

CHAPTER TWENTY-ONE

Only iron control kept Mac from running to the hospital room the next morning. Ridiculous, that it had taken him so long to get where he wanted to be.

But like it or not, he'd had no choice but to do his duty. Lina, despite her protestations, had been detained until Kate could make a statement. Of course she'd called an attorney immediately, who was already making noises about suing for false arrest, among other things.

He knew what he'd seen when he'd first glimpsed those figures in the clearing in the cemetery. Lina had been trying to get Kate to drink. And tests had shown that the bottle of wine had been laced with enough barbiturates to be fatal in combination with the wine. It was the same combination that had killed Jason.

Pushing the door open, he hurried into the room. Allison looked up from her position beside the bed, yawning. Kate lay in the bed, so still it was frightening until he realized she was breathing.

"Here you are at last." Allison stood and gave him a hug. "Stop looking so worried. She's going to be all right."

He moved closer. Kate's face was relaxed, the

lines of stress smoothed out. The hospital gown revealed the yellow-and-purple colors of her bruised head and shoulder.

"She's had a rough time of it since she came to Laurel Ridge." He touched the bruise on her shoulder gently.

"So someone will have to make up to her for that," Allison said tartly. "Any idea who?"

Mac shot her a look. "You're just meant to be sitting with Kate, not matchmaking."

"Hey, you did that yourself. I'm just the first one to recognize it." She waved her phone. "Nick went down for coffee. You want me to tell him to bring you one?"

"Not now." He sat down next to the bed, his hand clasping Kate's. "You probably should go home and get some sleep. I'll get someone else to come in when I have to leave."

"Your mother's on her way." At his glance, she shrugged. "You didn't think you could keep her away, did you?"

He had to acknowledge the truth of Allison's words. Mom would be here. Well, at least he'd know someone he trusted was with Kate. He didn't want her waking up alone.

Even as he thought it, he felt Kate's hand stir under his. He leaned over her, studying her face. Her eyelids flickered and opened. For a moment her brown eyes were unfocused, and then they turned frightened.

"No, no," she murmured.

"Kate, it's all right." He clasped her hand firmly in both of his. "You're safe. You're in the hospital. Do you understand? You're safe."

The fear faded. Her gaze lingered on his face, and it seemed to him that for the first time, Kate was completely transparent to him, with all her barricades gone. He could only hope that she saw the same when she looked at him.

"Mac." She said his name softly. Then her brow clouded. "Lina?"

"Safely locked up," he assured her. "You don't have to worry about her. It's over, and you're safe."

Her eyes flickered shut. "So tired."

"I know. You sleep, sweetheart." It was the first time he'd used an endearment for her, and it felt good. "There will be plenty of time later for talking."

He watched as her breathing grew deeper and even, her hand relaxing under his.

Plenty of time. He hoped so. But if Kate decided that Laurel Ridge held too many bad memories for her, there might be very little time at all.

"There, all signed." Kate finished affixing her signature to the statement she'd made and handed it across Mac's desk to him. "Now, please tell me Lina is going to prison for what she did to Jason."

Mac pulled his chair around the desk so that he sat knee to knee with her. She could read in his face the thing she didn't want to hear. "She's going to jail, all right. But I doubt that we can convict her on Jason's murder."

"But she did it." Even knowing the truth of what he was saying, she still had to protest. She wanted Jason's innocence to be established now and forever.

"Yes, she did. I have no doubt about that. But we can't prove it. We can, however, prove that she attacked you with murderous intent. You understand, don't you?"

Kate nodded reluctantly. "I suppose, but I still wanted to see Jason's name cleared."

"I know you did." He reached out toward her tentatively and put his hand over hers. "I wish we could, but the DA refuses to bring a case based on so little evidence when we've got two solid charges we can prove."

"Two?"

"Auditors have combed through the records of the investment company. There was something wrong, all right. Lina has been diverting money from clients' accounts to her own for nearly two years, as far as they can tell. All the clients were Russ Sheldon's. I think she wanted to be able to blame him if things went wrong."

"She didn't count on Jason finding anything." Satisfaction went through her at the thought. She wasn't the one who'd uncovered an embezzler. That had been her little brother.

Mac nodded. "I don't suppose Lina ever dreamed Bart would bring in an intern. Or that it would be someone as smart as Jason." His lips quirked. "Bart now says it was Lina who suggested that Jason was responsible. He may just be trying to make himself look better. Lina knew how he'd react."

"She manipulated all of them."

"Yes." Mac pulled something from his pocket. "We found this when we searched her house. Since it won't be entered into evidence, I thought you should have it."

It was the silver dragon charm. Kate's heart seemed to stop for a moment. "She took it. Why would she do that?"

"Looks as if the little ring it attaches to is broken. I'm guessing it came off his key ring at some point that night, and she picked it up. Why she kept it—well, that's anyone's guess. You'd need a psychiatrist to answer that one."

She held the charm against her heart for a moment. The whole story was surprisingly clear in her mind now, and she realized that was because of Jason. Lina had been the shape-shifter of his imagination, the creature playing one side against the other for her own benefit.

Mac frowned. "I should have seen it. If I'd

been able to get the story out of Bart or Nikki to begin with . . ."

He was blaming himself. At one time, she'd have been eager to blame him, too, but she knew better now. She clasped his hand firmly, loving the way his fingers closed over hers in response.

"You couldn't have," she said flatly. "Don't start accepting responsibility for something you couldn't possibly have known. If it hadn't been for the video journal, the truth would never have come out."

"In a sense, Jason brought his own killer to justice. With your help." Mac seemed to study her face, his gaze lingering on her lips. "And I owe him a vote of thanks, because he brought us together."

"Mac . . ." she began, half longing to hear what he was about to say and half-fearful.

"Don't." He squeezed her hand. "Don't tell me about how this can't work, and how you hate cops, and how you can't take a chance on loving me. Just let me tell you what I feel."

She started to protest and then folded her lips together, nodding.

Now that he had her attention, Mac hesitated. His fingers moved absently over her hands, caressing her skin and setting up frissons of warmth that rippled across her.

"We haven't known each other very long," he said at last. "But I know you. Bone deep. Better than I've ever known anyone. And I know I love you. For good. Forever." He raised his hand, cupping her cheek, and the warmth spread and multiplied. "You can tell me it's too soon . . ."

"No," she said quickly.

"No?" He looked taken aback.

"No, it's not too soon." She smiled, feeling the movement of her cheek against his palm. "Anybody who knows me will tell you that I know what I want. I want you. This. Us together."

"Even if that comes with Laurel Ridge thrown in?" he asked.

She was making a choice between the adventurous life she'd thought she wanted and a real life with someone who cared for her. Someone with whom she could build the kind of family she and Jason had never had.

She answered him with a question. "Do you think the *Laurel Ridge Standard* might have space for another staff writer? I'll cover PTA meetings and parades and Sunday picnics. But I won't write anything critical of the police chief."

"I think they might." Mac rose, pulling her up with him. He held her for a moment, studying her face. "You're sure it won't be hard, living here where Jason died?"

"Where Jason lived," she corrected. "He had a lot of good experiences here, too. And people here will know he was innocent. Jason would be happy, I think."

The tiny doubt fled from Mac's face, and he drew her against him. She went eagerly, her arms going around him as she lifted her face for his kiss.

She'd come home. She had no doubts at all. And when Mac's lips claimed hers, she knew it was going to be better than her wildest imaginings.

GRANDMA'S HOMEMADE NOODLES

Making homemade noodles is a tradition in Pennsylvania Dutch families, and my grand-mother's recipe has been passed on for generations. In fact, I recently taught one of my granddaughters the secret!

Beat together one whole egg and three egg yolks. Add flour, stirring constantly, until a stiff dough forms. Turn the ball of dough out on a well-floured board or waxed paper and knead lightly for a few minutes, working in a little more flour until no longer sticky to the touch. Cover and let rest for fifteen minutes. Then roll out, incorporating more flour as needed, into a very thin circle. It should be about the thickness of a dime. Cover with tea towels and let dry for several hours. Cut into four pieces. Roll up each piece, jelly-roll style. Using a thin, sharp knife, cut into very thin slices. Gently shake out the rounds of dough into strips. Drop the noodles into boiling chicken broth and simmer for twenty minutes. The broth will thicken as it cooks, so stir occasionally to prevent sticking. Do not drain. Just serve as is, broth and all. This may be put on top of mashed potatoes as if it were gravy or served separately as a side dish. The dough is sometimes cut into squares to use in chicken pot pie. Enjoy!

Books are produced in the United States using U.S.-based materials	Books are printed using a revolutionary new process called THINKtech™ that lowers energy usage by 70% and increases overall quality	Books are durable and flexible because of Smyth-sewing	Paper is sourced using environmentally responsible foresting methods and the paper is acid-free

Center Point Large Print
600 Brooks Road / PO Box 1
Thorndike, ME 04986-0001 USA

(207) 568-3717

US & Canada:
1 800 929-9108
www.centerpointlargeprint.com